My One True Highlander

SUZANNE ENOCH

St. Martin's Paperbacks

This is a work of fiction. All of the characters, organizations, and events portrayed in this novel are either products of the author's imagination or are used fictitiously.

MY ONE TRUE HIGHLANDER

For information address St. Martin's Press, 175 Fifth Avenue, New York, NY 10010.

ISBN: 978-1-250-09543-5

Our books may be purchased in bulk for promotional, educational, or business use. Please contact your local bookseller or the Macmillan Corporate and Premium Sales Department at 1-800-221-7945, ext. 5442, or by e-mail at MacmillanSpecialMarkets@macmillan.com.

Printed in the United States of America

St. Martin's Paperbacks edition / April 2017

St. Martin's Paperbacks are published by St. Martin's Press, 175 Fifth Avenue, New York, NY 10010.

10 9 8 7 6 5 4 3 2 1

Also by
SUZANNE ENOCH

Hero in the Highlands
Some Like It Scot
Mad, Bad, and Dangerous in Plaid
Rogue with a Brogue
The Devil Wears Kilts
The Handbook for Handling His Lordship
A Beginner's Guide to Rakes
Taming an Impossible Rogue
Rules to Catch a Devilish Duke

For Jack, whose teenager logic I find
endlessly fascinating and useful,

and

For Ryan, who would totally have
pet foxes if we'd let him

Prologue

"Oh," Lady Marjorie Forrester muttered, taking a hasty step backward to avoid Lord Belcast and his wildly unpredictable walking cane. "Well, a good day to you anyway, my lord."

Pulling her shawl more closely around her shoulders against the October chill, she even gave a polite half curtsy at his swiftly retreating backside for good measure before she continued up Bond Street. One never knew who might be observing, after all. The Season had ended weeks ago, and only those lords and ladies with the most urgent business chose London over the countryside and hunting, but Mayfair was never empty. And so she kept her eyes level, her chin high, and her expression a pleasant half smile. Ladies didn't show perturbation. Everyone knew that.

Everyone, Viscount Belcast included, also knew that a gentleman didn't ignore a lady and nearly trample her, either—which meant, clearly, that he didn't see her as a lady. He should have; she'd been to boarding school and a reputable finishing school, after all. She knew which utensils to use when, in which order guests entered a dining room, just how many waltzes could be played at a soiree without risking scandal, and a thousand other things merely awaiting the proper moment to be enacted.

And so she remained a perfectly refined, poised lady on the outside. Inside, though, Marjorie seethed. She tightened her fingers around the ribbons of her reticule and clenched her jaw. For nearly three months she'd faced this daily nonsense, and for nearly three months she'd told herself that eventually Lord Belcast or Lady Ingram or Lord Albert Masters or someone would look her in the eye and nod or tip a hat or inquire as to how her day was proceeding. Clearly, though, she'd miscalculated.

Keeping her steps measured, she strolled past the milliner's where she'd intended to purchase a new straw hat, and instead turned up Brook Street in the direction of the supremely fashionable houses on Grosvenor Square. It made no sense to purchase a hat when no one would ever acknowledge her existence, much less her choice of chapeau.

Two houses from the corner she passed through the open wrought-iron gates and up the half-dozen shallow steps to the grand double doors of Leeds House. As she reached the top step the left-hand door swung inward and the long-faced butler standing there in black livery inclined his head.

"My lady. We didn't expect you back so soon," he intoned.

Marjorie put on a smile. "I decided the day was too pretty for shopping," she said. "I'd rather spend it out in the garden. Winter will be here before we know it."

"Of course, my lady. I'll have Mary fetch your gloves and pruning shears."

"Thank you, Michaels."

"And Mrs. Giswell is in the breakfast room. She . . . expressed surprise that you'd gone out so early—and without an escort."

"If I'd required anyone else's presence, I would have requested it," she returned, disliking the brusque tone she heard in her voice and too annoyed still at London to be able to suppress it. "Please tell her that she can do as she wishes for the remainder of the day. I won't be going out again."

The butler nodded, then cleared his throat. "If I may, Lady Marjorie, I believe it will only be a matter of time before your esteemed peers see you for the gracious young lady you are."

She'd become completely transparent, then. "Thank you for saying so, Michaels, but I think we both know the truth."

Everyone knew the truth. She'd simply become the last one to acknowledge it. A few months ago, when she'd been Lady Sarah Jeffer's companion and living in a tiny room in a tiny house that smelled of cats and mildew, she'd been perfectly acceptable. Perhaps she hadn't attempted to shop on Bond Street, but no one had pretended not to see her. Lord Belcast had even nodded at her once, even if it had only been to acknowledge that he'd nearly stepped on her.

"They haven't had the privilege of speaking with you, my l—"

"There you are, Lady Marjorie," the exceedingly proper voice of Mrs. Giswell exclaimed.

Inwardly Marjorie winced. "Yes, here I am," she said with forced lightness, when she would rather be punching something. "I'm off to the garden, as a matter of fact."

"Michaels said you'd gone out. I know I do not need to remind you that the sister of a duke does not go anywhere without an escort. Particularly a sister who is barely one-and-twenty years of age and unmarried. If you wish to be accepted by your peers, you—"

"I would do well to be seen with a proper companion," Marjorie finished, since she'd memorized this particular speech weeks ago. "Especially one who served as a companion to Princess Sophia." She didn't quite understand why Hortensia Giswell held up that bit of her employment as exceptional; Princess Sophia was the sister of the Prince Regent, of course, but there were also all those nasty rumors about an illegitimate child. Perhaps that was why Mrs. Giswell had left the royal household, though. Either she'd failed in her duty, or more likely, she found the scandal too unladylike for her sensibilities.

"Precisely," Mrs. Giswell returned, clearly not reading Marjorie's thoughts. "I know my way around etiquette and protocol. And, if I may point out, *you* were the one who hired *me*."

"I recall," Marjorie said, sighing. And she'd done so with good reason. Not only did Society dislike her in general, but even under the best of circumstances she would be considered too young to run a household on her own. Everyone knew a young lady did not introduce *herself* into Society, either—she always had a mother or an aunt or at the least a more mature female as family or friend who would show her about.

She, however, didn't have anyone to step in as her mentor. And until very recently she'd never thought a mature female would be required, except to serve as her employer. Young ladies of her station—well educated, but three or four sidesteps away from the peerage—became either governesses or companions or the wives of shopkeepers. If she'd found a successful barrister or a parson, well, that would be the epitome of the level of comfort she might have hoped to find. And so she'd applied to be the companion of Lady Sarah Jeffers, a minor earl's youngest sister, and had spent eight months fluffing pillows, hurrying out to purchase hair ribbons or sweet biscuits, and pushing cats off her lap. Until just under three months ago, she'd thought to spend the remainder of her life being someone's paid . . . slave. This morning, she remained unconvinced that her new circumstances marked much of an improvement. Yes, she was the one doing the hiring, but she could well imagine cats in her future.

"Well, if you wish to stay by my side and protect my reputation today, Mrs. Giswell," she said aloud, "I'll be pruning back the rhododendrons in the garden."

"You still need a new bonnet to wear to Lady Faresie's breakfast," the older woman countered. "She invited you, and so you must not embarrass her."

Marjorie sighed. "I think she invited me precisely so her other guests will have someone at whom to point and whisper."

"That is very likely. And it is still your first invitation to a proper gathering. In my opinion, you *must* attend. At this time of year you won't be facing the heart of the *beau monde,* but the fringes. You won't have a better opportunity to begin to fit in."

That encouraging talk followed Marjorie all the way out to her garden, which spoke well for Mrs. Giswell's determination even if it also made her own head pound. All of the opportunities in the world wouldn't matter if Society had already decided that the sister of a jumped-up duke didn't deserve recognition.

Heavens, when she'd read that Harold Leeds, the Duke of Lattimer, had died and apparently left no heirs, she hadn't even dreamed that she and her brother might be Lattimer's last surviving relations. Gabriel certainly hadn't considered it; he'd been far too occupied with the war on the Peninsula to even read London newspapers. But there they were, the army major who became a duke and the lady's companion who became a duke's sister.

At first when Gabriel had told her about the unexpected inheritance and then given her Leeds House for herself, she'd thought all of her dreams had come true. *Ha.* Yes, she now resided at one of the grandest houses in London, and yes, she would never have to seek employment again. And for that she did feel blessed.

Marjorie frowned as she snipped off spent pink blooms and errant branches. A comfortable home and an income. Balanced against being snubbed by viscountesses and pushed away by former schoolmates afraid of losing their own positions in grand households if they were seen with her, perhaps she had nothing at all about which to complain.

"Am I expecting too much?" she asked aloud.

"That isn't for me to say, Lady Marjorie," Mrs. Giswell returned. The lady's companion sat on a bench, a parasol in one hand and a book in the other. Evidently gardening wasn't ladylike enough for her. "You must be content with doing your utmost, and leave the rest to hope. Certainly your plan to remain in London throughout the winter can only help. Your peers who come to visit Town will begin to view you as a familiar sight."

"I'm remaining in London because I have nowhere else to go," Marjorie countered. "This is the residence Gabriel gave me. Whether it does me any good to stay here or not is a moot point, is it not?"

"But you can see to it that being here *does* serve you well."

Marjorie shook herself. Growing up with only an absent older brother for family, one who'd made certain to send her to the best boarding schools he could afford, she'd never felt the need to complain. She'd been grateful for it. Now, when she had so much more, noting every instance of someone being unkind to her seemed ridiculous and ungrateful.

"I apologize, Mrs. Giswell," she said, straightening to face her companion. "All we can do is our best, and you've certainly encouraged that in me."

The older woman smiled. "And I shall continue to do so, my lady."

Before she could resume her pruning, Michaels appeared from the side of the house. He carried a silver salver held out in front of him, and Marjorie took a breath. Could it be that she'd received another invitation? It would mark only the second one in three months.

"My lady, a letter has just arrived for you," the butler announced, his own hopeful expression probably a mirror of hers.

Stripping off one glove, she took the folded missive off the tray. The heavy, precise script spelling out her name and the Leeds House address both made her smile and lifted her heart a little. "It's from Gabriel," she said, breaking the wax seal and unfolding it.

Over the years she and her brother had had more conversations via letter than in person, and she'd become accustomed to his brief, straightforward style. Even so, she had to read the dozen lines twice before her mind grasped precisely what it was he was saying. "Goodness," she breathed, reading the note a third time just to be certain.

"I hope it isn't bad news, my lady," Michaels offered, evidently intending to stand there until dismissed.

"No. No, it isn't bad news. It's very good news, in fact. I think." She looked up. "My brother's getting married."

For the briefest of moments Mrs. Giswell looked . . . disappointed, but she affixed a smile on her face so swiftly that Marjorie couldn't be certain if she hadn't just imagined it. Her companion set down her book and clapped her free hand against the fist holding the parasol. "Oh, splendid news indeed! Who is she? The new Duchess of Lattimer could pave your way into the very heart of Society with barely a flick of her fingers."

"I . . . um." Marjorie gave a short laugh that sounded a bit brittle even to her own ears. "He's marrying Miss Fiona Blackstock. His Lattimer estate manager."

Now Mrs. Giswell looked like she'd swallowed a bug. "A miss?" she forced out. "A Scottish miss? Not the daughter of a marquis or even an earl? But—"

"My brother," Marjorie interrupted, "has spent most of his life as a soldier. I doubt a pretty curtsy and a 'lady' before a female's name would impress him."

"Well, he certainly hasn't done you—or his new dynasty—any favors."

Gabriel and his new dynasty more than likely would stay as far away from London and proper Society as he could manage. But that didn't signify at the moment, not when abrupt and unexpected excitement tugged at her insides. "He says they'll marry next month, but that the weather then will be too harsh for visitors, and so I may come see them in the spring."

"That, at least, sounds reasonable," Mrs. Giswell seconded, nodding. "No civilized person would wish to travel to the Highlands in November. I daresay if he waited until spring, though, he could wed properly here in London, perhaps even at St. Paul's, during the little Season."

Marjorie pulled off her other glove and set both of them together with the pruners on Michaels's tray. "Gabriel and I have missed celebrating Christmases, birthdays, Easters, and every other holiday together since I turned eight and he joined the army at seventeen. He will not wait for spring, or London, and I am *not* going to miss his wedding."

"It seems to me that he very clearly stated his wishes, my lady," her companion countered. "As both your older brother and the Duke of Lattimer, he is to be obeyed regard—"

"You may obey him, then," Marjorie cut in. A month

or two away from the diminished hordes of the *haut ton* who pretended not to see her, from day after day of feeling more lonely than she ever had as a paid companion, and given the idea that she would now have a sister, a third member of their very small family—waiting until spring would be intolerable. "I'm leaving for Scotland tomorrow."

Chapter One

G raeme, Viscount Maxton, stripped off his heavy work gloves as he strode up the hill toward the house. "Calm yerself, Connell," he urged, "before ye split the seat of yer trousers."

His youngest brother continued circling and leaping about like a pine marten after a mouse. "But it's the Maxwell!" the eight-year-old exclaimed, grabbing one of Graeme's hands to pull him along. "Ye said after last year he'd nae darken our doorway again, but there he is, himself! The Duke of Dunncraigh! And two grand coaches!"

Two coaches? That didn't bode well. Eight, nine men plus the coach drivers, all of them following after the dinner scraps of the chief of clan Maxwell. "Where are yer brothers?" Graeme asked, sending a glance across the field. Old Dunham Moore stood hip-deep in the irrigation ditch digging out an old tree limb, but other than that the field and green slopes beyond stood empty. Even the crows had flown elsewhere to search for a meal.

"Brendan says he's making a fishing lure," the eight-year-old offered, "but I ken he's writing a love poem to Isobel Allen or Keavy Fox because he locked his door."

Locked in a bedchamber was good, whatever the actual reason for it. "And Dùghlas?"

"He's the one who sent me oot to find ye, Graeme. I heard the Maxwell say he was growing into a fine young lad."

Graeme tightened his grip on Connell's hand, drawing him to a halt. "I ken ye're excited, duckling, but I need ye to go help old Dunham in the ditch right now. And I need ye to stay there until I or one of the lads come and fetch ye."

The boy's light gray eyes narrowed, then widened. Swallowing, he swiped his too long brown hair from his face. "I can go fetch Uncle Raibeart," he offered, his young voice quavering a little. "I'm nae tired at all."

The offer tempted Graeme. If it had been one of the older boys, he might have agreed to it. But under no circumstances did he mean to send Connell running two miles across the countryside while the Duke of Dunncraigh's brutes wandered about. "I dunnae think we'll need Raibeart," he returned, "but I do need ye close enough to hear trouble and far enough to stay oot of it. One of us has to be ready to run fer help."

Connell nodded, swallowing again. "I'll be ready."

Smacking the boy on the arse to speed him on his way, Graeme topped the hill. He knew by heart every inch of this land, of the white and gray walls of Garaidh nan Leòmhann, but the two heavy coaches and accompanying quartet of saddled mounts crowded on the front drive were new. His groom, Johnny, was nowhere in sight to collect or even water the animals, which hopefully meant the stay would be brief.

As he reached the front door it remained closed; either Cowen was occupied elsewhere, or the butler was in hiding. Graeme lowered the handle and shoved the heavy, stubborn oak open with his shoulder.

"So ye decided to make an appearance after all," a low

voice drawled from the morning room doorway. "I dunnae ken if that makes ye brave, or stupid."

"A bit of both, I reckon. I see ye still dress English," Graeme returned, debating whether to push past the Maxwell's nephew or wait for an invitation. "Good fer ye, Artur. I thought after the duke's dealings with Lattimer, he might have ordered ye to stop wearing Sassenach clothes."

Artur Maxwell squared his shoulders. "That's fairly bold talk, Maxton. I dare ye to repeat it in there." Shifting out of the way, he indicated the depths of the morning room.

Keeping his own expression neutral and his work gloves clenched in his left hand, Graeme walked into the room. "Yer Grace," he said, inclining his head.

As the Duke of Dunncraigh turned from gazing out the front window, Graeme took a swift measure of everyone else in the room. His younger brother Dùghlas sent him a relieved look, which told him the fourteen-year-old at least had the sense to know that the Maxwell's visit here rarely boded anything but trouble.

He knew all but one of the other men crowded into the small room. Five of the Maxwell's bruisers, all related to the duke in one way or another and ready to bloody, shoot, or set fire to anything their master looked at sideways. The other one had the same look about him, and Graeme shifted his attention back to the duke and the stiff-spined other man who stood close by the Maxwell—no doubt ready to wipe Dunncraigh's arse if asked to do so.

"Ye took yer time getting here," the duke stated, his green eyes flat and emotionless beneath a shock of white hair.

"I was moving a plow and the handle cracked," Graeme returned, stepping over to tousle his younger brother's brown mop of hair and shove the lad toward the door. "Ye owe me some arithmetic, as I recall," he said for good measure. Once his brothers were out of immediate danger, he would deal with what seemed to be a hostile visit—another hostile visit—from his clan chief.

"Ye're plowing yer own fields now, are ye, Maxton?" the Maxwell's arse-wiper drawled. "Do ye milk the cows and cut the peat yerself, as well?"

Graeme kept his gaze on the steely-eyed duke. "I reckon ye brought Sir Hamish with ye as yer jester, but as we both ken we arenae friends, I'd prefer if ye'd forgo the theatrics and tell me what's brought ye oot here."

Sir Hamish Paulk's heavy face folded into a scowl. "That's bold talk fer a chieftain who cannae pay his own tithing, ye damned—"

"Considering ye just lost the tithes and loyalty of all the tenants of the Duke of Lattimer's ten thousand acres, I suggest ye nae go aboot insulting yer remaining clansmen, Yer Grace," Graeme cut in. "Or allowing yer other chieftains to do so."

"Sir Hamish doesnae have my patience," Dunncraigh returned. "I find myself more curious over what else ye think ye ken aboot the goings-on at Lattimer. I'd have thought ye had enough of yer own worries, what with three younger brothers and a large patch of poorly protected land of yer own." The Maxwell moved closer. "I reckon it's helpful that ye *do* know an English duke has taken our ancestral land and turned a good handful of our own against us."

That wasn't all Graeme had heard, but repeating rumors about the Maxwell failing to purchase Lattimer and then resorting to sabotage and threats in an attempt to turn the tenants against their lord—which efforts hadn't turned out at all well for Dunncraigh—seemed a very poor idea at the moment. "And why is that?" he settled for asking.

"Because I'm feeling a particular dislike for Gabriel Forrester, the damned Duke of Lattimer, and I'm inclined to feel a particular generosity toward any of my clan who might . . . discover anything useful against him. Or who might cause Lattimer a measure of consternation. Do ye ken what I'm saying, Graeme?"

"Aye. And I've nae liking fer any Sassenach. But I reckon I'm content to keep to my own affairs."

The duke nodded. "Yer land borders his, so I ken ye wish to be neighborly. All I'm saying is that if ye should happen to have or overhear any dealings with Lattimer that someone might be able to turn against him, and if ye tell me of them, ye might find yer herds have increased and that any tithes ye might owe have been forgotten. If someaught unfortunate befell the duke himself, well, I'd nae mourn his loss."

He clapped Graeme on the shoulder. Making a supreme effort not to level his clan chief with a punch to the jaw, Graeme took a moment to wonder if anyone serving clan Maxwell under Dunncraigh's leadership actually liked the man. For him, even beneath the dizzying barrage of faux fatherly advice and barely veiled threats, the duke was to be tolerated, placated when possible, and obeyed when necessary—and otherwise ignored.

Dunncraigh and his sycophants stomped back out to their coaches and mounts, and he followed them outside to make certain no one lingered. One of the luckier things about owning a rundown manor and a property of a mere thousand acres was that the likes of a duke, especially one who happened to be the head of clan Maxwell, had no wish to remain under his roof for long.

"Ye'd best do as he asks, Maxton," Sir Hamish said, watching as the duke settled into the lead coach.

"So ye're giving me helpful advice now, are ye, Paulk? I reckon I'll give that all the consideration it deserves."

"If ye sell off any more land ye'll barely qualify as gentry, Maxton. So take the advice given ye and smile while ye hear it. With but two hundred cotters ye're already underqualified to be a clan chieftain. Make yerself useful, earn yerself some blunt and some gratitude, or he may decide ye're of nae use at all."

"Do ye recommend I follow yer strategy? Stay so close to Dunncraigh's arse that he thinks ye a pimple?"

"Go to the devil, ye useless sack of shite. Ye're the same as yer father and yer grandfather, stubborn fools. There are consequences fer failing yer betters. With yer brothers to look after, ye'd best remember th—"

"Hamish," the duke called. "I've nae wish to remain here till Christmas."

The other Maxwell chieftain present held Graeme's gaze, clearly meaning to intimidate. *Not bloody likely.* Graeme tilted his head, then took a quick half step forward. When Paulk flinched back, he curved his mouth in a smile he didn't feel. "It'll take more than yer beady eyes glaring at me to give me a fright," he murmured. "Now run off, dog. Yer master's calling ye."

"He's yer master, too. Ye'd best realize that before he decides the wee bit ye contribute isnae worth the aggravation ye cause." With that, Sir Hamish turned on his heel and stepped up into the coach.

Graeme stood on his drive of crushed oyster shells and gravel to watch the coaches and riders rumble down the hill and vanish into the scattering of trees and boulders beyond. Once he was certain they were well away, he turned back to the house—to find Dùghlas and Brendan standing in the open doorway, both of them holding rifles. Cowen stood just inside the foyer, armed with an old claymore the butler had likely pulled off the wall in the drawing room.

"Do ye mean to murder yer own clan chief then, lads?" he asked, proud that they'd had the presence of mind to arm themselves, and alarmed at what would have happened if a battle had erupted in his morning room.

"They threatened ye, Graeme," Dùghlas said, blowing out his breath as he lowered the weapon to point at the floor. "I nearly pissed myself when Cowen showed 'em into the hoose."

"Why would the Maxwell think ye'd want anything at all to do with the Sassenach Lattimer?" Brendan took up. "Mayhap we *should* go shoot the grand Gabriel Forrester so Dunncraigh will leave us be." He hefted his rifle.

Eyeing the sixteen-year-old, Graeme frowned. "I'll agree we could use both the money and gratitude that being Dunncraigh's lapdog would give us, but the Duke of Lattimer's nae done a damned thing to me. So ye mark me well, Brendan; nae a soul here is to harm Lattimer or those under his protection. Do both of ye brutes ken what I'm telling ye?"

"Aye."

"Aye, Graeme."

"Good. Dùghlas, go fetch Connell. He's doon by the ditch with Dunham past the south field."

Handing his rifle over to Cowen, Dùghlas trotted across the drive toward the near field. Brendan, though, stepped forward and spat onto the gravel. "After losing a thousand Maxwells to that Sassenach, Dunncraigh should be more grateful to ye and yers. Ye should have told him that, Graeme."

"I'll agree that a Maxton has been a clan Maxwell chieftain fer better than two hundred years, if ye'll agree that our da and I've nae spent much of that time bowing to Dunncraigh. I reckon we'd fare better if I bowed more, but I'm nae murdering anyone in exchange fer a pat on the head."

The brother nearest him in age continued to look angry and defiant, as offended and righteous as any well-protected and stubborn sixteen-year-old could be. Graeme put a hand on his shoulder and squeezed. The lads had been much easier to manage when they were bairns, and the eleven years that separated him from Brendan had seemed much wider. Just a few years ago he could tell them the way things were and they didn't question a damned word of it.

"Tempers are boiling now," he continued, "what with Lattimer getting his gamekeeper to swear that he was taking blunt from Dunncraigh in exchange fer causing trouble. The Maxwell's embarrassed, I reckon. And he wants blood. But winter's nearly here, and everything'll quiet doon. By spring we'll be talking aboot calves and lambs and all this will be forgotten. So be patient. Dunncraigh willnae be sending us posies, but he'll likely go back to ignoring us again—which is damned fine enough fer me."

Finally Brendan nodded, his fingers easing their grip on the old rifle. "I ken, Graeme. Ye want us to stay quiet, like wee church mice, even though we havenae done a damned thing wrong."

Graeme knew some who could debate the last part of that statement, but now wasn't the time for that discussion. "Aye. And now ye can come help me fix that plow and drag it back to Widow Peele's before the snow and wet rot the rest of it."

"Dunnae we have men to do that?" Brendan returned, abruptly sounding like a young lad again.

"Aye, we do. And today their names are Graeme and Brendan."

When Connell trotted back up with Dùghlas, the eight-year-old needed more reassurance that they weren't about to be murdered. The animosity between the Maxtons and Dunncraigh had begun well before he'd inherited his father's role as chieftain, but he could take steps to mend the break if he felt so inclined. His brothers shouldn't have to be frightened of their own kin and clan. Causing trouble for a neighbor, though, English or not, didn't sit well. Lattimer had brought some changes to the Highlands, but none of them had harmed him or his. If not for Dunncraigh's public condemnation of the man, Graeme would have been tempted to go make his acquaintance. They were neighbors, after all, even if their homes lay six hours' distant from each other.

Once he'd sent the younger lads back into the house and Brendan on his way to the field, Graeme gestured at Cowen. "Send fer Boisil Fox and his brothers," he muttered, moving closer to the butler. "I want an extra watch on the hoose tonight."

The butler nodded, his gaze moving toward the treeline. "Ye reckon we're in fer it, Laird Maxton?"

"Nae. I dunnae want Brendan sneaking off to go shoot the Duke of Lattimer."

The older man's expression eased. "Yer *bràthair*'s a good lad, if a mite hotheaded."

"He's a mite hotheaded the way the Highlands are a bit nippy in January. We'll be back by sunset."

"I'll keep an eye oot until then, m'laird."

Hopefully keeping his brothers close by until their tempers cooled would see them past the worst of this. The Maxwell's rare visits had never yet boded well for the Maxtons, and this time was no damned exception. As Graeme made his way back through a deepening drizzle to the widow's old plow, he spared a moment to wish that he could stop being civil to a man he disliked on principle, and stop worrying over three younger brothers, a half-dozen servants, and roughly two hundred cotters currently residing on his land.

With that kind of freedom, the only question would be who he went after first—Lattimer, for simply being there and being English; or Dunncraigh for fifty years of bitter vitriole. But that was also a question for a man who lived a different life—and one with far less responsibility than he had.

Lady Marjorie Forrester took the coachman's outstretched hand as she stepped down to the muddy ground. She'd worn her most practical walking shoes, but they immediately disappeared beneath thick, sticky brown halfway up her toes.

"For heaven's sake," Mrs. Giswell exclaimed from the coach doorway, "someone—you, sir!—move those planks over here before we drown in the mud!"

"I'm nearly to the inn, now," Marjorie returned, nevertheless favoring the large bearded man with a smile as he slogged over with an armful of planks and began laying them between the vehicle and the coaching inn. "Thank you for your assistance, sir."

"With that woman screeching at me, I was scared she'd put a curse on me if I didnae do as she said," he returned in a thick, drawling brogue, grinning back at her.

Once the planks covered the mud, Mrs. Giswell stepped down gingerly to follow Marjorie. "A lady does not screech, sir," she stated in her coolest tones. "A lady merely speaks up when an expected and needed chivalry is not offered."

"Och, a chivalry," the large man took up, tugging on his thick brown beard. "Ye hear that, lads? I'm a bloody knight!"

The half-dozen men scattered about the small courtyard laughed. "Aye! Sir Robert the Blacksmith, ye are," one of them called out.

"Aye, and the lot of ye bow when ye see me from now on."

The conversation amused her, and Marjorie smiled, starting a little when Mrs. Giswell put a hand on her arm.

"A lady is not amused by brutes and their foul language," she said. "Now let's get you inside before you catch your death, my lady."

The wind did have a definite bite, but she wasn't yet chilled enough to feel more than a sense of exhilaration. The accents in the Lowlands had been charming as the coach drove north, but now just from the thick brogues surrounding her she knew they'd reached the Highlands. For heaven's sake, they might even be on Gabriel's land; Lattimer Castle's property consisted of ten thousand acres—or so her brother's solicitors had informed her.

Taking a breath, she pushed open the inn's faded green door and stepped inside. According to the sign hanging outside this was the Cracked Hearth, but at first glance the old stone fireplace seemed to be perfectly intact. The place had a low ceiling braced with massive wood beams, leaving Marjorie with the sensation that she was too tall for the room—despite the fact that she was far shorter than some of the very large men inside.

And it wasn't just men having luncheon or escaping the rain at the Cracked Hearth; a dozen women and a handful of children sat at the tables or played in the corner, as well. The sight of families left her feeling easier about being in the cavernlike setting, but it also made her very conscious of how . . . out of place she looked there.

She'd chosen her London-made green and cream walking gown because the color of it had enchanted her, and the heavy Parisian shawl of green braided wool because it was warm and French-made when such things were almost impossible to get. Six months ago she wouldn't have been able to afford either of them, or her walking shoes, and perhaps they weren't exactly plain even by London standards. The novelty of being able to purchase whatever she wanted still hadn't quite faded. Now, though, picking her way through the luncheon crowd to find an empty table at the Cracked Hearth, she wished she'd been a bit more discerning.

"You should be accustomed to being noticed," Mrs. Giswell whispered from behind her. "A lady doesn't acknowledge stares."

"I'm frequently noticed," she returned in the same tone. "In London it's followed by people turning their backs on me. Here they keep looking."

"And they will continue to do so, no doubt. They don't seem to be any better mannered than those men outside who laughed while we waded through the mud."

That seemed severe. Dwelling on ignorance versus rudeness, though, would keep her from listening to the very boisterous banter going on all about the large, low room. Doing her best not to return their attention or smile at the young boy with the red hair and pretty gray eyes sitting with a group of boys three tables away, she sat and stretched her fingers out to the candle there to warm them. "I'll be perfectly satisfied with hot tea and a warm meal," she returned.

Mrs. Giswell gathered her dark brown skirt and took a seat on the opposite bench. "You might have taken a private room, my lady. A duke's sister should not be dining with commoners." She leaned closer. "And while I commend you for traveling with your own driver and coachman, I still believe you should also have employed at least two outriders and someone to travel a day ahead of us to arrange for proper accommodations and announce your coming."

"That's a bit grandiose, don't you think?" Marjorie returned. After five days of being confined in a coach with her paid companion, the endless litany of what a lady should and shouldn't do had lost much of the limited appeal it had once had. That didn't make it less necessary, but it had definitely become less interesting. "I did attend finishing school, you know. I have some expertise in etiquette and propriety."

"Yes, but that was when you were preparing for employment as a governess or a companion. Not the sister of a duke. You hired me to assist you with settling into the aristocracy. If I may be so bold, I daresay I've spend more time amid the *beau monde* than you have, Lady Marjorie. And wherever you travel, you must always keep in mind that you are the Duke of Lattimer's sister."

"I do thank you for your boundless wisdom, Mrs. Giswell." Boundless and endless, but she had hired the woman for precisely that reason.

And Mrs. Giswell made a very good point. Because while she had excelled at both boarding school and finishing school, she'd had a very keen insight about the restrictions her birth and income placed on her future. If not for the death of a great-great-uncle to whom she hadn't even known she was related, the education she'd received would have been completely adequate.

When a soft-faced young man approached the table, Mrs. Giswell placed a request for tea and two servings of roasted veal—evidently the proper meal for a midday rest and a change of horses—so that she wouldn't have to converse with any commoners, herself. Marjorie settled for giving him a smile, which for once earned her a friendly nod.

Whatever Mrs. Giswell thought was proper, Marjorie didn't want someone riding ahead to prepare the way, both because it seemed even more frivolous than her wardrobe, and because for once she meant to surprise her brother. That was the true reason for her hurry—because she wanted to arrive before the final preparations were made for his wedding. The rush and her decision to forgo outriders had nothing to do with this being her first and only excuse to flee the emptying streets of London before she was the only soul left in Mayfair. Nor was it because she'd felt like she'd been alone from the moment she'd taken up residence at Leeds House. Before that even, but she'd expected it, then.

"Have you considered yet who you might have sponsor you in the spring so you may have your Season? That would see you introduced to the best families, and would diminish any reason they might have to slight you." Mrs. Giswell cut her veal into delicate portions, every motion proper and feminine and precise. "I have several suggestions, though any of them will likely require a generous gift on your part."

Marjorie took a moment to properly dissect her meal, as well. "So I must purchase this female's friendship." Not for the first time, she wondered if fitting in with the aristocracy was worth the effort. As a girl she'd dreamed of being a great lady, of men who tipped their hats and bowed at the very sight of her. Abruptly she *was* that lady, only to discover now that the deference of others could evidently be purchased.

"You purchase their cooperation and assistance," Marjorie's companion corrected. "In time you might find acceptance and even friendship, but only the first is necessary to your success." She took another dainty bite, chewed, and swallowed. "As you already know, being an aristocrat is an expensive proposition. And not every title comes with as much wealth as your brother's. The offer of a new carriage, say, to an appropriate, established household, should secure you a marchioness or a viscountess with good connections."

Bile rose in her throat, and she drank down half a cup of weak tea to drive it back down again. "Let us discuss something more pleasant, Mrs. Giswell. We can develop our strategy for acceptance when we return to London."

After that she had to listen to a twenty-minute discussion of the general unpleasantness of Scottish weather. Finally she couldn't stand it any longer, and rose. "I'm going to stretch my legs before we return to the coach."

Mrs. Giswell started to her feet, as well. "Of course."

"You stay here. I'll remain in the courtyard, well in sight of Stevens and Wolstanton," she said, naming her coachman and driver.

"My lady, that is not—"

"Please, Mrs. Giswell. Give me a moment to breathe."

The older woman snapped her mouth closed and sat again. "Of course, my lady. I did not mean to offend."

"You didn't off—Oh, for heaven's sake. I'll be back in ten minutes." And she would apologize when she returned, because as frustrating as Mrs. Giswell was, Marjorie knew blasted well that she needed the woman.

She would have preferred not to have to carry the image of her companion's hurt expression with her as she traipsed through the mud. Every time Mrs. Giswell opened her mouth, her own circumstances seemed more . . . hopeless. Even if she succeeded in winning over the aristocracy, even if they all accepted her and invited her to every soiree and luncheon, she would know she'd only arrived there because of carefully placed gifts and a large quantity of money. The magic of the song vanished once she joined the chorus, apparently. But still, to hold grand parties and chat with well-spoken, well-educated folk about important topics . . . It could still happen. If she was patient, and generous to the correct people.

The light drizzle, the cold pricks of water soaking through her shawl and onto her skin, actually felt refreshing. She nodded to her coachman and driver, seated on boxes beneath an overhang and eating something that steamed in the chilly air.

Five or six more hours, tomorrow morning at the latest if they decided to stop for the night, and they would be at

Lattimer. It wouldn't be just her and the constantly Society-minded Mrs. Giswell. Perhaps her brother or his betrothed would even have an alternate plan to her purchasing a carriage for some woman who otherwise couldn't be bothered to look in her direction.

A face appeared around the corner of the building. The young boy with the pretty gray eyes smiled at her. Marjorie grinned back. "Good afternoon, sir."

His nose wrinkled. "I'm nae a sir."

"Why not?"

"Because I'm eight, I reckon." He beckoned to her and backed around the corner again.

"I'm not following you, sir," she called, pulling her shawl closer around her shoulders. "It's raining." If not for the prospect of six more hours in Mrs. Giswell's company she would have returned to the inn already. Perhaps she should, anyway; the last thing she wanted was to be bedridden at Lattimer once she finally arrived there.

The boy appeared again, a very young black and white kitten cradled in his hands. "I only wanted to show ye the kittens in the haystack," he said, his Highlands brogue rendered even more charming by his youth. "I reckon I'll keep this one, name him Bruce."

"Oh, he's too young to leave his mama, don't you think?" she returned, walking up to gently scratch the adorable little thing between the ears.

"If I wait, someone else'll take him. Or the foxes will. And they'll get the other wee ones, too."

"Perhaps you could find a box and take all of them and the mother home with you."

He wrinkled his nose again, clearly considering. "I reckon I can do that, if ye'll help me collect 'em. I counted seven bairns, plus the mama."

She hesitated, perfectly aware that duke's sisters did not climb into haystacks after cats. Especially not when they wore gowns that cost more than six months of her old salary.

The boy tilted his head, red hair falling across one eye. "Are ye scared of me, miss? Everyone says the English are cowards, but I didnae ken ye were afraid of kittens. Of course I've only met one English before, but he wasnae a lass. He's a peddler who comes by to sell pots and pans and he's English, but he says he's nae been to London so I dunnae know if I believe him."

Stifling a grin, Marjorie sighed. "No, I'm not scared of you, sir. My name is Marjorie. What's yours?"

"Connell."

"Let's go rescue your kittens, shall we, Connell?"

He smiled widely. "Aye."

Hiking her skirts, she stepped into the unkempt grass behind the stable. A half-collapsed pile of wet hay leaned against the back of the building, kept mostly out of the rain by the deep eaves. In the eyes of a female cat it was probably the perfect place to have a litter.

"I'll get the mama and three kittens," she said, crouching where he indicated and leaning down to spy an unhappy-looking tabby. "Can you carry four kit—"

Something pulled fast and hard over her head from behind. She lost her balance, flailing backward. Hands far stronger than the boy's would have been grabbed onto her wrists and bound them together in front of her. Shaking herself out of her shock, Marjorie took a deep breath to scream.

"Make a sound, and it'll be the last one ye make," another voice growled. "Ye ken, Sassenach?"

Since he'd just ordered her not to talk, she settled for nodding beneath the heavy material covering her head and shoulders. Fear stiffened her muscles, making her feel heavy and uncoordinated as she worked to sit upright.

"Good. On yer feet, then. Try to make a run fer it, and I'll shoot ye in the leg and ye'll still be coming with us."

"If ye make the lass faint we'll have to carry her, so shut up," another voice muttered.

Including the devious little boy there were at least three of them, then. Hands grabbed her beneath the arms and yanked her to her feet. The tall, wet grass tangled around her feet and the hem of her gown, but they continued hurrying her along. The already faint sounds of the courtyard faded, but she had no sense of which direction they were heading.

Her heart pounded so loudly she thought it might burst from her chest. If she could manage to pull the covering off her head she might at least have a chance to escape, but to where? For all she knew, everyone at the Cracked Hearth worked together to kidnap travelers. For ransom, she supposed—and hoped. If this was for money, then she had a chance to survive it.

She swallowed, her throat so tight she almost choked. If this wasn't about money, if she'd been grabbed because she was English, or because they regularly grabbed and murdered strangers . . . Oh, good heavens. Marjorie stumbled.

"Keep her on her feet," the voice on the left ordered, pulling her upright again. "We're nearly to the wagon."

"I'm trying," the voice on her right returned. "Ye'd best be certain she is who ye think she is, or we're all in fer it."

"I heard it plain. She's the Duke of Lattimer's sister."

They sounded young, or younger than she was, anyway. The two who held on to her were at least her height, though, and she doubted she could wrestle free of one, much less two or more.

"Her name's Marjorie. That's what she told me," the boy Connell said from a few steps behind her.

"And ye told her yer name, duckling."

"She asked me," he protested. "Ye didnae say I should lie, Brendan."

"Saint Andrew's arse. Stop talking, bairn."

"Dunnae yell at me. I did what ye said."

"I'm . . . I'm nae yelling. Go hold the horses while we load her in."

She bumped into something wooden at the level of her thighs and nearly fell over again. It felt safer to simply do as they said, but Mrs. Giswell and Stevens and Wolstanton were somewhere behind her. The wagon would not be taking her anywhere she wanted to go. Oh, the lectures she would be getting from Mrs. Giswell after this. And she would deserve them.

That thought actually steadied her a little. Squaring her shoulders, she dug the toes of her walking shoes into the soft ground and locked her knees. "It's time for you to let me go," she said in her calmest voice. "We'll call this a jest, and I'll be on my way with no one the wiser."

"Ye're nae to talk," the left voice, Brendan, countered. "Step up."

"No. You'll have to shoot me. Which will make a great deal of noise, I'd like to point out."

What sounded like Gaelic profanity followed. Then came another few words she didn't understand, and one of them seized her shoulders. The other one lifted the sack half off her head and then pulled a strip of cloth tight around her mouth and knotted it.

Marjorie kicked out, but someone grabbed her foot. Pulled off balance, she half fell onto what she assumed was the back of the wagon. Fear stabbed through her again. She squirmed, punching out with her joined hands and connecting with something solid.

"Hold 'er still, fer Lucifer's sake," Brendan hissed, falling across both her legs.

"She hit me in the damned eye," the other one grunted.

"We'll tie her arms doon, then. After I get her legs. I told ye we'd need all this rope."

No class in boarding school or finishing school had ever dealt with how to avoid or fight against a kidnapping. And wrestling and fighting were so completely unacceptable they weren't even mentioned. Several headmistresses would be receiving a sternly worded letter if she survived this. *When* she survived this, she hurriedly corrected. Yes, she seemed to be thinking very frivolous thoughts, but school, the order and . . . safety of it, felt very comforting right now. And anything that helped keep her calm could be useful.

"There," the one named Brendan said, his weight finally leaving her legs. "Ye'd best settle yerself, Lady Marjorie Forrester, because ye've got a bit of traveling to do. Ye can blame yer Sassenach bastard of a brother fer it, but ye're going to help make things right. Fer all of us."

Chapter Two

"With the wagon?" Graeme Maxton asked, handing his wet coat over to the butler and shaking rainwater out of his too long hair. With the money troubles he had, a visit to the barber seemed like a luxury, but if he didn't hack some of the mess off soon, he wouldn't be able to see.

"Aye," Cowen returned. "Aboot an hour ago Connell and Dùghlas came galloping up, fetched Brendan, and the three of 'em headed oot in the wagon together."

"Well, it's the wrong time of year fer kits and goslings or whatever other baby animal Connell likes to rescue, so hopefully Dùghlas shot a buck and we'll have venison fer dinner."

"It makes my mouth water just thinking aboot it. How did ye find Hugh Howard, then?"

"His spine's still a bit stiff, but his boy Gordon and I mended the roof. I doubt Hugh'll wish to be climbing ladders fer a time even after he's able again." He headed down the hallway to his small, cluttered office. "Let me know when the lads return. I reckon we'll have snow on the ground by nightfall, and I dunnae want Connell catching a raw throat again."

"If I dunnae see 'em within the hour, I'll send Johnny
oot to fetch 'em back," Cowen returned, naming the head
groom. "And I put yer correspondence on yer desk, as ye
asked."

Graeme nodded. More mail meant more bills, but neither of them cared to say that word aloud. If debt was
something he could stab or bludgeon or pound senseless,
they would all be in a much sounder state. Debt, though,
had as much strength as he did, and a much larger share
of patience.

As he topped the stairs a small gray cat jumped up to
perch on the bannister and gaze at him with yellow eyes.
Absently he reached over to scratch it beneath the chin,
and its purr rumbled against his fingers. He needed to curb
Connell's penchant for rescuing wee animals soon, but he
kept putting it off. Breaking his youngest brother's heart
could damned well wait if it gave the eight-year-old time
to outgrow his obsession.

He walked into the office, stepping over yet another cat,
this one an orange tabby, as he did so. Between the five
cats of which he knew, the two pet foxes, and the gander
that lived in the stable, the humans who lived in his house
were outnumbered as it was. And that didn't count the trio
of orphaned rabbits he knew Connell currently had hidden in his bedchamber.

When he looked up again he'd managed to find the
funds to pay the drovers who'd taken the sheep to market,
and the thirteen pounds he needed in order to purchase a
new plow horse. The outcome surprised him; perhaps luck
had finally begun to swing back in their favor.

"Graeme," Brendan exclaimed, out of breath as he skid-
ded into the room.

Alarm rumbled through him. "What happened?" he
asked, shoving to his feet. "Where are yer brothers?"

The sixteen-year-old frowned. "Naught's happened.

Ye always think I've caused ye trouble. Well, this time I havenae. I've found a way to save the lot of us." His dark gray eyes narrowed. "I'm nae a wee bairn any longer, Graeme. I'm a man grown, and I can help ye." He backed up and gestured out the door. "I *have* helped ye. Come and see. But promise me ye'll nae say a word until ye've heard me oot."

That all sounded dubious, but if it meant Brendan had finally begun to shoulder some responsibility instead of going about starting fights, Graeme remained willing to give him a chance. And if he could close both eyes tonight for the first time in a week without worrying about the Duke of Lattimer's continued health, so much the better.

"Lead the way, then," he said, and followed his brother up the long ground-floor hallway to the small sitting room at the back of the house where Connell's young foxes spent most of their time.

Dùghlas and Connell waited in the hallway, and the un- settled sensation in his gut deepened. "What happened to yer eye?" he asked his second-youngest brother.

With a glance at Brendan, Dùghlas jerked his thumb toward the door.

"There'd best nae be a deer or a wildcat in there." Graeme reached for the door handle.

Before he could push it open, Brendan stepped in front of him. "Ye said ye'd listen, first. Ye gave yer word."

"Then get on with it. I've little enough patience to be- gin with."

Brendan nodded. He took a deep breath, the motion re- minding Graeme that the lad only lacked four or five inches on him. If the sixteen-year-old couldn't manage to put reins on his temper fairly soon, they'd all be in for it.

"Dùghlas and I both heard what the Maxwell said to ye last week," his brother began, putting up a hand when Graeme would have interrupted to remind him that this was none of their damned business. "I ken ye think it's nae fer us to trouble aboot, but if the Maxwell decides ye shouldnae be here, that damned well affects us, too. And ye also said I wasnae to murder the Duke of Lattimer, so I havenae."

"Well, thank Christ fer that."

"Graeme, ye're to let me finish."

"He practiced," Connell put in. "We had to listen to him muttering all the way home."

"Shut yer gobber, duckling, before I ferget what I'm saying." Brendan took another breath. "Whatever pride ye have, we need to earn Dunncraigh's gratitude. That would mean safety and blunt fer all of us. And I—we—found a way to earn it."

"Which way?" Graeme asked slowly, a heartbeat away from shoving through the door, his brother's pride be damned.

Brendan beat him to it and opened the door a crack. Graeme leaned in to look—and his heart stopped altogether.

They'd dragged a chair into the middle of the room. On it, sat a lass. Or he assumed the figure to be a lass, anyway; a heavy sack covered her head down to the shoulders, and a wet and muddy gown of some shade of green clung to a slender figure bound around the ankles, knees, waist, wrists, and forearms. Very quietly he pulled the door shut again.

"Who—who the devil is that?" he growled, grabbing Brendan by the collar and pushing him back against the opposite wall.

"She's Lady Marjorie Forrester," Dùghlas put in, backing farther down the hallway and pulling Connell with him. "Lattimer's sister."

Graeme stared from one to the other of his brothers. He couldn't possibly have heard that correctly. Brendan's

defiant expression didn't alter, but Dùghlas had the sense
to look worried. Connell looked ready to cry.

"Ye . . . Ye kidnapped Lattimer's sister," he said aloud.
"Why by all the bloody saints would ye do that? Are ye
feverish? Or just that dim-witted?"

"The Duke of Dunncraigh would pay good blunt to get
hold of her," Brendan insisted. "She's a new herd of sheep,
all the tithes we've missed paying, and enough lumber to
repair every cottage on the property."

Graeme closed his eyes for a moment, still willing all
of this to go away. "Where'd ye get her? We'll put her back,
let someone else find her, and be done with it."

"She saw Connell, and she knows his name because the
duckling told her. He told her my name, too."

A large tear ran down the eight-year-old's cheek. "Are
the English going to hang me, Graeme? Brendan said I
should bring her to the back of the inn. He made me do it!"

The inn. "Ye took her from the Cracked Hearth? Ye
load of half-wits! Yer wagon tracks'll lead them directly
to our front door."

"Nae. They willnae," Brendan protested. "We spent an
hour driving all over the countryside. Nae a man can track
us, and the Sassenach has nae idea how far she is from the
road."

His jaw clenched so hard it creaked, Graeme took a half
step back. "Go sit in the front room," he finally ground out.
"Dunnae speak, dunnae look at each other, dunnae go any-
where else. After I figure oot what to do with her, I reckon
I'll see to the three of ye. Until then, nae a damned word.
Now nod at me that ye ken what I'm telling ye, and go."

One by one they nodded and stomped off to the morning room, Brendan at the back and still looking as angry
as he did concerned. All the sixteen-year-old saw, though,
was the brilliant plan he'd laid out. As usual, the idea of
consequences completely eluded him.

The consequences did *not* elude Graeme, however. The female knew two of his brothers' names, and at the least, the name of the inn from where she'd been taken. She might have people out looking for her already. Letting her go or handing her to her brother would both cause a tremendous degree of trouble for both him and his brothers with the law—if any sane man could call possible imprisonment or being transported for life merely "trouble"— but if the Maxwell heard about any of it, all the Maxton lads would be banished from the clan, and he could well find himself at the bottom of the nearest loch and his siblings vanished.

The alternative would be to do as Brendan planned and hand her over to the Duke of Dunncraigh. God knew what would happen to her if he did so, not to mention the outcome for Lattimer and all the Maxwells—former Maxwells, since Dunncraigh had banished the lot of them from the clan—on Lattimer's land, though he had more than a hunch that it wouldn't be anything pleasant. Dunncraigh wanted to own Lattimer Castle and its ten thousand acres, and this would give him a way to do so.

As Brendan had said, the Maxtons would benefit from aiding their clan chief. A bit of relief from debt, the prospect of making a profit from wool and crop sales and not having it immediately eaten by upkeep and taxes. He couldn't even imagine it. All that in exchange for a spoiled aristocrat with whom he had no connection, and certainly owed no kindness. Hell, this would likely be the most good she'd ever done anyone else in her entire life.

Graeme faced the door again, then resumed pacing instead. Whatever the devil he meant to do next, he needed to do it soon.

More stomping, heavier and angrier—if bootsteps could sound angry—than before. Marjorie took a deep breath.

Being tricked by a young boy certainly wasn't her fault; any true lady would of course offer assistance to a child in need. But those weren't the footsteps of boys, now. And disbelief, affront, or annoyance no longer felt adequate. Boys, or not, this was unacceptable. Now, sitting in a hard chair with her hands bound and a smelly sack over her head, she didn't feel simply put out, the victim of some naughty boys' prank. With those last bootsteps, this stopped being a rare misadventure and became very, very serious.

At least she'd managed to slip the awful cloth off her mouth, so she no longer felt half suffocated and completely helpless. If she had her voice, she had something. Not much, because both her hands and arms were growing numb, but more than she'd had ten minutes earlier.

"Steady," she whispered to herself. Yes, she knew how to be polite and proper and appropriate. Evidently those very things were what had gotten her into this mess. But losing her wits now certainly wouldn't help anything. Because that last, angry pair of boots didn't belong to any boy, and she couldn't keep pretending that she was having a very bad dream.

The door creaked open, and the footsteps entered the room, clattered around a bit, then retreated again to the entry. She held her breath, listening for anything that could give her a clue about who seemed to be standing there, staring at her. The silence, though, dragged on for what felt like hours.

"Whatever this is," she finally said, trying to keep her tone calm and civilized despite the very uncivil circumstances, "I assure you that my main interest is being returned to the Cracked Hearth Inn and my carriage. The rest doesn't signify."

"It doesnae signify to *ye,* yer highness," a low-pitched, very Scottish voice replied, "but it damned well signifies to me."

"I'm not royalty," she returned, seizing on those words. The young men had known her name, but if this was a case of mistaken identity, well, thank heavens. "I'm just—"

"I ken who ye are, Lady Marjorie Forrester," he interrupted. "Sister of the Duke of Lattimer, the man most hated in these parts by the chief of clan Maxwell. And that's where ye are, lass. In the heart of Maxwell territory."

Her heart stammered. Had she stumbled into a war? Her brother was quite fond of battle, after all. "If you know who I am, sir, then you also know that my brother is not someone with whom one trifles. And he would not look favorably on anyone who harmed his sister."

"And *that,* yer highness, is precisely my problem." Three fast footsteps moved toward her, and then the sack yanked free of her head.

She wanted to look. She wanted to see who'd ordered that boy to trick her into wandering off, and then tied her up and dragged her off . . . somewhere. But Marjorie shut her eyes tight. "If you're worried about trouble, then make certain I can't see you," she said. "Just drop me by the roadside, and we can forget this ever happened."

The silence seemed to drag on forever. "Ye saw my brother, lass," he finally returned. "And ye know the names of two of them. That's the rub. Seeing me should be the least of yer worries."

"I won't tell," she insisted, putting every ounce of sincerity she possessed into those three words.

"I'm nae willing to risk my family's necks on the word of a Sassenach," he said. "Especially one accustomed to having her own way. Open yer damned eyes. Ye look ridiculous."

If there was one thing worse than being ignored, it was being called ridiculous. "You and your brothers kidnapped me," she retorted. "Don't expect me to take your criticisms seriously." With that Marjorie opened her eyes—and her heart stopped beating. A lion—a lion god—leaned against the door frame, arms crossed over his chest.

A mane of dark brown hair shot through with deep red hung almost to his shoulders, stray strands half covering one eye and not at all lessening the impact of steel gray looking directly back at her. His nose was straight, his mouth spare and unyielding. And unsympathetic. She'd once seen a lion in the Tower of London, and the way he'd gazed at her—the undisputed king languidly sizing up a gazelle and deciding whether she was worth devouring or not—had made her shudder. And she shuddered now.

For heaven's sake he was big; tall, broad-shouldered, and looking like he could lift a horse over his head. She would have been willing to wager that everything beneath that worn shirt and coat and those buckskin trousers was muscle. *Think,* she ordered herself. This was not the time for ogling like some schoolgirl, however striking this man's appearance.

Like the young boy's, his clothes weren't crisp and new. Unlike Connell's, this man's shirt and trousers were streaked with dirt. His nails were neatly trimmed, but one of them was bruised black, and all of them were dirty. What was he, a stable boy? A farmer? Certainly he wasn't an aristocrat. Not with hands like that. And not with the way he'd called her "highness" a moment ago. Marjorie willed herself to begin thinking again, instead of simply staring. With all those muscles and the way he seemed to be actually using them, he likely didn't have any spare space for thought. Perhaps she could use that to her advantage.

"Well," she ventured, very aware of her hands bound in her lap, "I've seen you now. My offer still stands, however; return me to the Cracked Hearth, and I won't speak a word about you. Or your brothers."

Pushing upright, he strode up to her. "And I still

dunnae believe ye," he stated, and pulled a knife from one boot.

"No!" she shrieked, ramming her head into his chest. The impact made her blink stars.

He grunted. "I'm nae going to murder ye, yer highness. Nae today." Grabbing her shoulder, he leaned over to slice through the ropes binding her arms and then the ones holding her hands together. "If ye try to run, ye'll be back in this chair," he said. "And because I'm nae as much of a fool as ye English like to think, I've two guards by the door and a shackle and chain locked to a bed upstairs. That's fer the night."

The idea that she wouldn't be seeing her brother Gabriel and his betrothed at the end of the day, that she didn't have her clothes or her hairbrush or any money with which to purchase replacements, that she truly wouldn't be going anywhere unless someone else allowed it— Marjorie abruptly wanted to scream and cry and pound her fists like an infant. "And then what?" she made herself ask.

The big man shrugged, returning the knife to his boot and backing toward the door. "And then we'll see. I reckon ye can untie yer own legs." He tilted his head, the fall of that lanky hair making him look oddly vulnerable. "There's a bowl of water there by the wall, a mug of milk, and a slice of mutton. I reckon it's nae as fine as ye're accustomed to, but I wasnae expecting guests."

"I am not your guest," she retorted, and those gray eyes assessed her all over again.

"Nae, ye arenae. Ye're a pile of trouble that my brothers have dumped on my lap. And now I have to figure what use to make of ye."

"And you're blaming me? Don't be absurd. Let me go before this gets any worse. I've been missing for an afternoon. I can explain that away. Overnight won't be as simple, sir." And it would likely ruin her—if that hadn't happened already. She took another breath, trying to slow her pulse. One thing at a time. Escape first, then worry over her reputation, and about how much more difficult this would make her plans for acceptance in Mayfair.

"Naught aboot ye is simple, lass. But dunnae expect me to give in to yer doe eyes and long lashes when lives are at stake. So ye'd best calm yerself and get someaught to eat before ye faint dead away, and I'll come fetch ye later. If ye care to curse anyone beneath yer breath, I'm Maxton. Graeme Maxton."

"What do you mean, 'she isn't there'?" Hortensia Giswell demanded, keeping her expression one of matronly annoyance despite the tightening of her throat. *Not again.*

The coachman brushed at the water soaking into his coatsleeves. "I went around the back of the stable where Lady Marjorie was headed, not five minutes after I lost sight of her. She wasn't th—"

"You let her out of your sight?"

"No need to be shrill, Mrs. Giswell," Stevens countered with a frown that looked more put upon than concerned. "It's raining; she won't have gone far. Did you look inside the inn? She might have come back in through the kitchen. Maybe even took a room to warm up and dry off."

Hortensia made herself take a slow breath. "I will go ask again. In the meantime, take Wolstanton and don't simply 'look.' Find Lady Marjorie, or none of us will ever find employment in London again. You do recall who she's on her way to visit."

Finally the coachman blinked, nodding. "Yes. Of course. Wolstanton and I will search the stable and the area around the inn. Thoroughly."

"Good."

Gathering her appropriately matronly skirts, unmindful

of the continuing drizzle despite the fact that it was likely turning her tightly bunned graying hair into a shiny helmet, Hortensia hurried back inside the Cracked Hearth. The luncheon crowd had thinned somewhat, which she didn't like. Not only had she lost potential witnesses, but any one of them who'd vanished might have made off with Lady Marjorie. She was pretty, wealthy, unmarried, and English. Anyone with avarice in his heart might have taken her away.

Oh, she'd been right to suggest outriders, protection, someone to alert the Duke of Lattimer of their approach. The duke might even have sent men to meet them. Why had she stopped at mere suggestions, though? She knew the proper etiquette, for heaven's sake. This had been such a bad idea—everyone knew the Highlands were dangerous, and Highlanders even more so.

The innkeeper, apparently also aware of the reputation of his countrymen and of the impact a kidnapping would have on the popularity of his establishment among English travelers, escorted her to every room in the inn, and opened every door himself. No Lady Marjorie. If she'd been a lesser woman, Hortensia was certain she would have begun hand-wringing and possibly fainting by now. A lesser woman might also believe she'd been cursed.

When Princess Sophia had disappeared, she'd known almost immediately that the willful girl had arranged it herself, with substantial aid from that dastardly and utterly unsuitable glorified groom of a beau. Yes, the queen had managed to find her wayward daughter fairly quickly, but the mere fact of the princess's absence had been enough to see Hortensia sacked. And the babe that had resulted nine months later had cemented, or so she'd thought, her reputation as the worst companion in London.

She'd thought her career as a mentor and companion utterly and forever destroyed. For heaven's sake, she'd taken work as an assistant in a series of dress shops for twelve horrific years—until Lady Marjorie Forrester had posted a request for someone of precisely her qualifications. Her second, and last, chance at redemption. And now this. It simply wasn't fair.

An hour later Stevens the coachman sat down across the table from her in the low-ceilinged common room of the Cracked Hearth, the arrogant man. "We didn't find a damned thing," he panted, taking off his gloves and setting them on the worn tabletop. "No tracks, no bits or baubles off her clothes, not a soul who saw anything. Or at the least not anyone who would admit to seeing anything."

Hortensia nodded, taking a last sip of her cold tea. "I found nothing, either."

"Well, Wolstanton's hitching up the team as we speak. I reckon if we push for it, we'll reach Lattimer Castle just after dinner. His Grace'll have men down here before daylight."

"No!" she squeaked, then cleared her throat to try to cover the outburst.

"No?" the coachman repeated, furrowing his brow.

"The only way for the three of us to keep our positions is if *we* retrieve her from wherever she is and deliver her safely—and gratefully—to her brother's care. We'll take rooms here. With enough questions asked and enough of Lady Marjorie's money delivered to the right hands, someone will talk. She didn't simply vanish into thin air."

"You're jesting, I hope," Stevens returned. "The only thing worse than being sacked immediately for this would be what will happen when His Grace discovers that we knew about it and didn't notify him. I'd rather be unemployed than arrested."

"That will only happen if we don't find her, which we will." She reached out to seize his hand, squeezing it. "We must."

Stevens grunted, his precise black hair only a little dented by his coachman's hat. "We'll stay the night. If we've learned nothing by morning, we'll . . . reassess our plans."

Hortensia withdrew her hand. A lady's touch, when rarely given, could have a very potent effect, indeed. "Thank you, Stevens. Fetch Wolstanton, and we'll divide our efforts appropriately."

Once he'd left the table, Hortensia took another drink of her long-cold tea. The barmaid really needed to bring around a fresh pot of hot water. The lack of civility and attention to detail she'd found thus far in the Highlands could prove to be very problematic—especially when she had a rescue to perform, and a very limited amount of time in which to do it.

Chapter Three

B y the time Graeme left the sitting room and pulled the door shut behind him, every servant in the house had gathered at the head of the hallway to whisper and mutter among themselves. Even if he'd wanted to keep his captive a secret, it was far too late to do so now. The best he could hope for was to keep the household from gabbing about it outside these doors.

"Nae a soul's to speak to her, and she's nae to leave that room," he ordered, pushing his way though the half-dozen men and one woman—the manor's formidable cook, Morag Woring. "Cowen, set Boisil and his lads outside until we can get a spare room upstairs ready and the windows nailed shut."

"Aye, M'laird."

His brothers sat close together on the sofa in the front room, though at this point he wasn't certain whether it was a show of united defiance or an attempt to hide how nervous they were. He hoped it was the latter.

For some reason he hadn't expected the woman beneath the sack to have black hair. Why that mattered he had no idea, but it felt significant. As did the bright blue eyes, and the way he'd wondered whether the color would deepen to sapphire in the sunlight. Graeme blew out his breath. The parts of her didn't matter. All that *did* matter was that the whole of her was in his house, and that she was there against her own will.

He dropped into the chair opposite his brothers. "What did I do wrong in raising ye," he asked, "that ye reckoned kidnapping a lass would solve yer troubles?"

"It's nae just *our* troubles," Brendan returned. "If the Maxwell turns against ye, we'll all be in fer it. And ye're so bloody stubborn ye'd risk all of us, Connell too, to yer damned pride."

"The Maxwell barely remembers we exist," Graeme retorted. "I reckon he visited every clan chieftain between Lattimer and Dunncraigh to vent his spleen about how much he hates Lattimer and how grateful he'd be if someone else saw to the problem fer him. It's nae pride; it's ignoring someaught that'll be trouble fer us."

"But we're Lattimer's neighbor," Dùghlas put in, always the most logical of the three. "Dunncraigh expects us—ye—to do someaught. Otherwise he wouldnae have bothered coming by here at all. He's nae more stomach fer ye than ye do fer him."

"What he might expect and what he'll receive are two very different things, lads."

"Why? She's here! All ye have to do is send word to Dunncraigh and tell him so. We've solved yer troubles fer ye, *bràthair.*"

Graeme contemplated Brendan for a long moment. Sixteen. When the devil had that happened? And why had he only noticed when Brendan began kidnapping delicate-looking young Englishwomen? "Fer the sake of argument," he returned slowly, "let's say I do just that. What do ye reckon happens next?"

"The duke sends someone to fetch her, uses her to purchase Lattimer from the Sassenach, and clan Maxwell unites again. And *we* did it, so we get the Maxwell's gratitude and a sackful of blunt."

"Uses her how?" Graeme pressed. "Ye're leaving oot some details."

Brendan folded his arms across his chest. "That will be fer Dunncraigh to decide, and has naught to do with us."

"Are ye certain of that? Because *ye* took her away from safety." Sitting back despite the fact that he'd never felt more alert, Graeme stretched out his legs. "I dunnae ken if ye've noticed, *bràthair,* but the Maxwell prefers other men dirty their hands so he can avoid trouble. What if he asks *me* to ransom Lady Marjorie Forrester to her brother? Dunncraigh may get Lattimer, but I reckon I'll get prison. Or a hanging."

Connell's eyes widened. "They wouldnae! The Maxwell asked us to help him, so it's his fault."

"The Maxwell asked us to hurt a man who, from what I can tell, inherited some property and is working to improve it. I found his request selfish. But nae, he didnae ask ye to kidnap anyone."

"He would have, if he'd known Lattimer's sister would be aboot."

That was likely true. "Say he did, then," he agreed. "And say Lattimer, being a bloody English soldier, tells Dunncraigh to go fling himself into the loch. And then Dunncraigh asks us to get rid of the lass before Lattimer can track her here. Would ye shoot her, Brendan? Cutting her throat would be quieter, of course."

His youngest brother sniffed. "She was going to help me rescue Mouser's kittens from the haystack. Ye cannae murder her fer that, Brendan."

"So I should be like ye, Graeme, and do naught while we watch our property rot away?" The sixteen-year-old stomped to his feet. "*I* did someaught, and it wasnae just fixing old plows or pulling sheep oot of ravines." Pushing open the door, Brendan slammed it closed behind him.

"What are we going to do, Graeme?" Connell asked, still teary-eyed. "I dunnae want ye to hang."

"I dunnae want that, either. Go up and change oot of yer wet clothes, and stay away from the back sitting room while I figure oot this mess."

The two remaining boys shot to their feet and fled.

"And dunnae think ye'll be escaping withoot punishment," Graeme called after them.

Once they'd gone, he sat forward to rest his elbows on his knees and his face in his hands. If he caused his brothers some worry, then good. They should be worried. This was not sneaking out to go spy on the half-dressed lasses dyeing wool down by the river.

And however serious they thought this might be, it was even worse than that. The lads had dropped them directly into the middle of a fight between two of the most powerful men in Scotland. He'd always preferred action to words, but at this moment he'd be walking into cannonfire either by releasing her or sending her on to Dunncraigh.

Cowen knocked on the half-open door. "M'laird, she—the grand lady, that is—is pounding on the door and demanding to see ye. She asked fer ye by name, sir."

Graeme pushed to his feet. "That's because I gave her my name."

"Why in God's name would ye do that?" the butler asked, clearly dismayed.

"So when everything goes awry she'll accuse me instead of Connell or Dùghlas or Brendan." He paused in the foyer. "Did ye drag that chain oot of the cellar?"

"Aye. And we've nailed shut the windows in the bedchamber beside yers. I reckoned ye'd want her close by."

"Thank ye, Cowen." He glanced over his shoulder at the older man as they continued down the hallway and the trio of stairs that marked the lower back half of the house. "Ye seem to be settling into this fairly easily."

"I'm all a-tremble inside, Master Graeme, but I reckoned it wouldnae do any good to let the rest of the staff see it."

The muffled pounding ahead of him grew steadily louder as he approached. "I know someone's out there!" she called. "I demand to speak to Graeme Maxton at once!"

"Och, ye *demand,* do ye, yer highness?" he returned, glad she met his expectations of a rich, delicate, spoiled aristocrat. While he couldn't quite manage to blame her for all of this, to himself he could agree that she likely deserved a little fright and discomfort. "I'm here, then, so stop yer yowling. What do ye want?"

"There . . . There are foxes in here."

Graeme shared a glance with Cowen, amusement pulling at him. Served her right, the spoiled miss. "Foxes, ye say?"

"Yes. Two of them. They're both staring at me with their beady eyes, and one of them is growling. And they stole my mutton."

He didn't want her bitten, damn it all. Turning the key, he shoved open the door. The lass staggered backward, and he caught her arm before he could stop himself. Her skin was soft and warm and smooth, and he released her the second she got her feet under her again.

"You see?" she enunciated in her precise English tones, pointing beneath the small couch. "Foxes."

"Daisy. Pete. Go find Connell," he ordered, stepping farther into the room.

The pair of foxes bounded out of the sitting room in a flash of red fur and white-tipped tails. It wouldn't do for the foxes to reside in Connell's room while the lad had rabbit kits hidden there, but once he moved Lady Marjorie to her guest bedchamber they could return to their sitting room den.

"Better, m'lady?" he asked, finally giving her his full attention. Black hair, aye, a bit disheveled after the sack and the travel in the back of the wagon, but still long and curling and soft-looking. She likely had a maid brush each strand a dozen times before bed. That wouldn't be happening tonight, however.

"Yes. Thank you. Though you might have told me they were pets."

"I might ask in return whether ye reckon all Highlands hooses have wild foxes settled in their sitting rooms," he commented, folding his arms across his chest. Graeme cocked his head at her. "How the devil did ye manage to get stolen by a handful of bairns? Or are ye daft enough to think yerself safe alone in the Highlands?"

"I'm not alone," she retorted, managing to look regal despite the half-fallen hair and the mud-edged green gown. "I stepped away for a breath of fresh air, and the little boy lured me away by asking for my help." She put her hands on her slender hips. "Do you often use children in your nefarious dealings? That is shameful, sir."

"Ye've mud on yer cheek," he noted, curling his fingers against the desire to brush it away. "Ye'd look more indignant if ye were clean and yer hair put back up, I reckon."

"I *was* clean and my hair put up, before your hoodlums kidnapped me," she retorted. "And my goodwill is swiftly vanishing. Set me free by sunset, or—"

Graeme closed the distance between them. "Or what?" he murmured. "Dunnae make threats against me or mine, lass. Ye've nae idea what's afoot here, or how very restrained I'm being."

She lifted her chin to continue meeting his gaze. "Clearly I don't know what's going on. All I *do* know is that I was on my way to see my brother and now I'm Graeme Maxton's prisoner somewhere in the Highlands. You tell me not to threaten you, but you've already done far worse to me, sir."

A man could get lost in those sky-blue eyes of hers, he decided. And she'd likely smile and dance away and entangle the next unfortunate lad who crossed her path, and then the one after that. "I'll find ye someaught else to eat, ye'll stay here another hour or so, then we'll move ye into somewhere a mite more comfortable. Likely nae as luxurious as what ye're accustomed to, but it'll have to do."

"And then?" she demanded, looking fierce but for the ghostly pallor of her cheeks—unless the hue of fine porcelain was her normal color.

Deliberately he smiled. "And then we'll see."

The door closed and locked behind him again, and Marjorie took a deep, steadying breath. Oh, he aggravated her. If she still felt frightened, well, she wouldn't admit that even to herself. It did her no good, and quite possibly only aided him.

She stalked over to the nearest window again, shifting the heavy curtains a little with her fingers to peer outside. A vast countryside spread out before her, broken by stands of trees and rocky hills and soft-edged patches of snow. She'd ridden in the back of that wagon for well over an hour, and in God-only-knew what direction. She could be three hours from Lattimer Castle, or nine.

That still wouldn't have stopped her from attempting an escape, though. Eventually she would stumble across someone who would help her, or at least point her in the correct direction. Grimacing, she settled her gaze on the man who stood beside an overgrown birch tree, a floppy-edged hat pulled low over his eyes and his attention squarely on her. She'd already looked out the window facing a wild-looking river, and seen the other man waiting there.

Both wore heavy kilts of red and black and green plaid—the clan Maxwell tartan, she assumed, since Graeme

Maxton had informed her that she was in the middle of Maxwell territory. He wore trousers and muddy work boots, but she had to presume he was also part of the same clan.

Letting the curtain fall closed again, she made another circuit of the small room. A blue couch, two overstuffed chairs of the same blue material, the hard-backed chair to which they'd initially tied her, four small tables scattered about, and a writing desk between the river-facing windows. She'd already searched it for weapons, but the boys had evidently removed everything sharper than an inkwell.

Clobbering Maxton with that might feel satisfying, but it wouldn't gain her an exit from the house. And when she made an attempt, she meant for it to be successful.

Above the writing desk a small glass-doored cabinet had been affixed to the wall, the seashells and driftwood and small, polished river rocks it held pretty, but completely ineffective as weapons. Closing the doors again, she eyed herself in the slightly warped reflection. A smudge of dirt crossed her left cheek, just as Maxton had pointed out, and her hair could likely frighten a scarecrow.

Scowling, she pulled out the few remaining pins and used her decorative green hair ribbon to tie it all back in a tail. It was horribly informal, but leaving it loose would be scandalous even in these circumstances.

Marjorie began to rub at her cheek, then stopped. What was she cleaning up for? Because he'd noted that she was dirty? Well, she certainly hadn't done that to herself. And if she looked disheveled and out of sorts, she had a right to do so.

After another few minutes spent studying the half-dozen paintings on three of the walls, she sat on one of the blue chairs. Two of the paintings, a man and a woman, weren't of any particular quality, but looked to be the parents—or perhaps even the grandparents—of Connell and

Graeme, the two Maxtons she'd seen. The woman shared their gray eyes and open, direct gaze, while Graeme, at least, had as much in common with the hard jaw and straight slash of eyebrows that marked the man. He'd seemingly picked up a combination of their hair colors, for the lady boasted a curling mass of deep red hair, a stark contrast to the short, straight brown of the other portrait.

Why in the world his hair color mattered except so she could adequately describe him to her brother and the local authorities she had no idea, but she had nothing else to do but contemplate it. Him, rather. Now that she knew the foxes were tame, she almost wished she hadn't complained about them. They would have helped keep her thoughts distracted, at least.

With no clock in the room she could only guess the time, but the lone candle they'd left her had burned quite low. Perhaps Maxton meant for her to go mad or expire from boredom. Grimacing, Marjorie stood and stalked up to the door again.

"Hello?" she called, knocking.

Silence.

"Hello? I know someone's out there. If I'm to remain trapped in here, I require another candle. And a book, for heaven's sake. I've never seen a sitting room before that didn't contain even a single, solitary book on a shelf somewhere."

Listening carefully, she heard muttering and then fast-retreating footsteps. Quite possibly she shouldn't have insulted the lack of literature; she had no idea, after all, if any of these heathens could read. But for once her instinct to be kind and proper and polite could go hang itself. If she'd been less polite she might have ordered Mrs. Giswell to leave the table at the inn so she could dine in peace, and she would be within sight right now of Lattimer Castle and Gabriel. But because she'd bit her tongue against her frustration and left to clear her head, she was here. And she didn't want to be here.

Heavier, booted footsteps approached, and she backed away from the door. She'd nearly fallen over the last time he'd stomped into the room, and she had no wish to be grabbed again. Far too many people had grabbed at her today.

The door opened, but this time he didn't enter. He didn't really need to, though; big and broad-shouldered as he was, he filled the doorway. He leaned against the doorjamb to gaze at her, a long strand of his unruly hair falling forward halfway down his cheek. "A book and a candle?" he finally drawled.

"Unless I'm to sit here in the dark, yes," she returned.

"Ye can if ye like. Or ye can come with me, yer highness."

Marjorie folded her hands in front of her, wondering why in the world she could look at a man who'd kidnapped her and kept her trapped in a room and still be able to notice that he had fine gray eyes, a lean waist, and an indescribable . . . something that made her want to keep looking at him. "You're leading me to my prison cell, I suppose?"

"Aye." He narrowed one eye. "It does have a fireplace and a warm bed. I reckon ye're chilled."

"I've been sitting in a cold room and in a damp gown for hours. Am I supposed to be grateful that you've finally realized I might be uncomfortable?"

"Nae. Ye could stop yammering aboot it and follow me to where it's warmer, though." With that he turned his back on her and walked out of the doorway.

The man was a barbarian. That was the only conclusion that made sense. An uneducated, unfeeling, arrogant barbarian. "Heathen," she muttered, stalking after him.

"I didnae quite hear ye," he returned, slowing his march up a long hallway.

"I called you a heathen," Marjorie said distinctly.

"Ah. That's what I thought ye said."

An older man in black livery emerged from a side door to fall in behind her. Someone to make certain she didn't run out the large double doors ahead, she supposed. Still, at least now she knew precisely where the exit lay. She would have to find some paper and begin sketching out a map of the house and countryside around her. When an opportunity to escape presented itself, she meant to make use of it.

In the small foyer, Maxton turned to face her, lifted an eyebrow, then headed up the stairs to her left. All along the wall portraits hung, men in the same plaid as those she'd spied outside, some bearded and glowering, others looking more contemplative, and most of them with the gray eyes and red-brown hair of her so-called host. Evidently his ancestors made a habit of marrying redheaded women.

If this house belonged to him, and despite his worn, dirty clothes, he didn't seem to be some common farmer after all. This was no farmer's cottage, at the least. Simple and rather austere, yes, but the size alone said it belonged to a family of some rank and importance. Shepherds didn't have portraits of their ancestors lining the walls.

The doors on either side of the upstairs hallway stood closed, probably so she couldn't see into the rooms that lay beyond. It would never do for her to discover where the muskets or swords were kept, after all.

Maxton stopped two doors short of the windows that marked the end of the hallway. Making a show of producing a key from his coat pocket, he unlocked the door and pushed it open. "In here," he said, gesturing for her to precede him.

The door itself looked very solid and somewhat intimidating, but Marjorie kept her shoulders squared and stepped inside. A large bed stood close by one wall, while a small fireplace on the opposite wall sent warmth and light into the room. A comfortable-looking pair of chairs squatted before the fire, while a huge, heavy-looking wardrobe shared the wall with the fireplace. If this hadn't been a prison, she would have called it welcoming.

"The windows are nailed shut," Maxton said, strolling in behind her. "If ye think to set fire to the hoose and escape that way, keep in mind that ye'll be the last soul to be rescued—and that's after the foxes and the cats. In fact, I may nae get up here to ye at all."

The words sounded easy and amusing, but she didn't mistake for one second the steel behind them. "No matter the circumstances," she retorted, "I would never endanger young Connell in that way. I'm not the barbarian here, sir."

"That's good to know," he returned, eyeing her again. Whatever he looked for, she hoped she left him wondering. "Ye'll find a bellpull by the bed," he went on after a moment, "should ye need to summon me."

"Summon you?" she repeated, seizing on the words. "Are you the butler, then?"

"I'm the man ye'll be dealing with. The only one."

"Well, how pleasant for both of us." She took another turn about the room, not about to sit in his presence. "I don't suppose you've considered that I have no change of clothes or even a hairbrush? Not to mention the fact that I just spent hours racketing about in the back of a filthy wagon in the rain."

Gray eyes assessed her from toe to head, the slow lift of his gaze making her heart skitter. With boarding school, and finishing school, and then serving Lady Sarah and her cats, followed by months of being ignored by everyone in Mayfair, she'd never had many dealings with men. By the time she'd received Gabriel's letter, she'd actually begun to anticipate the inevitable crowd of fortune hunters. At least a man who needed her income would have reason to be polite to her. Even a fortune hunter, though, wouldn't look at her the way Graeme Maxton did—with the gaze of a predator assessing his next meal.

"The room across from ye has a bathtub," he said after a moment. "We'll fill it fer ye once I'm finished here. And there are a few things in the wardrobe that might suit ye. Nae as fancy or grand as what ye're accustomed to, I imagine, but they're clean. And dry."

She nodded, expecting him to leave and lock her in again. Instead he remained in the middle of the bedchamber and continued looking at her. "Don't expect me to thank you, Mr. Maxton," she finally said, as the silence began to stretch on. "I'm not here because I chose to come visiting and got caught by the foul weather."

"Nae, ye arenae here because ye decided to come calling," he agreed. "Until I decide what's to be done with ye, though, ye might consider trying to be more pleasant." He inclined his head, the gesture graceful but not looking terribly practiced—as if he didn't bow often, or willingly. "I'll fetch ye when the tub is full. And if ye're going to keep snapping back at me, it's Laird Maxton. I'm a damned viscount, m'lady."

A moment later she was alone again, locked into yet another room with nothing but the clothes on her back, a small tray of food, and deep dark night out the pair of windows behind her. With a shudder she pulled the heavy green curtains closed. For all she knew those men still stood outside, watching her from below.

A viscount. *Him.* She never would have guessed that in a hundred years. Callused hands, worn clothes, his plainspoken, rude manner—the only aristocratic thing about him was his arrogance. If he was what passed for nobility in the Highlands, she'd be doubly happy to return to London.

A tear ran down her cheek, and she brushed it away. Tears wouldn't get her out of this mess. And screaming out her frustration would only convince her captor that she should never be allowed out of this room.

Hm. Perhaps Lord Maxton's comment had some potential. Perhaps being polite and pleasant and demure would gain her some trust. If so, Graeme Maxton had given her the key to his own downfall. Because the moment they turned their backs, she meant to escape. And no aggravating, arrogant man—handsome or not—would be able to stop her.

Chapter Four

As usual during the short days of a Highlands autumn, Graeme rose well before sunrise. This morning as he finished shaving and cleaning his teeth he wondered why he'd bothered to go to bed at all. He damned well hadn't slept enough to make it worthwhile.

The source of his unrest was likely dreaming away the morning in the bedchamber beside his. And while the idea annoyed him, they'd all be better off if she remained sleeping. He needed to figure out what to do about her when he couldn't send her on to Dunncraigh, and wouldn't simply return her to the Cracked Hearth. And while he could keep her prisoner here for the moment, that came with its own set of additional problems—and expenses.

For one damned thing, he was going to have to hire a female to look after her. A lady required someone to brush her hair, help her dress, and myriad other things he couldn't even imagine. Mrs. Woring the cook would never do; he trusted her to keep her mouth shut about their unwanted visitor, but the woman regularly beat venison into submission. A gentle hand, she did not have.

Keeping grand Lady Marjorie here only prolonged the

danger to the lot of them, anyway. Whether she remained for one day or one week, her tale to the local constabulary wouldn't change. Nor could he bribe her to keep her silence. Her impractical shoes—which he remembered with annoying clarity—likely cost more than he'd had to spare all year. And hell, aside from bribery, the only two other ways to keep a lass from speaking out against him were to kill her, or to marry her.

To marry her.

A knock sounded at his door. "Enter," he called, jumping.

"M'laird," Cowen said, stepping into the room, "she's pounding at the door again. Nearly rang the bell off its hook, too."

Graeme took a deep breath. Whatever he'd abruptly begun to contemplate, he needed more than two seconds to figure it out. "Likely she needs someone to open the damned curtains fer her," he muttered absently. "Have a plate of breakfast made up, will ye? And some tea. Ladies like tea, I hear."

"Aye." The butler cleared his throat. "I thought to send Taog doon to the Cracked Hearth for a bite this morning."

"That's a good idea, Cowen. I'd like to know if I'm aboot to have half the Sassenach army riding doon into my valley." And Taog the footman had a good portion of sense, so the lad wouldn't be likely to gossip, or to miss any clues that the Maxton household was about to be in for a great deal of trouble.

"That was my thought, too."

Graeme followed the butler into the hallway, then watched the older man hurry down the stairs on his errands. Five servants, Garaidh nan Leòmhann had, when back during his parents' time the so-called Lion's Den had boasted a dozen. He would almost rather have seen the house go up in flames—dead and ruined all at once. This way, the slow decline and ruin they'd been facing for the past dozen years or so brought a little pain with it every damned day.

The lass pounded on the far side of her door as he reached it. The lass who happened to be a damned heiress. And a privileged, spoiled Sassenach. But for what he required, that really didn't matter. Graeme made a fist and pounded back. "I'm here, fer God's sake!"

"You're a very rude man," she returned, her voice a little muffled through the thick oak.

"I dunnae recall claiming anything different. What do ye want? Ye'll have yer breakfast in a minute."

"I . . . I require some assistance."

Clenching his jaw, ordering himself not to imagine her still in her night rail with her long dark hair loose over her shoulders, he pulled the key from his pocket, unlocked the door, and shoved it open.

Lady Marjorie was not wearing the night rail he'd scavenged for her, nor was her long, dark hair loose. And although he didn't see what he'd imagined, the sight before him left him more unsettled than disappointed. She'd found the light blue muslin gown that had once belonged to his mother, the fit a little tight across her bosom. And she'd somehow tamed that hair into an elegant coil atop her head. If she was attempting to convince him that she was an angel and that her halo, however, she would firstly have to be other than a Sassenach, and secondly not be the physical representation of just how much trouble he'd likely found himself, whatever he decided to do with her.

He shook himself. "What assistance?" he demanded. "Ye look fairly decent to me."

Her pale cheeks darkened to a soft rose. "I—yes. It's the buckle on my shoe. I put them on the hearth to dry, and when I tried to put them back on, one of the buckles broke off."

"Yer shoe."

She frowned. "Yes, my shoe. Do you expect me to go about barefoot? There's snow outside."

"I dunnae expect ye to go aboot outside at all," he countered. Just the thought of one of Dunncraigh's men spying Lattimer's sister on *his* property . . . The coolness between the Maxwell and himself would seem like a handshake compared to what would happen if that occurred. Of course if he had under his control the money to challenge the Maxwell's stranglehold, the story would have a very different ending.

"I am not going barefoot," she stated. "A lady wears shoes. It's bad enough that this is a house dress I will have to pair with walking shoes. If I—"

"Fer glory's sake," he muttered. "Where are the damned things?"

"On my feet. I wasn't about to admit you into my presence while my feet were naked. And your language, sir. If you please."

Graeme clenched his jaw, choosing to concentrate on the second part of the statement even while the first part had him conjuring more than her feet naked before him. Damnation. He needed to go visit Morag Polk or Juno Allen in Sheiling. Three younger siblings and a host of cotters under his protection or not, a man like him wasn't meant to be celibate for . . . God, how long had it been? A month? No wonder he was imagining a proper English lass naked. Of course if he married her, he could damned well see her naked. Even a marriage of convenience—his convenience, in this instance—needed to be consummated.

"My language?" he repeated, fighting his way back to the conversation at hand. "Ye're the one came to the Highlands, lass. Dunnae ye dare complain aboot our way of speaking."

Color touched her cheeks again. "I meant the profanity. Not your . . . way of speaking."

"Oh." Had he cursed? He couldn't recall, though odds were that he had. "Well, I reckon I'll speak as I wish."

She folded her arms over her chest, which sent his attention back to the snug fit of the blue muslin. "Physically I am your prisoner, Mr. Maxton. My mind and my opinions, however, remain my own."

"That's bloody fine with me," he returned, lifting his gaze to her face again, using profanity deliberately. He was well versed in it, and that was damned certain. "Give me yer damned shoes."

"I . . ." She made a sound very like a growl. "I will not surrender my only footwear."

"God save us from the plague and Englishwomen," he muttered, altering his grandfather's favorite saying a bit to fit the circumstances. Old Uisdean Maxton would no doubt approve, given his well-documented suspicion of any Sassenach. "Cowen!"

The door opened so quickly that the butler must have been listening just on the other side of it. "Aye, sir?"

"Find me some lass's shoes. I dunnae care if they're milking shoes or dancing slippers, as long as they'll fit our guest, here."

Bobbing his head, Cowen backed out of the doorway and vanished again. Female shoes were a rare commodity at the Lion's Den, but they'd managed to find a handful of gowns in the attic. The butler was a resourceful lad; he'd manage.

"Thank you."

That captured his attention. "So ye're a polite lass now, are ye?" he asked, cocking an eyebrow.

"I am your captive, sir. I'm hoping for kind treatment."

She had no idea how very kind he was being to her, considering the purpose his idiot brothers had in mind for her, and how much blunt handing her over to Dunncraigh would likely earn him. In fact, the only thing that would likely earn him more would be to keep her for himself. That would definitely set him against Dunncraigh, but at least he'd have the income to make it a good fight. Could he do it, though? To her?

He certainly didn't owe her anything; she was a foolish, self-important Sassenach who would have fared far worse if someone else had found her. As for him, an heiress would provide what he required. After she gave him an heir he could go elsewhere for sex, and he'd never looked for anything beyond that. He never would. "Do as ye're told and I'll be kind enough," he returned belatedly.

A female with any sense would have curtsied and gone over to sit by the fire until he could fetch her breakfast. This one, though, stood her ground in the center of the room and continued gazing at him with those eyes the color of the midday sky. For Lucifer's sake, he would be tempted to marry her whether she had money or not. "And what is it I'm to do, then?" she asked. "No one's told me anything about why I'm here except to say that my brother and I are English and you're all from clan Maxwell. Surely we aren't the first Englishmen who've ever ridden through Maxwell territory."

"That would be the problem, yer highness," he said, wishing Cowen would hurry the devil up and find some shoes for the lass so he could go away somewhere and catch his breath and his wits. Just standing there in her presence he couldn't seem to pull enough air into his lungs—and he couldn't blame it all on his contemplation of a marriage. He'd gone bride hunting once or twice before, after all, only to be thwarted by Dunncraigh and one of his many sons and nephews. He hadn't noted the lass's appearance, then. Now, though, he couldn't seem able to look away. That aside, Marjorie Forrester was someone the Maxwell didn't know about. Nor would the duke, until it was too late. If Graeme found her physically attractive—and he damned well did—then he would count that as an unasked-for bonus. "Ye arenae the first English to cross our path. And the previous . . . visitors, we'll call 'em, werenae very kindly."

"Out of curiosity, did you kidnap any of these so-called visitors? That might explain their lack of friendliness."

Damned impossible woman. "Nae. Nae me personally, anyway. But I reckon ye'll do fer the moment."

Not him personally. He was trying to be flippant or sarcastic, no doubt, but Marjorie seized onto those particular words with all her strength. Her kidnappers—his younger brothers, she now knew—had been full of derogatory statements about her fellow countymen and her in particular, but despite his threats and arrogance and intimidating presence, Maxton seemed mostly to view her as . . . She wasn't certain, but it made her breath quicken.

But he didn't seem to have anything against the English in general, or her in particular. Her first thought after making that realization was that perhaps she could convince him, then, that setting her free would be to everyone's benefit. She needed a plan first, though. He wanted to protect his brothers, and so she would have to figure out how to convince him that they wouldn't be blamed for this—whether she meant to keep her word or not.

"Nae response to that, yer ladyship? Have I broken yer spirit, then?" he prodded.

Ha. Not likely. "My continued well-being would seem to be at your whim, sir," she returned. "I wouldn't call that level ground for an argument."

A slight smile curved his mouth. "Ye do have a point."

Arrogant man. Smiling at her as if he knew exactly how handsome he was and meant to use that to sway her weak little female brain into think him charming. *Ha*. And *ha* again. "I know I do."

Another man, this one younger and taller than the one she'd assumed to be the butler, appeared in the doorway. The scent of the tray he carried made her stomach rumble, and for once she didn't care how unladylike that might be. She should probably refuse to eat as a protest against her captivity, but if she starved herself she wouldn't be in any condition to escape when an opportunity presented itself.

"Ye requested breakfast for the lady, sir," the young man said, his clearly curious gaze fixed on her. "I've brought it while Cowen's searching fer shoes."

"Thank ye, Ross," Maxton said, taking the tray. "Oot with ye."

The young man fled down the hallway, and with one foot her captor hooked the door and pushed it closed behind him. "It isn't proper for you to be in a room alone with me," Marjorie stated, mostly to see how he would react to that. By London standards she'd been ruined the moment she vanished from the inn. Of course by London standards she wasn't qualified to be in any of their fine ballrooms and parlors, anyway. This man didn't know that, though. And anything she could do to keep her distance from him had to be to her benefit. It seemed like it should be, anyway.

"So ye say," he muttered, and set the tray down on the small table beneath the two overstuffed chairs. "Sit doon and eat."

"I prefer not to dine with you standing over me and glowering."

He sat down in one of the two chairs and with his boot kicked the other out for her. "Sit doon and eat," he repeated.

"But I just said it isn't proper for—"

"Ye're a damned captive, lass. Ye dunnae make the rules here. And I'll nae ask ye again. If ye dunnae sit doon, I'll eat yer breakfast myself. And I'm damned hungry, so dunnae think I wouldnae do it."

With a stifled sigh, dragging one foot a little so the unbuckled shoe wouldn't come off and trip her, Marjorie sat at the table opposite him. A cloth covered the plate, presumably to keep the items beneath it warm, and she removed it to set it across her lap. Despite her hunger she poured hot tea into her teacup first, then dropped in one lump of sugar while he frowned. Hm. Was sugar dear here? Deliberately she took a second lump and stirred it in the tea. Then she found the fork and knife and cut herself a bite-sized slice of mutton.

"How long does it take ye to eat?" Maxton asked, setting an elbow on the table and his chin on his clenched fist.

Marjorie chewed and swallowed. "I beg your pardon?"

"The food's better when it's hot," he continued, light gray eyes meeting hers and then lowering to the utensils in her hands. "At this rate it'll be ice before ye finish."

"I suppose you grab great chunks of meat in your hands and rip off mouthfuls with your teeth?"

"I dunnae dine with my pinkies sticking up in the air."

She glanced at her hand and curled her fingers back into her palm. "I do what is considered proper. And in my opinion you have no grounds to criticize *my* behavior. Kidnapping someone is far worse than drinking with a straight pinkie—which is proper etiquette, by the way."

That only made him grin again, the insufferable man. "If ye'd stayed in London where ye belong," he commented, "ye could be wielding yer cups and glasses however ye chose, with nae a soul to criticize ye."

"Ha!" she bit out. "That shows how little you know." With that she returned to consuming her breakfast, which he seemed for some reason to find fascinating. Perhaps utensils *were* foreign to him, after all.

"And ye'd nae be ruined, with but one way to save yer reputation."

That stopped her for a moment, stopped her breath and her heart. "I don't know what you're talking about, my lord," she said, even though she had a very good idea. He thought they needed to marry? *No!* He was a mannerless, kidnapping barbarian, and she—she had plans, blast it all. Plans that didn't include the Scottish Highlands or marrying for other than love. Not now, when she could afford to be both unemployed and unmarried.

"If ye mean to wound me by pointing oot how little I ken aboot London, ye might as well save yer breath, yer ladyship."

She set down the fork and knife and touched the napkin to the corners of her mouth, willing her fingers not to shake. "That, Lord Maxton, is a splendid idea," she returned, deliberately misinterpreting his comment. "Until you tell me why I'm here and what you mean to do with me, I'm finished chatting with you." She folded her hands into her lap.

The viscount sat back. "Despite the fact that I've dragged ye off, tied ye to a chair, and locked ye into a room, ye reckon that threatening me with yer silence will move me to tell ye all my evil plans?"

Tilting her head, she met his gaze. "As a point of clarification, *you* untied me, provided me with a bath and clean clothes, and sat with me while I ate breakfast. *You* didn't kidnap me." She paused to take a breath. "In fact, I think you had no idea that any of this was going to happen until you saw me sitting in that chair with a sack over my head. And the question I demand you answer is what you mean to do with me now that I'm here."

"Ye've some wits aboot ye," he said, reaching over to

collect her knife and fork before he pushed to his feet. What ye need to ken, lass, is that this *is* all my doing. I'll swear to that on a stack of Bibles. And now that ye *are* here, I reckon I'll do what's right."

"And what might that be?" she demanded, even though she didn't want to hear what she very much thought he meant to say next. "You're letting me go, I presume?"

"Nae. I've decided I'll marry ye."

She gasped as he spoke the words aloud; she couldn't imagine a circumstance where she would have been able to stifle the sound. "No, sir, you will not! I refuse!"

His humorless smile appeared again, more offputting than friendly. "Ye can refuse fer now; it'll take a few days fer me to get a license. In the meantime, ye can stay in here and consider what I'd have to do with ye if I couldnae count on yer cooperation. Ye may nae like the idea, but it's the best way fer both of us to stay alive and protected. I'm nae the biggest fright in the Highlands, lass."

"I'm afraid I must disagree with that, Lord Maxton."

At least Maxton hadn't nailed boards over the windows, even if he had nailed them shut. At least, Marjorie reflected, she had daylight and a view. She'd dragged a comfortable chair over nearly the moment he'd locked her in again. Now, as she sat sipping the cold dregs of the tea that he'd left her, she had to concede that this particular corner of the Highlands was very . . . picturesque. Mountains capped with snow, a river running past jagged rocks while old, twisted trees climbed up the far bank, deep greens broken by shrinking patches of brilliant white—she'd never seen anything so rugged and wild.

She wanted to walk out into it. As firstly she remained a prisoner and secondly no one had appeared with shoes, however, that didn't seem likely to happen. Nor did she have any idea how long her present circumstances would last—or now, if this would ever end. She should likely be cowering in terror, fainting, demanding a physician to tend her—but while likely a fitting reaction, it didn't seem particularly useful. And in truth, while she felt angry, annoyed, frustrated, and supremely uneasy about what her future might hold, she was more angry than anything else.

Marrying her? It would have been gallant, she supposed, coming from someone who owned a sense of nobility or decorum. Marjorie didn't believe for a second that Graeme, Viscount Maxton, was motivated by either of those things. If it wasn't for her benefit, though, it had to be for his. As his wife she wouldn't be able to speak against him in court, which might indeed save him from imprisonment. It wouldn't save him from her brother's wrath, though perhaps he hadn't considered that. She would make certain he did.

There was also, of course, her money. She had an admittedly limited view of this house, but what she had seen looked quite shabby. An influx of thousands of pounds would make a tremendous difference. Perhaps it made sense to him, then, but she had no intention of going along with it. She'd spent far too much time and effort and education to end up as some odious man's purse. For heaven's sake, London fortune hunters were the only aristocrats who'd deigned to speak to her, and thus far she'd sent them all away.

He'd said he wasn't the most frightening thing in the Highlands. And whatever that thing was, he'd also implied that by marrying her, he would be saving her from it. At first she'd thought she would be ransomed to her brother in exchange for some of his money. Or perhaps cattle, or sheep. Highlanders did like their sheep. But Maxton hadn't been talking about a ransom, clearly. Was it somewhere else she might be sent, then? Someone else who'd decide to marry her without her having any say in the matter? *Men. Highlands men, especially.*

Silently, because a lady didn't utter such words aloud, she cursed her brother. Not because he'd written her, but because he'd only bothered to send the one letter. When they'd met in London better than three months ago and Gabriel had told her of his unexpected inheritance and given her Leeds House, he'd promised to write more often. If he'd done so, she might have known that clan Maxwell seemed to be at odds with him. She might have known not to make the journey north to surprise him, for heaven's sake.

Something behind her rustled, and she whipped her head around, half expecting to see more foxes, or perhaps a wildcat, invading the bedchamber through some hole or other. A folded sheet of paper slid into the room, however, through the narrow crack beneath the door. Marjorie stood, her heart skittering. Did she have an ally?

Moving as quietly as she could in her broken shoe, she hurried over to retrieve the note. Her hands unsteady, she unfolded it—to see a child's uneven, untidy printing sprawled across the page. "Dear Lady Marjory," she read to herself, "I am vary sory I helpt my brothrs kit nap you. And please do not be mad at Graeme, becuz it was Brendan and Dùghlases faults, mostly Brendan. I hav baby rabits in my room to. Do you want to see them? Youre friend, Connell Maxton."

Well, the spelling and grammar were both atrocious, but at least someone had apologized for dragging her into this mess. And it confirmed what she'd suspected—that the lion-maned oldest brother hadn't planned on her being there—though that didn't seem to have stopped him from taking advantage of her presence. *Marry her?* Ha. She'd jump out the window first.

Even more importantly, *did* she now have an ally? She

pressed her cheek against the cool wood of the door. "Are you still there?" she whispered.

"Aye," young Connell's hushed voice returned. "Did ye get my note?"

"I did. And—"

"Write me back," he interrupted.

Marjorie closed her mouth again. However serious and precarious her situation, to the eight-year-old this was clearly a game. And an ally was an ally. "I don't have anything to write with," she whispered back.

The stub of a pencil rolled beneath the door. She picked it up, frowning as she turned the boy's note over. Just how desperate was she, to be willing to use a child? And how ridiculous was she, to turn away possible help because she would have preferred that it came from someone tall and handsome and considerably more mature?

"Are you going to wait for my response?" she whispered.

"Nae. I'm supposed to be doing my lessons," came back. "Graeme filled two damned pages with arithmetic problems. If I dunnae do them, it'll be nae supper fer me. Before sunset I'll knock three times, then two times. Then ye'll ken it's me, and ye can send the note under the door."

At least that would give her time to decide how dastardly she was prepared to be. "Very well," she said, and a moment later heard his light footsteps retreating.

Young Connell had already proven to be a valuable source of information today. Through the boy she'd learned that Graeme hadn't ordered her kidnapping. Even more surprising, the barbarian wrote out arithmetic equations for his brother's study. Heaven help them all if that man was solely responsible for educating his brothers—though that did explain everyone's liberal profanity.

Marjorie sat at the writing desk and pulled a fresh sheet of paper from one of the drawers. If she did decide to make use of Connell Maxton she could certainly blame it on his oldest brother; whether Graeme had been behind her kidnapping or not, he was the one who'd decided what to do with her. And he'd been exceedingly rude and arrogant about it.

As handsome as he was, if he'd been more patient and considerate, he might—*might*—have had half a chance of winning her affection. Or at least she could pretend that. Because she could imagine kissing him, and enjoying it. That had more to do with how . . . alone she'd felt than with his supposed charms. And it was *only* in daydreams, anyway.

Grimacing, she set pencil to paper. Manners, etiquette, propriety—she'd spent years mastering all the rules and nuances necessary for survival in proper Society. But this concerned morality, and she remained fairly certain that she and Society had some disagreements in that area.

The fact remained, though, that she needed to return to Society, because her house sprawled in the center of it, and she needed to live in that house, with those people around her—and the longer she went missing, the less likely any of them would be *ever* to accept her. All they would need was an excuse to dismiss her as ruined, or scandalized, as if being the sister of an upjumped duke wasn't enough to earn their scorn. But the wife of a probably destitute Scottish viscount? That would finish off her chances as surely as the news that she'd been kidnapped in the first place.

She hid the letters old and new beneath the remaining blank papers in the desk, and slid the pencil into an old-looking, empty vase on one shelf. In her opinion it hardly qualified as a weapon, but it *had* been something Maxton didn't seem to want her to have. Perhaps he worried a crow might fly down the chimney, giving her the opportunity to tie a message to its leg and send it off for help.

Her door rattled. Marjorie jumped, nearly pulling the

vase onto the floor. She had hours to wait before Connell and his secret knocks, but before she could convince herself that the youngster had been too excited to wait for sunset the heavy thing swung open. It wasn't the boy.

Chapter Five

"So am I to have no expectation of privacy?" she blurted, sidestepping away from the vase.

The broad-shouldered, russet-haired lion strolled into the room. "Were ye up to someaught that required privacy?"

"No. That isn't the point."

"I cannae decide if ye're a madwoman, or just relentlessly contrary," he muttered, hefting the cloth sack he carried from one hand to the other.

If he meant to put that thing over her head again, she would punch him in the nose. "Am I causing you some difficulty?" she asked, allowing the sarcasm she felt to color her tone.

"Damned right, ye are. Sit doon." He gestured at the chair she'd dragged beneath the window.

Marjorie folded her arms across her chest, mostly so he wouldn't see them trembling. "I will not be blindfolded again, you oaf. Not to be dragged to the altar, or anywhere else."

One straight brow lowered, and he looked at the sack

in his hand as if seeing it for the first time. "It's shoes," he said, eyeing her again. "So ye arenae fearless."

"Point me to anyone who is, and I'll show you a fool."

"Meaning me, I suppose. Sit yer arse in the chair." He dragged his free hand through his auburn hair.

"I told you that I don't like to be loomed over."

With an even more exasperated glance, Maxton grabbed the back of the other hearthside chair and dragged it over to face the one she'd placed earlier. Then he dropped into it, lifting both eyebrows as if daring her to find something else about which to complain.

While she might have rightly pointed out that a gentleman wouldn't seat himself before a lady, she kept her mouth shut. Neither of them thought him a gentleman, and reminding him of that might also remind him of other things men who weren't gentlemen might do with a captive female—other than announcing they were to be married, that was. A shiver ran up her spine, not unpleasantly. Trying to ignore why her mouth had suddenly gone dry, she seated herself with every ounce of grace she possessed and folded her hands on her lap.

He set the bag between his booted feet. "Give me yer foot," he ordered.

"I am not sticking my foot up in the air."

"One day I hope ye'll realize how far I've been bending over to be kindly to ye, yer grandness," he drawled.

"And one day I hope you'll realize that nothing you do can possibly convince me that marrying you is in my best interest." A bit harsh, perhaps, if she needed his goodwill, but for heaven's sake, telling her that he was being kind, *while* he kept her prisoner?

Uttering something unflattering-sounding in Gaelic, he slid forward, dropping from the chair onto his knees. It was a vulnerable position; light gray eyes beneath unexpectedly long lashes lifted to meet hers, something secret and enticing in his gaze.

Stop it, Ree! she ordered herself, but by the time she realized she should have kicked him somewhere sensitive and fled out the unlocked door, he'd already slid a hand around her ankle and grasped it quite firmly. Brushing the folds of her skirt aside with his other hand, he drew her foot forward to rest on one of his bent knees.

"This is . . . not proper, sir," she gulped, her cheeks heating.

"Well, which is less proper, then?" he retorted, taking the heel of her walking shoe and pulling it off her foot. "Me touching yer foot, or ye wearing broken shoes?"

As utterly certain as she was that it was the former, Marjorie hesitated to answer. Men didn't kneel in front of her, much less touch her legs and pull off her shoes. The sensations running up the back of her legs and along her spine had nothing to do with being captured, and everything to do with a man—this man—touching her.

He set the broken shoe aside and, still holding her ankle in one hand, dug into the sack with the other. The shoe he produced was old, the burgundy satin across the top frayed on one side. Despite that, the quality of it was obvious, from the faded gold embroidery around the ankle to the tight, precise stitches above the short heel. Lowering his gaze, he slipped it onto her foot.

"Well?" he prompted after a moment. "Do ye reckon ye can stomp aboot in that?"

This seemed to have much less to do with shoes than it did with him attempting to make her . . . trust him? To agree to marry him even after her vehement protests? Was that it? She flexed her toes. "A lady doesn't stomp. But yes, it seems to fit rather well."

He switched his hand to her other foot and replaced that

shoe as well, moving far more slowly than she knew to be necessary. Marjorie didn't like it, didn't like the intimacy of it or the way his touch made her heart beat harder. This man was actively ruining her life; she should be trying to kick him in the face, not fighting against . . . lust or whatever it was that made her want to run her fingers through his disheveled hair.

Realizing she still sat there with one foot in his big hands and resting on his knee, she yanked free and firmly set both feet on the floor. "Don't expect me to thank you, Maxton. My shoes and I would be perfectly fine if not for you."

Reaching out, he tugged down the hem of her skirt. "I dunnae expect yer gratitude, yer gloriousness. I'm only glad my rough hands didnae scratch yer delicate skin."

That prompted an unbidden image of his palms sliding up her bare legs. She shook herself, wondering if perhaps she had a fever. She had been driven about in the rain, after all. "I don't find you at all amusing, sir. I have shoes to wear, but unless you mean to release me, I would prefer if you didn't keep barging in here to harass me."

He straightened, still looking up at her. "Och. I'm harassing ye now, am I? By agreeing to wed ye and save yer reputation?

"And *your* purse, I would imagine," she retorted. "I'll risk being ruined, thank you very much."

Maxton inclined his head. "If that's how ye feel, I'll leave ye to converse with yerself. It'll give ye a taste of how a ruined lass spends her days, nae doubt. And hopefully ye'll appreciate yer own loftiness more than I do." Dropping her discarded shoes into the sack, he stood. "I brought ye someaught to read, but now I'm thinking it might be too plain fer ye. Best I leave ye to prance aboot on yer pedestal alone."

Marjorie shot to her feet. "Something to read?" she repeated aloud, the prospect of another half-dozen hours of solitude abruptly pushing at her. Corresponding with the boy could occupy her for a few minutes, but it didn't remove her from a locked room the way reading could.

He faced her again. "Aye. Someaught to read."

"Let me have it, then."

His sensuous lips curved just a little. "Nae."

"No? Why not? You've already brought it here; you may as well give it to me."

Gray eyes looked her up and down, making her feel hot—but on the inside, beneath her skin. "I reckon I'd like to hear ye ask me nicely," he said after a moment, "being that we're betrothed. And give me either a curtsy or a kiss. I'll let ye choose which. This time."

Oh, dear. More than likely he meant to embarrass her, to remind her just how little control she had over anything here. Still, she had to weigh the alternatives—a second evening of nothing but her own worried thoughts to keep her company, versus a show of respect, a curtsy, to a villain. Because she certainly wasn't going to kiss him. Not for all the tea in China, or an original folio of Shakespeare's.

Squaring her shoulders, Marjorie sank into a deep curtsy, her skirts flowing out around her. Heaven knew she'd had enough practice at it; the art of the curtsy had actually been a class at finishing school. Aside from that, previous to three months ago practically everyone she'd encountered in Mayfair as she ran errands for her employer had outranked her.

For a long moment after she lifted her head again, Maxton gazed at her. In all likelihood no one had ever curtsied to him before, so it was entirely possible that he was at a loss for words. She'd felt like that, the first time a man had bowed to her—and that had been all of seven weeks ago.

Visibly shaking himself, Maxton dug into the sack and produced a leather-bound tome, which he held out to her.

"Very prettily done, lass," he drawled. "I didnae think ye had it in ye."

She took the book, being careful not to touch his fingers. "The entirety of what you know about me, sir, wouldn't fill a teacup," she returned, cradling the thing to her chest. "Now please leave. And knock before you come in, next time."

"Aye, and I'll dress in my finest and slick back my hair fer ye, too, shall I?" he retorted, amusement touching his voice again.

"Well, someone should do something with that lion's mane of yours."

He turned for the door, then stopped to swing around and look at her again, an unexpected grin touching his mouth. "A lion's mane, is it?" he asked, dragging his fingers through the auburn mass. "I like the sound of that."

Graeme pulled the door closed behind him, turning to lock it and then pocketing the key. Whatever he thought of her kind in general, Lady Marjorie had some spirit. Nor did she seem quite as empty-headed as he'd expected—after better than a day of captivity the duke's sister should have been in hysterics, throwing things and demanding a maid to help her brush her hair.

And damn it all, she should have been grateful to have a viscount—any viscount—agree to marry her. He'd read stories where a kiss or an ill-timed laugh had ruined some English lady's reputation. This one had gone missing for better than a day already. However lofty her friends, he doubted they'd overlook the damage. She could announce that she didn't care, but he didn't believe it. Not for a single bloody minute.

When Cowen appeared in front of him, he just barely kept from jumping. Damn it all. In a house stuffed with three unruly lads, he couldn't afford to be lost in his own thoughts. "Send these to the cobbler," he said, holding out the sack of shoes. "And a chicken fer payment; God knows he'll nae be getting coin fer it."

"Aye, m'laird. And ye wanted to know what yer *bràthairs* are up to. I couldnae say, but all three of the lads are in the billiards room."

Nodding, Graeme turned back up the hallway. It had become apparent yesterday that he'd been far too lenient with his younger siblings, far too concerned with keeping a roof over their heads to notice the nonsense going on *in* their heads. And it was dangerous nonsense, as he'd witnessed yesterday.

He shoved open the closed billiards-room door. "So ye think ye get to play after ye tie up a lass, frighten her half to death, and then dump her in my lap?"

Three pairs of eyes, all various shades of gray, looked up at him. "We're nae playing," Brendan announced, returning to the papers they had scattered across the billiards table.

"Nae a newspaper says Lady Marjorie's gone missing," Connell announced, shredding a dandelion leaf and dropping the bits into his rounded coat pockets.

"Nae a newspaper ye've seen," Graeme amended. "We'll nae have a London paper to hand fer days."

"Even so," Brendan countered, "Sam Woring put in a notice aboot a missing pitchfork. A duke's sister's more important than a pitchfork, and there's nae a mention of her."

To himself Graeme could admit the omission was a bit . . . odd, but the silence didn't mean his slender, blue-eyed problem had vanished. "Is that yer concern then, Brendan? That nae a soul knows what ye've done?"

"Isn't it yers too, Graeme? That she doesnae bring us more trouble?"

Just gazing into her eyes was trouble. "That's *a* concern," he conceded. "My largest worry is over why ye and

Dùghlas even thought of kidnapping a lass, and why neither of ye decided against it." He stepped deeper into the room, closing the door behind him. "Dunnae ye understand? Ye put yer hands on a lass, dragged her away from her friends and family, and both scared her and made her—and her brother—into our enemies."

Brendan pounded a fist against the table's surface. "Aye, we've made a Sassenach an enemy, but that's because ye and Papa made an enemy of our own clan chief. If ye do what we planned, ye'll have Dunncraigh in yer pocket. And then with all of clan Maxwell behind us, nae English trespassing duke could stand against us."

"Ye—"

"We were desperate to help ye, Graeme," Dùghlas interrupted. "Ye kept saying ye'd manage the Maxwell, but then ye ignored him. And so when we saw the lady there at the inn, we couldnae pass by our chance."

Graeme blew out his breath. Lucifer's balls, they still didn't understand. They saw Lady Marjorie as nothing more than leverage. And perhaps he was guilty of the same thing. Or perhaps he was making the best of a bad situation. "Well, now that ye've dragged her here and ruined her reputation, I reckon it's up to me to decide what's best fer the lot of us. I've sent a note to Father Michael inquiring aboot getting a special license so I can marry Lady Marjorie Forrester."

All three boys looked at him blankly. "But—" Brendan finally stammered. "She's to go to the Maxwell, so he can take back Lattimer. If ye—"

"If I what?" Graeme prompted. "If I marry her, we'll have the blunt to stand against anyone. Hell, we might even gain Lattimer as an ally."

"If he doesnae murder ye for marrying his sister," Brendan retorted.

"Ye should only marry her if ye're in love with her,"

Connell said, with all the conviction his eight years gave him. "And ye've only known her a day. What if she doesnae like cats?"

"I'll risk it," he returned. "And love is nae a thing I'm looking fer. Her money'll do just fine."

"She willnae be able to bring charges against us, either," Dùghlas noted. "If ye're doing this fer us, Graeme, ye shouldnae—"

"Of course it's fer ye, ye heathens," Graeme cut in. "Ye did wrong. I'm making it right, in the way that works best fer all of us, the Sassenach lass included."

"We could just ask her to be quiet aboot it," Connell insisted.

"She doesnae owe us that. Or anything." And that was the crux of the problem.

She owed him no kindness, no favors, and even if she swore not to mention the lads' names, he had no reason to believe her. He would be better off bricking her into the room and never mentioning her again.

Just the idea of that, however, made his chest tighten. The day the Maxtons of clan Maxwell were desperate enough to commit murder—the day *he* became that desperate—he would walk away from the Highlands altogether. Even so, he wouldn't be digging through old trunks to bring her any more pairs of shoes, even if he did find her absurd insistence on propriety amusing.

When he'd put his big, rough hands on her damned dainty ankle, though, he hadn't felt amused. He'd felt . . . Devil take it, he didn't know what he'd felt, but he knew he shouldn't have been feeling it. Not toward a damned nose-in-the-air Sassenach with the power to see him imprisoned or transported. Who could see his brothers imprisoned or transported. *That* was why he needed to marry her. The money made it more tolerable. The rest . . . didn't signify, whether his cock tried to convince him otherwise, or not.

"We've got her here now," Brendan took up, clearly not confused by the damned female's presence at all. "And we cannae let her go. Ye may as well hand her to Dunncraigh and have some good come of this. Let her be *his* worry."

"I'll nae be taking advice from ye until ye've at least grown some scruff on yer cheeks," Graeme retorted. "And nae until yer first solution to trouble isnae to kidnap a lass."

Brendan's cheeks darkened. "But ye're willing to marry her. How are ye any better?"

Graeme scowled. "That's cowardly to say, when ye ken damned well I willnae fight a bairn as wee as ye are, Brendan."

"I'm nae wee! Or a bairn! I only lack four inches on ye, Graeme Maxton, and I'll fight ye any damned day of the week."

It was true the lad had come within two inches of six feet, but Brendan remained skinny, and nearly as gangly as Connell. In another three or four years, aye, he might put on the muscle to make a fight interesting. Today, though, a brawl would only serve to embarrass the boy, get his back up. That would only ensure that not a one of them learned the lesson he badly needed to teach them.

"Well, it willnae be today, because Sean Moss's son Will has a fever, and ye'll be helping to sack the grain at the mill. Ye and Dùghlas, both."

Brendan slammed his fist against the paper-covered surface of the billiards table. "Send us to shovel shite if ye want, Graeme, but ye're still a stubborn fool."

"I dunnae want to shovel shite," Dùghlas countered.

"Shut yer gobber, Dùghlas," his older sibling grunted. "I'm making a bloody point." The three lads started for the door.

"So am I," the second-youngest returned. "Aboot shite, and how I dunnae want to shovel it."

"Dùghlas, ye're a—"

"Connell," Graeme broke in, reaching out to catch the eight-year-old by the collar. "Ye stay here."

The boy frowned. "The lads watch after me."

"Aye. And the last time they did, ye lured a lass into a kidnapping. Stay aboot the hoose."

"Fine," Connell grumbled. "But I dunnae like it."

"Good. Ye're nae meant to."

When the older boys had gone, Connell faced him again. "Would the Maxwell hurt Lady Marjorie?" he asked, dipping both hands into his pockets to absently pet the rabbit kits Graeme wasn't supposed to know about. "Is that why ye want her to stay here?"

"I dunnae ken if he would or nae," he returned, putting a hand on his youngest brother's shoulder and guiding him back into the hallway. "If I gave her over, and if he did hurt her, it would be on my head, though. And I've enough to worry over withoot adding that."

Connell nodded. "Mayhap we should let her go, then, while the lads are at the mill. Ye could tell 'em she escaped."

"I would, if I could trust her nae to accuse ye three muttonheads of dragging her off." And if he could be sure that whatever tale she told wouldn't reach Dunncraigh and cause even more trouble between him and his clan chief— if he didn't end up in prison, which seemed the most likely scenario. "Between ye and me, duckling, marrying her is the best plan I have."

"Well, I hope she likes us, if she's to be part of the family."

Hm. She would be a part of the family, which meant she would be about sensitive, impressionable Connell. "If she doesnae like us, she's mad. But dunnae worry yerself aboot it, duckling. I'll sort it oot."

The eight-year-old chuckled as he headed up the stairs toward his animal-filled bedchamber. "Aye. The way ye sorted oot Fionan Polk?" He mimed swinging a punch. "The blood went everywhere! I even got some on my shoe."

Graeme grinned. "She's a lass, so I reckon I'll try to be more delicate."

This time Connell laughed. "Ye're nae delicate, Graeme."

His brother had a point. Four lads in the house, three of them his responsibility since his twentieth year, meant that more often than not he solved problems with a loud voice and a short, hard punishment, a smack across the arse, or a toss into the river Douchary. Ham-fisted, but effective.

Until now, anyway. Completely aside from the *way* she'd arrived, having a female beneath his roof changed everything. The last woman in residence had been their mother, and while Graeme remembered her well enough, mostly he recalled how petite she'd been, how delicate-seeming, and yet how utterly ferocious. This lass seemed more sharp and more helpless, but he had no inclination to compare the two females, anyway. Marjorie Forrester was very much not his mother.

Was she a wife, though? And why had it begun to matter to him that she liked them? Liked him? She was a damned prisoner, and should be grateful for any solution he offered.

"M'laird," Cowen said from the foyer before Graeme could even reach the landing, "Father Michael's here. He said ye're to go over the schedule for the Samhain fair."

And that would take the remainder of his day. For a moment Graeme contemplated giving the scheduling duties over to Cowen, but the task traditionally belonged to the clan chieftain, and that was him. Aside from that, he'd requested a marriage license this morning. Graeme had asked for discretion, but neither would he be surprised if half the valley knew he'd decided to wed.

"Did ye put him in the morning room?"

"Aye. With some of that black tea he favors."

Graeme nodded, heading back down the stairs. "Come find me in an hour with some disaster or other, or I'll sack ye." He paused. "And nae a word aboot our guest."

"I wouldnae," Cowen returned. "I can only imagine how many hours he'd preach aboot that."

Suppressing a shudder, Graeme walked into the morning room. The priest sat by the fire, tea at his elbow and his Bible and well-worn, much-marked plan for the fair in his lap. "Father Michael," he said, offering his hand as the priest rose.

"Graeme. I apologize fer being late. Morag Moss finally lost her cat Tabby, and asked me to pray over him, and then she insisted on baking some shortbread fer me."

"That was kind of ye," Graeme noted, taking the seat opposite. Privately he thought Morag Moss had simply wanted to keep the white-haired, distinguished-looking priest about—especially since today was wash day and half the village would note who'd called at her cottage.

"She's a very pious lass. And all alone, with her husband and now her Tabby gone."

"Aye."

The priest sipped his tea, eyeing Graeme over the rim of the old cup. "Well, lad? Are ye going to tell me who's finally caught yer heart?"

Graeme snorted. "Nae a lass has caught my heart, Father. But I have decided it's time to marry."

"But lad, ye—"

"I've nae agreed with ye yet on the topic of love, so dunnae expect me to do it today." If that was harsh, the priest should expect it by now. For eight years they'd been having the same conversation.

Father Michael cleared his throat. "Ye're wrong, but I'll respect yer opinion. Who is she, then? And does she ken she doesnae have yer heart?"

"I've nae a particular lass in mind yet," he said slowly,

wondering if there was a worse sin than lying to a man of God. "But I mean to marry soon, and I want nae delays when it's decided. Did ye send the request?" If he hadn't been a viscount he wouldn't have bothered with a license; handfasting was more respected than a piece of paper in the Highlands, anyway. But with a title involved, the Crown had to make certain things were official.

"Aye. With the mail coach. It'll be a few days before we hear back from Canterbury, but with ye being a viscount I dunnae see any difficulties. When ye *do* find a lass, though, Graeme, I hope ye can—"

"Nae more aboot marriage," Graeme interrupted. "Ye're here to speak against dancing at Samhain, I reckon."

Father Michael sighed. "Have it yer way, lad. Ye're more stubborn than a mountain. Aye. I object to the dancing, though I dunnae expect to sway ye this year any more than I did last year." The father dropped another lump of sugar into his tea. "By the way, ye ken I dunnae hold with gossip, but as the Maxwell chieftain hereaboots ye *are* aware of the English who took rooms at the Cracked Hearth, aye?"

Graeme kept his expression neutral despite his internal leap to attention. "Nae," he drawled, drawing out the word. "Should I be? They do travel across my land, from time to time."

"Of course they do. But these three, two men in livery and an older woman, claim the woman's niece has gone missing. I thought someone might've informed ye, so ye could have the folk hereaboots keep an eye oot fer the lass."

Someone damned well should have informed him. News about Lady Marjorie was to be kept secret from everyone outside the household. Not from him. Bloody hell. If Taog had returned from the inn and declined to tell him what was afoot there, the lad would be polishing bannisters for a fortnight. "I'll ride doon in the morning and talk to this woman myself," he said aloud. "I've nae fondness fer any Sassenach, but if we can help find this lass, we'll do it, of course."

Father Michael nodded. "That's good of ye. Aside from the blessings due any Samaritan, having the news get oot that an English lass has gone missing in the area willnae serve anyone." With a brief smile he returned the teacup to its saucer. "Now. I ken all the lads favor a drinking contest at the fair, but dunnae ye think it a trifle . . . sinful? Perhaps we could substitute a good pie-eating competition in its stead."

He didn't want to talk about beer drinking or pie eating, or the brawl that would likely ensue if he canceled one in favor of the other. He wanted to gallop down to the end of the wide, curved valley, across the river Douchary, and see for himself who was looking for Lady Marjorie and why they were describing her as "an English lass" instead of the sister of the Duke of Lattimer.

That didn't make sense. However Highlanders felt about the English, naming the missing woman and thereby the amount of the reward for her safe recovery would have provided more than enough incentive for the local residents to scour the area clean looking for her. Her companions, though, hadn't done that. Not yet, anyway. But why not?

". . . agree that the dancing is far too provocative," Father Michael went on, and Graeme blinked, not certain how long the priest had been droning on. "I suggest a group reading of appropriate scripture regarding fall harvest and the inevitable onset of winter."

"Perhaps we should all lie doon in the graveyard in the spot where we mean to be buried."

The priest's cheeks reddened. "I'm trying to shepherd a flock of hot-tempered sinners, lad, ye among them. I'd appreciate if ye'd nae jest aboot it, or the calling to which I've dedicated my life."

Graeme drew a hard breath in through his nose. "I apologize, Father Michael. God knows I dunnae envy ye yer task."

"Thank ye, lad."

"But I reckon yer sinners will be more likely to listen to yer good words if they've a bit of beer and dancing to reflect on."

The old man sighed. "I find it helpful to remind myself that if we had nae sinners we'd have nae need fer sermons."

After some negotiation both beer drinking and pie eating stayed on the list, and mainly out of pity Graeme allowed for a religious embroidery display beneath one of the canopies. It would be a long day of mayhem, but a last bit of fun before the heavy snow set in at least made the winter seem shorter.

As the topic shifted back to a suggestion of local lasses of good character and family and how important it was for a clan chieftain to ensure the continuation of his line, Cowen barged into the room. "Laird Maxton, the . . . ye . . . there's someaught wrong with one of the upstairs windows," he panted.

"Surely ye dunnae need to trouble the master of the hoose aboot a window," Father Michael said.

Graeme was already on his feet. God, had she broken out? Jumped? Fallen? "See that the Father has more tea," he snapped, striding past the butler. If she'd been injured . . . "I'll be back in a moment."

He took the stairs two at a time. And he wasn't thinking about the ramifications to him or his if something had happened to her, or about the loss of blunt and corresponding loss of power. He was thinking about *her*. One of the house's two footmen, Ross, pounded on the locked door at the end of the hallway, his unanswered calls sending Graeme's heart into his throat. Aye, she was a rich Sassenach with the world at her feet, but she had a backbone, too, when he hadn't expected that.

Shouldering the footman aside, he dug into his pocket for the key, unlocked the door, and slammed into the room. His breath catching, he looked toward the windows. Neither was broken, both were still shut, and the lass herself stood there between them with a lit candle in her hands.

"I am not going to be bullied into marrying you," she stated, her chin lifted.

As his heart resumed beating again, Graeme took another look at the windows. *Devil a bit.* Slamming the door closed on Ross's surprised face, he stalked up to her. Holding her gaze, he first blew out the candle, then swiped a hand through the reversed letters she'd spelled out across the glass in what looked and smelled like strawberry jam.

With the light behind the ten-inch letters, HELP must have shown bright and red in the window for anyone passing by to see. If Father Michael had arrived an hour later, or left a few minutes early, their discussion about the missing English lass—and his impending marriage—would have gone very differently.

The cleverness of it—he would admire that later. At the moment he needed to stop this from happening again.

"Aren't you going to say anything?" she demanded, the lifted chin and defiant gaze betrayed a little by the shaking at the edge of her voice. Then she didn't like being loomed over, and he definitely loomed now.

He loomed inches from her face, from her firmly closed mouth and full, rose-petal lips, as anger, fury, admiration, frustration, and desire all slammed through him. Taking her shoulders in his big, jam-covered hands, he held her

back against the narrow wall between the windows. And
then he bent his head and kissed her.

Graeme wasn't gentle about it, either. Once he touched
her, lightning skittered beneath his skin, heated and elec-
tric. Her mouth moved against his, likely protesting his un-
gentlemanly behavior, as her fists clenched and unclenched
against his chest.

When he'd had a good taste of her, he lifted his head
again. "Never been kissed by a barbarian before, I'll wager," he muttered, using every ounce of self-control he possessed to keep from kissing her again.

"I . . . will not dignify that with a response."

"I told ye there would be consequences, yer highness."
Firming his grip on her shoulders, he twisted her, pushing
her backward toward the bed.

She tried to jerk away from him, her blue gaze shifting
between him and the bed. "You wouldn't dare, sir! I
would . . . I would see you hanged!"

For the briefest of moments he was tempted to play the
heathen she clearly thought him. Want heated his blood.
Proper female that she was, she would definitely have to
marry him once he'd bedded her. If he gave in, though,
with her clearly frightened and unwilling, he would deserve
the hanging she threatened—if he didn't, already. Word-
lessly he shoved her backward onto the bed. As she strug-
gled to sit upright he crouched down, grabbed the
shackle he'd declined to use last night, and swiftly locked
it around her left ankle.

"I thought . . . I thought . . ."

"What, lass?" he prompted. "Ye thought I meant to have
ye against yer will?" Graeme straightened, taking a step
backward before she could recover her wits enough to kick
him in the head. "If I were that sort of man, ye'd be wiser
nae to test me, dunnae ye think?"

Lady Marjorie tugged, but the chain didn't budge. "I will not be chained like some animal, sir," she retorted, wielding the "sir" like a weapon and only the shaking of her voice telling him it wasn't just anger she felt.

"And I'll nae have ye endangering me and mine," he retorted. "This isnae yer soft London where ye and yer friends play games aboot who ye dance with and who ye talk to. Here the games end bloody. I dunnae have many rules here, but ye'll damned well follow 'em, or ye'll stay chained to the bed until doomsday."

He wanted to remain in the room to bellow at her, to make damned certain she understood that he wasn't jesting, to inform her that he could damned well bully her into marriage if he chose to do so. She'd curled her feet up beneath her, though, and shifted as far as she could away from him on the bed. Aye, they'd all fare better if she feared him, but the part of him that had given in to the absurd impulse to kiss her didn't like the idea of her shrinking away from him.

Clenching his jaw, Graeme turned for the door—and then flinched as a teacup hit him in the back. The delicate porcelain fell to the wooden floor and shattered into a dozen pieces. Well, he hadn't broken her spirit, anyway. Continuing forward, he pulled open the door. "Cowen, have Ross clean off the window and the mess on the floor," he ordered, and handed the door key to the butler. "Two of ye in here, and neither of ye talk to her majesty. Lock her in and bring me the key when ye've finished."

"We'll see to it, Laird Maxton," the servant replied. "Dunnae ye worry."

Graeme sent a glance back at the slender figure curled on the bed. He *was* worried, but not about what Lady Marjorie Forrester might attempt next. Rather, he was troubled because in all of her protests over her treatment and what she would and wouldn't tolerate, she hadn't uttered a single protest about the kiss.

He had no complaints about it, for damned certain. In fact, he wanted to kiss her again. And that would only make things worse—for all of them.

Chapter Six

The blasted chain and shackle reached far enough that Marjorie could sit in the closer of the two chairs the servants had carried back over to the hearth, but the window and even the door were several feet out of her reach. Her leg felt awkward and oddly weighted, a clear sign that she'd badly miscalculated.

Given the house's location on the rise, and her windows up on the second floor, the odds of someone seeing her request for aid had been fair. She'd watched people come and go all day, after all. And all she needed was one pair of eyes, one person whom Graeme Maxton didn't control, to take notice and tell someone—anyone—what he'd seen.

Marjorie shifted again, trying to find a position where the heavy chain didn't threaten to drag her out of the chair and onto the floor. In none of her wildest imaginings could she have conjured anything as outlandish as her being chained to a bed in a pleasant-looking house in the middle of the Scottish Highlands while a strapping Highlander threatened to marry her. And she certainly couldn't have imagined her captor kissing her—or that she might possibly have enjoyed it.

The way he'd swooped in, as if he couldn't quite stop himself, his warm mouth on hers, the scent of whisky and wilderness . . . She touched her fingers to her lips. Her first kiss—and an ironic one when she considered that her dreams after she'd become Lady Marjorie and moved her scant few personal possessions from Lady Sarah Jeffers's attic room into massive Leeds House, had been filled with handsome, young, well-born men who waited in a queue to fall in love with her.

Yes, despite the passive . . . disdain with which she'd been treated since Gabriel had been elevated from army major to the Duke of Lattimer, she had seen a handful of gentlemen callers—all of them fortune hunters. She'd seen to it that none of them got near enough to kiss her.

Maxton was a fortune hunter, as well, or half one. She remained uncertain whether his primary goal in forcing her into a marriage was to gain her money, or to protect his family from her untrustworthy Sassenach ways. After they'd kidnapped her and dragged her into this, or course. But given his ham-fisted assertion that he was saving her reputation and then the way he'd chained her to the bed and locked her in a room while yelling at her to behave, she didn't think he'd intended that kiss. And she knew for blasted certain that she should have been as offended by it as she was at the idea of being forced into a marriage.

For heaven's sake, she should be fearing the loss of her virtue, the ruin of her reputation, and the torching of her future prospects for a proper beau and a proper marriage in London. Mostly, though, she wished he'd brought her something more engaging to read than *Culpepper's Medicinal Herbs.*

And in her heart, she knew why she was more aggravated than fearful. Yes, she could apply everything she'd learned in boarding school and finishing school, use all the advice from the ever-optimistic Mrs. Giswell, but she knew. Years of patience and generous gifts to strategically placed persons might earn her a few dinner or soiree invitations, the least thank-yous anyone could manage without being considered impolite, but if she wanted to go to the theater she would have to rent her own box. If she wanted to attend a grand ball she would have to hold it, and then expect that no one else would attend. If she wanted to marry within her own, new station, it would have to be to a man who needed her money. But damn it all, he would ask her and she would accept. Not force her into something and announce that it was for her own good.

Marjorie sighed, tugging on the ridiculous chain again. It must have been forged to restrain a draft horse, or perhaps an elephant. Graeme Maxton now held two keys to her imprisonment. And now that he'd made this a challenge, well, she'd make certain her next attempt at escape went better—or at least caused him more trouble.

A trio of knocks sounded low on the door, startling her. Two more followed. Then, before she could say a word, another note slipped though the narrow opening and floated for several inches along the floor. *Blast it.*

"Connell, I can't reach the door," she said, as loudly as she dared.

"But ye said ye would have a note fer me."

"I do. But your brother chained me up, and I can't get to it. Or to the door."

"Is that because ye spread jam on the window? That was a mad thing to do."

She frowned at the door. "Yes, I suppose it was. I had to try something, though."

"Ye shouldnae make Graeme mad at ye. He walloped me across the arse once when I brought home a pine marten I'd caught. I hid it in the stable, but it got oot and killed nine of our chickens. That's nearly half of 'em. And it put the other ones off laying, so we had nae an egg fer nearly a fortnight."

"How long has Graeme been looking after you?" she asked, unable to help being curious. About him, about this place, his family, and what in the world had led them all to the point that kidnapping her seemed their best course of action.

"Fer eight years," the boy answered promptly. "Since I was a two-day-old leaking duckling of a bairn. And I smelled bad, too." Connell sighed audibly. "Are ye going to marry Graeme? He says ye are. Do ye like cats?"

She certainly didn't like Lady Sarah's fat, spoiled cats who had always eaten better than she had. "I would have to meet the cats to know if I liked them, and if they liked me. And no, I'm not marrying your brother."

"Well, that willnae make him happy, either. And how are ye to answer my letters if ye cannae reach the door?"

"I don't know. Perhaps you could have a word with your brother and suggest to him that I don't need to be chained to the bed."

"I'll give it a try," he returned, sounding reluctant. "Graeme's stubborn, though. He made the lads go help at the mill to punish them for kidnapping ye, and I heard him say we all have to go clean oot the damned irrigation ditches tomorrow, before the water freezes."

All of them? Did that mean Graeme, as well? If so, that could be her chance to run. First, though, she needed to get free of the chain. "Anything you can do would be appreciated. This shackle is rubbing my ankle."

"I'll let ye know what happens; listen fer my knock after dinner."

"Thank you, Connell."

After his footsteps padded away, Marjorie leaned over to turn up the oil lamp on the nightstand. She could only guess the time, but she knew this late in the year sunset came early to the Highlands. Four o'clock? Half-four? Several hours before the brute brought dinner, anyway—

unless he'd decided she should go hungry tonght. Considering her left shoulder smelled of strawberry jam and her stomach already growled because of it, *that* wouldn't be a particularly pleasant prospect.

Instead of dwelling on that, she tallied up what she knew about this place and her captors. Four brothers—Graeme, Brendan, Dùghlas, and Connell Maxton. A butler named Cowen, a footman called Ross, and a female cook who didn't appear to be anywhere near her size.

They owned a wagon, had somewhere over a dozen chickens—or they had, before the pine marten got to them. A mill lay somewhere close by, and it was a punishment to send the boys there to work. From the view she'd had out the window, a wild, swift river ran across the property just down the hill and past what looked like the main road. The house had a stable with at least two riding horses, and the hay came in a wagon from somewhere to the east. Could that be where the mill lay?

The two horses could be useful. Given that the residents of the house were all male, neither of them had likely been broken to the sidesaddle, and she'd never spent much time on horseback anyway, but if it meant escaping she would ride astride—or even bareback—if she had to. At that point she would need a better idea of where she'd be most likely to find help. The miller would be loyal to the Maxtons, so she could rule out east. That still left three other directions and a great deal of very cold, very rugged territory.

She did have one thing in her favor; given Graeme's reaction to her writing "help" on the window, she would be willing to wager that his neighbors didn't know about her. Her brother and his men were likely searching for her by now, alerted by Mrs. Giswell, so the more people whose attention she could attract, the better. Gabriel could even offer a reward for her safe return, which a few months ago would have been impossible.

"Leave it there, Ross. I'll take it in."

Marjorie started. Good heavens, how long had she spent plotting? When she glanced over her shoulder at the window, the sky beyond the closed curtains was dark. And then she caught sight of the note in front of the door.

Oh, no! Connell's new missive. Stifling an unladylike curse, she lurched to her feet and limped forward—only to be brought up short by the chain. Swiftly she sank to her knees and stretched out her right hand. *Damnation.*

Metal slid against metal as he pushed the key into the lock. "Don't you dare come in here without knocking first!" she ordered, and sank down onto her stomach. *Almost . . .*

The door swung open. Booted feet approached, stopping directly in front of her. "What do ye think ye're doing?" he asked in a low voice touched with amusement.

Marjorie scrambled back to her knees, using the moment ostensibly to straighten her dress, but instead shoving the missive down her front before she stood. "I wanted to see if I could reach the door," she returned, brushing at her skirt. "I leaned too far. I told you not to come in without knocking."

"But then I would've missed that."

She glared at him, mostly for effect. His brother's note—and his brother's . . . friendship with her, she supposed it was—were both secure. "You don't possess even an ounce of propriety and politeness, do you?"

"Nae. I dunnae. Sit in yer chair if ye want dinner." He hefted the tray in his arms. "Ye decided against punishing me with silence, then?"

Making a show of limping and struggling with the heavy chain, she seated herself. "I decided my silence would appeal to you. Since you have no morality, perhaps you'll bend to excessive nagging."

Laughter burst from his chest, deep and surprisingly infectious. "Sassenach or nae, I do like yer wits, m'lady." Setting the tray on the table, he moved the second chair back over and sat opposite her as he had at luncheon.

He liked her wits. Graeme Maxton's approval happened to be the last thing in the world she sought. She wore the evidence of his brutishness, after all. And yet in the back of her mind she couldn't help acknowledging that she'd never received a better compliment.

Teachers, tutors, dance masters had noted her fine posture, her pretty face, the artful shape of her hands, and the grace of her movement. Until now, no one had complimented her mind. Marjorie cleared her throat.

"Nae response to that? Och, ye dunnae care what I think, do ye?" he went on after a moment, his charming smile fading. "Ye're a grand lady, after all."

"I never said any such thing," Marjorie retorted. "Though I have no idea why you think I should care a whit about anything you utter. And if you value my wits, perhaps you should listen to what I have to say instead of trying to force me into something neither of us wants."

He folded his arms across his chest. "I havenae said I dunnae want it, lass, though I'm beginning to think ye may be a madwoman. Now eat yer damned venison."

"I am not your lass, and I would like to be returned from whence I came."

" 'Whence,' is it?" he repeated, clearly amused.

"Yes. 'Whence.' That is the correct word."

He was right about one thing—she'd clearly begun to go mad, and after only a few days of captivity. She had no other explanation for the nonsense running through her mind. Squaring her shoulders and trying to set all that aside, she picked up the knife and fork.

"Ye've never been truly hungry, have ye?" he asked after a few moments, rudely staring at her mouth as she ate.

"No, I haven't." Until very recently she'd eaten simple

fare, but Gabriel had always managed to send her enough of his salary to pay for her schooling, her clothes, lodging, and her meals. "Have you?"

"I've gone withoot from time to time. But with three brothers, if I took as long as ye do with every bite, I'd starve to death."

"So none of you have manners. What a surprise. I imagine even the sight of me combing my hair must seem outlandish to you. Good heavens, what might happen if your brothers saw someone using utensils?"

"I reckon they'd think someone was aboot to start a fight," he returned, more mildly than she expected. "Ye've the right of it. We're a pack of hounds here, sleeping on piles of hay and gnawing on bones. Ye're lucky the cook remembered how to roast that venison, or ye'd be eating it raw like the rest of us."

Whatever he claimed, she did know that even the youngest of them could read and write, but she couldn't say that without admitting she and Connell had been corresponding. It made her curious, though, about why he persisted in characterizing himself and his household as barbaric. Of course he *was* a barbarian, but he actually seemed . . . proud of that fact. Highlanders, Mrs. Giswell had claimed, couldn't be explained, and he was living proof of that.

"Will you at least give me the opportunity to prove that you can trust me? That I won't cause trouble for you or your brothers?" she ventured.

"Nae. I willnae. Anything else ye want to ask me?"

The answer didn't surprise her. "So you've made your decision and won't be swayed. Before you reach the point of no return, though, consider that a special license still requires a priest, and that I will not remain silent, and I will not agree to marry you."

He cocked his head. "Do ye want me to get doon on one knee?"

"I have a life elsewhere, sir, and I have no desire or incentive to give up that life for you. Even—"

"Ye have a beau in London, then, do ye?" he asked, his voice flattening a little.

It was on the tip of her tongue to say yes, but the part of her that remained supremely annoyed wanted him to acknowledge that the fault lay with him, and not some imaginary suitor. "Would it make a difference to you if I did?"

"Nae. I'm thinking ye dunnae, anyway. Ye wouldnae be so prickly if ye did."

"I am not—" She took a breath, setting down her fork. "For heaven's sake, you don't even know me—nor I, you."

"That's yer objection, then? We're nae acquainted?"

Impossible man. "That's *one* of my objections, yes. Of course there's also the matter that I have a shackle on my leg, and that I don't like you!" She took a breath. Ladies didn't yell. He was simply . . . maddening beyond all sense and reason.

That attractive smile curved his mouth. "I think ye *do* like me. Ye just dunnae like that ye do."

"Oh, for . . ." This was getting her nowhere. Either he was intentionally aggravating her, or he had a supreme lack of self-awareness. She tended to think it was the former, but she wasn't going along with his plans, regardless. "Think whatever you wish, Lord Maxton. I'm more interested to know if you own a book other than *Culpepper's Herbal Medicine*. I would prefer something more literary." She paused to take another bite, chew, and swallow. "And my gown has jam on it. Might you spare me some water and a scrub brush?"

That made him look her up and down again, which sent odd tingles down her spine. "After ye change into yer nightclothes, toss yer gown by the door. I'll knock before I fetch it."

She shrugged to cover her discomfiture at the idea of

him coming in to see her naked—or nearly so. "Don't expect me to be overcome with dizziness at the idea of you touching a dress I won't be wearing."

Maxton tilted his head, a lock of his lion's mane falling across one eye. "Tell me someaught. If I werenae marrying ye, ye'd be ruined in English eyes, aye?"

"I've been alone without a chaperone and in male company for over two days. That doesn't earn me a parade. It earns me gossip and whispers and considerably fewer invitations to soirees." Not that she had any to begin with, but he didn't need to know that.

"Wouldnae marrying me fix that?"

An honest question? "No. You're a viscount, yes, but no one in London knows your . . . pedigree. And you're Scottish."

"But they wouldnae call ye ruined."

Marjorie sighed. "Please don't pretend you're attempting in any way to help me. We both know I'm still here because you want my money."

He leaned forward. "That's nae all I want of ye."

Abruptly her cheeks warmed. "I'm certain I have no idea what you mean."

His gaze held hers for a moment, then he settled back in the chair again. "Marrying ye's nae the only way fer me to gain some blunt, lass. If I told Dunncraigh who I have beneath my roof, he'd likely throw enough money at me that I could purchase a London lady fer a wife." His direct gray gaze unsettled her. "That could only happen if ye were never heard from again, though, so be careful who ye choose to ally yerself with in the Highlands."

Fear brushed at her, cold and dark—the first time she'd truly felt it in his presence. "Why in the world would the Duke of Dunncraigh wish me harm? I've never met him, and never heard of him except to read his name from time to time in the newspaper."

"He and yer brother are at war, lass. Lattimer may think it's over and done with, but Dunncraigh's nae finished with him, yet."

Oh, dear. "Then bring me to my brother. Ransom me to him. Or simply be a good Samaritan, which I promise not to dispute. He will reward you."

"Ah, lass, if Dunncraigh ever heard that I'd helped Lattimer, that I'd given ye to yer brother and nae to him, *I'd* be the one to disappear. And I wouldn't even be the first to do so. That would be one thing if it was just me, but I've my brothers and a hundred cotters relying on me." Almost absently he lifted her glass of wine and took a sip of it. "So now ye ken my dilemma. I dunnae wish to be yer enemy, or yer captor. But ye've nae offered me a better opportunity than the one I lit on—marrying ye."

She nodded. "I do understand. But I still won't cooperate. I wish you would believe that if it comes to it I will not name your brothers. I wouldn't name you, either, my lord."

"What I'd like to do and what I can afford to risk are two different things. So ye stay in this room, and in that shackle, until ye come to yer senses."

This was worse, much worse, than she'd even imagined. This Dunncraigh, who from what she'd read had recently been accused of threatening and neglecting his own clan Maxwell, wanted to do harm to both her and Gabriel. And she'd landed squarely in Maxwell hands. "I shouldn't ask," she said quietly, working to keep her voice steady, "but why haven't you given me to Dunncraigh in exchange for those piles of gold?"

Graeme drew in a breath, then stood. "I reckon I'll be keeping my own counsel on that count."

"But if you married me, he would certainly find out."

"Aye. He would. And if he came after me, I would firstly have the funds to make it a fight, and secondly I'd have yer brother nae wanting anything to happen to ye and so helping me go after the Maxwell. I dunnae see anything fer me to regret."

"But you don't know me! You certainly don't love me!"

He shrugged. "I've nae known that to be a requirement fer a marriage. I prefer it that way."

"That's very . . . sad."

"In yer opinion." Silently he gathered up the utensils, empty plates, and glasses, leaving her with a single tin of water—presumably so she couldn't break it over his head. He carried the tray to the door and pulled the heavy thing open to set his armload down in the hallway.

Marjorie sighed, grateful for some time now to think. But then he faced her again. "Now," he murmured, softly closing the door behind him and then strolling slowly back to her, "one more thing fer me to see to tonight, lass."

Even knowing what she did, knowing he'd just more or less said he had no use for love, her heart skipped a little when he said "lass" in that low, intimate brogue of his. Marjorie climbed to her feet, resisting the urge to smooth her skirt. A lady did not show uncertainty, because a lady always knew the correct thing to do. And of course if he tried to kiss her again, the correct thing would be to slap him. Except that she wasn't certain she wanted to slap him—and she couldn't explain why, even to herself.

He stopped a foot in front of her, his gaze roving her face as if searching for . . . something. Truth? Trustworthiness? Interest? Desire? When he reached out to cup her cheek in his hand, she stopped breathing. He was a foot taller than she was, far stronger, and as long as he kept hold of those two keys he had complete control over her physically. It almost seemed to his credit that he hadn't tried to do more than bellow at her—but this, the way he looked at her now, could be far more dangerous.

His mouth, warm and surprisingly sensuous for such a

heathen, touched hers. It made her want to melt into him, to feel his strong, hard arms around her. This was so, so wrong, but it didn't feel that way. And she could tell herself that perhaps, just perhaps, if he liked her enough he would realize the true best option was to let her go.

He put a hand on her shoulder, deepening the kiss as he trailed one finger along the conservative neckline of her gown. She should be scandalized; a proper lady would never allow such an intimate touch from a man, whether he'd declared that he meant to marry her or not. None of her instructors had ever been in this circumstance. Of that she was certain.

Still kissing her, still touching her in a way that made shivers chase each other down her spine, he hooked his fingers into the front of her dress—and slid out the folded note she'd stuffed there. At the same moment he took a long step backward.

"Give that back!" she demanded. *Blast it all*. He'd outmaneuvered her, and she'd fallen for it like some moonstruck nodcock. Marjorie stomped after him, only to be brought up short by the blasted chain.

And there he stood, just out of her reach, his unreadable gaze on her as he unfolded the missive. Then he looked down, his jaw visibly clenching. "Ye have an admirer, do ye?" he asked gruffly. "He's eight years old, and ye'd try to turn him against his own family?"

"I would do no such thing," she protested, even though she'd actually considered it. "And he would be very hurt to hear you say that."

Graeme narrowed his eyes. "I dunnae need ye to tell me how to raise my brother. And since he says he wants to show ye how to fish in the river, I'm thinking ye told him to help ye escape."

Thank goodness she hadn't put any of that in writing. And really, all she'd suggested even aloud was that he ask if she could be unchained so she could reach the door and the writing table. "Nonsense!"

"Then why did ye hide it from me?"

"Because you're an annoying, arrogant man and I didn't feel like explaining myself to you." She scowled. "But I promised not to get him into trouble, so look beneath the blank papers in the drawer." She jabbed a finger at the small writing desk.

Even well out of her reach he backed toward the desk, as if he didn't trust her enough to take his eyes off her. She, on the other hand, wanted a quiet moment or two to further contemplate that kiss. If it had been meant only as a distraction, Graeme Maxton was a consummate liar, because she hadn't felt anything but curiosity and desire. Or perhaps that was just her—in which case she needed to stop it immediately.

"His note came first," she said by way of explanation, as Maxton pulled the pages from the drawer. "And you might consider that I didn't have to tell you anything about them."

He glanced down at the notes, then pocketed all three of them. "I'll give ye ten minutes to change oot of the dress and toss it by the door." With that he headed out.

"I . . . I can't reach the night rail," she said, wishing it didn't sound like an excuse to have him stay.

With another sharp look at her he altered course for the wardrobe and pulled the night rail off its shelf. Then he bunched it in his hands and lifted it to his face, and breathed in.

Good heavens. Shivers started along her arms all over again. "That is not appropriate, sir," she managed, her cheeks heating.

"Lemons," he said, lifting his head again.

"I put sliced lemons in my bath when I can," she stated. "I like the smell of it in my hair."

"So do I." He walked forward and handed her the garment, their fingers brushing as he did so. "I'll have another bath drawn fer ye in the morning. I dunnae promise ye lemons."

Marjorie lifted her chin. "I didn't ask for any."

"I know."

Chapter Seven

G raeme walked outside to a light snow flurry and the
gloom of predawn. His heavy coat kept the cold at
bay, but it did nothing for the darkness. The lass would be
awake in an hour or two and expecting breakfast and a
bath, though, so he needed to see to his errands while he
could and before the next disaster came calling.

As Johnny saddled Clootie for him, he leaned against
the wall of the stable and pulled her letter from his pocket
again. It wasn't addressed to him, and she'd certainly
meant it to draw Connell into a friendship. Whatever her
motives, though, something about it fascinated him.

It might have been the neat, lovely printing—no doubt
simplified for Connell's benefit. "Dear Connell," he read
to himself, for the fourth or fifth time, "Thank you so much
for your letter. Of course I accept your apology; I have an
older brother, too, and as a young girl I followed him
everywhere—and frequently got into trouble because
of him."

The brother she referred to was of course the Duke of
Lattimer, the reason for all this bloody mess. Lucifer's
balls, she was clever, pointing out to Connell that the lad

and the duke had common ground. Enough to launch a hundred questions about why the Maxwell had declared Lattimer an enemy, at the least. Thank Lucifer he'd intercepted the letter before the duckling could get hold of it.

"I would love to see your baby rabbits. Are they as soft and warm as I imagine?" she went on, of course admiring Connell's fondness for young animals. "And you must tell me about your foxes! Do they get along with the rabbits? As I cannot visit them at the moment, perhaps you could draw me a sketch of them. Also, when you write me back, please tell me the name of the river I can see from my window. I don't think I've ever seen anything quite as lovely. Your friend, Ree Forrester."

So she was after clues about where she was, however prettily she asked for them. He could hear her voice as he read, the smooth words and cultured accent. Aye, she knew how to use words, flinging them about sharp as a blade, even when he had an eye and an ear out for trouble from her. And mayhap some of what she said made sense, but it all came down to trust—and he didn't trust her.

Straightening, he refolded the note and slipped it back into his pocket before he swung up on the gray gelding. "I'm off to the Cracked Hearth for breakfast, and then to see to Pòl Maxwell's deer troubles," he told the head groom, stuffing his rifle into the scabbard on the saddle.

"I heard the pesky things ate all his wife's cabbages," Johnny returned, slapping Clootie on the rump as Graeme trotted out of the stable.

He had at least three other things to attend to this morning, and that was before he dragged his brothers out to help clear the irrigation ditches with the rest of the local cotters. Aye, they'd be frozen in a month, but the last thing he wanted was for some old tree branches to get caught in one of the gates and smash it to the devil when the ice twisted them around.

As he rode away, he couldn't help glancing up at the line of dark windows along the house's upper floor. With the shackle on her leg she couldn't be watching even if she was awake, but even in the dark, even asleep, he felt her presence. And even with the way she'd put him behind in his duties, he wanted to go watch her eat breakfast, wanted to hear what insult she would aim at him this morning—even if it did include reasons she wouldn't marry him.

The last thing he wanted her to know was that she had him hesitating—not because of her pretty, biting words, but because he didn't quite feel the . . . satisfaction he'd expected at bringing a spoiled Sassenach lass to heel. She could indeed bring him wealth, and with that, power, but beneath all that he didn't like the idea that she would be sad and miserable here. He was a Highlander; he valued his freedom, and he didn't like having to chain her, even if that was to protect his family.

No, he didn't require love, and didn't want it, actually, but she seemed a lass made for it. Made for long, sweaty nights of sex, too, judging from that pair of kisses, but would she want him? Or would she consider it her wifely duty, which would make any physical contact considerably less interesting?

Trying to shake himself loose of her, he rode parallel to the river Douchary for a good mile and a half and then took the bridge where the rutted road crossed over it. At least Brendan had thought to drive about in circles before he brought her home—if she knew she was only three miles from the inn she might be trying harder to escape.

After another mile or so he reached the scattering of cottages and other buildings that marked the wee village of Sheiling. His village. Even with the sun barely a glow behind the mountains to the east, smoke already rose from most of the chimneys, and he could hear metal ringing against metal from the direction of Robert the blacksmith's.

As he swung down in the inn's stableyard one of the stable boys ran up, pulling on a wool cap as he came. "Good morning, Will," Graeme said with a smile, handing over the reins. "He's been fed, but if ye could find him an apple and a blanket to throw over him while he waits, I'd appreciate it."

The boy tugged on the front of his cap. "I'll see to the old devil, Laird Graeme. Dunnae ye worry over him."

Ree—Marjorie—did address him by his proper title, but she thought of him as just that and no more—a viscount, a minor noble in an uncivilized country, a lord last-name. He already had ample evidence that she didn't understand Highlanders or their ways. Because he wasn't just a lord. Here, he was the laird, the clan Maxwell chieftain responsible for keeping the people around him safe, for relaying the thoughts and wishes and rules that came from the Maxwell, for collecting clan tithes, settling disputes, and for maintaining the security of the clan and its interests in this part of the Highlands.

He pitched a penny to Will, then made his way through the fading snow flurries to the inn's front door. Coming here today could be a risk; on seeing him, someone might recall to Lady Marjorie's friends that his brothers had been about a few days earlier, just when she'd gone missing. But he needed to learn what they did know, what they'd said, and when he could expect the Duke of Lattimer on his doorstep.

In fact, as he walked into the warm common room he was surprised not to find the inn filled with her brother's men. And why weren't they here, looking for the missing sister of their lord and master?

"Good morning to ye, m'laird," the innkeeper called from across the room. "Maddie's just made some fresh bread, and the roasted ham is very fine this morning."

Sending the rotund man a nod and a grin, Graeme sat

at one end of the nearest of the long tables. "And some mulled ale, if ye care aboot me at all."

"Aye. It is a mite temperate this morning."

A minute or so later the innkeeper set the hot mug on the table, then sat on the bench opposite. "I reckon I know why ye're here this morning," he said, uncharacteristically lowering his voice.

Alarm bells began ringing in Graeme's skull, but he kept his expression still. "I heard ye have some English visitors here, and a missing lass. What can ye tell me?"

"It's a bad business, m'laird. Pretty young lass, went oot fer a breath of air, and vanished." He leaned his elbows on the rough-hewn table. "Odd, though, that the woman here, Mrs. Giswell, says this lass is her niece, but the coach standing out of sight behind the inn bears the Lattimer crest."

Graeme didn't have to feign his frown. "That *is* odd," he agreed. "What's the missing lass's name?"

"Marjorie Giswell, or so they say. I saw her, ye ken. Pretty young lass, black hair and blue eyes, and nae resembling her so-called aunt even in the dark. On the other hand, Mrs. Giswell and the two men with her seem genuinely worried over the lass."

"Are they offering a reward?"

"Aye. A hundred quid—which makes her a princess, I reckon. It doesnae quite make sense, but she's definitely gone missing, and we definitely dunnae want Sassenach redcoats tromping aboot the moors looking fer her."

He agreed with all of that. As for no one in her party admitting that she was Lattimer's sister, it made sense when he considered it. But if they knew how dangerous it was for her to be in Maxwell territory, why had they allowed her to come in the first place, and much less to wander about on her own? And why hadn't *she* known about the risk she was taking?

"That's her now," the innkeeper said, angling his chin

toward the stairs that led to the half-dozen rooms for let upstairs. "Mrs. Giswell. I reckon she'll be headed up toward Garaidh nan Leòmhann in the next day or so; she and the two fellas and Robert Polk have been south and west the past two days."

"Robert Polk?" Graeme repeated, lifting an eyebrow. "They've hired our blacksmith?"

"Nae. I think he's sweet on the old lass. She called him 'sir,' and now his head's so big I'll have to widen my doors."

"His skull's big enough, already." With a grin, Graeme took a blessedly warm swallow of the spicy mulled ale. "I'll go talk to her, then, and offer my help."

"Ye stay here, m'laird. I'll bring her to ye, as is proper." The innkeeper stood.

"Thank ye, Ranald."

That was how it was supposed to be. Anyone staying more than a few days in a clan's territory was supposed to present themselves to a chieftain and state their intentions and reason for trespassing. And then the chieftain would decide whether the strangers would be allowed to stay or not, and whether the clan chief needed to be notified.

The power of the clan chiefs and chieftains had waned considerably since the bloody disaster at Culloden. Chiefs burned out their own cotters to make room for sheep in a desperate effort to keep from having to sell off their ancestral, hard-won land. And men like him, who disagreed too vocally with their chiefs and didn't have the resources to break away completely, fought tooth and nail to keep what they had.

And now his lunatic brothers had piled this on his head. If the British army became involved, he could lose not only his status with the clan, but his ability to help and protect his tenants. He could lose Garaidh nan Leòmhann, the Lion's Den, as they called it, named by fierce Highlands warriors and by their enemies who feared to tread there.

"Laird Maxton," the innkeeper said, inclining his head as the stout, gray-haired woman glided up behind him, "Mrs. Giswell. Mrs. Giswell, this territory's chieftain of clan Maxwell, Graeme, Viscount Maxton."

She sank into a deep, graceful curtsy, one of such perfection that it immediately reminded him of his sharp-witted would-be bride. "Lord Maxton," she said, in a supremely cultured accent. "I'm very pleased to meet you. I require your assistance, my lord. Have you been informed that my niece is missing?"

"Aye. I heard aboot it yesterday afternoon," he said, oddly glad that that, at least, was the truth. "That's why I'm here this morning. Sit and have breakfast with me, Mrs. Giswell, and we'll see what can be done to help ye."

Hortensia Giswell sat as gracefully as she could on the bench opposite the very fine-looking, if wild-haired, Viscount Maxton. Finally, someone who might be able to do more than recite how young English lasses shouldn't go wandering about the Highlands alone. She knew that. More importantly, Lady Marjorie knew that.

The sympathetic but supremely unhelpful innkeeper brought her hardboiled eggs and toasted bread, her usual breakfast, so she held in her impatience, kept her criticisms about Highlanders and the Highlands to herself, and dined with the Scottish chieftain.

"What's yer niece's name?" he asked, apparently finding something amusing about the way she ate. Perhaps he wasn't accustomed to someone who knew how to use utensils.

"Marjorie," she returned. "Marjorie Giswell." Whatever last name she gave, Marjorie would certainly recognize that she was the one being sought, which was all any of them required. "She's one-and-twenty, of medium height, and has blue eyes and very dark brown hair. She's not an heiress, by any means, but I am offering one hundred pounds for her safe return."

"That's very generous," he commented. "Tell me, does this lass have a beau? They could marry here in Scotland withoot residence or parental consent."

"You're suggesting she eloped? Ridiculous. Aside from the fact that it would surround her with scandal, she has no beau." After two months spent in the young lady's company, she would certainly know if there was a particular gentleman. And there hadn't been, the poor lonely girl. Hortensia had actually begun to wish there had been someone for her. Someone who wasn't a blasted fortune hunter. But then again, men were trouble. All of them.

"What brings ye to the Highlands, then?" he pursued, continuing to gaze at her as he downed a good portion of the steaming, cinnamon-scented ale in his mug. "Ye've nae sent fer help, Ranald tells me, so I reckon ye dunnae have relations hereaboots."

That charming accent of his didn't fool her for a moment. He'd likely been told about the Lattimer coat of arms on the coach, and he was fishing for more information. Well, she wasn't about to declare to the world that an heiress, an English duke's sister, had gone missing. If someone had the young lady, a hundred pounds would sound like a fair, generous offer. If they learned the truth about her, getting Lady Marjorie back would involve politics, a great deal more money, quite possibly the military, and would likely end with her being sacked.

"My late husband served with the Duke of Lattimer," she lied slowly, hoping the tale made as much sense aloud as it did in her head. "His Grace very kindly invited me to visit, even offered me the use of his London coach. But I don't care to travel alone, so Marjorie volunteered to accompany me."

He finished off a thick slice of ham. "My cotters are fairly well scattered, but I'll make certain word gets oot that ye've a missing niece and she's to be found and returned to ye safely," he said, washing down the remains of his breakfast.

At least he seemed to believe her story. If her keeping the truth about Lady Marjorie's identity from everyone somehow caused her harm, though . . . Hortensia would never forgive herself. Oh, she was adept at social machinations, but she'd utterly failed with her last charge when Sophia had disappeared, and this looked to be even worse.

She reached out to touch the back of Maxton's hand. "My niece is very dear to me, sir," she said, not trying to hide her concern. "You know the Highlands better than I could ever hope to. What do you think has happened to her?"

"This land has more sheep than it does people," he returned, looking down to fiddle with his fork. "And neither is likely to be especially kind to a Sassenach. An ootsider, that is. But a lass alone—it wouldnae be our custom to turn away someone who needs help. She could well be at some shepherd's cottage waiting fer ye to find her, or fer the shepherd to find the time to walk her back here."

"Oh, I do hope that's what's happened," she said, releasing his hand and trying not to imagine how unfriendly the sheep must be if they warranted such a warning. "I'll keep searching and be as patient as I can. But if I haven't recovered her in the next few days, I'll have to send to His Grace for more assistance."

A muscle in Maxton's jaw jumped. "Bringing in a Sassenach soldier and his men wouldnae be wise."

Hortensia hadn't thought that idea would go over well. It would provide a little more incentive for this "laird" to aid her, however. "I understand, Lord Maxton. I must consider the safety of my niece before everything else, though. I hope *you* understand that."

"What I understand, Mrs. Giswell, is that ye shouldnae have let the lass oot of yer sight in the first place," he stated, then took a breath that lifted his shoulders. "Ye keep looking, and I'll do what I'm able. If she's nae fallen into a loch or a ravine somewhere, we've a chance of finding her." He climbed to his feet, tall and fit and imposing. "Now if ye'll excuse me, I've some cotters to see, and a few trackers to put on the lass's trail."

She remained seated on the long bench for several minutes after he left. If anyone in this blasted tangle of trees and moors and lakes and ravines and impossible mountains could help find Lady Marjorie, Graeme Maxton seemed to be the one to do it. The poor young woman wasn't at all foolish, so whatever these Highlanders thought or said, Hortensia would have been willing to wager—if ladies wagered—that someone had taken her. The question was who'd done it, and where they'd taken her. And why, of course.

"I see Laird Maxton rode doon to see ye this morning, lass," a low, thick brogue commented from behind her, and she gave a quickly stifled smile. "That's an honor, seein' how much that lad carries on his shoulders these days." Robert Polk, the big, bearded blacksmith, circled around to take the seat Maxton had vacated.

"I am honored, of course," she said, nodding. "But Marjorie is still missing."

"Ye've the right of it, Mrs. Giswell. To ye, Graeme Maxton's a way to find yer niece, and nae a thing more than that. Is he calling men together fer a search? I can tell him where we've already been, if ye like."

"He said his tenants were scattered far and wide, but he would see to it that they knew to look for her, and that she was to be returned safely." Hortensia frowned. "Should he have organized a search party?"

The blacksmith rubbed his dark brown beard. "The winter fair's in less than a fortnight, and we'll all gather fer that. Pulling clan Maxwell together before then, what with everyone working to bring the flocks doon from the hills and harvesting the last of the crops before they freeze—nae, I reckon he did as he should."

That made sense, little as she liked hearing it. "Then I'll continue my search. I cannot sit and do nothing."

He smiled, his brown eyes crinkling. "I didnae expect ye could. Which is why I've already hitched up the wagon. What do ye say to heading north? The river Douchary comes within aboot a mile of here, and we can follow it fer a ways."

While most of the locals seemed content to shake their heads at the idea of an English lass foolish enough to wander off on her own, not all of them had been so unhelpful. When he stood and walked around the table to offer her a muscular, soot-stained arm, Hortensia took it. Sir Robert, as she'd accidently dubbed him and he now called himself, had been nothing but helpful and attentive since the moment Lady Marjorie had gone missing.

In fact, she had more than a suspicion that the big man might be sweet on her. Her, twenty years a widow. It was somewhat thrilling to have such a large, fit man mooning after her, even if his manners were barbaric and his grammar frightful. If she'd learned one thing in her years as a tutor and a companion, it was that anyone could be taught. The trick lay in finding the correct incentive.

But that could wait. First she needed to find and rescue Lady Marjorie. And that needed to happen very soon, for everyone's sake.

With her ear against the floor, Marjorie could hear the low rumble of Graeme's voice, and then his heavy boot steps climbing the stairs. Swiftly she looped the chain once around the wooden slat she'd managed to break and slid out from under the bed.

Her fingers were red and dented, and they and both of her arms and her back ached from pulling and shoving the heavy bed frame about for half the night. She'd warned him, though, that she refused to be chained. Rubbing her hands together briskly, she hopped onto the bed to pull the blankets up to her chin. The chain slapped against the nightstand, luckily in time with his knocking.

"Come in," she panted, running a hand across her face and loose hair and hoping she hadn't acquired any cobwebs.

A moment later the door opened, and he strolled into her room. "Why are ye wearing the bedsheets?"

"Because I'm in my night rail. What do you think, I'm secretly wearing a ballgown and mean to dance my way to freedom?"

A slight, lopsided grin touched his mouth. "I wouldnae be surprised if ye are and ye will, yer grandness," he returned.

She didn't like that she found his smile charming. "Well, I'm not. And so I require a gown, and you promised me a bath." One arm still smelled of strawberry jam, and she had just spent several hours crawling beneath the bed—not that he needed to know that.

"Aye. That I did." He continued gazing at her, then visibly shook himself and stepped forward, brandishing a key in his hand as he approached. "Ye'll have to give me yer ankle, unless that's too improper and ye'd rather keep the chai—"

She clenched her jaw and stuck her leg out of the blankets, only up to the knee. It still felt very scandalous, and the way he gazed at her bared skin didn't help, either. "If you please," she said brusquely, hoping her cheeks weren't as red as they felt.

"Hm? Oh, aye. Lost myself in thought there, fer a moment." Putting a hand firmly on her calf, he twisted the lock a little until he could reach it, and then inserted the key and turned it.

She sighed in relief as the heavy thing clanked to the floor. Only a heartbeat later, though, she realized he hadn't let go of her leg. In fact, he stared at her ankle, which she'd managed to scrape and bruise while trying to work the other end of the chain free. *Blast it.* If he realized what she'd been up to, he'd likely chain her to the wall in the cellar next.

"I'm sorry, lass," he murmured, instead of the tirade she expected. Then he ran his fingers very lightly over her bruised skin. "I didnae intend this."

He blamed himself for her injuries. True, he'd put the blasted thing on her in the first place, but she'd been the one wrenching her leg about. She opened her mouth to tell him how minor it was, all things considered, but stopped herself at the last second.

If she could use his guilt to her advantage, that was what she was supposed to do. Yes, he'd kissed her, and yes, she'd found it immensely unsettling in an exhilarating kind of way, but they weren't friends. And they definitely weren't allies. "It seems you didn't intend a great many things where I'm concerned, but they keep happening anyway."

The expression in his dark gray eyes cooled to ice, a sure sign that she'd scored a hit. Marjorie didn't feel at all triumphant or vindicated, though. She made a show of gathering the sheets around her and standing, anything to avoid his gaze. It didn't matter a whit if she'd hurt his feelings; *she* wasn't the villain of this piece. But it felt like it mattered, like she'd . . . cheated or something.

"Can ye walk?" he asked, his voice clipped.

Now would be the time to say something even more biting about how she would have to manage, because he certainly wasn't permitted to attend to her and he didn't seem to have anyone in residence who was. Instead she clung to the tightly wrapped sheets and limped for the door. "Yes. I can walk."

He'd evidently ordered everyone to stay clear, because the hallway stood empty and silent as she stepped out of the bedchamber. Whether that was for her benefit or theirs, she had no idea, but she did appreciate not being gawked at while all she wore was a thin cotton night rail and some sheets.

"Yer shift and gown are inside," he said, moving up behind her. "And yer shoes. I'll be right outside the door, waiting fer ye, so dunnae do anything foolish."

The most foolish thing she'd done was to go help a boy rescue some kittens. Since then, she'd done her best *not* to be foolish. Her annoyed glance back at him didn't have the desired effect, though, because his gaze seemed to be resting on her backside. Blushing, she hurried inside the small room and shut the door behind her. This one, of course, didn't lock. She wasn't the one deciding her privacy. And that fact could be even more troublesome than she'd anticipated.

Graeme Maxton said he had no use for love, but he did desire her. It certainly . . . felt that way whenever she caught him looking at her. And it wasn't because he meant to marry her, since he'd made it clear that *that* had more to do with strategy than with feelings. But that made his lust about *her,* and she simply was not accustomed to that.

She dropped the sheets to the wooden floor, then stepped out of her night rail. He—or someone—had left soap on a stool beside the steaming bathtub, so she could wash her hair this time, at least. A small covered bowl sat there as well, and with a glance toward the door she lifted off the rough washing cloth draped over it.

Lemons. Two thinly sliced lemons, peel, pulp, juice, and all, filled the bowl. With the cloth removed, the scent of them immediately lifted into the air to remind her of warmth and sunshine—two things that had been very rare since they'd begun the trip north. Abrupt tears filled her eyes and ran damply down her cheeks, and she brushed them away, surprised at how touched she felt.

He'd listened to what she said, and brought her a gift accordingly. Whether he meant it to placate her or to bribe her into being more cooperative she had no idea, but just seeing them, smelling them, meant a great deal to her.

Marjorie dumped half of the bowl's contents into the hot water of the bath. She'd save the rest of it for her hair. Then, very conscious that she was naked, she slowly padded back to the door. "Thank you for the lemons," she said quietly, putting one palm against the cool wood.

"Ye're welcome, lass," came almost immediately and from very close by. She could imagine him leaning his forehead against the door as she was, their hands touching but for an inch of old oak. The thought made her feel warm, and safe, in the least likely place in the world for her to do so.

Before the chill of the room could sink deeper than her skin she backed away and stepped into the bath. With blessed heat surrounding her she took her time soaking, and then washed her hair with soap and lemons and tried to convince herself that she was only smiling because it felt good to be clean, and not because her maddeningly stubborn captor was also proving to be far more considerate, and interesting, than she ever would have expected.

Chapter Eight

The moment he heard Marjorie step into the brass bathtub, Graeme pushed away from the door and moved quickly and quietly to his own bedchamber. The pale, perfect skin of her leg marred by purple and red bruises, wounds that *he'd* caused her—it made him angry. Furious. He'd fought people—men—before, caused and received cuts and bruises far worse than those she bore. But those had been fair fights, two opponents stepping forward willingly. Marjorie had had no choice in the matter, because he hadn't given her one. Not from the moment she'd arrived.

Cursing, he dug one of his softest linen shirts out of his wardrobe and with the help of his boot knife, tore it into long, wide strips. Gathering them up along with a heavy wool scarf, he returned to her room and sat on the floor to line the ankle cuff with the thick wool and then wrap every bit of it but the lock with layers of linen. He'd have to open the cuff a bit wider than it was now to fit it around her leg, but he'd be damned if he would lock it on her again without some padding.

He wanted to leave it off her altogether; in fact, he

wanted to yank it free of the bed and throw it through the window. If it had been just the two of them, he would have risked it, risked her getting away and sending the law and Lattimer after him. But as he'd been reminded every day for the past eight years, he couldn't make decisions based solely on what *he* wanted.

Because what he wanted happened to be naked just a few feet away from him. A proper, aristocratic, tight-bunned English female, and he wanted her pale, perfect skin against his, he wanted her mouth on him, he wanted to see her face flushed with passion and to hear her cry out his name as he came inside her.

That was why he'd asked her so-called aunt if she had a beau—though why in hell that should matter, he had no idea. He simply wanted her, and that had nothing to do with what an alliance with her could do for his corner of clan Maxwell. He wanted to know that a lovely duke's sister desired a near destitute Scottish clan chieftain who mended fences and sheared sheep and delivered calves with his own two damned hands.

With the cuff as comfortable as he could make it, he stuffed the knife back into his boot, placed the book of Robert Burns's poetry he'd dug out of the attic on the mantel where she could reach it, then returned to his watch by the spare room's door.

A few minutes later, that door opened, and Marjorie in shimmering emerald stepped into the hallway with the scent of steam and lemons swirling around her. Graeme's entire body reacted, and he had to work to remain where he was. To make it worse, her long, dark hair hung damply halfway to her waist, strands framing her own face and caressing her cheeks. She looked up at him, her deep blue eyes searching his.

Abruptly she blinked and looked down. "You found another dress for me," she said, brushing her fingers along the deep green satin of her skirt.

Thankfully they'd simply stored most of his mother's things away in the attic, along with his grandmother's and her mother's before that. "It was fairly fashionable ten years ago, I imagine," he heard himself say. "And it's a bit warmer than the other one."

Of course she wouldn't thank him for it, because she'd said she would do no such thing, but she did incline her head. "I don't suppose I could go for a walk?" she said, stopping short of the open door to her room. "Stretch my legs a little?"

Graeme knew he was being led about by his cock, but he was still tempted to take her for a stroll. "Nae," he said aloud. "The fewer people who know ye're here before I wed ye, the better fer all of us."

"For all of *you*, perhaps."

He grimaced. "I met Mrs.Giswell this morning," he offered, motioning her into the bedchamber. "She's calling ye her niece Marjorie, and offering a hundred pounds fer yer safe return."

She stopped again, facing him. "Why—"

"I reckon she figured with the way ye went missing, that ye'd been taken. And that if so, it'd be better if ye werenae known to be Lattimer's sister. A hundred quid's a damned fortune, hereabouts, but nae overly suspicious. Nae when it's offered by some mad old Sassenach lass."

"At least someone's looking for me," she muttered, limping past him and into the room.

"Aye. And we'd best come to an agreement, ye and me, before she brings yer brother and all of his MacKittrick men doon on my head."

"Who's MacKittrick?"

There likely wasn't any harm in telling her, and if it

distracted her for a time, so much the better. "Yer brother's started his own clan. Did ye nae know?"

She shook her head, the dark cascade of her hair falling over one emerald shoulder. "I had no idea that was even possible."

"It isnae, truly. But the castle, Lattimer, used to be called MacKittrick, after an old Maxwell chieftain. When all yer brother's tenants sided with him against the Maxwell—the Duke of Dunncraigh—they were booted from clan Maxwell. So they decided yer brother was Laird MacKittrick, and now they're MacKittrick's men. His clan, in the ways it counts."

"That's . . . Why in heaven's name didn't Gabriel write and tell me all this?" she burst out, stalking toward the window and then quickly turning back, as if she remembered she wasn't supposed to be over there. "Why didn't he tell me he was in the middle of a war with clan Maxwell? And that clan Maxwell apparently surrounds Lattimer?"

"It does," he commented. "And he didnae do ye any bloody favors by keeping silent, and that's damned certain."

She folded her arms across her chest. "Yes, I believe we can agree on that point. And your language sir, if you please."

Back to that again, were they? So be it. Neither of them had much incentive to change, so he'd imagined they'd be having the same argument until doomsday. "Aye. My filthy language. Ye can sit in the chair, or on the bed," he said, squatting to pick up the end of the chain. "I padded it, but I'll let ye choose which leg I put it on."

Marjorie scowled. "My right leg, then. At least I'll be able to sit in the chair more comfortably." With that she seated herself, graceful as any princess, in the old, overstuffed chair. "And however well you cover it, it's still a shackle, and you're still locking it around my ankle."

Graeme clenched his jaw. "I'm aware of that, lass. Agree to marry me, swear on someaught ye cherish, and I'll take it away."

She looked directly at him. "No."

"Stubborn woman," he muttered, unsurprised. Trying to ignore the lemon scent of her skin, the smooth warmth of her, he carefully locked the cuff around her ankle, made certain none of the metal pinched or even touched her, then straightened again. "I'll be back with yer breakfast in a bit," he said, retreating to the door. "Is there anything else ye require, aside from yer freedom and a coach with four white horses to carry ye away from here?"

"The horses don't have to be white," she returned. "I'm not particular."

Every time he thought he'd figured her out, every time he concluded that she was the grand, spoiled lady he'd expected, she said something like that and set him off kilter again. "I'll keep that in mind," he returned, pulling the door closed behind himself.

Another day or two of this and he was likely to become a raving lunatic. At the bottom of the stairs he summoned Cowen. "Has Mrs. Woring put a tray together fer our guest?"

"Aye, m'laird. I was aboot to have Ross fetch it fer ye."

"I'll fetch it. I need ye to send Ross doon to Mòriasg Hoose and have him tell my uncle I request his presence at his earliest convenience."

Raibeart Maxton was a practical man, and Graeme could damned well use some practical advice—and a plan that didn't end with someone imprisoned or dead.

"Ye should go talk to her," Connell Maxton urged, as he tossed bits of chicken into the air and his pair of foxes leaped after the morsels. If Morag Woring got word of where one of the chickens she'd set aside for dinner had gone, the lad wouldn't be able to sit down for the meal, but the foxes seemed happy enough.

"She's locked in," Brendan returned, frowning over a full page of complicated-looking mathematics. "And she's English. I dunnae want to talk to her."

"When Graeme marries her, ye'll have to talk to her," Dùghlas pointed out.

"Nae. I willnae." Brendan crossed out a line in heavy pencil. "Damnation. I'd rather be oot clearing the ditches than doing this."

"Graeme said the morning snow should be gone by tomorrow, and we're to do it then," Connell recited, as if they all hadn't heard the announcement four hours ago, over breakfast. "And why dunnae ye want to talk to her? Are ye scared? Of a lass? *I* talked to her."

"Aye, but ye make friends with frogs, duckling. And then ye weep when a hawk takes one. Dunnae make the same mistake with her. Stay well away from that woman."

In the chair beneath the window of the downstairs sitting room, Dùghlas set aside his own pencil and sighed. Generally afternoons were filled with Brendan's complaints about having to continue his studies at the old age of sixteen, while Connell worked through whatever passage he'd been given to read, and Dùghlas helped Connell and finished up his own studies.

Today, and for the past few days, the lessons had been more difficult and more lengthy, and they felt like a punishment—or a way to keep them inside the house. Dùghlas supposed that made sense, given the trouble they'd made for Graeme, but he wondered if their oldest brother had any idea how angry Brendan still was.

Aye, Brendan was angry nearly daily, but generally it was because a lass he liked had smiled at someone else. Then, his grumbling was full of plans to knock Rory Polk or Eran Howard on their arses. This, though, felt different. And when they'd tied up the lass, Brendan would have driven the wagon all the way to Dunncraigh himself, if they hadn't had Connell with them. He kept talking like he didn't care what happened to her now, even with the plans Graeme had made, and Dùghlas was beginning to believe that he meant it.

"Stop teasing Connell," he said aloud. "He likes the Sassenach, and ye ken the duckling has a soft heart."

"I dunnae have a soft heart; I have a big heart," the eight-year-old corrected. "And Brendan can say whatever he likes. I think he's just mean."

"It's nae mean to be willing to do what's necessary. It's practical. I'm practical."

Dùghlas snorted. "Ye're a bull in a bloody china shop."

"At least I've done someaught. Graeme would just as soon throw punches while the Maxwell threatens him—and us. Dunncraigh's supposed to be our ally, nae our enemy. And we can be back at the laird's table by sending one damned letter! If trouble comes of it, I'll take it on my shoulders. Graeme's needed here."

"And what would that make me," Graeme said from the doorway, "if I allowed anyone to take ye from here, Brendan?"

The sixteen-year-old slammed his fist against the tabletop. "I'm nae having this argument again, Graeme! Withoot blunt coming here from somewhere, ye'll have to sell Garaidh nan Leòmhann before Connell's old enough to go to university, even though ye'll nae have the blunt to send him anymore than ye will Dùghlas and me."

"I'm nae going to university!" Connell yelled. "I'm staying here and helping! And we willnae ever sell the Lion's Den, will we, Graeme?"

"Nae, we willnae," the Maxwell chieftain returned with a grin. "If we've nae money we'll sell Brendan to gypsies."

Dùghlas grinned too, relieved to see his oldest brother

in better humor again. "Well, that'll gain us a shilling or two, at least."

Brendan pushed to his feet, his face beet red. "Ye're all so damned amusing."

He stomped for the door, but Graeme didn't move. "Where do ye think ye're going?" he asked, lifting an eyebrow.

"The snow's stopped. Someone ought to go take a look at the irrigation ditches and see what's to be done tomorrow. So I reckon that's where I'm going."

With a nod, Graeme stepped aside. "Good. Stay away from Sheiling in case someone remembers ye were there the same day her ladyship went missing."

"Aye, Laird Maxton, my lord and chieftain."

Connell charged the door, too, the foxes on his heels. "I'll go fetch my coat and help him, then."

"Ye'll fetch yer coat *after* ye read me yer sentences," their oldest brother amended, putting a hand on the duckling's head to turn him back into the depths of the room.

"Damnation," Connell muttered. "Ye're truly nae going to sell Garaidh nan Leòmhann, are ye? And dunnae lie to me. I'm old enough to know the truth."

Graeme sat at the worktable. "I'm nae selling our home, Connell. And that is the truth. I may have to lease some of the hillsides fer grazing to some of our neighbors, but ye'll always have a home here. Except when ye go to Edinburgh to university, of course."

With a laughing yell of protest Connell launched himself at Graeme, and the two of them and the foxes ended up in a pile on the floor that only ended when Graeme stood and lifted the bairn over his head. "Who's the Bruce?" he demanded, lowering Connell's head until they were eye to upside-down eye.

The boy roared with laughter. "I'm the Bruce!"

"What?" Graeme spun him in a quick circle with the

foxes bounding into the air around them. "I couldnae quite hear ye. Who's the Bruce?"

"I surrender! Ye're the Bruce!"

With a triumphant bellow Graeme tossed Connell in the air and caught him again. In another year or two the lad would be too heavy for flinging about. Not today, though. Today he needed to hear the duckling's laughter as much as the boy needed a good laugh and a wrestle. Another thing he'd neglected over the past few days.

The next three things happened all at once.

Soft female laughter sounded from just inside the doorway behind him.

Connell squealed. "Ye set her free! I knew ye would, Graeme!"

Brendan pounded on the sitting room window from outside. "Uncle Raibeart's here! Sir Hamish Paulk's with him!"

This had been a good idea. Marjorie knew it had been. She'd sat in her temporary bedchamber for nearly an hour—after she'd clanked over to the door the second Graeme left to slide a piece of writing paper between the lock and the jamb to keep the door from locking, then removed the padding from the ankle lock and pulled her foot free. She still had no idea where to run, and he was likely to dog her heels unless he trusted her at least a little.

Before she could open her mouth to state that she might have run but she'd chosen not to do so, Graeme dumped his youngest brother onto the overstuffed couch cushions and strode forward to grab her arm. "Paulk's Dunncraigh's lapdog. So ye need to get back upstairs," he hissed, his face pale. "Now."

The flat, dead-serious tone of his voice convinced her as much as his grim expression. This was not him being angry that she'd escaped her prison. That would likely come later. With a brief nod she gathered her green skirts and hurried up the hallway—only to be blocked from the stairs by the two older men for whom Cowen had opened the front door.

The butler's eyes widened almost comically as he caught sight of her. "I—ye," he stammered. "Ye should-nae be here."

"Nonsense, Cowen," the taller of the two men drawled, favoring her with a smile that reminded her of Graeme's. "A lass here in the Lion's Den? Introduce us."

These two men were the reason Graeme had been more concerned with getting her out of sight than with figuring out how she'd escaped. The question for her, though, became whether they were more likely to offer her aid or to send her off to the Duke of Dunncraigh.

She did, however, have some skills at conversation that might assist her, and in more ways than one. She offered a polite curtsy. "Good afternoon, gentlemen. I've been told that one of you is Lord Maxton's uncle, and one of you is Sir Hamish Paulk, but I'm afraid I wasn't given a description."

The one who looked like an older version of Graeme put a hand to his chest. "Raibeart Maxton. This is Sir Hamish Paulk, chieftain of clan Maxwell."

"A chieftain? Like Lord Maxton is a chieftain?"

Steel-gray eyes took in the length of her before returning to her face. "Nae. I'm nae like Graeme Maxton. I dunnae ignore the Maxwell's wishes or fail to pay my tithes. And ye're English."

That answered that. She and Sir Hamish were not going to become bosom friends. "I am English."

"And what's yer name, then? Ye've held on to it fer a good bit, I reckon."

"Uncle Raibeart." Graeme's booming voice sounded from closer behind her than she expected. "Thank ye fer coming so quickly. And Sir Hamish. What brings ye this far from Dunncraigh's boots? And who's licking 'em while ye're away?"

"I came to see yer uncle and do some fishing at Mòriasg, nae that it's any of yer affair. Who's the Sassenach?"

Graeme glanced at her as he put himself between her and them. "Nae that it's any of *yer* affair, but this is Marjorie Giswell. She's to—"

"I'm Connell's new governess," she broke in hurriedly. *There*. That should put a stop to his marriage plans for her.

He sent her a black look. "Aye. Governess," he ground out.

"A governess?" Raibeart asked, lifting an eyebrow. "Ye're a mite young fer that, are ye nae, Miss Giswell?"

Yes, she'd out-maneuvered him, but her internal gloating only lasted a moment. Now she'd made herself a governess, the one thing she'd vowed never to become. A companion had been awful enough. Caring for and instructing someone else's children because she couldn't make a home herself had seemed the worst form of torture possible. Even so, it had to be an improvement over being anyone's unwilling bride. And for the moment, that was enough. Mrs. Giswell would faint at the idea that now she'd become an actress, a governess, and escaped a marriage, all in the same moment. She fixed a smile on her face. "I am one-and-twenty, sir. How old should a governess be?"

"She shouldnae be English, and that's fer damned certain," Sir Hamish put in. "Nae in a Scottish hoose."

Marjorie inclined her head. "Well, I cannot change where I was born, but if I can teach young Connell the difference between an exclamation and an interjection, I believe I will be satisfied." She backed down the hallway away from the three men. "Please excuse me. I didn't mean to intrude."

As soon as she turned the corner she found the nearest open room, slipped inside, and sagged against the wall. The moment Hamish Paulk set eyes on her she'd felt in more danger than she ever had in Graeme's presence. That didn't make any sense, of course, when one had been holding her captive and the other had only eyed her rather boldly, but she felt it down to her bones. She would not be throwing herself on Sir Hamish Paulk's mercy.

For the moment she wasn't a prisoner. But if she fled now, after she'd provided everyone with a reason for her to be staying, she'd raise even more suspicions. Considering that here she at least had food and warmth, the last thing she wanted was to end up on foot somewhere in the Highlands wilderness while at least two sets of men hunted her. Graeme's first priority was protecting his brothers. If she fled while his guests were here, he might well have no choice but to tell them the truth about her to save the boys.

Deciding all those things in two hard beats of her heart, she'd moved from being an adversary to an ally of Graeme Maxton—at least from her viewpoint. She had no idea how he would see it. All she did know was that she would not be wearing that shackle again. Not without a blasted fight.

"There ye are," a younger voice said.

With a surprised gasp she straightened. "Oh, goodness. You startled me."

Light gray eyes beneath a straight mop of dark hair regarded her. Was this Brendan, the one who, according to Connell, had been her chief kidnapper? Or the other one? He stood as tall as she did, which didn't tell her much, and though she'd heard both boys' voices during the long, bumpy wagon ride, she didn't know which voice belonged to which Maxton.

"How'd ye get oot?"

"I think I'll keep that information to myself."

A grin crinkled his eyes. "Are ye angry at Brendan and me? I reckon ye ken that ye cannae blame Connell."

So this was Dùghlas, the fourteen-year-old. She made a note of that for future reference. "I *was* angry," she admitted. "And I'm still not convinced you and Brendan don't deserve a walloping."

The boy nodded, his hair flopping across his forehead. All of the Maxtons she'd seen so far, with the exception of their uncle, badly needed a haircut. "That's fair enough," he said. "Ye're still nae to leave the hoose, if ye hadn't already figured that."

She cocked her head. "And you're to stop me if I do?"

"We're all to grab hold of ye and drag ye back upstairs. Ye're nae as delicate as I thought, but I'd wager two or three of us could manage that."

The matter-of-fact way he spoke actually left her feeling somewhat calmer. He wasn't angry, or frightened, or particularly worried over Paulk's presence, at least. Unless he didn't understand the implications. Or unless she had figured them wrong. "I imagine you could. Very well, then. I'll remain in the house."

"Good. Graeme's closed in his office with Uncle Raibeart and Sir Hamish, likely trying to explain why he needed to see our uncle. I'm to take ye back to the sitting room and show ye how I help Connell with his lessons so ye willnae look like a nodcock if they stay fer luncheon, which I reckon they will."

Of course the Maxtons would assume she had no idea how to be a governess; given the number of ways Graeme had referred to her as a princess, he probably thought she'd been born into wealth and position. He had no idea that she'd gone to school with the idea of serving in a household, even if it had been as a companion rather than as a governess or tutor. Well, for the moment she had no intention of correcting his misapprehensions.

"Lead the way," she said, gesturing. "And please tell me where things are in the house as we go, since I'll be expected to know."

"Nae. I'm nae telling ye a damned thing withoot Graeme's permission," he countered. "If ye need someaught, Connell or I'll fetch it fer ye."

Blast it. "Not Brendan, though?"

"Brendan thinks sending ye on to Dunncraigh is the answer to all our ills, so ye'd do well to stay away from him."

They walked back into the sitting room where Connell still sat on the couch, his eyes wide enough that he knew at least something of what was afoot. "Sir Hamish is here?" he whispered loudly. "Did Graeme tell him to come take ye to—"

"Hush, duckling," his brother interrupted, ruffling his brother's red hair. "All ye need to know is that this is Lady—I mean Miss—Marjorie Giswell, and she's yer governess."

"I'm too old fer a governess," Connell returned, not quietly.

"Then I'm your tutor," Marjorie amended. "And you should all call me Ree." She sat on the couch beside him. "I think I've only just taken the position, which would explain why we don't know each other well."

"Do ye know aboot my baby rabbits? Because Graeme doesn't know about them."

Beyond him Dùghlas rolled his eyes. "Ye really think Gr—"

"I think you told me about the rabbits because we're friends," she interrupted.

Connell nodded. "I think so, too."

" 'Friends'?" a deeper male voice echoed from the

doorway. "I'm nae yer friend. And I'm trying to decide why I shouldnae drag ye oot by yer damned hair and tell Sir Hamish exactly who ye are."

And that would be Brendan. As she looked over at him, Marjorie reflected that even if she hadn't known who he was, she would have known he was one of the Maxton brothers. Gray eyes, his narrowed, glared at her from beneath an unruly tangle of red-brown hair. He was thinner than Graeme, and a few inches shorter, but he stood taller than she did. And he was daring her to argue with him, to make one wrong step that would give him the excuse to do exactly as he threatened.

Marjorie folded her hands in her lap. "First of all, ladies do not care to hear a man cursing in their presence. Cursing makes a man seem impolite and inconsiderate, and no lady wants to spend her time with someone more concerned with proving how rough he is rather than with making her feel special. Second, m—"

"That would explain why Isobel Allen called ye a lunkhead and willnae go walking with ye, Brendan," Dùghlas put in.

Stifling a smile at that, she stood, keeping her gaze on the sixteen-year-old. "Second, my brother is the Duke of Lattimer. I am not some helpless female who screams and faints. Mistreat me, and I will be the worst enemy you can imagine. Be fair and kind to me, and I can be the best friend you've ever known." As she spoke she slowly approached him, stopping when they were merely two feet apart. Some of this she'd wanted to say to her neighbors for months, and she hadn't dared. It felt good to say it now. She only hoped she wasn't wasting a good speech for no good reason.

He didn't back down, and she held his gaze for a long moment, having to lift her chin a little to do so. The anger practically radiated off him, and she certainly understood wanting more and not being able to find a way to achieve it.

"You think I'm the means by which you can help your family," she said after a moment. "Perhaps I am; just not in the way you imagined."

"Ha," he retorted. "Ye'd help us, willingly, after what we did to ye? After Graeme tried to force ye to marry him? Ye wriggled oot of that like a clever lass. But I'm nae a fool, Sassenach. And we dunnae need English charity." With a scowl he turned around and stomped out of the room.

Marjorie let out the breath she hadn't realized she'd been holding. Brendan could still change his mind and go wag his tongue about her to Sir Hamish, and she wouldn't be able to do anything about it. Hopefully, though, she'd at least given him something about which to think. Something to make him hesitate before he acted.

"Ye made him stop arguing," Connell said, bouncing up beside her to take her hand as if they'd been allied for months rather than for the past ten minutes. "Usually Graeme has to drag him outside and throw him in the river before he'll shut his gobber."

"I didn't wish to be dragged off by my hair," she returned, pasting a hopefully convincing smile on her face. "Now. Please show me what you do for grammar and mathematics, if you don't mind." Because whether she wanted to be a governess or not, today she preferred that position to being locked up in a room again, or dragged off to the marriage altar because that was the least of several evils.

She wondered what Graeme might be telling his uncle and Sir Hamish Paulk about her, because she certainly qualified as an oddity in this household. Whatever his ultimate intentions, today he'd tried to protect her, keep her safe, and he'd lied to his clan to do it.

That certainly made her think about his kisses all over again, as well. And made her wonder whether she was still a captive, or somewhere in the past hour had become a mad, willing participant.

Chapter Nine

Of course I'd be honored to judge the jams and short-bread at the fair, lad," Raibeart Maxton said, a furrow appearing between his straight brows. "But ye might have sent me a note aboot that. I thought ye had someaught amiss here, sending for me at my 'earliest convenience.'"

As long as Hamish Paulk sat in the room with them, nobody would be discussing anything more troublesome than jams and shortbread. "Aye," Graeme said aloud, watching as the Maxwell's favorite chieftain poured himself a second, generous glass of the house's most expensive vodka. "I reckon Ross got overexcited when he delivered the message. That's why I was surprised to see ye."

"So we rode two miles fer nae damned good reason." Sir Hamish sat again to sip at his drink. "And I missed half a day's fishing." He rapped his knuckles against the surface of the old, worn desk. "I'd rather know where ye found that fine Sassenach lass. A fortnight ago ye couldnae pay yer tithe to Dunncraigh."

"I reckon if I decide to put the education of my *bràthair* ahead of sending the Maxwell a bit of coin he doesnae need, that's my affair," Graeme retorted. He didn't like the way Hamish called Marjorie "fine," as if the lass wasn't a good thirty years Paulk's junior. And he definitely hadn't liked the way the old man had looked at her.

As for that clever little trick she'd pulled, turning herself into an employee rather than a betrothed, in a sense he was relieved. More relieved than he'd expected. Aye, he would have married her, and she likely would have hated him for it. Now, he could pursue something more carnal, without feeling that he was pushing her into a union about which she had no real choice. Now she could tell him no— though he didn't think she would. Not if he'd read those kisses correctly. No, he wouldn't be falling for her, but wanting her felt safer now that they wouldn't be . . . permanent. Now that he could put distance between them if he wanted to do so.

"But an English lass, Graeme?" Raibeart took up. "Even I have to question that. Ye ken we've a handful of educated Highlanders who'd welcome employment at a fine hoose such as this. Lads, too, which I reckon would make a more proper tutor fer Connell."

"Ye ken we're at war with an English duke," Hamish put in. "Are ye trying to rile Dunncraigh even more than ye already have?"

Oh, for Lucifer's sake. "If there's one thing Garaidh nan Leòmhann doesnae have need of, it's another lad. With her aboot, at least they have to use utensils."

It had been twenty minutes now since he'd last seen her heading for the back of the house. He had to settle for hoping that Dùghlas had understood his hastily whispered instructions, that he'd found Marjorie, and that the fourteen-year-old had somehow managed to convince her to cooperate. Failing that, the lad and whoever he could round up to help him would have to throw her back into her bedchamber, when he didn't know how the devil she'd managed to escape in the first place.

"I heard someaught aboot a Sassenach lass going missing out of Sheiling," his uncle went on. "There's a reward fer whoever finds her. Wasnae her name Margaret or Marjorie?"

Damnation. "Aye, that's her," Graeme conceded, thinking fast. "Her aunt's staying at the Cracked Hearth while we open a room fer her. We didnae know she'd be coming fer a holiday. The old woman's a Bedlamite, nearly. I had to ride doon this morning to remind her that nae a soul's missing, that her niece is where she left her, and that this is Scotland and nae Prussia."

The two men continued to look skeptical, but when neither one said anything aloud he decided not to elaborate. The simpler the tale, the easier it would be to keep it straight later. At the same time, he knew he couldn't leave Mrs. Giswell at the inn where she could announce to all and sundry that her supposed niece was still missing. And that damned Lattimer coach needed to vanish, as well.

"Well, lad, as Brendan's nae burned doon the stable and Connell doesnae have a red deer living in the attic, invite us to luncheon and then we'll be on our way."

Graeme forced a smile as he climbed to his feet. "I dunnae believe he has a deer in the attic. I'd nae swear to it. But how long are ye staying at Mòriasg, Paulk? I'd like to know when I can next go visit my uncle withoot seeing ye there."

"That depends on the trout, I reckon," Sir Hamish returned flatly. "Of course when Dunncraigh finally decides ye're nae worth the trouble ye cause, this is all likely to be my territory, too, since I'm the nearest chieftain. Mayhap I'll stay a bit longer, to get the lay of the land."

They couldn't strip him of his house, or of his property, but with him no longer considered part of clan Maxwell, remaining would be a very unpleasant prospect. He would lose cotters, and income, and then debts might well take what Dunncraigh couldn't. It wasn't a pleasant prospect, but it didn't mean he would bow to a man who endangered and mistreated his own. Not while he had the choice to do otherwise.

Marjorie had altered the plan he'd concocted to deal with Dunncraigh, but he'd only known her and her circumstances a few days—a short enough time that the idea of rising to victory in this fray seemed a fleeting dream, at best. A dream that had slipped through his fingers before he'd even had a chance to clench his fist.

The two men seemed determined to remain on his heels, so he informed Cowen they'd have more for luncheon, sent up a quick prayer to whoever might be listening, and headed for the sitting room. In the doorway, though, he stopped.

Marjorie sat at the small worktable beside Connell. Something in his chest unclenched as he took in the curve of her neck, the loose, tangled bun of dark hair at the top of her head, the close-fitting, too-fancy emerald gown that clung to her bosom, and the slight smile on her face as she glanced up to meet his gaze. She hadn't tried to flee. She was still there. He hadn't lost her.

He tried telling himself it was relief he felt, relief that she hadn't complicated things even further, but the exhilaration coursing through him seemed closer to anticipation. She'd stayed. He didn't know why, but for the moment, at least, he could imagine they'd chosen the same side.

"I'd nae have learned a damned thing if she'd been my governess," Sir Hamish muttered, jabbing Graeme in the ribs with an elbow.

Connell looked up. "We dunnae curse in this hoose," he stated. "The lasses dunnae like it." He wrote something on the paper in front of him. "And Ree isnae my governess. She's my tutor. And Dùghlas and Brendan's."

Dùghlas rose from his usual chair by the window. "Duckling, ye've been wanting to show Uncle Raibeart the . . . new thing in yer bedchamber, have ye nae?"

The boy practically bounced to his feet. "Aye! Come and see! But Graeme cannae come."

Graeme gestured the lot of them toward the hallway, clapping Dùghlas on the shoulder as his brother passed. "Thank ye, Dùghlas," he whispered. Eventually he would "accidently" discover the three rabbit kits, but for now they could remain Connell's poorly kept secret—especially when they provided an excuse to get everyone else out of the sitting room. "We'll sit fer luncheon in twenty minutes. I need a word with Miss Giswell, in the meantime."

Sir Hamish looked as though he'd rather stay behind, but keen-witted Dùghlas pulled the chieftain into a conversation about grouse hunting, and in a loud moment the four of them were gone up the stairs. Pulling in a slow breath, Graeme faced Marjorie again.

"I want the nails gone from those windows," she said, standing, "and I'm not stepping into that room again until *I* have the key to the door."

If he'd thought for a second that she would simply play her part—her new part—without comment, that had only been in his dreams. "If ye think I'm letting ye leave here to cause havoc, ye'd best reconsider. I could still wed a tutor. Or a governess."

"And I could have left this morning, and I didn't," she pointed out.

"Aye, and why didnae ye do that, exactly?" he returned, folding his arms over his chest.

She took a quick breath, grimacing and likely trying to decide the pretty lie she meant to tell him. Perhaps she would say she'd fallen head over heels for him and couldn't bear to leave his company. That would be nice to hear—

even if he wouldn't believe a word of it. Not when he half wanted to hear it.

"I considered leaving," she said finally, "but I'm not dressed for the cold weather. Neither do I have any idea in which direction I'm most likely to find assistance. Nor do I want you riding me down and dragging me back to force me into marriage. So I thought to prove to you that I'm not a threat to you or your brothers. When the lot of you come to your senses, I'm hoping you'll see fit to return me to my companions and my family. If you require monetary compensation for your . . . hospitality, *I* can arrange that. Without my brother knowing a thing."

Honesty. He damned well hadn't expected that. "Today I reckon we'll all fare better with ye here," he returned. "If ye like, we can begin negotiations again tomorrow."

She gave a curt nod. "Fair negotiations."

He almost smiled. "Aye. Fair ones."

"Then in light of our temporary alliance I would like to point out that you gave me the name Marjorie Giswell, the female for whom my so-called aunt is searching."

"I recall. I told my uncle she's batty."

Her lips twitched. "She won't approve of that."

God, he wanted to kiss her again. This time, though, he didn't have an excuse or an ulterior motive. He wasn't trying to intimidate her or distract her while he stripped her of a letter she was trying to hide, or attempting to get her to agree to a union she didn't want. This would simply be because he found her attractive and he wanted her.

Generally desiring a lass was enough to get her into his bed; even with his dour finances he was a viscount and a clan chieftain with a fine, grand house, and the lasses claimed that he had a handsome face and knew his way about a bedchamber. And he'd never heard any complaints, if he said so himself.

But those lasses were Highlanders, accustomed to Highlands ways and content with their Highlands lives. Not a one of them had been the sister of a duke, a lass who'd already dined with more lords and ladies than he'd likely ever meet in his entire life. No, he wasn't lowborn by any means, but as she'd said, being a viscount and the master of Garaidh nan Leòmhann didn't give him much of a pedigree by English aristocratic standards.

"So ye'll cooperate, then," he said aloud, mostly because he'd begun to worry that she would be able to hear his cock creaking against his trouser seams in the silence. It was certainly bellowing loudly enough in his head, telling him to ignore the nonsense of kidnappings and marriage and politics and bend her over the worktable.

"Today, I'll cooperate," she agreed. "If you give me the key to that bedchamber. I won't wake in the morning to find myself locked in again." She held out her delicate, long-fingered hand, palm up.

"And tomorrow?" he asked. "I'll nae have ye running oot the door fer soldiers to come arrest my brothers."

"I already told you that I would send any soldiers I might find after *you*. I give you my word about that. But I'm certainly not going to otherwise promise to behave myself to your satisfaction."

Warmth coursed beneath his skin, and he couldn't have helped grinning even if he'd wanted to. "I'd prefer if ye didnae behave yerself, Ree, so I dunnae mean to ask ye to do so."

She flushed. "I didn't mean it that way," she retorted. "I meant I will not obey your ridiculous commands."

Graeme took a long step closer to her. "I'd rather ye did mean it the other way, but I'll make do fer now." Taking the old iron key from his coat pocket, he placed it onto her palm and then closed his fingers around her hand. "Ye're still mine, ye ken," he murmured.

Her sky-blue gaze locked with his. "I beg your pardon?"

"My prisoner," he clarified though that hadn't been at all what he meant.

The last woman in the world he should be lusting after, the last woman in the world who would have any reason to look at him with anything but fear and contempt. Disaster waited directly ahead of him, and as little as he could afford more trouble, he had no intention of moving aside. It wasn't love, he reminded himself, because he was fairly certain love was loftier than the carnal thoughts running through his head. No hearts, no broken hearts, and none of the damned, selfish tragedy that came with that.

"Laird Maxton," Cowen's voice came from behind him, and he immediately released Marjorie's hand and stepped back.

"What is it?" he asked, his gaze still on her.

"Father Michael's here," the butler returned. "He spied Sir Hamish and yer uncle and he's already blessed himself twice and invited himself to luncheon."

The pastor had a better sense of smell than a deerhound, when it came to opportunity. Clenching his jaw, Graeme nodded. "Set a place fer him."

"Aye. I apologize fer nae tripping him at the front door, but I dunnae attend church as often as I should, anyway."

"It's fine, Cowen. Go see to it."

This complicated things even further. Having Hamish Paulk remaining in the area should have been trouble enough. But Father Michael appeared at the door almost daily with the fair on the way, and once he met the lads' tutor he would expect to see her . . . tutoring. Locking Marjorie up again after this visit would now be impossible. She'd bloody well outmaneuvered him for now, but he still had a special marriage license heading this way. If everything else fell apart, he could still fall back on that.

Graeme needed her cooperation not just through luncheon, but for the remainder of her stay. In addition to that, Father Michael was a notorious gossip. Once he knew about Marjorie Giswell, everyone would know. The Giswell woman at the inn would know—and once she realized who'd done the kidnapping, she would be off to Lattimer to inform the duke.

The sins piling up on his doorstep looked to be higher than the winter snow. Even so, he had every intention of keeping his greatest temptation as close to him as he could manage, whether she had any strategic value, or not.

Her eyes beginning to droop closed, Hortensia Giswell poured herself a last cup of tea and sent the driver and footman upstairs to the room they'd been sharing. As loath as she was to admit defeat, she had to face the fact that Lady Marjorie had been missing for over four days now. What had begun as a hopeful, possibly heroic attempt to find her was now on the verge of becoming a self-serving, irresponsible attempt to save her own employment and reputation. And if something happened now, she wouldn't be able to live with it.

Tomorrow. First thing in the morning she would hire a horse for Wolstanton and send the coach driver six hours north to Lattimer Castle. By midnight the duke would be here, and he and his men would hopefully find more cooperation than she had. Of course Gabriel Forrester was English, as well, but he nevertheless wielded a great deal of power, and he could offer a great deal more money, or threats if that proved necessary, for his sister's safe return.

The inn door opened, but the hopeful accelerated heartbeat that had been accompanying that sound for the first two days had given up the effort. An older man in a plain brown coat and the red, green, and black plaid of clan Maxwell on his kilt strolled inside to take a look about the nearly empty common room. Apparently seeing no one he knew, the old fellow turned around and left again.

She wasn't surprised to see him go. From the complaints of the other patrons, the beer and spirits at the Cracked Hearth got weaker as the night progressed. Even Robert the blacksmith had kissed her hand, declared that he would rather drink cow piss than more of the inn's swill, and departed some thirty minutes ago.

Stifling a tired groan, she stood and sent Ranald the innkeeper a nod, then slowly climbed the stairs to the private rooms on the first floor. Because of her searches she was coming to know the territory for several miles around the inn fairly well, not that it had done her any good. Today, at least, she would have called the land that spanned the river Douchary and its surroundings lovely, if it hadn't been so empty of Lady Marjorie. By the time she left here, she imagined she would detest every bit of the Highlands as the location of her latest, greatest, and last failure, but for the moment she could still admire parts of it.

Once inside the small, plain room she shut the door and then sat on the edge of the bed to remove her shoes and stockings. As she straightened, the bed creaked behind her. For a startled, fleeting second she thought Sir Robert had decided to try to tempt her into sin. Then, before she could do more than gasp, a cloth went around her mouth and pulled tight as something smelly and heavy dropped over her head.

No! She swung backward with an elbow and struck something solid, eliciting a pained grunt. *Ha!*

Despicable scoundrels, attacking virtuous women! Was this what had happened to Lady Marjorie? Oh, the horror! Hortensia rolled sideways on the bed, kicking as she went.

"Ouch," a low male voice muttered. "Ye didnae say she was a fighter."

"I didnae think she was," came the reply. "But make certain ye dunnae hurt her."

Two of them at least, then. Hands grabbed at her again, and in response she rolled back in the other direction—and smacked her head against a bedpost. The blow stunned her. Before she could recover her wits they'd twisted her up in ropes and blankets so tightly she couldn't even wiggle her toes. *Blast it!* Defeated by her own momentum.

"Are ye injured, lass?" the second voice whispered, close by her ear.

She tried whacking at him with her head, but only struck air.

"I'll take that as a nae."

"How the devil are we supposed to get her oot the window?" the first voice hissed again. "I didnae realize she was so stout."

The nerve! To kidnap her and then insult her figure! With a growl she tried to kick out again, but only managed a motion she imagined looked something like a beached whale.

"I reckon ye've made her angry," the second voice observed, humor in his tone. "Tie the rope aboot her waist and we'll anchor it to the bed. Once we get her lifted into the window, we'll lower her doon to . . . our friend."

Three of them, then. And while they might be trying not to hurt her—likely so she'd fetch a better price from some foreign prince or other—she had no such qualms about hurting them. Ladies didn't fight, but neither did they willingly surrender their freedom or virtue.

She flopped about again, but didn't manage to strike anyone. Breathing hard, she had to settle for growling under her breath. "Easy, lass," the second despicable man murmured. "We're taking ye to see yer mistress."

She made what she hoped was a derisive sound.

"Ye dunnae believe me? I cannae blame ye fer that. But

how else do ye reckon I know she's nae yer niece, and that she goes by Forrester and nae Giswell?"

He knew something, clearly. And furious as she was at being manhandled, the slightest bit of hope sneaked back into her heart. If they were both kidnapped, she still had a chance to redeem herself. She could save them both—perhaps not their reputations, but she wouldn't be stranded on the outside and forced to watch the inevitable unfold without being able to help.

She nearly changed her mind about cooperating when the two men hoisted her into the air and then left her hanging there with her head pointing downward. The jolts and jumps that rattled her teeth and cut off her breath seemed to go on forever, but finally another pair of hands spun her right way up just before she thudded dully onto the cold, hard ground.

A moment later she heard the two men climb down the wall behind her. "Ye might have backed the wagon beneath the window, lad," the first voice panted.

"That's nae stealthy. Ye told me to be stealthy."

"Well, now we'll stealthily lift her into the wagon," the second voice whispered. "Now, before someone walks by and we have to snatch him, too."

Hands pawed at her legs and her shoulders and—good heavens—her backside, and then she went back into the air and settled onto what must have been the bed of the wagon. It creaked and shifted around her, and then began bumping and rattling as it rolled forward.

Poor Wolstanton and Stevens would be beside themselves in the morning, with no idea where she'd gone or why. Hopefully they wouldn't conclude that she'd decided to head to Lattimer Castle herself. Given the driver's reluctance to travel through the barbaric Highlands alone, though, they might well conclude that she *had* made the trip just so they could justify staying put, themselves.

At least she would be with Lady Marjorie. Once the two of them put their heads together, no ropes would prevent them from escaping to rain fierce justice down on these savages.

The one clever thing his brothers had done when they'd kidnapped Marjorie had been to drive the wagon in circles for an hour before they turned for home. By the time Graeme had duplicated their maneuver and driven up the long drive to the Lion's Den, his old pocket watch in the moonlight read nearly four o'clock in the morning. He closed his eyes for a moment, tired and knowing he wouldn't be sleeping for a good twenty hours, at least, before he hopped to the ground.

Strategically this made sense; the local cotters would know shortly, thanks to Father Michael, that the grand house employed a lass named Marjorie Giswell and that the lass's aunt had been looking for her and offering a reward for her return. He'd taken his own steps to spread the rumor that Mrs. Giswell was something of a lunatic, and now in addition he could say that she was residing with them while she recovered her senses. The searches would stop. The rumors of a Sassenach female going missing would stop. And no one would dig deeper to discover who these mad Englishwomen truly were.

It gave him what he needed most: time. And thanks to the lengthy wagon ride and covered eyes of his new captive, while his neighbors would know where the two English ladies were, the lasses themselves would have no idea. She—they—hopefully wouldn't be trying to flee.

In fact, the largest difficulty he could foresee was that he was running out of spare rooms with locks on the doors. "Let's get her inside," he intoned, lowering the back gate of the wagon.

"And up the stairs?" Cowen said woefully, still looking

uncomfortable out of his usual livery. All three of them had donned the Maxwell plaid beneath plain, coarse coats, as well, in the hope that no one would notice three more cotters lurking about the Cracked Hearth in the middle of the night.

"Aye. If ye can heave her over my shoulder, I'll carry her up."

"Ye'll break yer back, Lai—lad," Ross protested.

Another muffled, annoyed *whumph* emanated from their cargo. "I'll manage," he countered, ducking as the two servants lifted her, and declining to remind them of other heavy things he carried on a fairly regular basis.

He mostly wanted to make certain his other guest hadn't slipped out during the night, but that would have to wait until he had this one secured. He'd set guards, of course, but that didn't guarantee anything. She'd said she stayed because she still believed they could come to an amicable resolution. Graeme didn't know if he believed that, but he'd accept it mostly because he wanted to. At the same time, he could not—would not—allow her to flee if they *didn't* reach an agreement. And it didn't have as much to do with protecting his siblings as he kept claiming; she'd assured him they would be safe, and he believed her. No, this odd need of his to have her close by was something as primitive as the need to protect, but it was at the same time much warmer and sharper.

They'd already prepared a second bedchamber for another unwilling guest, nailing shut the windows with the nails they'd pried out of Marjorie's, and attaching the chain to a much sturdier part of the bed—though how petite, proper Marjorie had managed to break that slat, he still had no idea. The woman was a marvel, a bolt of lightning hidden beneath a smooth, soft, delicate-looking exterior.

Finally he pulled the sack from his newest captive's head, to be rewarded by a pair of narrowed green eyes attempting to stare him down. A heartbeat later they widened, and she mumbled something around the rag he'd tied over her mouth.

"Ye recognize me, then," he said. "Good. I'm going to cut the ropes and pull off the gag, and ye're going to behave yerself and keep yer voice doon or they'll all go back on again. Nod if ye mean to go along with that."

A few more indecipherable words—ones he imagined weren't all that ladylike—followed that, and then she nodded. These proper women were a damned handful. Leaning in, he unknotted the rag and pulled it free.

"Where is Lady Marjorie?" she demanded.

"Ye'll see her shortly. I give ye my word."

"You also gave me your word that you would help me find her and see that no harm came to her."

"So I have, and so I shall," he returned, cutting through the last of the ropes that bound the blanket around her. "There's water on the table, there, and all yer things from the inn are in yer trunk." Graeme gestured at the heavy, leather-bound behemoth Cowen and Ross had carried upstairs.

"I don't know what game you're playing, sir," she said as he turned for the door, "but I believe it to be a dangerous one."

He nodded. "Aye. That it is."

And it would continue to be dangerous as long as he refused to return Marjorie Forrester to the glamorous life she'd lived before they met. But the idea of sending her back to where he'd have no reason or excuse ever to see her again troubled him even more than the realization that he would very likely be going to prison for keeping her.

Chapter Ten

Marjorie awoke to the sound of a soft knock on her door. For a moment she waited to hear the click of the key in the lock, before she remembered that she had the key. Sitting up, she reached beneath her pillow for the cold iron.

Pulling the coverlet around her shoulders and slipping into her walking shoes, she yawned and crossed the room to the door. "Who is it?" she asked, leaning against the hard oak.

"It's me, lass," Graeme's low voice returned.

"What time is it?" The sky beyond the curtains remained black, as it would until nearly nine o'clock in the morning here, but it felt early. Very early.

"It's half five. Open the door before I wake the rest of the hoose."

"Come back at a more decent hour. A lady doesn't receive callers before sunrise." It was about time she was the one deciding when her door should open, and for whom. And the fact that she could practically hear his teeth clenching made even this small victory all the sweeter.

"I brought ye a gift," he said after a moment.

"You may show it to me at breakfast."

"It's likely to spoil before then," Graeme returned.

Spoil? Had he brought her an iced cream? Or a rare, night-blooming flower? Neither would be appropriate, considering that she was not his guest and he was not some potential beau, but the idea of him finding something she might enjoy and then not even waiting for dawn to bring it to her . . . Her pulse shivered a little. "Very well," she said, trying to sound reluctant.

She turned the key and pulled open the door. And her heart skittered again. In the hallway's dim lamplight a scruff of dark whiskers shadowed the lower half of his face, softening the hard, precise line of his jaw. His hair hung long and damp around his face, disarming and enticing all at the same time. As her wandering gaze lowered past an old, dark shirt and coat, she paused again.

He wore a kilt. A few of his men did, as she'd seen from the window before he'd chained her away from it, but this was the first time he'd worn one in her presence. The red, green, and black plaid suited him somehow, fit the wilder, more dangerous, more rugged part of him that he generally hid behind a grin and a lifted eyebrow.

"Do ye want to know what's underneath it?" he murmured, and caught her mouth in a kiss that scratched her lips and shivered all the way down her spine.

She twined her fingers into his lapels, pulling herself close against him. Oh, it was so, so wrong, and she'd never experienced anything nearly as exhilarating. Was this her gift? She couldn't—shouldn't—accept, but for heaven's sake she wanted to. What did it matter? She was ruined anyway. Everyone would whisper behind her back that she'd shared a bed with him, so she might as well do it.

Before she wanted him to, he broke the kiss. "Ye're a damned tempting lass, yer highness," he whispered, cupping her cheeks in his hands. "Come let me show ye yer gift." Shifting, he took one of her hands in his, twining his fingers with hers.

The intimacy of that simple gesture thrilled her. Had she truly lived a life so proper and so isolated from the . . . warmth of others that a mere handholding could stir her blood? The idea shocked her, and yet the evidence lay in her fingertips. This was the same man who'd tried to force her into marrying him, true. But this morning he was asking—and that made a great deal of difference.

He led her to one of the doors at the front end of the house, then faced her again. "Before ye try to club me, I had a reason. I'll explain it to ye after ye stop cursing me."

Marjorie lifted both eyebrows, watching as he pulled another key from his pocket and unlocked the door. "A lady doesn't curse," she said automatically.

"Ye will."

Graeme opened the door, nudged her inside, then shut it again as she faced it. She listened, abruptly cold and worried again, for the sound of the lock turning, but he didn't do it. If he had, all chance at an alliance would have been lost.

"My lady!"

Whirling back around to face the dim, candlelit room, and nearly tripping beneath the heavy bulk of the coverlet around her, she gasped. "Mrs. Giswell!"

The stout woman sat on the single, plain chair by the wall, her hair a disheveled crow's nest and her simple muslin gown wrinkled and more than a little askew. Even more telling, she was barefoot. Mrs. Giswell stood, a chain rattling along the floorboards in response, and Marjorie flung out her arms to envelop the older woman in a tight hug.

"That damned barbarian," Marjorie snapped. "What in the world happened?"

"Oh, my lady, you vanished into thin air!" Mrs. Giswell

sobbed. "We looked everywhere for you, asked everyone we met, but no one knew anything! I should have sent for your brother immediately, but I . . . I was selfish, and I didn't wish to be let go for losing you. I'd decided to send Wolstanton to fetch him this morning, but I should have done it much, much sooner. I am so, so sorry. Can you forgive me?"

Gabriel didn't know she'd gone missing? That could be good for Graeme, but that shouldn't be the first thing that occurred to her, blast it all. "Of course I forgive you," she returned, patting her companion's shoulder. "For goodness' sake, *you're* the one in a locked room with your ankle chained to a bed."

"Better me than you." Mrs. Giswell took a deep breath, clearly trying to gather her wits back around her. "I might have fought harder when they captured me, but that man told me he would bring me to you, and that you were safe."

"And so I am."

She settled Mrs. Giswell back into the chair, perched on the edge of the bed, and tried to explain the last five days. She left out the kisses and her unexplainable . . . interest in Graeme, but she included everything else—ending with the fact that she was now posing as a tutor for Graeme's younger brothers.

"That was very clever of you, to announce that you were a tutor in front of witnesses. That fortune hunter! Shocking."

"It wasn't as straightforward as that, but no matter the circumstances I am not about to put my future into someone else's hands," Marjorie returned. "Not when I finally control it myself." Or what remained of it, anyway.

"I knew we should have hired outriders," Mrs. Giswell returned, shaking her head. "Though if I'd had any idea how dangerous it would be for you to be up here, I would have objected to this trip much more strongly. Highlanders? A clan war? Good heavens."

"I'm only thankful that you didn't race about the countryside announcing that Lady Marjorie Forrester had gone missing. You kept things from being much worse. But yes, the bit about the clan war with Gabriel would have been nice to know."

Never making this journey, though—not only would it have meant not meeting her brother Gabriel's betrothed, whether she would ever have a chance to do so now or not, but it would have meant that none of the last five days had ever happened. That she wouldn't have met Connell or his brothers. Or his oldest brother. If nothing else, she'd felt more . . . alive, more challenged than she could ever remember. And for that, she had to thank Graeme.

Of course, that didn't mean she wouldn't be having a very stern word with Graeme once she left Mrs. Giswell. That last kiss, especially, left her feeling uncertain of her balance, as if the floor wasn't quite firm beneath her feet. And this had been after he'd given her the key, after he'd lost the ability to lock her in a room. For that moment she hadn't been his prisoner, nor he, her captor. She'd liked that kiss, very much. She wanted to repeat it. And heaven help her, she *did* want to see what he had beneath his very fine kilt.

But those thoughts certainly weren't appropriate when Mrs. Giswell sat in chains. She shook them off, or at least managed to push them back a little. "Can you remember the route you took to get here?" she whispered, not certain how close by Graeme might be. "We could follow it back to return to the inn."

"They put a smelly sack over my head," her companion said with a sniff. "All I know is that we drove for hours and hours."

"Yes, that was my experience as well, blast it all."

"Lady Marjorie. Your language."

Ah, she had her conscience back, not that she generally needed reminding. "My apologies." She stood. "Now. See if you can get some sleep, and I will see if I can get that barbarian to take that shackle off your leg." She headed for the door, belatedly noting in the growing glow from outside that this room was much smaller and plainer than hers. Not that that signified.

"Remember that a lady who controls her temper, controls her situation."

Abruptly she also remembered why she'd once wished that the trip north had been considerably shorter. Marjorie smiled. "I shall keep that in mind."

She opened the door and shut it behind her to give Mrs. Giswell some privacy. When she turned around, though, Graeme wasn't lurking in the hallway. Nor was he on the stairs or in the foyer when she leaned over the railing to look.

Fine. This would be a conversation best had after she was dressed, anyway. Deliberately going out and kidnapping Mrs. Giswell, *after* he'd agreed to terms with her, and after he'd claimed to be so angry with his brothers for doing the same thing to her. The nerve of that impossible, arrogant man.

Stalking back to her room, she shut and locked the door. The only gown to hand was the fancy emerald one, and so she cleaned up, dressed, and put up her hair as swiftly as she could. Graeme Maxton needed a lesson taught him, and she would have to be the one to do it.

Leaving the room again, she started for the stairs, but stopped when she heard a sound coming from the half-open door beyond hers. The room at the very back of the house belonged to Graeme, so she turned around and marched up to it.

He stood in the middle of the large bedchamber, his back to the doorway, and his rough shirt and coat on the floor at his feet. All he wore, in fact, was the kilt belted around his hips. As she watched, he ran a wet cloth over his face, under his arms, down his chest, and around the back of his neck. The play of the muscles across his back, the flex of his arms and shoulders—it left her mouth abruptly dry and sent warmth between her legs.

Marjorie had always been a logical woman; she'd never been able to afford to be otherwise. Flights of fancy were for the rich. Given her birth and her monetary circumstances, she'd known for a very long time where to set her sights, in which direction lay the chance for her best possible life. She'd landed precisely where she'd aimed, becoming the well-educated companion to a short series of wealthy, elderly women. It hadn't been particularly fulfilling, but it had provided her with lodgings, spending money, and a certain degree of freedom during the few hours each week she wasn't needed.

Even now, in possession of more money than she could possibly spend in a lifetime, employing her own companion and with boundless free time, she approached her life logically and cautiously, supported the correct charities, did her shopping at second-best stores where her being an upjumped duke's sister would cause the least commentary, expended countless sleepless nights worrying that she would never fit in despite her efforts and careful planning.

This, though—that man and what she badly wanted of him—had nothing to do with logic, or the future he'd tried to force on her. This was about her dreams, and her much-denied desires. It had everything to do with how she felt when she looked at him, and when his dark gray eyes met hers.

His actions and those of his brothers had ruined what small chance she did have to settle into proper Society, and his so-called offer of marriage wouldn't have altered that. It might have saved him, but not her. He owed her something for embroiling her in this mess, didn't he? Even if the warmth and intimacy she craved from him was fleeting, she would at least know what it was like to want someone so badly she shook at the very sight of him, and to have him touch her in return.

Marjorie squeezed her eyes shut. Yes, she found him handsome and attractive, and she even admired the way he, at twenty years old, had stepped up to become the de facto parent of a newborn and two other young brothers. That didn't mean she could—or should—ignore the other things. No, he hadn't kidnapped *her,* but he had prevented, and still prevented, her from leaving. And just hours ago he'd snatched Mrs. Giswell, probably frightened the poor woman half to death, and chained her to a bed.

That was what she needed to keep hold of, for her own sake. The anger, the righteous fury at the way he decided *his* troubles should be resolved, and damn everyone else. He'd never even asked if she'd been happy with her life before he'd ruined it, though he seemed to assume that she had been.

Squaring her shoulders, she shoved open the door, marched in, and pushed it shut behind her. As he faced her, she ignored his bare, muscular chest with its light dusting of hair and instead kept her attention on his face, on the half smile he'd assumed when he saw her—as if he knew precisely how attractive she found him.

"How dare you?" she snapped, and slapped him hard across his handsome face.

His smile dropped, and he grabbed her wrist before she could swing it out of his reach. "If I hadnae fetched her," he said flatly, "how long do ye reckon it would have been before she told someone who ye truly are? Especially once she heard from Father Michael where ye are? And then how long would it be before Hamish Paulk heard it? He's but two miles from here right now."

"You called her my 'gift,'" she retorted, wishing she'd been taller so she wouldn't have to lift her chin and stand

on her toes to look him in the eye. "Is that it now? If someone might—*might*—cause you trouble you simply grab her
and utterly destroy her life, her reputation, and her future?"

"I dunnae think we're talking aboot Mrs. Giswell, are
we?" He yanked her closer. "I didnae grab ye, lass."

"No, you merely locked me in a room and put a chain
around my leg, and kept me here long enough that no one
will ever risk sending me an invitation to a ball or a dinner,
or ask me to go driving in Hyde Park. Not one of my pointy-
nosed neighbors wishes me a good morning as it is. My
own neighbors, in a place I've always wanted to live. And
now it won't just be a nightmare. It will be impossible."

She lifted her free hand to hit him again, but he grabbed
that wrist, as well. "Are ye mad at me fer that, or fer
snatching Mrs. Giswell? Ye need to decide, though ye do
look very fine standing there with yer eyes glinting like
sapphires."

"I—you—I don't need to 'decide' anything," she retorted, refusing to be distracted. "I'm mad at you for everything, including making marriage a threat. Now let me go."

"So ye can hit me again? Nae. Ye can just stand there
and glare at me."

Marjorie tried to pull her wrists free, but she might as
well have been wrestling with a wall. "I demand that you
at least free Mrs. Giswell."

"Nae. I'll nae risk Sir Hamish stumbling across her.
Ask me someaught else, and I'll do my damnedest to
give it to ye."

"Let *me* go. And don't make me ask you again, you heathen."

"Ah, heathen, is it?" Maxton bent his head and caught her
mouth in a hard, demanding kiss. "Then I'll be a heathen."

She couldn't stop herself from kissing him back. Oh, my,
she wanted to kiss him back. Wanted to feel his hands on
her, and his mouth on her, and she wanted to run her palms

along his skin—except that he still had her wrists and she couldn't move. Marjorie kissed him again, hungrily. "Let go," she muttered, her voice muffled against his mouth.

The second he released her arms he swept her up in the air and carried her to his bed, his mouth teasing and nipping at hers until she couldn't even breathe, much less think. He set her down and followed her onto the soft bed, dark gray eyes meeting hers for a long moment before he sank over her onto his elbows.

"This is wrong," she managed, her voice breathy and not sounding like her at all.

His mouth stopped its very wicked trail along the base of her throat. "Ye willnae marry me, but ye said ye were ruined, lass," he murmured, his mahogany hair falling across his eyes as he lifted his head to look at her again. "I aim to make certain of it." With his left hand he gathered up the material of her skirt so he could rest a palm on the inside of her thigh.

Oh, good heavens. "I've spent a very long time being proper, you know."

The hand began sliding upward. "And answer me someaught, Lady Marjorie. Ree. Has being so very proper gotten ye what ye want? Has it made ye happy?"

"You should have asked me that days ago." If she had any coherent thoughts left in her head, that would have been a very complicated question, she was certain. At this moment, with the weight of him across her hips, his hands on her bare skin, and his teeth—ohhh—nibbling on her earlobe, all she could recall was how hard she'd been trying, and with no detectable results. "No, it hasn't," she breathed.

"Then try someaught else."

"But I'm your prisoner."

"I havenae let ye go," he agreed, and shifted to tug her gown down past her shoulders. "I dunnae ken if that makes ye still my prisoner, but I've a mind to keep ye here a bit longer, regardless."

He kissed her again, his fingers trailing down in exquisite shivers to circle her breasts closer and closer until his thumbnail scraped lightly across a nipple. Marjorie jumped, digging her fingers into his tawny, red-tinged hair, and he did it again.

Before she could catch her breath, he lowered himself along her, replacing his fingers with his tongue. She jumped again, arching her back as swirls of pleasure jolted down her spine. Evidently he knew exactly the effect he was having on her, because he chuckled, the sound muffled against her skin, before he licked her other breast and then put his mouth over it to suck.

She arched again, shifting to curl her fingers into fists and press herself against him. This was what all those looks he'd given her meant. This was what he'd wanted of her. And so far, she liked it. She liked it very much.

He slid down still further, bunching up her skirt and sliding his palms up between her legs. When he dipped a single finger up inside her, she thought she might faint. Her heart beat so hard he could surely hear it, and she felt hot beneath her skin.

"Sit up, lass," he muttered, taking her hands to pull her upright—which was a good thing, because she didn't think she could have managed it on her own. Her grasping arms and legs didn't even feel like they belonged to her any longer, but they seemed to know what to do without her even consciously having a thought about it.

He knelt in front of her, leaning in to kiss her again, and reached around to undo the ribbon at her waist and the single button at the back of her neck. Then he took the hem of her dress and her shift in his hands and lifted them off over her head.

With him stretching up in front of her, the bulge in the

front of his kilt was unmistakable. She'd wanted to know what lay beneath there. Very conscious of his rough fingers roving across her skin, Marjorie tentatively reached a hand out to brush across the front of the plaid. He jumped, slowing his own exploration to watch hers.

Emboldened by his quick intake of breath and the half smile on his very capable mouth, she scooted a whisper closer and ran a hand from his bare knee up his thigh and beneath the kilt. Two round, velvety-soft . . . orbs, she supposed, and a hard, jutting rod that felt both warm and full beneath her fingers. And very, very large. Looking up at him, she found his amused, hungry gaze squarely on her. Still looking at her, he unfastened the pin at the bottom of his tartan, then unbuckled the waist and drew it off, dropping it to the floor.

And there she sat, with her fingers wrapped around his manhood. Before she could decide whether she felt more wanton than embarrassed, he put his hands on her shoulders and pushed her down onto the bed again. This time she could taste the hunger of his kiss as he plundered her mouth, the play of the muscles across his abdomen and his back as he settled his knees between hers.

Putting his hands back on her thighs, he slowly spread her legs wider, until his manhood brushed against her innermost place. She gasped again at the sensation, at how vulnerable and yet . . . safe she felt in his arms, when she really had no reason in the world to trust him. And yet trust him she did.

Lifting his head a little, resettling his arms on either side of her shoulders, he looked down at her as he canted his hips forward. She worked to meet his gaze, refusing to shut her eyes even at the thick, filling sensation of him sliding into her. When she felt resistance she knew he did as well, but with a whisper of something in Scots Gaelic he continued to press slowly deeper.

At an abrupt, sharp pain she cried out, and he caught the sound against his mouth before she could stifle it herself. "I'm sorry, Marjorie," he breathed, holding himself still inside her. "It'll pass in a moment, and I have it on good authority it'll nae happen again."

So that was how a physician could tell if a female had lost her virginity. She'd always wondered. She'd never expected the experience of doing so to be so intimate, somehow. "I'm fine," she muttered after a moment. "What happens next?"

" 'Next'?" he repeated. "We've barely begun, *mo boireann leòmhann.*"

"What does that mean?"

His smile deepened. Without answering he moved again, entering her fully. She couldn't help crying out again, but not from pain. The sensation of him moving inside her, filling her and retreating again, over and over— the mewling, wanton sounds coming from deep inside her barely sounded human, much less like something a proper female should ever make.

He rocked into her again and again, the bed creaking in time with his thrusts. Graeme kissed her, then bent to take a breast in his mouth, and all she could do was dig her fingers into his back as she drew tighter and tighter inside. With another muffled cry she shattered into a thousand bright, floating pieces, everything fading into darkness but the two of them, locked together and moving in rhythm.

His pace increased, and with a delicious, primitive groan that all by itself nearly sent her over the edge again, he shuddered against her, inside her. With a last thrust of his hips he lowered his head against her neck, and she lifted her hands to tangle them through his damp hair. Heaven. This was how heaven felt.

God above. He damned well hadn't intended for that to

happen this morning. But then she'd stomped into his bedchamber looking so . . . fiery, as if for once he could see through all the propriety in which she wrapped herself like a blanket. Or a shield, more like.

Graeme lifted his head to gaze down at her. "Do ye still think that was a mistake?" he asked, belatedly reflecting that he shouldn't ask a question if he didn't want to hear the answer.

She looked back up at him, her hair a dark, curling halo around her head, and her eyes a clear blue even in the firelight. "Yes, I still think that was a mistake," she answered, running her fingers along his shoulder. "But I wouldn't mind repeating it."

For the life of him, he couldn't figure her out, and that fascinated him. Her answer required a kiss, her soft lips molding against his and making his heart skip a beat or two. He didn't want to move, wanted to stay inside her until his cock was up for another go. Not just because he still wanted her, but because once they dressed again all the troubles around him, most of them concerning her, would come rushing back in barking at his heels.

At eight-and-twenty and with three younger brothers and what equaled a small army of folk depending on him, he generally avoided complicated females—or any female after more than the night's pleasure he was prepared to offer her.

If Samuel Johnson's *Dictionary* had a sketch next to the word "complicated," though, it would be of Lady Marjorie Forrester. She was English, highborn, well educated, civilized, and the sister of the duke on whom his clan had all but declared war. And that didn't even take into account the fact that he'd kidnapped her—and done what he was beginning to realize was the stupidest thing he might have attempted; he'd attempted to bully her into marrying him. This . . . was much better, even with no reward he could hold in his hands.

Before he became too heavy for her, he reluctantly removed himself and turned onto his side next to her. "I've a query," he said after a moment, as he pulled the remaining pins from her hair and set them aside. Goose bumps lifted on her arms as he drew his fingers through the lemon-scented mass.

"About what?"

"Ye said yer neighbors didnae so much as bid ye good morning. Did ye mean they willnae, now that ye'd been kidnapped and deflowered by a strapping Highlander?"

She grinned, but shook her head. "I moved into Leeds House over three months ago, right after my brother inherited the property. As unnoticed as I was before, within two days everyone in London seemed to know that before I became Lady Marjorie I was Miss Forrester, a paid lady's companion. And they were all horrified, as if they worried they might catch some commoners' disease or something from me."

Of all the things he'd thought to hear, that hadn't been one of them. He didn't know much about Gabriel Forrester other than the fact that he'd been serving on the Peninsula before he inherited Lattimer, and that some of the local soldiers who'd returned said he'd acquired the nickname the Beast of Bussaco. Likewise he'd just assumed the Forrester siblings had wealth and station before the brother had inherited the title from his uncle, or great-uncle, or whoever old Lattimer had been to them. He'd bloody well never thought that Ree hadn't been born Lady Marjorie. She carried herself like a damned queen, and that was certain.

"Well?" she prompted, still watching him. "Are you horrified now, as well?"

"What? Nae. I'm just surprised. When I called ye yer grandness or yer highness ye didnae bite back at me."

She shrugged, the motion doing some very pleasant

things to her tits. "You're the first man ever to think me grand, even if you did mean it as an insult."

"Ye want to be seen as grand, then."

"Gabriel—my brother—saw to it that I received the best education an army officer could afford. I learned all the same things the daughters of marquises and earls did, and then I spent three years in the spare rooms of some fine gentry houses, and I joined some wellborn ladies on their shopping trips to Bond Street or when they took the waters in Bath. I ran their errands and fluffed their pillows, and listened to them complain about ungrateful relations and how much they used to love to dance, and they paid me for it. Until Gabriel called on me that day, I thought I'd seen what the entire rest of my life would look like. And I didn't care for it."

"I can understand that," he said quietly. "Ye've spirit, lass. Ye werenae made to spoon-feed soup to old women."

"Well, I don't have to do that any longer. The—"

Small footsteps pounded up the hallway. With a curse, Graeme rolled Marjorie off the far side of the bed onto her gown and slid beneath his blanket just as Connell flew into the room.

"Brendan says he's going to enter the archery competition at the fair," his youngest brother announced, clambering onto the edge of the bed. "What competition should I enter?"

Graeme tried to angle his thoughts away from the lovely naked lass just out of sight on the floor. The lass who was turning out to be nothing like he'd expected. "There's to be a pie-eating contest. Ye could enter that."

"Nae. If Rob the blacksmith competes, I'm likely to get eaten along with all the pies."

Laughing, Graeme tousled the lad's red hair. "Ye make a fair point. How aboot a foot race?"

Connell cocked his head. "A foot race fer everyone? Because Dùghlas has longer legs than me."

"So ye want a contest ye're certain to win, do ye?"

"Well, that would be brilliant, I ken."

"I reckon so. And I also reckon ye'll be more pleased to earn what ye get. So two foot races. One fer lads under . . . ten years old, say, and one fer the older lads."

His younger brother grimaced. "Ye should make it under thirteen years old, then. Because Jamie Howard's wee, but he's twelve, and he'd nae have a chance otherwise."

Graeme smiled at him. Every once in a while he could believe that he'd done something . . . proper in raising his brothers. This felt like one of those times. "And that, duckling," he said aloud, "is one of the many reasons I'm proud to be yer *bràthair*. Now, go away and pester Mrs. Woring in the kitchen. I'll be doon shortly. And shut the door."

With a backward wave Connell scampered off, doing as he'd been asked. As soon as the door clicked shut, Graeme rolled onto his stomach to peer over the edge of the bed. Marjorie, Lady Marjorie, lay there on her back with his kilt covering her most intimate bits, a grin on her soft lips.

"My sincere apologies aboot that," he said, holding down an arm to help her up. "I generally lock my door when I dunnae want company, but ye surprised me a bit."

"Mm-hm."

As she stood, handing over his kilt as she did so, he noted that he liked seeing her in Maxwell plaid. The thought startled him to his bones, but after a stunned moment he realized it didn't signify. He wouldn't be marrying her. And what she most wanted was to be in London and have her damned pointy-nosed neighbors wish her good morning.

And that was one thing he could never give her even in his wildest, maddest dreams—especially considering that he'd been the one to take away any chance she might have had at seeing it happen. And now he'd done it twice over.

"I still want Mrs. Giswell out of that shackle," she stated, digging her shift out of the pile of clothes on the floor and pulling it on.

"Only if ye convince me that ye've convinced her to follow my rules," he returned. "I'll nae have her roaming aboot whispering that she's been kidnapped and offering a huge reward to whoever sends fer Lattimer."

"And what about me?"

He looked at her standing beside the bed, the light from the low fire outlining the edges of her shift in red, an ancient Celtic goddess come to life. That, despite the fact that she was English. Or perhaps he'd lost his mind; he hadn't slept in better than a day, after all.

"Ye're nae leaving. Nae with Hamish Paulk so close by here. Ye can interpret that however ye please." Aside from the politics and the danger to his family, once she left he would never see her again. And so he wasn't prepared to allow her to go. Not yet, and not after this morning.

For a moment she regarded him, her gaze thoughtful. "Just keep in mind, Graeme, Laird Maxton, that my location may not always be up to you."

"I will. I'll also keep in mind that ye said ye were surprising yer brother with this visit of yers. Lattimer's nae expecting ye, and he doesnae know ye're missing."

She wrinkled her nose. "I said that when we—when I—"

"Was it a lie, then?"

"No."

"Then dunnae expect me to disregard it."

"Barbarian."

"Princess."

She blinked, clearly surprised that he'd returned her insult. Rather than replying, though, she slipped on her emerald gown and knotted the ribbon around the high waist. Before she could reach around for the button at the nape of her neck, Graeme climbed to his feet.

"I'll do that, lass."

"You do recall that you're naked," Marjorie pointed out, taking a long moment to look him up and down before she turned away.

Just her gaze made his cock stir again. "I thought I felt a breeze up my backside." He took his time with the button, breathing her in all over again. Lemons had never been so arousing.

As he finished he pulled her long, loose hair back from her shoulders again. He'd never been a delicate or a gentle man, because he'd never found much use in it. His three brothers damned well didn't require subtlety. Likewise the Highlands lasses with whom he'd spent an evening now and again knew they weren't there for wooing or courtship.

Neither was Marjorie, but she was—despite what he now knew of her past—every inch a lady. He wanted to be gentle with her. He wanted to know every inch of her, spend long evenings before the fireplace in her company, wake to find her sleeping in his arms. Graeme took a hard breath in through his nose. Next he'd be writing poetry to her, trying to rhyme all the pretty words he generally avoided like the devil.

Damnation, she was going to be more trouble than he'd ever anticipated. If he had any sense, he *would* send her away. Now. And he would burn the marriage license the moment it arrived.

"I'm going to fetch breakfast and bring a tray up to Mrs. Giswell," she announced into the silence, shaking him out of his daydream. Or nightmare, rather.

Evidently she'd been less unsettled by the sex than he was. Graeme clenched his jaw. "I'll join ye after ye've had a chance to talk to her. I suggest ye be persuasive." He put a hand on her shoulder. "Ye should leave yer hair doon."

"And see myself called a lightskirt in addition to an up-jumped heiress?" Her shoulders lifted and fell, and then she moved away from him.

Graeme didn't want her leaving the room, not until he figured out what it was about her that he found so compelling, but he held himself still, anyway. He'd put enough chains on her, both literal and figurative. This one thing should be her decision.

With a hand on the door, she faced him again. "Why don't you wear your kilt more often?" she asked, her cheeks darkening.

"Because the Maxwell and I arenae seeing eye to eye, and I suppose it's my way of protesting his nonsense." Though with the way she kept looking at him this morning, he meant to wear the tartan more often.

"Ah." She turned away again and pulled open the door, then abruptly shut it again and strode back up to him, not stopping until she'd wrapped her arms around his shoulders, lifted up on her toes, and kissed him openmouthed. Then she fled the room, pulling the door closed soundly behind her.

Graeme blew out his breath. No, this wouldn't be complicated at all.

Chapter Eleven

I think if you look at it as items rather than numbers, you'll have an easier time of it."

Connell scowled. "What the devil are ye talking about?"

Stifling a grin, Marjorie stood up to pull a jar of smooth river pebbles off a shelf. "Put five of them on the table."

"I ken how many five is, woman. And ye're only pretending to be my tutor."

"True enough. But if someone should ask what I've taught you, I'd like you to be able to answer without having to lie."

"I suppose that makes sense," the eight-year-old said grudgingly. "But I dunnae like it. I have to let ye know that."

Marjorie wondered if perhaps she shouldn't have so readily dismissed the idea of being a governess back in finishing school. Connell in the short time she'd known him was already more interesting than Lady Sarah Jeffers, and she'd spent nearly a year with that moldy-smelling woman. "I completely understand. Put five more pebbles on the table, separate from the first ones."

She sat back to watch as he placed three more piles of five pebbles on the tabletop. Yes, he was definitely funnier and more sharp-witted than Lady Sarah. And, as she'd been discovering, he had no qualms over dishing out interesting tidbits about his oldest brother, a man the boy clearly adored.

"I've put yer damned—yer blessed, I mean—rocks on the table. Now what?"

"What is four times five, then?"

"I told ye that I dunnae know."

"But you do." She indicated the first pile. "How many?"

"Five."

"And here?" She pointed to the second stack.

"Five, fer God's sake. And five, and five again."

"Push two of the stacks together. How many are there, then?"

He moved his mouth, otherwise counting silently. "Ten. What good does that—"

"Push the other two together."

Connell did so. "Fine. And there are ten here, too, so dunnae ask me."

"I won't. Push the two tens into one pile. How many are there?"

"Ten and ten is twenty. I'm nae a bairn."

"Separate them into four equal piles again. How many are in each pile?"

"Five. Did ye think I'd ferget?"

"No, I didn't. What is five pebbles times four stacks?"

He looked down at the stones, then up at her again. "It's twenty. How did ye do that?"

She chuckled. "Well done, Connell. I didn't do anything. You did." As she spoke the hair on her arms lifted, and she turned her head to see Graeme leaning in the doorway and gazing at her. Warmth swept through her like a summer breeze.

For heaven's sake, she wasn't even certain she liked him. She craved him; especially after this morning. Especially since he'd donned his kilt again, and she knew what lay beneath it. In her defense, he had a great deal to recommend about him. Firstly, he was handsome as the devil, with that careless hair and graceful physicality that reminded her of a lion on the hunt. In addition to that, he'd taken on the task of raising his own brothers, doing that while seeing to the wants and needs of a hundred other families scattered in valleys and villages for miles around.

At the same time, she remained a prisoner here, unable to leave the mansion and with her own lady's companion still locked in a room upstairs. The most reasonable explanation for her attraction seemed to be that she'd simply lost her mind. If she accepted that idea, at least she could follow her impulses and fall into bed with him at the next—and every—opportunity. Madwomen did mad things, after all.

"Graeme!" Connell said, heaping up the pebbles again. "I can multiply now."

"I saw ye. Keep those river rocks handy fer a time." He pushed upright. "Do the other equations I gave ye while I have a word with Ree."

Marjorie had no idea where he'd discovered her nickname unless it had been from the letter she'd written to Connell. He definitely hadn't been present when she'd told his brothers to call her Ree. She liked the way he said it in his deep brogue, when only a very few of her schoolmates and her brother had ever addressed her that way. Only her friends. And lately those had been very hard to come by.

"Yer grandness?" Graeme prompted after a moment, both pulling her out of her reverie and reminding her that they weren't precisely friends. Not precisely, and not yet. What they *were* was something she hadn't quite figured out yet. She couldn't remember the last time she'd encountered something so . . . out of her realm of experience. And given the results, perhaps she should venture there more often.

Leaving Connell to his pebbles, she rose and walked over to join Graeme in the hallway. "Have you reconsidered Mrs. Giswell's prison sentence?" she asked.

"That's why I'm here. She demanded to see ye and then turned her back on me. Now she willnae speak, and she's better at silence than ye ever were."

Marjorie allowed herself a brief smile. "Oh, dear. She's given you the cut direct. It's the greatest show of disdain a lady can give a gentleman."

He lifted a straight eyebrow. "Ye've nae cut-directed me," he returned. "I recall a slap direct, though."

She'd begun to wonder if he was baiting her on purpose. "There's no such thing. And a slap isn't ladylike. I blame you for inspiring my misbehavior, though."

His grin warmed her insides. "I'll accept that responsibility. And I'll be encouraging ye again, I imagine."

Desire touched her, heady and welcome. But she was still a prisoner, and until that altered, she couldn't be certain how much of this was her free will, and how much she merely wanted it to be. "Perhaps a cut direct would teach you some manners, sir." With a sniff she preceded him up the stairs.

Graeme caught hold of her elbow and pulled her around to face him. With her a step above him, for once they stood eye to eye. "Ye can turn yer back on me, *mo boireann leòmhann,* but dunnae stop talking. I like the sound of yer voice." On the tail end of that, he leaned in and kissed her.

Now that she knew what lay beyond his kisses, they seemed even more intoxicating, like the heady scent of fine brandy and melted chocolate. Touching him made her want to forget or excuse what he'd put her through, made her want to believe that Dunncraigh was a force so evil and powerful that kidnapping a female first to assuage him and then to stand against him not only made sense, but was perfectly logical.

After a delicious moment he straightened a little. "Of course there are occasions when yer silence suits me, too," he murmured, gray eyes dancing as he grinned.

"Arrogant man," she muttered back at him, turning around again and stomping away from him up the stairs so he wouldn't see her grin.

She stopped in front of her companion's room and made a point of knocking politely. "Mrs. Giswell, you wanted to see me?"

"Is that insufferable Highlander with you?"

"Yes, but he's agreed to wait in the hallway." She sent him a pointed look.

"Thank heavens. Do come in please, dear."

Graeme pulled the key from his pocket. "If ye mean to convince her to nae make trouble," he whispered, "do it soon. I've an appointment with Father Michael and two of my cotters in twenty minutes. "Ewen Sturgeon and Kitty Howard want permission to marry."

"Permission from you?"

"Aye. I'm their chieftain. I approve all the marriages on my land."

"Do you ever deny your permission?"

"Once." Rather than elaborate, he gazed straight back at her, as if daring her to continue a discussion of marriage in his presence.

Well, *she* hadn't done anything wrong in that respect. "Are you allowed to approve your own marriage, or does Dunncraigh have to do that? Because that might have put a damper on your grand plan to marry me and defy him."

"He should be the one to approve my marriage, aye," he returned easily. "But part of the defiance plan would have involved defying him, ye ken."

She made a face at him. "Insufferable."

In truth, the way he didn't seem angry over his botched wedding plans left her relieved. Odd though it might be, she didn't want him as an enemy. Someone with whom she could argue, yes. But not someone she disliked. Oh, it was very complicated, and her few remaining propriety-minded friends would be fainting left and right if they knew what she'd been up to and with whom she'd been doing it. She, on the other hand, wanted to do it again.

"What are ye thinking aboot?" he murmured, and she shook herself.

"Kilts," she answered, half truthfully, and then refused to drop her gaze as he turned the key and opened the door. She removed the key herself so he couldn't lock her in with Mrs. Giswell, and then slipped into the room.

The lady's companion had turned her chair to face away from the doorway, but after a glance over her shoulder, likely to see if Graeme had indeed waited out in the hallway, she stood and turned around. "I'm glad that man permitted you to see me again. After I refused to bow to his demands earlier, I wasn't certain he would."

And while Mrs. Giswell had been worried over their captivity, she'd been eating in the breakfast room and helping Connell with his mathematics. Guilt pinched through her. "Lord Maxton is only worried about his brothers' safety, I believe. If you would give your word that you'll stay inside the house here and not speak to anyone outside of the residents and staff, I believe he would remove the shackle and let you leave this bedchamber."

"If he's worried over his brothers he should have raised them not to kidnap highborn ladies. And he shouldn't have rolled me into a blanket like a sausage and then toted me over his shoulder like I was no more than a sack of potatoes."

"I agree. I think a lady would have found a much more diplomatic way to deal with this. Perhaps arranged to have a conversation with you before resorting to kidnapping." In response to that she was almost certain she heard

Graeme in the hallway muttering something in Gaelic, but if he continued to think kidnapping was the first solution to trouble, the house would be stuffed to overflowing by the end of the week.

"I would certainly have been willing to listen to him. And I might have taken a moment to tell Stevens and Wolstanton to remain at the inn while I came to see you. I might have been able to offer a diplomatic solution. Now I have no idea what your men will be doing, after awakening to find me gone."

That probably wasn't the most helpful thing she could have said. Marjorie stifled a frown. "The situation is as it is," she said aloud. "This isn't where I planned on being, by any means, but I believe I'm safer here than I would be anywhere else except for Lattimer itself. Agree, give your word not to go about shouting to all and sundry that I'm the Duke of Lattimer's sister and we require a rescue, and you may have the run of the house."

Graeme hadn't explicitly promised any such thing, but locking people up wasn't aiding anything. When he didn't barge in to counter her statement, she had to assume he agreed.

"You're being held captive in a heathen household of barbarian Highlanders," Mrs. Giswell countered. "And you hired me to help you find your way in proper Society. These two things couldn't be further apart. What am I to do about that?"

"Be patient," Marjorie returned. "And in the meantime, civilize the barbarians."

Mrs. Giswell grimaced, but finally nodded. "Very well. I agree. I will remain in the house and not reveal your identity to anyone—which I haven't done anyway, by the by."

"And for which I sincerely thank you, Mrs. Giswell. I shall be back in a moment."

She ducked out of the room to see Graeme leaning back against the near wall, arms crossed over his chest and his head bowed. Even with his height and muscular frame the pose made him look oddly . . . vulnerable, as if she could see the weight that rested on his shoulders. He bore it so well that even though she knew about his responsibilities, this was the first time she'd seen the toll they took.

Abruptly he lifted his head to look at her. "I didnae agree to that," he said beneath his breath.

"She gave ground and so now you give ground. Give me the key to the shackle."

"Ye're quite the diplomat, Ree."

"Thank you." She held out her hand.

"Ye're also relentless." With an exaggerated sigh he put the key into her palm, running a finger up her wrist. "Ye ken I'm trusting ye with the safety of my brothers."

Marjorie nodded. "I understand."

"Ye'd leave in a heartbeat if ye could, aye?"

That was a strange question coming from a jailor to a prisoner, but neither was the answer as straightforward as it would have been a few short days ago. "Not in one heartbeat," she whispered, and went to go release her conscience and fellow captive. And for one more heartbeat she wished Mrs. Giswell hadn't agreed to anything and would stay locked up in a room, away from this odd little . . . refuge she'd found from the world.

"Ranald the innkeeper says the Sassenach still at the inn dooned aboot half a keg of rum yesterday and havenae stirred from their room except to eat and piss. I reckon ye've the right of it; they're nae going anywhere."

Graeme nodded at the groom. "Thank ye fer riding into Sheiling fer me." He patted Clootie on the withers as Johnny led the gray gelding back into the stable. With only two saddle horses at the house, Clootie was as likely to carry the lads to the loch for fishing as he was to carry him on his rounds to visit the cotters.

"I needed to see aboot getting a bridle mended, anyway," Johnny returned. "Couldnae find the blacksmith, though. Ranald says Robert Polk's been stomping aboot the countryside fer two days, bellowing fer some lass named Hortensia." The groom grinned. "Sean Moss said he figured that might be a cow, and that Rob's finally gone oot of his head."

Hm. Hortensia sounded like an English name to him. And as it didn't belong to Marjorie, that narrowed down his suspicions considerably. It meant more trouble in his path, but at the same time he found it hilarious that the gruff, determinedly unmarried Robert Polk was roaring after a proper, mature Englishwoman.

Then again, he was a determinedly unmarried lad roaring after an English lass himself, and he'd wager his prospects were much poorer than Rob's. He had a newly minted heiress desperate to fit into Society, while he lived literally and figuratively as far from proper as anyone could get.

That shouldn't have mattered when he meant to be rid of her as soon as he could do so safely, both for her and for him and his. Except that she'd given her word to keep the Maxtons out of any story she told, and he believed her. He'd kept her there, especially over the past four days, because he wanted her there. Because he didn't want to let her go. What that meant, he refused to consider.

Back inside the house he heard her laughing about something, Connell's giggle mingling with hers. For as long as he could remember the mansion had been chaotic and wild, and overwhelmingly masculine. Marjorie seemed to like the chaos, but even with the circumstances of her arrival she'd brought a peace and a thoughtfulness that filled the house with unexpected warmth. She brought him a . . . contentment mixed with excitement. He'd never experienced the like. It was addictive, and he craved her, craved being around her. And he would continue telling himself it was because he enjoyed bedding her, and nothing more. Nothing more was allowed.

"Laird Maxton," Cowen said, from the direction of the kitchen, "I've been instructed to tell ye that young Connell requests an audience with ye, at yer convenience."

"Well, that was pretty."

The butler blushed. "That was how the duckling said it, and he made certain I would tell ye the same thing precisely."

"Ye sounded very proper. Was Lady Marjorie anywhere aboot when this conversation took place?"

"Oh, aye."

Of course she had been. "I'll see him now, then. Do ye know the wheraboots of Mrs. Giswell? I request an audience with her, at her conv—"

"God's sake, m'laird. Please dunnae. All these polite, twisty words are giving me the shakes."

Graeme chuckled. "Ye're a man after my own heart. Just go find her, will ye?"

He expected to find Connell and Ree in the downstairs sitting room, but the continuing laughter led him upstairs to Connell's bedchamber. The door stood open, but considering the formality of the request, he knocked before stepping inside. "Ye wanted to see me, duckling?"

His brother and Marjorie sat on the floor, scooping the trio of baby rabbits he wasn't supposed to know about into a basket. Connell stood up, squaring his shoulders. "Aye. I did want to see ye."

"Here I am, then."

Glancing down, the lad took a deep breath. "Garaidh nan Leòmhann is yer responsibility, and ye need to know what's afoot beneath yer own roof. I have a duty to tell ye, then, that I rescued three rabbit kits when a hawk carried off their ma. Their names are Fluff, Gray, and Hop, and even though ye said we had enough animals in the hoose, I'd like to keep them. They're very nice, and Daisy and Pete havenae tried to eat them yet, and the cats think they're cats. I'm teaching the lot of them to be friends."

Marjorie knelt behind the boy, her expression proud as she practically mouthed the words of the speech along with him. She was back in the first gown he'd found for her, the pale blue one. Damnation, he needed to find her more to wear. A lady required more than two gowns. And he liked taking them off her.

"Graeme?" Connell prompted. "They're too little to go off alone, and Brendan said if ye knew aboot them ye'd have Mrs. Woring cook them in a stew." His light blue eyes filled with tears.

Oh, for Lucifer's sake. "I did tell ye nae more pets, Connell," he said slowly. "I reckon ye didnae have a choice, though, with a hawk taking their ma. Ye can keep 'em. Remember, though, the foxes and the cats might ferget they're all to get along."

The lad bounced on his toes. "Now that ye know about them and I have yer permission, I can build a hutch in here where they'll be safe."

"Mm-hm. Have Johnny help ye. He built the chicken coop. And I'll have Brendan lend a hand, too." He'd also have a chat with the sixteen-year-old about frightening their youngest brother for no good reason. "And Connell?"

"Aye?"

"Thank ye fer telling me."

Putting on a huge grin, Connell nodded. "Thank ye, *bràthair.* I couldnae leave them there in the heather withoot their ma."

With a return smile, Graeme tugged his brother's ear. "I know ye couldnae. Now take Fluff and Hop and Gray and go tell everyone, so we'll nae have any surprises." The boy fled, and Graeme squatted down in front of Marjorie. "How much convincing did that take ye?"

"Not much. I think he wanted to tell you, but couldn't figure out how to do it." She put a hand on his knee, beneath the hem of his kilt. "He's been very worried you would find out and make him let them go."

"Nae. I may nae be a civilized man, but I do ken when a boy who didnae know his own mother needs to rescue bairns who've lost theirs. Every animal beneath this roof's an orphan, me included."

"I am, as well. Gabriel and I lost our parents when he was seventeen, and I was eight. His answer was to join the army and use his pay to send me to boarding school."

"Ye were the age Connell is now, and ye went off on yer own to boarding school?" He couldn't even imagine his youngest brother sent away from his siblings. The abrupt anger he felt toward the mighty Duke of Lattimer made his jaw clench.

"We couldn't keep the house. The money for it paid off our parents' debts, bought him a commission, and paid for my acceptance and first semester of school. If Gabriel hadn't done that, I don't know where I would be now."

His anger eased again, though he remained certain he would have found a way for him and his siblings to stay together. "Ye dunnae think that wherever ye might have ended up would be better than being kidnapped by three nodcocks and held prisoner in the Highlands?"

She grinned at him. "Considering I'm alive to be kidnapped, I'd have to say no."

Graeme leaned forward, resting his weight on his bent knuckles, and kissed her. She cupped his face in her hands and kissed him back. Time seemed to slow, the sounds of the noisy house faded, and he could swear sunlight burned through the clouds outside to shine down on the countryside.

The door stood wide open, so as much as he wanted to prolong the moment, as much as he would have done so with anyone but this propriety-obsessed lass, he straightened and stood, holding down a hand to help her to her feet. Aye, he would let her go for now, but tonight he meant to visit her. Two evenings without her was two evenings too many, as far as he was concerned.

"You've never mentioned your father," she said, nudging his mind off its trail and into the shrubbery. "Do you mind my asking what happened to him?"

Since meeting her, he'd only wanted to forget. And yet by one action the dead man dictated the way he meant to live the remainder of his life. "My mother died giving birth to Connell. Brian Maxton was always mad fer her. Two days after she passed, he walked oot to the river and shot himself in the head."

Her dark blue eyes widened. "Oh."

"Dunnae ye dare call it romantic," he stated, accustomed to hearing those murmurs from every lass in the countryside. "He left three boys under ten years old with nae a parent."

"That's why Connell said you'd been looking after him since he was two days old."

He nodded. "Aye." Graeme forced a smile he didn't feel. "Ye may nae believe me, but at twenty I was a wee bit uncivilized. I did my damnedest, even thought aboot finding a bride to help me raise them, but it seemed like someaught I should do myself. They—all this—were my responsibility." Everything became his responsibility, all at once. Whether he'd been successful or not wasn't for him to judge, but no one could say he hadn't done everything he could.

"You? Wild?" She tugged on the black sleeve of his coat.

"You summoned me, Lord Maxton?" Mrs. Giswell's precise voice came from the doorway.

Marjorie immediately lowered her hand as he straightened. "Aye," he said, keeping his expression neutral as he faced the woman. Brown hair turning to gray, sharp green eyes, a mouth presently pinched a little in disapproval. She had a grand bosom, large and prominent enough to support a tea tray, while the rest of her went down in a straight line past her hips and then to a sturdy pair of legs.

"I insist you cease ogling me, sir," she stated, clasping her hands in front of her bosom.

"I wasnae!"

"Good," Marjorie murmured from beside him, almost soundlessly. He heard her, though, and her response warmed his insides. She did like him, or at least want him, whatever she might prefer to have him believe.

"I've word that the blacksmith in Sheiling has been looking fer a lass named Hortensia fer the past few days," he told Marjorie's companion. "Loudly."

Her cheeks darkened to crimson. "I have in no way encouraged any such thing," she said, a slight squeak in her voice. She fanned at her face with both hands.

"Regardless, I cannae have him stirring up questions."

"Please don't tell me you mean to kidnap him," Marjorie put in, clearly only half jesting.

"And what do ye suggest, then? That I kill him? Have him over fer tea?"

Making a face at him, she turned to Mrs. Hortensia Giswell. "Is he . . . trustworthy, do you think?"

"I . . . How in the world would I know?"

"Mrs. Giswell, this concerns the safety of those young boys," she pointed out, making Graeme want to kiss her all over again.

"Oh, dear." The companion sank into a chair. "Yes, I think he could be trusted with the truth. But not if you kidnap him."

"Yes, then," Marjorie said, looking over at him again. "Have him over for tea."

"Oh, aye. And biscuits. That'd nae make the blacksmith suspicious at all." *Women.* One of them had proved to have some tolerable ideas, but they were both definitely English. "I'll ask him over to look at horseshoes. Ye can chat with him in the morning room. And be convincing, if ye please. I dunnae think that shackle'll fit his mighty leg."

"Well, thank goodness for Mr. Polk's large ankles." Marjorie took Mrs. Giswell's arm and the two women left the room.

Now he needed to let someone else in on the goings-on at the Lion's Den. If this continued, everyone in the valley would know. Most of them he would trust with that information, but there were a few who were more loyal to Dunncraigh than they were to him, particularly with the limited aid and charity he could grant them.

On the other hand, he still didn't quite trust Brendan even though his brother's threats and complaints about Ree had subsided over the past few days. And yet he sent Brendan out nearly every day to help the cotters with the preparation for the heavy snow—where the sixteen-year-old had numerous opportunities to betray the lot of them.

Complications piled on top of lies spread over trouble. And in the middle of it, when he should have been concentrating on finding a way to get Marjorie Forrester out of the valley, he continued to look for every possible excuse to have her stay.

Chapter Twelve

Graeme met Robert Polk in the stable. The black-smith's dark beard looked less well tended than usual, and the typical grim smile with which he greeted every new challenge had been replaced by a deep scowl. "Laird Maxton," he said brusquely. "Ye've a horse needs shoeing? I'll see to it, but I've other worries today."

The two of them stood about the same height, but the smith had shoulders molded by years of wielding a heavy hammer, and the rest of him built to match his shoulders. Graeme had never considered having to fight the man, but today could be that day. It would be interesting, at the least.

"Come inside with me, then," he said aloud. They could do much more damage in the house.

"Yer horse is inside the hoose, then?" Rob asked, lifting an eyebrow.

"Nae. I want a word with ye."

"I'm here, then. I dunnae belong in a grand hoose."

Graeme took a half step backward into the muddy stableyard, trying to lure the smith into the open before they spooked the livestock. "I've someaught to tell ye, Rob, and

I need ye to listen to the end, and to keep what I say just between the two of us. Aye?"

Following him outside, Robert rubbed his beard. "I reckon I can do that. Ye've my word."

"To begin with," Graeme began, making certain he had room to move if the blacksmith came after him, "ye know Dunncraigh and I arenae bosom friends."

"Ye dunnae hold with the way he treats the outlying Maxwells. I've nae argument with ye there, as I'm one of the outlying Maxwells."

Resisting the urge to smile mostly so that his amusement wouldn't come back to bite him in the arse in a few minutes, Graeme nodded. "Thank ye fer that. Anyway, my brothers overheard my last argument with the Maxwell. Then at the Cracked Hearth they realized the Sassenach lass who'd just arrived was the Duke of Lattimer's sister."

The smith's mildly impatient look dropped. "Hortensia's niece is Lattimer's sister? Why didnae—"

"Hortensia," Graeme cut in, the companion's Christian name odd on his tongue, "isnae Marjorie's aunt. She's Marjorie's companion. When my boys took Ree, Mrs. Giswell didnae want anyone knowing they had a grander prize than they realized."

"That's clever, I suppose, but she could have told me the truth." Slowly he lifted his gaze toward the house. "Hold a bit. Ye mean to say this Marjorie's been here all along?"

"Aye. I couldnae see my brothers arrested fer taking her." Graeme inhaled a deep breath. This next part would be tricky. "Once word got oot that I had a Marjorie staying here, I didnae want to risk Mrs. Giswell sending fer Lattimer or soldiers. So I had to . . . move her here."

"Ye moved her here," Robert repeated. "And she didnae bother to tell me where she was headed? The lads got a note to stay put, but I didnae get a thing."

She hadn't written the note to the two English servants,

but that wouldn't matter to the blacksmith. "I didnae ask her permission first."

"Ye . . . Och. Ye kidnapped her. Just like yer *bràthairs* did with the other lass."

"I—"

"I reckoned she'd gotten tired of having a rough lad like me following her aboot." Abruptly the smith rounded on Graeme. "Is she well? Because my chieftain or nae, if ye've harmed her I swear ye and I are going to have a tussle."

Graeme inclined his head. "I could give ye my word that she's fine, but I reckon ye'd rather see fer yerself."

"That, I would."

So far, at least, that had gone better than he expected. He led the way into the morning room where both ladies sat, standing back as the furry bear of a man wrapped his arms around the proper and stout Mrs. Giswell and lifted her into the air.

"Are ye well, lass? I thought ye'd gone searching on yer own and gotten yerself lost. Those boys of yers said ye'd gone, but ye didnae leave me word. I looked everywhere fer ye."

"My word! Put me down, Rob. For heaven's sake."

"He knows what's afoot," Graeme told them, stepping away from the doorway. "I'm trusting the lot of ye from here on."

Did the blacksmith and the lady's companion have a future together? He hoped so; they seemed genuinely enamored of each other. They had no other familial or clan responsibilities that he knew of, nothing to keep them apart but the one being Scottish, and the other English. As far as he knew Hortensia Giswell had no secret desire to be accepted by the bluest bloods of the London *haut ton*.

A hand touched his arm. "Thank you," Marjorie said. "I know including Mr. Polk went against your better judgment."

"Well, once ye ask me to grant ye a wish, lass, there's nae stopping me."

"You haven't let me go," she reminded him.

"That's because ye being here is the one thing *I* wish," he muttered, resuming his walk through the foyer. Canopies and tables for the fair would be arriving beginning today, and they had wooden planks to lay over the muddiest parts of the meadow adjoining the house. It had given him another excuse to get Brendan out of the house and away from their female guests, but sooner rather than later he needed to have a serious chat with the lad.

A hand gripped his, pulling. "What did you say just then?" Marjorie demanded.

"I said I granted ye what ye wished," he returned, facing her. "Care to come see the meadow we're readying fer the winter fair?"

Her mouth opened and closed again, her pretty eyes widening just a little. "Of course I do. I've been wanting to go outside for days. But will my being seen put your brothers at risk?"

"I reckon by now everyone fer ten miles around knows I've an English governess here. If ye dunnae claim to be anyone but Ree Giswell, ye'll be naught but a minor curiosity."

"'A minor curiosity'?" she repeated. "That would be a lovely change." Wrapping her fingers around his forearm, she walked beside him out the front door and onto the rutted oyster-shell drive, and he pretended that his heart sped because the wind was brisk.

When she stopped to look back at the house, he paused beside her. She'd never seen it from the outside, he realized belatedly. Graeme looked at Garaidh nan Leòmhann, the Lion's Den, again himself. Pale gray stones, a rose trellis climbing up the wall beside the morning room window, two stories and an attic in a large, blocky rectangle that had definitely seen better days. Better centuries, more like. With the roses more or less untended for the past eight years and dying back now in the cold, trim peeling away from the window frames, and the corner of the small, weed-dotted garden in view, it looked . . . tired.

"It's nae much to look at," he said aloud, "but I reckon it has heart." A more gentle and compassionate one since she'd arrived, but he wasn't going to tell her that.

"I can imagine a dragon nesting on the roof," she returned. "A medium-sized one, looming in the fog. A large dragon would be a bit much, I think. And very clichéd."

Hm. He hadn't expected that response. "Dragons?"

"Just one. As a child I always thought dragons lived in the Highlands. This would be a splendid place for one to reside. The Lion's Den is quite . . . magical-looking, you have to admit."

Graeme looked all over again at the house in which he'd been born. Magical? Perhaps too many nonmagical things had happened there, but he didn't see it. "I like that ye can see it that way," he said after a moment. "I've heard tales that it used to be a much prouder place."

After that she wanted to see the stables and know the names of the two saddle horses and two cart and plow horses residing there, then he led her down to the bank of the river Douchary. Where the water widened and slowed, the banks were frozen out two or three inches. Soon the wide strip of free-flowing water in the middle would begin to narrow, and by January they'd be hammering through the ice to get fresh water.

"I didn't expect to see so many trees in the Highlands," she commented, her gaze on the scattered stands of birch and mountain ash that made their way along the far bank of the river.

Did she see them as a promising place to hide if she ever attempted to escape? He hoped not, because she'd never make it across the wild, white-spitting river. "Anywhere the wind cannae howl through, the trees dig into the ground and rise up as far as they can. Most of the valley here is trees and hollows and rivulets. My ancestors built on this side of the river because the winds keep the trees back. Highlanders prefer to see who's riding up on them with torches and cannon."

"It's very pretty," she said, freeing her hand to rub both her forearms. To a lass from the soft, warm south, the air must be biting cold today. He shrugged out of his coat and draped it across her shoulders.

"I need to find ye some warmer things to wear."

"I'm fairly handy with a needle and thread. If you don't mind me altering a few of your mother's things, I believe I can make do. Though you kidnapped Mrs. Giswell's trunk along with her, so I suppose you could go back and do the same thing with mine."

"I didnae kidnap her trunk. I wanted her to be more comfortable than I ken ye've been. I do try to learn from my mistakes, which is why I suppose I'll be going back for yer things, now." He preferred not to, as it would make it easier for her to flee, but the lass needed her damned clothes.

A smile touched her sweet mouth. "I imagine my wardrobe troubles could have been much worse. And I'm lately feeling somewhat . . . mollified."

He drew her a breath closer. "Are ye, then?"

"Graeme!" Connell's voice came from the direction of the stable. "Honker's oot! We have to get 'im before he's ate by a wildcat!" The bairn went charging up the rise toward the meadow.

"Honker?" Marjorie asked.

"Connell's greylag gander. He lives in the stable."

Marjorie gathered her skirts and hurried after Graeme, but as he headed after his youngest brother at a run, she

might as well have been standing still. A goose, multiple
cats, a pair of foxes, three baby rabbits, and heaven knew
what else, but Graeme had hundreds more lives stacked on
top of that. And he still took the time to chase down a pet
goose with his eight-year-old brother.

Halfway up the hill, though, she stopped. What in the
world was she doing? Whatever he said about keeping her
and his family safe, whatever she'd agreed to, she was still
a prisoner. And just across the rather formidable-looking
river behind her lay freedom.

Even as the thought occurred to her, though, she knew
she wasn't going anywhere. Perhaps she did know approx-
imately where in the Highlands she now found herself, but
she still wasn't prepared for a hike through the wilderness.
And she . . . didn't want to go. She wanted to stay, at least
until she'd figured out why she found this man—a barbarian and a heathen who seemed to enjoy nothing so
much as flaunting the rules and dragging her along with
him—so compelling. Until she'd rid him from her thoughts
and felt ready to return to her very large, comfortable
house in London.

Still panting, she resumed her sprint to the top of the
rise. She definitely needed to go for more walks, if she could
possibly arrange it. The meadow spread out before her,
piles of wood planks stacked here and there among rolls
of heavy canvas and two dozen men marking things with
stakes and string.

In the middle of all that, a large blue-gray goose honked
and flapped, dodging Connell, Graeme, and anyone else
running after it. She recognized Brendan as he made a
dive, only to get tangled up in twine. And Graeme, in his
white linen shirt and kilt with work boots, looked magnificent but wasn't faring much better. Connell, flapping and
squawking himself, seemed more excited than worried.

Finally Graeme made a twisting leap, scooping the

gander up in his arms and rolling several times before he came to a stop. Marjorie put both hands over her mouth, trying to stifle her laughter, as Connell flung up his arms and then collapsed beside his brother.

"Well done," she called, clapping. Marjorie picked her way over the remaining stakes and twine to stop beside them.

Breathing hard, Graeme grinned up at her. "If he ever figures oot how to fly, we're done fer."

"He cannae fly," Connell put in. "A wildcat tried to eat his wing when he was a bairn."

As she looked at Honker more closely, she could see the long length of featherless wing on one side. Another orphan Connell had needed to rescue. Another lost soul Graeme had allowed his brother to bring into the family.

Had she been one? Was that the real reason Connell had noticed her and had gone along with his older brother's plan? Was she a lost soul trying to fit into a place that neither needed nor wanted her presence? But where, then, was she supposed to go? She had the education and the sophistication to be an aristocrat, a house nicer than half the dwellings in Mayfair, and tradition had affixed "Lady" in front of her name the moment they'd recognized Gabriel as the Duke of Lattimer.

No one, though, had given any indication that she belonged among the blue bloods of London. And after her escapade here in the Highlands, she never would. Where, then, did she belong? Where would she feel that she'd achieved what she'd spent most of her life pursuing? Was—

Connell sat upright and took her hand, pulling her down to sit beside Graeme in the damp grass. "Pet him, Ree. His name's Honker. He's very friendly, but he likes to run aboot in the meadow."

With Graeme still on his back and the gander cradled against his chest, she reached over to run her fingertips against the soft feathers of the bird's breast. The head swiveled, beady black eyes assessing her, until he curved his neck to shove the top of his head beneath her hand.

"Honker likes ye," Connell announced. "I told ye he was friendly."

"He's very soft," she offered.

"And cunning," Graeme added. "We'd best get him back inside and help restake the meadow before the lads decide we're more trouble than we're worth."

A hand lowered to help her to her feet. She took it and stood, looking up to see Brendan gazing at her. "Thank you," she said.

Gray eyes held hers for a short moment. "We dunnae all find ye as charming as Graeme does," he murmured, sent a glance at his older brother, and walked away again.

"Brendan," Graeme said sharply, as he stood. "What did he say to ye, lass?" Without waiting for an answer, he put the goose into her arms and strode after his brother, grabbing him by the shirt to haul him back in front of her. "Apologize, Brendan. Whatever ye said."

Putting a half smile on her face, she shook her head. "He said you think I'm charming." He had; she'd only left out the other bits because they were between her and Brendan. "That doesn't require an apology where I'm from."

The sixteen-year-old's sharp eyes glanced at her and then away. "Satisfied, ye great lug?" he grumbled, shrugging out of Graeme's grip and stalking away again.

"That's all ye have to say?" Graeme asked, eyeing her now.

She handed him the goose back. "Don't try to begin a fight with me, Highlander," she countered. For a minute there, before Brendan had reminded her that she didn't belong at the Lion's Den, either, she'd almost felt like a part of the Maxton family. And for that brief moment, she'd liked it. "I haven't done anything."

"Aye," he said, blowing out his breath. "The lad has the right of it, ye ken."

The right of what? That almost no one here found her charming? That she didn't belong here any more than she did anywhere else? "Oh?"

The fingers of his free hand brushed against hers. "Aye. I do find ye charming."

This time she felt her smile all the way to her insides, and the world seemed to right itself again. When his opinion had come to mean so much to her she didn't know, but it clearly did. "You have your moments as well, I suppose," she conceded. "When you're not trying to bully me." Aside from those long, delicious moments in his bedchamber, she liked seeing him with his brothers. The warmth and affection they felt for each other was palpable—and very compelling.

"Johnny," he called, as the groom finished untangling himself from still more twine and approached. "Take Honker back to his pen, will ye, lad?"

"Of course, m'laird." The groom took the gray-blue bird. "So ye think ye can escape, do ye? We'll see if ye get that extra measure of corn tonight." The gander honked at him. "Och, dunnae try apologizing. Ye made a mess of the meadow."

With her still laughing at the exchange, Graeme moved closer to her. "Ye didnae try to run," he murmured.

She nodded. "I considered it," she admitted. He would only call her a liar if she claimed the thought had never crossed her mind. "We know Sir Hamish is nearby, so I decided not to risk stumbling across him."

The explanation made sense, at least. Otherwise she was going to have to face something that made no sense at all; in spite of being kidnapped, locked in a room, chained to a bed, and very nearly forced into a marriage, she . . . liked it here. Being among the wild-hearted, unconventional

Maxtons made her forget how badly she'd been failing in London.

It wasn't merely that she'd been occupied with pretending to be Connell's tutor, either. When she'd served as a lady's companion she'd frequently spent her nights lying awake as dread shoved down her throat until she nearly suffocated from it. A lifetime spent fluffing pillows and fetching tea for women who'd likely failed their own run at Society had felt forever and empty and useless.

She didn't feel that, now. But what in the world did that say about her and her life, if staying in her captor's house in the middle of the Scottish Highlands left her happier than having money and status in London?

"What's troubling ye, lass?" Graeme asked, stopping her at the front edge of the drive.

"I hadn't realized how much I miss walking," she improvised.

"Liar," he returned, and moved past her into the house.

Well. "What makes you think I'm lying, you rude man?" she retorted, pursuing him down the hallway.

"Because ye didnae weep when the lads dragged ye off to Garaidh nan Leòmhann. Missing a stroll wouldnae make ye so much as blink. If ye dunnae want to say why ye're crying, just tell me so. Dunnae lie aboot it."

"I'm not weeping," she stated, wiping a tear from her cheek. "I got goose down in my eye."

"And I've got goose down in my brain, then," he countered, striding into his office.

"You said it; not I."

As she pushed inside the room after him, Graeme sidestepped, yanked her over by the desk, and shut and locked the door behind them. She opened her mouth to protest once again that she wasn't weeping, and to point out that a gentleman didn't pursue such a line of questions, but he stopped her words with his own mouth as he kissed her. Their tongues tangled, her pulse skimming and skipping as he slid his hands around her hips and pulled her against him.

"That's better," he finally said, lifting his head. "It'll do until tonight, anyway."

It took a moment for her to gather her thoughts enough to form words again. "What's tonight, then?" she asked, even though that kiss gave her a very good idea.

"Tonight's when I'll have ye again, Marjorie," he drawled, running a finger along the neckline of her gown. "I've been patient fer two days, and I'm nae a patient man."

"What about all the lasses in the area, Graeme? Surely any number of them would be eager to share your bed. To have a place by your side, even. Connell's not an infant any longer, and you don't have to continue to do this alone."

He frowned. "Dunnae ye want me, lass?" he murmured, turning the attention of his mouth and lips to her jawline.

Did she want him? She could scarcely think of anything but being naked with him again. "That's not the point," she insisted, her eyes closing at the lightning shivers his touch elicited. "A chieftain of clan Maxwell needs a wife and heirs. I . . ." *Oh, goodness, what was she saying?* "I mean to say, I'm not . . ." She cleared her throat. "I'm ruined now, as I've said, and as such I have no objection to a dalliance. But Connell—and Dùghlas and Brendan—need a female influence in their lives. Badly. And a little bit of taming wouldn't hurt you, either. Perhaps, then, you shouldn't be wasting your time with me."

Somewhere in the middle of all that he'd stopped those toe-curling, feather-light kisses and straightened, gazing at her. Marjorie didn't know which would be more painful—to have him agree that she was a dalliance when he had better things to do, or to hear him say that she needed to mind her own business because she was, after all, just a Sassenach surrounded by Highlanders.

"Ye sound like Father Michael," he finally said, "always trying to get me leg-shackled to some 'promising' lass or other. I'm nae a monk, Ree. Ye're nae the first lass to lie in my bed."

Well, that hurt. "I didn't think I was," she said stiffly. "But that—"

"I'm nae some moonstruck bairn who needs to be led aboot. I have eyes . . . and I'm looking at ye." He stirred a little. "And since we both know ye'll be gone as soon as I let ye, then I dunnae see any hearts in danger of being broken. I ask ye to share my bed. If ye've nae objection, then leave yer damned door unlocked tonight."

"I have no objection," she whispered, so he wouldn't hear the trembling of her voice. Nothing permanent, but together as long as she was there. She could manage that. Until, perhaps, she decided to go, or he decided it would be safe for her to leave. That, however, wouldn't be today.

And if part of her wished that Sir Hamish's fishing holiday was proceeding so splendidly that he would decide to extend his stay in the valley, well, she didn't need to admit that to anyone but herself.

Hortensia backed away from the office door, careful not to rattle the old china tea set on the tray she carried. And she thought *she'd* gone astray. A few kisses and some discreet handholding, though, could hardly compare to what she'd just overheard.

Of course it would take a herculean effort to salvage Lady Marjorie's reputation should any rumors about a kidnapping emerge. What neither of the two young people in the office had grasped, though, was that at this moment no one outside of this ramshackle mansion knew there had even been a kidnapping. No one knew Lady Marjorie Forrester was missing.

For heaven's sake, did the young lady think her companion had learned nothing after the disaster with Princess Sophia? The fewer people who knew anything was amiss, the fewer who could wag their tongues about it. If they needed an excuse, they would have the time and opportunity to conjure one.

In fact, Lady Marjorie seemed to be creating the one possible complication herself. A pregnancy would dash any chance for her to emerge unscathed. On the other hand, a child could always be a foundling or the child of some deceased friend or distant relation or other. A good handful of "foundlings" resided in perfectly respectable households with their perfectly respectable "rescuers." Everything could be managed, as long as a modicum of discretion accompanied it.

The three younger Maxtons trudged into the house, and she stepped to one side of the hallway to let them pass. Little ill-mannered heathens, even though two of them were taller than she was. Someone should have taken a switch to them years ago. Now it was likely too late to rehabilitate any of them but that Connell—and given the way he preferred to nest with wild animals, even that would be a challenge.

". . . doesnae mean anything," the oldest one was saying, as he wrapped an arm around Connell's waist and hung the boy over his shoulder.

"It means she could've had ye shoveling shite in the stable, and she didnae," the middle, more clever one pointed out. "And that's after ye stole her, threatened her, and insulted her. I'd have walloped ye fer every single one of those things."

"Ye'd have tried, horseface."

"Cow lips."

"I'm the Bruce!" Connell yelled, for no apparent reason, and then they were past her and up the stairs.

Madmen. The lot of them. But then Lady Marjorie

emerged from the office, her hair coming loose from its pins on one side and her lips swollen. With a smile at the door she turned for the stairs, only to begin humming that song about two bonnie maidens, which everyone knew to be about the Jacobite rebellion. Of course it was good fun to sing it in a horrid brogue in London drawing rooms, but here it seemed very questionable and likely scandalous.

Hortensia opened her mouth to caution her mistress, but stopped herself when Lady Marjorie flung out her arms and twirled in a circle. In the two months she'd known the young lady, Marjorie had never hummed or sung, and she'd certainly never spun.

"Oh, Mrs. Giswell," the young lady exclaimed, stopping in mid-hum and blushing. "I didn't see you there."

"I'm bringing tea to Sir Robert. To Mr. Polk, I mean. Entertaining him in a room with just the two of us isn't exactly proper, but with no female servants but that savage cook in residence, I'll simply have to leave the morning room door open and make do."

"He seems very respectful of you, in any case," the lady replied.

"He is. Not that anything could come of a Scottish blacksmith and an English lady's companion, but flirtation is an art and should be practiced from time to time."

"Just a flirtation, Mrs. Giswell?" she said, her eyes sparkling with good humor. "Your Mr. Polk seemed excessively relieved to see you in good health."

"Yes, I think he was. But our time here is both unwilling and temporary, my lady, so what could it be if not a flirtation?"

The teasing grin on her employer's face fled, her gaze lowering. "Yes, of course you're correct. What else could it be?" She smoothed her skirt. "The priest is due here shortly. You haven't seen Connell, have you?"

"Upstairs with his brothers, I believe."

"Thank you. And please, be certain Mr. Polk remembers the roles we're playing if he speaks to Father Michael."

"I will, my lady. My niece, I mean. Ree."

With a flip of her hand and an utterly fake smile Lady Marjorie walked up the stairs. Her thoughts roiling, Hortensia watched her out of sight. *Oh, dear.* This was far more serious than she'd realized. However this misadventure had begun, Marjorie was . . . happy. Here. Perhaps she hadn't even realized it, but no one who hummed and smiled and spun in private—or what she'd thought had been private—was unhappy.

Hefting the tea tray, she pushed backward against the mostly closed morning room door and slipped inside, only to have strong, warm hands close over her shoulders. "A flirtation, am I?" Sir Robert muttered, leaning around with his bushy beard to kiss her on the cheek.

"I wanted to remind Lady Marjorie that she has plans, and that they don't include Graeme, Lord Maxton." She set down the tray to pour him a cup of tea with four lumps of sugar. After ten years of marriage to the very plain and practical Mr. Giswell, she appreciated a man with a sweet tooth.

"But what aboot *yer* plans, Hortensia?"

With a sigh she handed him the cup and saucer and then sat down on the couch beside him. "As long as she needs me, I go where Lady Marjorie goes."

"Then mayhap ye shouldnae be pointing oot that she has other plans, lass."

She lifted an eyebrow. "Stay here, you mean? Lady Marjorie wants to be a success in Society. She can't do that here." Aside from that, happiness and success rarely had anything to do with each other. So while she might find one here, she certainly wouldn't find the other.

The blacksmith shrugged. "Mayhap she'll change her mind aboot what she wants."

If Marjorie wasn't careful, she might find herself without a choice altogether. And that would leave her with neither happiness nor success. Nor any need for a lady's companion, because she would no longer be considered a lady.

Chapter Thirteen

Graeme could swear the number of cats in the house had multiplied. They might well have done it on their own, as cats were known to do, or Connell might have smuggled more inside on the chance that no one would notice. Either way, some of them were going to have to go out to the stable.

Nudging a brown and white one aside with his bare foot, he closed himself out of his bedchamber and padded next door to Marjorie's room. Aye, she'd tried to set him after some of the local lasses, but luckily she'd done it so awkwardly that he hadn't thought her serious.

He'd be damned if he'd knock tonight, so he pushed down on the door handle. It gave, and he let out the breath he'd held. She hadn't changed her mind about sex with him—at least not yet. If it *had* been locked he likely would have forgotten about being stealthy, put his shoulder to it, and knocked the door off its hinges.

She'd moved the two shabby, overstuffed chairs back in front of the window, and as he closed the door he could make out her silhouette against the silver-touched night beyond. "Did someaught catch yer eye oot there?" he asked quietly, moving up behind the chair so he could run his fingers though her loose, dark hair.

"Connell spent an hour before dinner trying to convince me that he'd found a pair of faeries living in a hollow tree just past the river, and that I would be able to see them after dark because their wings glow silver."

"And ye're expecting to see them, then?"

"No. But I wanted to look, anyway. It seems a good night for faeries—and elves and selkies and banshees and all the other magic folk who seem to live in the Highlands. Why do you have so many mythical creatures here?"

"Mythical creatures need wild places. There's nae a place in the world more wild than the Highlands."

"I like when you talk about the Highlands that way."

Graeme lifted an eyebrow. "Which way is that?"

"Like you cherish it."

The Highlands wasn't the only thing he was coming to cherish. That thought—the realization of just how vital this Sassenach was becoming to him and after such a short time—terrified him in a way nothing else ever had. A man in the Highlands needed to be strong, sturdy, and self-sufficient. He'd seen up close what happened to a man who gave up too much of his happiness, of himself, to someone else. And he'd vowed it would never happen to him. Hell, he'd been ready to marry a stranger, a Sassenach lass he'd thought stuffy and spoiled. If he didn't love her, she couldn't hurt him.

And yet he thought about that same lass every waking hour, dreamed about her at night, craved her endlessly. Just the scent of lemon put a damned tent in his kilt. She was a flame, and he, a moth.

Perhaps it was all lust, tied up in pretty ribbons. Aye, that could be it; he needed to purge her from his thoughts, and the only logical way to do that was to sate himself in her. Immediately and repeatedly, until he could breathe and think again.

She looked up over her shoulder at him. "You're being very quiet," she observed. "Do you not enjoy it here? I know for a fact that there are *easier* places to live."

"Nae fer me, lass," he said, shaking his head. "I went to London. Aboot nine years ago. Warm days, flowers, sweating in my fancy clothes, parasols and wee yapping dogs riding with lasses in their carriages."

With a chuckle Marjorie turned around to kneel on her chair, her arms folded beneath her chin as she gazed up at him. "Is that all you remember?"

Graeme shrugged. "I remember people looking sideways at me, hearing them wonder if I was a Jacobite spy—as if they'd forgotten aboot Culloden and what the redcoats did to the Jacobites. I bloodied my share of noses, got myself challenged to two duels, and got handed a lifetime ban to some place called Almack's." It had been more troublesome than that, but he reckoned she understood the underlying message—that he and London hadn't been compatible. At all.

"Ah, Almack's. Everyone wants an invitation, and everyone loathes attending," she said, nodding. "I've never been invited, myself."

"And do ye want to be?" For a lass with as much sense as she had, it seemed a very odd, and very hollow, goal.

"It's a sign of acceptance." Marjorie visibly shook herself. "But I don't want to talk about London any longer tonight."

"Nae? Did ye have someaught else in mind, then?" He put his hands on either side of her folded arms and leaned in to kiss her.

The moment she swept her arms up around his neck he took her by the waist and lifted her over the back of the chair. Even with all the uncertainty sitting between them, the questions that all came down to when and how she would leave, *this* was certain. The desire between them was both genuine and unmistakable. And he damned well knew what to do about that.

Graeme stood her beside the bed, took the bottom hem of her night rail, and lifted it off over her head. Her small breasts with their pebbled nipples practically begged for his attention, but tonight he had something else in mind. "On the bed," he instructed, shirking his own shirt and kilt.

She lay down with her head on the pillow as she had two nights ago. With a grin he wrapped his fingers around her ankles and pulled her around sideways so she lay crossways across the bed, her legs parted around his thighs as he stood on the floor. Holding her gaze, he knelt, caught hold of her right leg, and kissed the back of her knee. With kisses and nips of his teeth he made his way toward the apex of her thighs.

When he kissed her there, she jumped. "Graeme, that's very naughty," she managed in a half moan.

"Aye," he murmured back, and deliberately licked her. While she groaned and writhed beneath his ministrations, he parted her folds and continued introducing himself with his mouth and fingers.

As he slid a finger inside her damp heat she abruptly came, spasming around his digit. His cock jumped in response. If only the rest of their time together was so simple and straightforward, he would never have to let her go.

When she tangled her hands into his hair to tug him up along her body, he didn't resist. Pausing to circle his tongue around her breasts, he then lifted his head for an open-mouthed, tongue-tangling kiss. "Please, Graeme," she muttered huskily.

With her face flushed, her blue eyes searching his face and her breathing reduced to shallow, moaning pants, he couldn't have resisted if he'd wanted to. Still standing beside the bed, he used his knees to further part hers, gripped her wrists above her head, and pushed inside her.

Tight, shivering heat surrounded him, and he had to close his eyes to keep a modicum of control. Her slender body trembling, he withdrew and entered her again, with every thrust claiming her for himself. They could call it whatever they chose—answering a temporary mutual attraction, passing the time. It didn't matter. What mattered was their bodies twined together, their hard, mingled breathing, the deep, hungry, rhythmic coupling. With her he had a partner, a heart to beat in time with his.

As she began to pulse again he came, emptying himself into her, another claim on her. He could tell himself, both of them, that she was already ruined and so it didn't matter. Except that it did matter, because if she became pregnant he would have another reason never to let her go.

Graeme stretched, then opened his eyes when his hand touched nothing but well-rumpled sheets. For a minute he couldn't remember in which bedchamber they'd spent the night; for the past four they'd alternated even though his bed was both larger and softer.

"I think you'll have good weather for your fair," she said from the direction of the window.

He sat up. Ah, his bedchamber. "If I'd realized how much ye like looking oot windows, I'd nae have shackled ye away from them," he drawled, stifling a yawn.

"In London I looked out my window waiting for visitors," she returned, padding over to stoke the fire. She'd donned her night rail, which didn't bode well for more sex this morning. Still, he could be persuasive. "Here, it's just beautiful." She sighed. "Dùghlas told me a saying, that if you don't like the weather here, just wait a minute. The views seem to operate the same way."

"Aye. The most changeable thing here is the weather. Nae the people."

"And today I look forward to meeting some more of them."

After she said that, he closed his mouth over the suggestion that she remain inside the manor house for the duration of the fair. Aye, she would be safer inside, but by now everyone between Sheiling and Loch Achall knew he'd hired an English tutor for the lads, and that her aunt was holidaying with them as well. The cotters who hadn't met her yet would expect to do so, and he actually wanted her to meet them. If he could do anything to convince her that Garaidh nan Leòmhann was superior to London without him explicitly saying so and getting her back up, he meant to attempt it.

"Just promise ye'll keep me in sight," he said, pulling her back beneath the warm covers beside him. "Uncle Raibeart's nae gotten rid of his houseguest yet, so I've good reason to think Hamish Paulk will be aboot today to sour the milk and put the bairns off their mama's teats."

"I'll *try* to keep you in sight," she countered. "We both know you'll be blanketed by eligible females the moment you step outside."

"And ye dunnae mind that?" For Lucifer's sake, he wanted her to be jealous. He wanted her to be as desperate for him as he was for her. Instead, she kept talking about the future, *his* future, which didn't seem to include her in it.

"What I mind doesn't signify."

Well, that sounded promising. "Lass, we've been sharing a bed. Of course it signifies."

"No, it doesn't." She tried to shove away from him, but he held her there against his side. "You need to find a bride sooner or later, Graeme, and I need to go see my brother and then return to London."

"Ye want to. Ye dunnae need to." He turned her onto her back, so she had to look up at him. "Why would ye *need* to go back to that hoose where yer neighbors willnae give ye a single greeting?"

"Oh, stop it," she snapped, shoving at his chest. "You couldn't possibly understand."

"I couldnae, could I?" he returned. "Ye ken I could've married if I'd wanted to. But I didnae. I saw . . ." He stopped, taking a breath, then released her and rolled out of bed, himself. "I'll go doon and have a bath drawn fer ye."

He reached for the dress kilt he'd set out for the day's festivities, but she snatched it away from him. "You saw what?" she prompted, dancing out of his reach.

"Do ye truly want to know, or do ye just like seeing me naked?" he asked, folding his arms over his chest, and feeling somewhat gratified when her gaze dropped below his waist.

"I don't believe the two need to be mutually exclusive," she said after a moment, meeting his gaze again. "But since it's fine for you to decide whether or not I *need* to return to London," she said, exaggerating the word as he had, "then you can tell me what you saw that's kept you from marrying some pretty local lass."

He lunged forward, grabbing her wrist and yanking her up against his bare chest. "Ye think I'm Connell, that ye can play aboot with yer pretty words and get me to do what ye want?" Before she could kick or hit him somewhere sensitive he removed the kilt from her other hand and backed away to knot it around his waist. Getting it on properly could wait until he could lie across it without worrying over being tromped on.

"You are a bullheaded man," she announced, her hands on her hips.

"And ye're a bullheaded woman." Graeme jabbed a finger at her. "I saw my father love a lass so far beyond sense and reason that he shot himself rather than making an effort to take care of her boys, the things she most treasured in this damned world," he snapped, striding to the hearth and back.

"You told m—"

"Someone—I—had to look after those lads. And so I decided no lass in the world would make me ferget my duty or lose my damned heart. A bit of fun fer a night, aye, but nae more than that. I couldnae—wouldnae—risk getting twisted up with a female as long as one of those bairns still needed me. Now do ye ken?"

Her hands had lowered from her hips, and instead she reached for him, then apparently decided against it as she lowered her arms again. "No, I don't. Because you keep suggesting I stay, when y—"

"I dunnae ken, either!" he exploded. "Because from the first second I set eyes on ye, all I've wanted to do is hold ye in my arms and keep ye there. Ye've blasted away all the oaths I swore to myself, and I dunnae even care. But it doesnae signify, because all *ye* want to do is go back to London and pretend those bloody blue bloods want anything to do with ye, when ye already know they couldnae care less if ye live or die."

With that he strode for the door, stooped to pick up his boots, and left his bedchamber. He wouldn't have to worry about his heart now, at least, because she'd likely never want to look at him again. And that would be a good thing. It would damned well make his life less complicated.

Now, though, he needed to figure a safe way for her to get past Hamish Paulk and up to Lattimer. She wouldn't be safe anywhere on the road in between, especially if someone noted the crest on her coach as she drove away.

But it would have to be soon, because he wasn't certain how long he could tolerate her being under his roof but not in his arms. He didn't like irony. Not when the bastard did things like this—make him want to marry her when he didn't much respect the life she'd chosen for herself, and make him want to send her away when he'd begun to adore her.

"Come in, Mrs. Giswell," Marjorie called, as the knock sounded at her door.

Her companion walked in, made a clucking sound, and immediately shut the door behind her again. "You shouldn't be standing half naked in here with the door unlocked, my lady," she chastised. "Any of these madmen could stomp in, and then where would we be?"

"I have five buttons undone," Marjorie countered, eyeing herself in the small, cracked dressing mirror. "Up my back. That's hardly half naked."

"Just because we're in the company of heathens doesn't mean we should fall into their heathen ways."

Arguing with the woman would only earn her a tired tongue. And she'd done enough arguing already today, anyway. "Of course you're correct, Mrs. Giswell. Will you please button me?"

"This is the gown you altered, isn't it?" the older woman observed, moving up to fasten the gown. "That rose brings out your color. And the green pelisse is very fashionable, despite its age. It's very lovely, Lady Marjorie. Well done."

"Thank you." She'd chosen the gown from one of the chests in the attic, and then intentionally kept the alterations and progress to herself so she could surprise Graeme with the final result today. Now it seemed rather silly, and he likely wouldn't be sparing her a second glance, anyway.

If she was supposed to be flattered when a man pushed her away *because* he liked her, she'd missed that lesson. He took risks in his life all the time, but apparently he remained unwilling to take this one.

"Are you certain you shouldn't be wearing something

plainer today, however?" Mrs. Giswell went on. "I wouldn't mind if we were to be recognized and rescued, of course, but it's far more likely one of these burly fellows will be overcome with desire at the sight of you, sling you over his shoulder, and carry you off to his stone and moss hut to ravage you."

That made Marjorie grin. "You've thought that scenario through very thoroughly," she said, trying to hide her amusement behind her hand.

"Well, it could happen just as easily to me as to you, Lady Marjorie."

"Ree, please. Remember, I'm your—"

"Niece. Yes. And you should be calling me Aunt Hortensia, then, at least in front of the cotters and villagers. Though I still think it would be wiser to remain inside."

"I want to see the fair. I attended one on a school holiday in Derbyshire once, and I remember it being quite fun. I imagine this one will be even more so. I've never celebrated Samhain."

"A heathen ceremony for heathens." She sighed. "At least you'll have Lord Maxton to keep watch over you. I have no idea how he manages to keep his attention on everyone at once, but he does."

"My goodness. That sounded very nearly like a compliment."

Her faux aunt grimaced. "Well, perhaps he's part wolf, or wildcat."

"Lion," Marjorie countered absently. She didn't like what he'd said this morning. He was a man with a clan— or a section of one, anyway—and so he needed stability. As far as she knew, the best way to achieve that was through marriage and children. He shouldn't be denying himself that, whether it was with her or someone else. His brothers had his affection and love, clearly. It made no sense to deny that affection to someone else simply because it might hurt later, no matter what example his father had set.

He'd sworn some oath never to fall in love? In some ways she understood and sympathized with his reasoning, but then . . . Goodness. First to hear that he liked her, that he wanted her to remain here, and then to listen to all the horrid things he had to say about her return to London— it felt deliberate and mean-spirited. He'd made an oath, but so had she. And hers included being in London and being accepted by all those people who'd never deigned to look at her before three months ago. How dare he ridicule her for holding her course just because he'd . . . faltered in his?

"Lady Marjorie?"

She jumped. "Mrs.—Aunt Hortensia. I apologize. I forgot you were there."

"Is something troubling you?"

Oh, so many things. "Do you think I'm being stupid to want to be accepted in London?"

"What? Of course not. However unexpectedly it came about, you are a duke's sister. Your blood is as blue as anyone else's in Mayfair. If your mother hadn't kept you ignorant of that side of your family, the *ton* would have become accustomed to the idea of you and your brother inheriting ages ago."

Marjorie nodded. "Yes, perhaps. Our monetary circumstances would have been just as dismal, however."

"Oh, pish. Do you have any idea how many aristocratic families are just one step ahead of debtor's prison? A great many of them."

"You do make it sound plausible," she returned slowly, though she still doubted that anyone would have accepted an eight-year-old girl forced to leave London for boarding school and a seventeen-year-old young man determined to join the army to provide for the two of them. She and Gabriel would have had no London residence, no other

London relations but old Lattimer—who, from what she read, hadn't been a very pleasant fellow, anyway. "Of course it's all moot, now that I've been missing for a fortnight."

Mrs. Giswell took a breath. "May I speak honestly, my lady?"

"Of course," Marjorie replied with a frown. "Always."

"Very well." The companion folded her hands in front of her. "You have no friends in London."

"I—"

"Other than a governess or a companion here and there, I mean. No one of quality or influence."

This was beginning to sound like one of Graeme's speeches. She wasn't certain she could bear to hear it all again today. "We have been trying," she reminded her companion.

"Indeed we have. My point is, no one knows where you've gone or when you're expected back. Not even your brother. As far as he's concerned, you're still in London. If you appeared on his doorstep tomorrow, he would have no cause or reason to believe you'd been delayed somewhere against your will unless you told him so. As far as anyone in London is concerned, if they've noticed your absence or inquired at the house as to where you might be, you're at Lattimer Castle and have been for the past fortnight."

Marjorie stared at her. Mrs. Giswell had it all figured out. If no one knew she'd gone missing, no one could even suggest she'd been ruined. A few people here knew, but they and their opinions mattered even less to London than she did. In addition, they'd have little reason to suspect that Ree Giswell and Lady Marjorie Forrester were one and the same. She wasn't ruined—except, of course, for the fact that she was.

"You see? Everything can be managed. As soon as this

abominable Sir Hamish Paulk leaves the area, so will we. And no one will be any the wiser. Except for us, but we won't be telling anyone."

She should have been relieved. She could return to London in no worse a position than she'd been in when she left. But she didn't feel relieved, because part of Mrs. Giswell's logic had stabbed at her—the assertion that not a soul in London knew or cared to know where she'd gone.

Not a single soul in an entire town cared a single fig about her, her well-being, her life, or her death. No one. "No one cares," she said aloud.

"Well . . . no, but they aren't yet acquainted with you. We will make them care. In another year or two, well before you're ready to be put on the shelf, your absence will cause an uproar and make unmarried men weep in worry that you've given your hand to someone else."

She couldn't quite imagine that even in her wildest daydreams. If three months of effort hadn't even netted her a wave, she could hardly expect to warrant weeping two years hence. For goodness' sake, she'd grown up accustomed to being more or less alone, but even that was different than being present but utterly ignored.

A young fist pounded on her door. "Ree!" Connell called. "Are ye in there? I'm nae to come in unless ye say, because Dùghlas told me if ye see a lass naked ye have to marry her."

Mrs. Giswell gave a delicate snort. "He isn't wrong about that."

And Marjorie knew someone who'd seen her naked nightly over the past few days. "I'm dressed, Connell. You may enter."

Her door swung open, and the eight-year-old strolled in together with the pair of foxes and a big yellow cat. He wore a kilt, as well, a smaller version of Graeme's. "I see ye've noticed," he said, putting his hands on his hips. "I look very fine."

"Yes, you do. Quite handsome. You may well catch some lass's eye."

At that he frowned, stalking forward. "I dunnae want to catch a lass's eye. I'm too young. And the Lion's Den is a hoose of bachelors."

And would apparently remain so, in part because she was an idiot and hadn't somehow seen that she could enjoy a future with Graeme back when he'd first demanded that she wed him. He hadn't mentioned marriage since, of course, or love at all, but he had said he wanted her to stay. Here, in the middle of nowhere. How could she call this an improvement over civilized, sophisticated London?

". . . amnae a heathen, Mrs. Giswell," the boy was saying. "I washed behind my ears just this morning. Graeme said we must look shiny fer all the folk who come so far to see us."

"Shiny, hm?" the companion repeated skeptically.

"Your clan will be very proud of you, Connell," Marjorie interrupted, before Mrs. Giswell and her narrow definition of proper appearance and behavior could hurt the boy's feelings.

"Thank ye, Ree. And now ye're to come with me. Graeme said to fetch ye to see the lads march up the hill, all in the Maxwell tartan and with bagpipes."

Graeme had thought of her? Her heart lifted a little, as silly as it was. Barbarian or not, he'd said he liked and admired her. That meant something to her, whether it should have signified or not. As for how she felt about him—she couldn't even decide whether to face north or south. All the rest was too much, too unexpected, and too far removed from a lifetime of dreams for her to make any sense of it or her feelings at all.

"It was nice of Graeme to think of me," she said aloud,

trying not to linger over his name. "I know he has a great many things on his mind today."

"Aye. He told me to stay close by ye and watch over ye, because he couldnae take the time to do it."

Oh. "Well, of course not," she said briskly as those few words sent her world tumbling down around her again. "Lead the way."

A lady didn't show an excess of excitement or distress. A lady did not weep in public, even if her heart had just been broken into tiny fragments. A lady always maintained her composure, because in crisis others would look to her for clues as to their own behavior.

How long had those words guided her life? A decade? More? She could scarcely remember a time when she didn't recite various versions to herself, mostly to reassure her that she'd behaved properly in the face of some challenge or other.

Today, though, as she descended the stairs and walked outside in the gown she'd chosen because she thought Graeme would like seeing her in it, the words felt hollow. She smiled as a large group of women hurried past them toward the meadow, receiving excited grins and waves in return. On the inside, though, she wanted to race back to the house and throw herself on her bed to weep.

She'd met someone whose attention and companionship she genuinely enjoyed, someone hard and wild and at the same time gentle and intuitive. And because she'd dared to keep hold of her own plans and he, his, he'd evidently decided he was finished with her. As if his opinion was the only one, and the correct one. As if the nearly empty Highlands had more to offer her than a whirlwind life in London.

And what had he offered her as an incentive to stay, anyway? An admission that he liked her against his will? A suggestion that he liked her, but meant never to love

her? Given the fact that she was still being kept there
because he'd commanded that she not be allowed to leave,
she supposed she should expect to be shackled to the bed
again the next time he disagreed with something she said.

Ha. Oh, being angry was a great deal more pleasant
than feeling sorry for herself. Graeme could try to avoid
her, but the next time they crossed paths she had several
choice things to say to him, impossible, arrogant man.

Chapter Fourteen

E asily more than two hundred men, women, and
children gathered in the meadow, more people than
Marjorie had seen in one place since she'd left London.
They all faced the same direction, toward the scattering
of boulders and birch and oak and aspen at the far end of
the green space.

At the distant, thready wail of a single bagpipe, Connell clutched her hand and squeezed, his face a vision of
tense excitement. "This is it," he whispered, practically
shaking.

A second and a third bagpipe joined in, raucous and
discordant, until abruptly the three twined together in a
strong, fast-tempoed harmony. Male voices yelled something in Scots Gaelic—a deep, primal roar that made the
hairs on the back of her neck lift.

Then the deep rumble of drums joined the pipes, a slow,
low thud that seemed to match the beat of her heart and
resonate in her chest. Through the light fog hanging between the trees, a figure emerged, followed by a second
and a third and then a dozen, then more. Goose bumps
lifted on her arms at the sight of fifty men dressed in red,

black, and green plaid kilts marching forward, heavy-looking broadswords in hand.

The big man in the lead raised his sword over his head, and that roar sounded again. Long red-brown hair lifted in the breeze, gray eyes challenging the crowd. Graeme Maxton. In his full kilt, draped across his chest and over one shoulder and down to his knees, accelerating into a trot with warriors following behind him, he looked like an ancient Celtic god.

The gathered crowd, Connell included, answered the challenge, and as the two groups met the warriors jabbed their swords into the ground to be greeted with cheers and handshakes and hugs and sloshing mugs of beer and ale.

She had no idea what it meant or symbolized, but it looked magnificent. Before she could ask Connell, he dragged her forward into the crowd. "Come on! We have to greet Graeme!"

Someone handed her a mug, and she drank a generous swallow as they made their way forward. If she was to greet Graeme as a lady should, a quantity of beer would be vital.

"My L . . . Ree," Mrs. Giswell chastised from somewhere behind her.

Marjorie took another drink. "When in Rome, Aunt Hortensia," she said over her shoulder.

She turned forward again—and nearly slammed into Graeme's broad chest. He looked down at her, his jaw clenched. "Miss Giswell."

Now she felt like a green schoolgirl all over again, facing a popular Adonis and with no idea what to say. She gulped down more beer. "Is this a commemoration of a particular battle?"

"Aye. Bannockburn. Our clan marched with Robert the Bruce and helped rout Edward the Second."

"Sent him fleeing back to England," Connell piped in, "his damned tail between his legs!"

That elicited another cheer, and Connell pumped his fist at the sky. Stifling a smile, Graeme glanced at her then quickly away, before he hefted his brother up to sit on his shoulders. "Bannockburn!" he bellowed.

"Bannockburn! Robert the Bruce!"

In a second the Maxton brothers had moved past her to mingle with the rest of the crowd.

"They're celebrating the victory of a clan that finds them disgraceful," a low drawl came from directly behind her.

Her spine stiffened. Turning, she pasted on her best, most ladylike smile. "Sir Hamish."

The Duke of Dunncraigh's close friend and chieftain gazed down at her. Even if she hadn't known how much trouble he could mean for her, she wouldn't have liked him. He dressed more English than anyone else she'd met here, but something about him made her skin crawl.

"Miss Giswell. This is yer first Scottish fair, I assume?"

"Yes, it is. If you're about to offer to show me about, I would prefer that my guide be less cynical about the gathering."

He narrowed one steel-gray eye. "The truth isnae cynical. It's naught but the truth."

She needed to keep her mouth shut. A lady didn't argue, and particularly not with someone who seemed intent on beginning trouble. If Graeme were forced to step down as clan chieftain here, Hamish Paulk would step in, and his own power and influence would increase as a result. He wanted Graeme gone. And Marjorie was very conscious that she could be the means by which it happened.

"No response to that? Then walk with me, lass."

Marjorie reluctantly wrapped her fingers around the

forearm he offered her. She was a tutor, a governess. She didn't rebuff men who outranked her. "Since you persist, I have to assume you have some information you want to impart to me. Or you're attempting to discomfit me for some reason," she went on conversationally. It wasn't a rebuff, but she didn't have to be cowed by him, either.

"Ye're an uppity lass, I see," he said, leading her to where a half-dozen ladies sat beneath a canopy kneading freshly dyed wool yarn. "My niece is an uppity lass, too. It got her betrothed to a damned Sassenach duke, but it also got her booted oot of clan Maxwell on her arse. Her and a thousand of her kin."

She nearly stumbled, and covered by bending down to adjust her newly repaired shoe. From what Graeme had told her about Gabriel's war with Dunncraigh, the niece in question had to be Fiona Blackstock, her brother's betrothed. And this man was her uncle—and therefore soon to be an in-law of the Forresters. Of hers.

"Does the Duke of Dunncraigh often banish members of his own clan?" she asked. "How many could he possibly have remaining?"

"More than enough to teach that Sassenach *and* damned Maxton a lesson or two aboot humility and their proper place in the world. And ye can tell him I said that."

For a horrifying second she thought he meant she could inform Gabriel, and that he'd figured out who she was. In the next moment she realized he meant her supposed employer, Graeme. "I'm certain that's none of my affair," she offered as smoothly as she could. "I'm only here to tutor Connell, and the other two as needed."

A young lady about Brendan's age approached to give her a shy smile and Sir Hamish a nervous, rough curtsy. "M'laird. And ye're Miss Ree, aye? Is it true ye've come all the way from London?"

"It is," Marjorie answered. This could be a tricky conversation. With Hamish standing there, she would have to be doubly careful about revealing her life in England.

"Have ye ever seen Prince George? The Regent, I mean?"

"The woman who employed me once sent me for fresh daisies. His coach drove right past me, stopped, and then a pale, plump hand stuck out the window. 'A flower from a flower,' a lisping voice said."

The girl put both hands to her mouth, her brown eyes wide. "What in the world did ye do?"

"I removed a flower from the bouquet, put it in his hand, and curtsied. I never did see his face." For once she felt gratified to have been a lady's companion. At least it made her present, faux employment seem plausible, and she could share a tale here that she never would have dared repeat in London. Not when she'd been doing everything possible to forget every bit of her life before the last three months.

"Och, I'd have fainted dead away!" the girl exclaimed. "I'm Isobel. Isobel Allen. Ye must come meet my ma and my sister. They'll nae believe that ye gave a flower to Prince George!"

Smiling and supremely grateful, Marjorie released Sir Hamish's arm and took young Isobel's. "If you'll excuse me, sir. I know you have more important things to do than show a child's tutor about the fair. Thank you for your indulgence."

"Oh, I'll show ye aboot," Isobel took up, giggling as she waved at a gathering of young misses. "But ye'll have to talk aboot London until yer tongue falls oot."

If there was one thing she did know, it was London. "I would consider that a fair trade," she returned, chuckling.

Over the next few hours she was fairly certain she met every single cotter, fisherman, farmer, drover, and shepherd—and their families—for five miles around.

People kept putting food and drink in her hands, and she even spied Mrs. Giswell dancing a reel with Robert Polk to the exuberant sounds of fiddles, fifes, drums, and bagpipes. She received dinner invitations to a dozen houses, and one marriage proposal from a very inebriated shepherd everyone called Goat. She cheered the foot races, laughed and applauded for the pie eating and an impromptu caber toss some of the men set up close by the river.

As Isobel hurried off to congratulate her mother for baking prize-winning shortbread, Marjorie turned around to find Brendan Maxton behind her. "Brendan," she said, inclining her head. If he'd decided to announce to all and sundry who she truly was, she didn't think he could have picked a better—or worse for her—moment.

He narrowed one eye, cocking his head. "I saw ye making Isobel Allen laugh. She doesnae laugh when I'm aboot her. What did ye say?"

Goodness. From his hard, wary expression he was waiting for her to tease him. At this moment she couldn't think of a worse thing to do. "She seems to enjoy stories," she said slowly, considering. "But I would recommend that you not cast yourself as the hero. Perhaps tell her about how Honker the goose had you all running about a few days ago and you ended up tangled in twine. And then congratulate her on her mother's baking ribbon. Then you might even ask if she's thought about entering any of the competitions."

"Ye'd best nae be bamming me," he muttered.

"I'm not. Try it. What have you to lose?"

It was more likely *she* would have something to lose if he failed to impress, but she wasn't about to mention that if he wasn't. The sixteen-year-old nodded and backed a half step away from her before turning on his heel and walking away.

That felt like a fairly earth-shaking conversation, and

her first thought was that she wanted to tell Graeme about it. In the next heartbeat she remembered that he didn't wish to speak with her. Immediately the day seemed less bright, the wind colder, and the conversations with people who actually seemed pleased to make her acquaintance, less . . . joyous. Stupid, stubborn man.

"What was that aboot?" the stupid, stubborn man himself asked in a low voice just to her left.

"Oh, are we speaking now?" she returned sotto voce, keeping her gaze on the group of young, unmarried people practicing making marriage knots and laughing over the degrees in difficulty of untying them again.

"Dunnae push me, Marjorie. What did Brendan say to ye? Ye lied the last time, but this isnae just aboot ye, ye ken."

"Don't push you?" she repeated, a day's, a lifetime's worth of frustration and disappointment bubbling over. "Where were you when Hamish Paulk decided to show me about the fair? I thought his presence here was the entire reason it wouldn't be safe for me to leave. Was *that* a lie? Because you wanted me to stay and didn't have the spleen to tell me so until this morning? And then you stomped off because I won't give up my own plans?"

Silence, though she could practically feel the heat and anger radiating from him. "Aye," he finally growled. "Ye have every damned thing figured oot. Except fer yerself. Now. Did Brendan threaten ye?"

Just the way he pronounced every word spoke of fury. Putting her hands behind her back and clenching them together, she turned to face him. The icy steel of his gaze made him seem an utter stranger, not the man with whom she'd shared a bed for the last few, best, nights of her life.

"No," she stated between clenched teeth. "He did not threaten me. He asked me for advice, which I gave him." Marjorie stalked closer so she could lower her voice still further. "And why didn't you tell me that Hamish Paulk is the uncle of my brother's betrothed?"

A muscle in his jaw jumped. "Because I didnae want ye thinking he's anyone ye could trust. He isnae. He turned his back on his own niece in exchange fer Dunncraigh's table scraps."

For a long moment she held his angry gaze. "Well?" she finally asked, tapping her foot against the ground. "Do we stand here glowering at each other till moonrise, or are you going to apologize to me?"

Both of his brows lifted. "I'm nae apologizing to ye, Marjorie. I told ye how I felt, and ye stomped all over it."

The nerve! "You told me that you wanted me to stay. That's all. That doesn't say anything about how you feel. For all I know, you want me here because Connell does need a tutor, and the rest of you Maxtons need to learn some damned manners. Well, I am *not* a tutor, and I am *not* a governess, and I am *not* a lady's companion. Not any more, and never again."

"I havenae said ye were."

"You never say anything I want to hear." She could feel tears burning at the corner of her eyes, but she was not going to cry in front of him. Not for all the tea in China. "Now go away and be your clan's chieftain."

What the devil did that mean? *He never said anything she wanted to hear?* For God's sake, he'd told her the decision he'd made not to allow any lass a piece of his heart, and that she'd taken one anyway. Not in those words, but he didn't know how anyone could interpret it differently. He'd asked her to stay, when he'd determined that no lass would be sharing his life. If that didn't qualify as him telling her how he felt, he had no idea what did.

Graeme tangled with it, argued silently with it, all through the evening's bonfire and the carving of faces in gourds and vegetables to ward off evil spirits. The lads and lasses lit the candle stubs set inside the hollowed-out lanterns, leaving unsettling sets of yellow eyes glowing all around the meadow. If he'd been the superstitious sort he might think the eyes were all looking at him, accusing him of doing whatever the hell she'd said he'd done.

Sassenach women. Of course he knew better than to tangle himself up with one. In a sense, though, that had been part of the problem. He'd figured his attraction to Marjorie Forrester was lust. Lucifer knew he didn't have anything in common with her, or even much sympathy to begin with. And then with her sharp wit and her defiant spirit, her calm presence and kindness to Connell and the lads, she'd crept beneath his skin before he'd even been aware of it.

A small hand grabbed his. "They're hanging apples on strings. Can I try to catch one?"

Ruffling Connell's hair, Graeme shook his head. "Ye're nae old enough."

"If I stood on a chair, I could reach."

"Aye, but whoever snags the first apple will be the next one to marry. Do ye have a lass in mind?"

The eight-year-old made a face. "Brendan says he's going to do it, and he only just kissed Isobel Allen an hour ago."

Well, that straightened his spine. "How do ye know Brendan kissed Isobel?"

"Because I thought they were going to look fer rabbits and I followed 'em," the boy said matter-of-factly.

One kiss, and the lad was ready to catch an apple. Whatever Marjorie had advised the sixteen-year-old, he doubted she'd suggested marriage. But something had happened, because while Brendan pining after Isobel Allen was nothing new, her being impressed enough with him to grant him a kiss was.

He walked over to where most of the young people had gathered. Technically he supposed that at twenty-eight he could be considered one of them, but it seemed like a very long time ago in both age and distance since he'd nervously tried to bite an apple and then been supremely relieved when he hadn't managed it. And then, after the deaths of Deirdre and Brian Maxton, he'd never done it again. On purpose.

Brendan stood close by Isobel, which wouldn't make a conversation with his volatile brother any easier. Graeme draped an arm across the lad's shoulder. "After an apple, are ye?" he murmured under his breath.

"I told Isobel I mean to try," Brendan whispered back. "But nae, I dunnae mean to catch one. I cannae be a married man before I can manage to sprout enough chin hairs to need a razor."

That was damned unexpected, and refreshing. "Have fun, then. I think ye'll impress her just by stepping forward."

"Aye." He squared his shoulders and stepped forward out of Graeme's grasp. "I'm next, I reckon."

Some teasing and laughter followed that announcement, but to Brendan's credit he managed a grin before he had apples bouncing off his nose, mouth, chin, and one ear. He actually made it look like a decent effort before the unofficial timekeeper called him to step back.

"I'd have a time explaining a black eye from that," he said, chuckling as he returned to where Graeme and Isobel stood.

Considerably relieved despite the lad's assurances, Graeme watched the next few apple hunters before he slung Connell over his shoulder to go watch the bagpipe competition. He was halfway there when his brother nearly kicked him in the back of the head. "Wait. I want to watch Ree catch an apple!"

Graeme swung around so quickly he nearly flung Connell to the ground. The boy yelped, grabbing onto Graeme's head and obscuring one eye as he spied Marjorie stepping into the jungle of hanging apples. With her hands clasped firmly behind her back and an amused grin on her face, she went after a fat apple tied toward one end of the overhanging branch.

From the laughs and encouragement around her, she'd charmed his tenants as thoroughly as she'd charmed him. He wondered if she realized that—until his mind froze at the sound of an apple's juicy crunch.

"The first apple!" Connell yelled, his cheer echoed around the meadow.

The lass likely had no idea she'd done anything more than caught hold of the Samhain fair's first apple. And as he gazed at her accepting more cheers and congratulations, he knew the exact moment someone told her. Her fair skin darkened, her hands folded in front of her as if she was trying to protect herself, and her bright blue gaze darted about until she spied him.

She didn't look away. What the hell did that mean, though? Defiance? Reminding him that she'd definitively turned him down already? Daring him to make some comment about the abysmal odds of her finding someone lofty enough in London to be worthy of her hand? Or did she wish for a single, mad moment that he wasn't bound to the Highlands and she, to London Society? That was what *he'd* been wishing for the past week.

But she was a damned stubborn lass, and until she realized on her own that the dream she'd had for her life was just that, he and his ramshackle life didn't stand a chance with her. Graeme frowned. He'd kept his house and his family and his clan together for the past eight years on little more than willpower and sweat.

If he stopped bellowing at her for being pigheaded and

instead demonstrated what Garaidh nan Leòmhann offered, what he offered . . . It would be a damned sight better than watching her leave to return to a life he knew she found miserable. To a life she could hope to have until her dying day and never find—because it didn't exist. Not for her.

He slept alone that night for the first time in a week, and he didn't like it one damned bit. Not that he did much sleeping—Marjorie Forrester had claimed the first apple of winter. That meant she would be the next to marry. And if he had any say in the matter, she would be marrying him. And this time he would ask, and she would say aye.

The best part of coming to that conclusion was that completely aside from the fact that he wanted it, this marriage was something he could justify. He'd already justified it to himself, when all that mattered was what she owned, and not who she was. She'd grown up with an income as limited as his own. Now, and thanks to the generosity of her brother, she commanded nearly unlimited funds. A marriage to Marjorie would allow him to accomplish unfathomable good for his tenants and his village, his brothers, the Lion's Den, and his small corner of clan Maxwell, even if he'd decided not to wield her as a weapon against Dunncraigh.

When Ross came to wake him before dawn he'd already risen and dressed. Breakfast could wait, because he needed to return before Marjorie rose. Padding barefoot to the stairs, his boots in his hand, he stilled when a door at the opposite end of the hallway opened. It was likely Connell, and that could create some complications; he didn't want to explain what he was about, and if he did, the bairn would blab about it to everyone, including Marjorie.

A big, bearded shadow approached, work boots in one hand. *Well, fancy that.* He and the blacksmith nodded silently to each other, slipped quietly down the stairs, and sat side by side on the bottommost step to pull on their boots.

"Laird Maxton," the smith grunted, and opened the front door to head out on foot toward the road and Sheiling two miles distant.

"Rob." Graeme shut the door and walked up to the stable for Clootie.

"Ye certain ye dunnae want company?" Johnny asked, as he handed over the gray gelding's reins.

"Nae. I will take that tin bucket over there, if ye dunnae mind."

"The—Nae. Of course I dunnae mind." The groom retrieved it for him.

"Thank ye. I'll be heading upriver a mile or two, if someone needs desperately to find me."

In an hour or so workmen and villagers would be swarming over the meadow to remove canopies and planking and the remaining gourd and vegetable lanterns, but for now the hollow faces and dark, empty eyes continued staring at him as he trotted past.

It occurred to him that he needed to visit the village today, and that he also needed to begin his visits to all the outlying cottages to be sure every family had what they required to survive the winter. The Duke of Dunncraigh espoused that a family needed to be responsible for its own well-being, but that was something else about which he and the Maxwell disagreed.

Today, though, this morning, was about him and a lass. The rest of the world could wait its damned turn.

Marjorie took a last glance at the pretty rose-colored gown she'd worn yesterday, then closed the door on the small wardrobe. The contents had increased, at least; between Mrs. Giswell and herself she'd added five gowns to the selection, plus the few from her recovered trunk she'd deemed suitable for the setting and her faux position in the household. It was nothing compared to the shopping spree she'd embarked upon after moving into Leeds House, but it did remind her of how little she actually needed of what she now owned.

Today she wore a heavier brown and mauve gown with a gray pelisse. Those deep, rich colors seemed made for Scotland winters, and she smiled as she took a turn in front of the dressing mirror. Whether she and Graeme were speaking or not, at least she looked composed.

Mrs. Giswell reached the top of the landing just as she did. That wasn't surprising; they'd both stayed out of doors late into the night to watch the festivities. What surprised her was the wide smile on her companion's generally stoic face.

"You're in a pleasant mood this morning," she noted, leading the way down to the main floor.

"The fair was quite invigorating," her faux aunt replied. "And I imbibed a little more of the spiced rum than I should have, strictly speaking. You did say 'when in Rome,' however."

"So I did." Mrs. Giswell hadn't been the only one to overindulge, either. For heaven's sake, how was she to know that biting an apple could be so significant to the Highlanders? She'd wanted to sink into the ground from embarrassment. They'd all laughed and cheered for her, though, and no one had seemed affronted or angry at her stepping into the middle of their traditions.

"Oh, I nearly forgot," the older woman exclaimed, as they reached the foyer. "I spoke to Ranald, the owner of the Cracked Hearth, last night. He said my boys—by which I assume he meant Stevens and Wolstanton—were following my instructions and staying close by the inn."

"Your instructions?"

"Yes. Evidently I left them a note the night I vanished,

saying I'd gone on to Lattimer Castle, and that they were to remain there until I sent for them."

That would have been Graeme's doing, then. In all honesty, over the past days she'd completely forgotten about her coachman and driver. "Well, it's done, at least. And I can't fault Graeme—I don't want to see any harm befall Connell or the other boys. In fact, I'll write Stevens myself and ask that they cover the Lattimer coat of arms on the coach doors."

"I asked Ranald to do it nearly a fortnight ago," Graeme said, as he emerged into the foyer from the direction of the kitchen.

Her spine stiffened and her fingers clenched, her body wanting to fling itself into his arms, while her mind bellowed that the more distance between the two of them, the better it would be for her. "Well," she said aloud, "it's been seen to, then. Good."

He nodded, no sign of last night's anger on his lean face. "Aye. Are ye going in to breakfast? I've a few people to see, so I'll be oot fer a few hours."

"You don't need to report your whereabouts to me," she returned. "I said we'd remain here until Sir Hamish departs, and so we will."

"Then I'll see ye later." Without another word he headed up the hallway toward his office, entered, and closed the door behind him.

"So you are on the outs," Mrs. Giswell noted, moving into the lead. "I thought there was a chill in the air yesterday, but now I'm certain of it."

"I don't wish to discuss it."

"And *that* is how a lady puts a stop to an innapropriate conversation. I shall desist."

Wonderful. She'd finally mastered the art of being appropriately rude. Perhaps that was the key to success in London—to be direct, rude, and dismissive. Being friendly and hopeful certainly hadn't achieved anything. Not in London, anyway. Yesterday, in this small corner of the Highlands, she'd been appreciated, welcomed, and accepted, all with nothing for her to offer in return but a smile. Of course she'd lied about who she was, but she had the distinct impression that she cared more about that than they did.

"Who are ye going to marry?" Connell demanded, as she entered the breakfast room. All three of Graeme's brothers were there, in fact, the youngest one excited and the other two looking supremely amused. At her, no doubt.

"Why you, of course," she returned, swooping in to clasp his hand. "I must marry the first man who asks me."

"I didnae ask ye, and I'm nae a man," he exclaimed, pulling his fingers free. "I'm a bairn and a duckling."

"Oh, dear!" She put both hands to her cheeks. "Then I suppose I shan't marry anyone—because no one bothered to tell me what catching the first apple meant!" She kissed him on the cheek.

He wiped the kiss away with a grimace. "I was hoping ye were bamming me. I've had my eye on Jenny Moss fer some time now, anyway."

Brendan let out a shout of laughter, the first time she'd ever heard him do so. "Ye ken she's twice yer age, duckling."

"Aye, but she makes a very fine rhubarb pie."

"That's good enough fer me," Dùghlas put in, chuckling as well.

After Marjorie selected her breakfast she headed for the chair at the opposite end of the table from Brendan. If he'd decided he didn't hate her, she meant to make an attempt not to do anything to change his mind.

"Ye can sit here, Lady Marjorie," he said unexpectedly, indicating the chair to his right. "Ree, I mean. I've been thinking I might owe ye an apology."

"'Might'?" Dùghlas echoed. "This entire da—blasted mess is yer doing."

"I've been thinking about that," Marjorie interrupted, before they could begin quarreling, and took the seat beside the sixteen-year-old. "I was quite angry at first. But at the same time, I got to meet all of you, when I wouldn't have otherwise. And about that, I cannot be angry."

"You could still be angry aboot Brendan," Connell suggested. "He's only happy this morning because he finally got to kiss Isobel Allen."

The older boy's face flushed. "How'd ye like yer head dunked in the river, duckling?"

"Ye wouldnae, because I would tell Graeme, and ye'd be—"

"Isobel seemed very happy last night, herself," Marjorie broke in. "And if anyone has the right to applaud or complain it would be her, Connell. Ladies don't like it when you say things, true or not, that could embarrass them or hurt their reputations."

"Aye," Brendan seconded. "So keep yer gobber shut."

"I . . ." The boy stood up, then collapsed into his chair again, the very image of defeated youth. "Aye." In the next heartbeat he straightened up again. "I'm going up to the meadow after breakfast, if ye want to come, Ree. Last year I found two pennies, a button, and a seashell necklace."

She could use some fresh air this morning. Anything to help her think, to help her figure out how she would leave these boys behind when the time came to go. How she would leave the master of the house even when he was acting like a complete lummox. Returning directly to London had begun to make more sense; as long as she remained in the Highlands she wouldn't be able to stop thinking about him and all the might-have-beens he left in his wake.

"Certainly," she said aloud. "I'll go up and fetch my coat in a moment, if you'll wait for me."

"Let's go now. I dunnae want someone else finding all the treasures."

Well, she wasn't terribly hungry, anyway. "Certainly. Give me two minutes."

"I'll wait fer that long, but nae any longer."

This would be good. It would distract her, and perhaps one of the workers in the meadow might have overheard Sir Hamish discussing when he might be leaving. While Connell tried to recruit Brendan and Dùghlas and even Mrs. Giswell to join in the search for accidentally dropped treasures, Marjorie stepped around two cats and a rabbit and climbed the stairs again.

Pushing open the door she headed for her wardrobe—and stopped dead.

A large bouquet of thistles, late white roses, and long fern fronds stood on the table beneath the window, a ribbon of black, green, and red plaid around the neck of the vase. "Lovely," she whispered, crossing to them as the mild spice of the roses touched her.

In her entire life no one had ever gifted her with flowers. And these were wild and lovely and unmistakably hers. She cupped a rose in her hand, inhaling again. Then, her fingers shaking a little, she picked up the folded paper leaning against the base.

She knew who they were from, of course; while she'd met several pleasant and even rather handsome men at the fair, none of them had cause to send her flowers. Of course the man of whom she was thinking had no reason to do so, either—unless he regretted something he'd said yesterday.

With the note half unfolded, she paused. She wouldn't mind an apology for his rudeness, for the things he'd said that had made her question a lifelong dream. What if, though, the flowers were an apology for the kind things he'd said? What if she was about to read that he should never have suggested that she stay in the Highlands, because of course she belonged in London? What if he was apologizing for saying he liked her?

"Just open it, you coward," she muttered to herself, took a breath, and unfolded it.

"Marjorie," she read, his writing dark and surprisingly elegant, "The other night I called you *mo boireann leòmhann*. It means 'my lioness.' I reckon if I insult you in English, the compliments should likewise be in English. You fit here, at the Lion's Den. As long as you're here, I mean to keep pointing that out to you. Eventually maybe you'll believe me. Yours, Graeme."

Marjorie sat down in her chair and read the note a second time. And a third. It wasn't an apology. In some ways it felt like a declaration of war. He knew what she intended to do, and he meant to convince her that she was wrong.

At the same time, he'd called her a lioness. *His* lioness. He'd said it to her in Gaelic nearly a week ago, and every night since then—until last night, of course. A lady wasn't supposed to be flattered at being called a wild beast. But she did feel flattered. When he said it to her, even before she knew what it meant, the words had made her feel fierce and wanton. She'd liked being in his arms, liked being in his bed. Liked the feeling of him moving inside her. She craved it, even. When she didn't want to hit him over the head with something, she craved *him*.

What he'd said, though, that she belonged here—he couldn't know that. By an extreme oddity of luck and coincidence she'd ended up here, but to say she *belonged* at a place where she'd been—was still being—held captive? That was absurd. Arrogant, and absurd. She'd trained to be a lady, and now she had the chance to live like one. But not here. The Lion's Den was not a place for a lady. No soirees, no evenings at the theater, no carriage rides through Hyde Park. No civilization. And that was what she knew—civilization.

"Are ye coming doonstairs?" Connell yelled from the direction of the foyer. "All the treasures will be gone!"

Marjorie shook herself. She couldn't yell back, because that wasn't ladylike, but she did stuff the note into her pelisse pocket, pull the old, borrowed coat out of her wardrobe, and hurry out of the room. If she was a lioness, she seemed to be a cowardly one.

Chapter Fifteen

A scattering of cotters and other workers had already arrived to begin removing canopies and benches and planking from the meadow, their efforts hindered by a light scattering of snow that had fallen overnight. While Brendan and Dùghlas divided their time between toeing the low grass for treasures and helping carry things to the waiting wagons, Connell clearly only had one thing on his mind.

He slowly trudged across the fairgrounds, bent over at the waist with his hands on his knees for balance. Marjorie wasn't about to fold over like a rheumatic old man, but she did keep her head down and crouch to further explore any promising blemish in the white-dusted grass.

"We're too late," Connell muttered as he searched. "Naught's left to find."

Carefully Marjorie pulled a shilling from her pelisse pocket, waited until no one was looking, and pitched it into a small shrubbery before moving on. When Connell approached, she made a point of looking in a different direction.

"A shilling!" the duckling exclaimed, pulling it from the

bushes and holding it high in the air. "I knew there would be someaught!"

"Well spotted, Connell," she complimented, walking over to inspect his find.

"I'm a grand finder."

"That you are," she agreed, grinning at his excitement.

Over the next hour she managed to drop another shilling and twopence, which Connell found as surely as any hound. He also discovered a broken bead bracelet, a metal hair clip and, to his great delight, a small bone-handled knife.

"Ye should have Father Michael ask after anyone missing a knife," Dùghlas suggested.

"But *I* found it."

"But whoever dropped it might need it," his brother returned. "Dunnae describe it to Father Michael, but tell him if anyone claims it, they can come here and describe it to ye. If someone does claim it, though, ye have to return it."

The boy kicked a clump of grass, sending a small spray of white into the air. "Aye. I dunnae like it, but aye."

"That's very gentlemanly of you, Connell," Marjorie said, with an appreciative nod to his brother.

"Ye're English, aye?" one of the workers, an older man with short-cropped gray hair and a bushy mustache asked her.

"I am."

"I heard there was an English lass aboot. Could ye tell me someaught?"

"I'll certainly try," Marjorie returned, smiling.

There was something about Highlanders she found refreshing. If they didn't like someone, they didn't hide it or pretend to be friendly. They asked direct questions, and expected a direct response. It was . . . pleasant to always know where she stood with both aquaintances and strangers. In fact, her only shaky ground was Graeme.

"I'm on my way north to put some windows into an old war castle. An Englishman, Lattimer, is hiring Scots builders from all across the Highlands. But I've nae worked fer an Englishman before. Do I have to bow when he passes, or nae look him in the eye? That's what I've heard."

For a moment Marjorie couldn't find her words. "You're . . . headed to Lattimer Castle?"

"Aye. It's a bit north of here. Ye've heard of it, then?"

"Yes, I have."

This man could take her away from here. She could be at Lattimer Castle before midnight. They could leave this very moment, and with the boys distracted and an ever-increasing number of men arriving in the meadow, it could be an hour or more before her absence was even noticed.

She looked across the meadow to see Graeme. He squatted on the ground beside Connell, his brown and red mane touching his brother's red hair as they bowed over the duckling's treasures. No, she didn't fit here. She shouldn't *want* to fit here. Why, then, did she spend so much of her time smiling and laughing?

"Miss?"

She shook herself. "No, you don't need to bow," she answered belatedly, "and I believe the Duke of Lattimer would appreciate being looked in the eye. Are you going to be here for a while?"

"Fer a time," he answered. "They put oot word at the Cracked Hearth fer extra hands today, and mine are willing."

"May I ask your name, sir?"

He blushed, pulling his tam from his head to twist it in his hands. "I beg yer pardon, miss. Cooper's my name. Samuel Cooper."

"I'm Ree, Mr. Cooper. Would you excuse me for just a moment?"

"Aye. Of course."

Trying not to hurry her steps or to look back over her shoulder, Marjorie returned to the house. Once inside she did run, gathering her skirt and racing upstairs to her borrowed bedchamber. Keeping in mind how little time she likely had before Mr. Cooper resumed his journey north, she pulled paper from the desk drawer and the pencil from the vase where she'd hidden it.

At her elbow her bouquet still sat, full of white roses and deep purple thistle and the soft green of the forest ferns. *Hush,* she reminded herself. She could admire them later.

"I expected to find ye stuffing yer things into a sack," Graeme said from the doorway.

Marjorie started. "You're very stealthy for such a big man," she said, not turning around. "And no, I'm not packing. I'm writing a note."

"To yer brother? So he can come and fetch ye and begin a war?"

"To my brother, yes. To begin a war, no. And since you knew Samuel Cooper was headed for Lattimer and you let him remain here anyway, I have to assume you were giving me the chance to flee."

"Look at me."

For a moment she continued scribbling. Unable to resist her curiosity or the timbre of the command, though, she turned around. "What is it? I don't know how long he intends to be here."

Graeme walked forward and knelt beside her chair, so for once he had to look up at her. He wanted to grab the pencil out of her hand, and take the letter she was writing so he could introduce it to the fireplace. But she was correct; he had known where Samuel Cooper was headed, and he was giving her a choice. Apparently she hadn't taken the one he'd expected.

"Ye're nae leaving, then?" he asked, trying to sound cynical and not like some orphan watching someone else take the last scrap of bread he would ever see.

"Sir Hamish is still residing two miles away, his gaze turned here while he waits for you to make a mistake. I told you I would stay as long as he remains here. I don't wish to aid him in any way."

She continued to make this about her word, her honor, rather than about her emotions. He wanted to shake her until she understood. Until she admitted that she did want to stay here—and not just because being at Garaidh nan Leòmhann made her happy.

And it did. He knew it did. She merely refused to see it. "If ye dunnae mean to cause harm, then show me the letter."

Without any hesitation she picked it up and handed it to him. "Add something, if you like."

Graeme turned it right-side up. "Gabriel," he read to himself, "I wanted to inform you that I am presently in the Highlands. I'm staying with a friend half a day or so from Lattimer, and I do mean to come visit you and meet your Fiona. Be assured that I'm well—though I wish you'd bothered to inform me about the tensions between you and clan Maxwell. I just barely avoided trouble. You really do need to write more. If I choose to remain here longer than another week I shall inform you. Otherwise, you should expect me then. All my love, Ree."

The last four words kept his attention for an absurd amount of time. She wrote them so easily, more easily than he ever could, and yet he wondered if she'd ever thought of those words with regard to him. He hadn't said them to her, either, but that was about his own weakness, and not hers.

Slowly he handed the letter back up to her. "I dunnae need to add anything."

"I wanted . . . I wanted someone else to know my whereabouts. So if I was to disappear, at least one person who cared would notice."

He met her deep blue eyes. "I know yer whereaboots. And I care."

Marjorie nodded, turning away as she wiped a hand across her eyes. She wanted the conversation to end there, then, before she had to talk about how she felt and what she truly wanted. He took hold of the chair and pulled it—and her—around to face him again.

"I didnae want to meet a lass who could twist me up inside. I didnae want my heart to pound or my breath to catch when a particular lass entered a room."

"Oh, stop telling me why you don't want to like me," she snapped.

Hm. "I hadnae thought aboot it that way. What I'm trying to say, Marjorie, is that I only figured on the pain of it. Until I met ye I didnae realize there would be laughter, and arguing, and quiet, and calm, and peace, and heat, and strength, and two people feeling all those things at the same time, together."

He spoke slowly, trying to fit all the pieces together as he went. It *was* like putting together a puzzle, seeing the picture, and only then realizing an entirely different puzzle lay on the backside, just as pretty and important as the first.

She wasn't still protesting, and she hadn't tried to turn away again or leave, so he went on. "I'm a man with more responsibility than I figured to have at my age, and so I'm cautious of making a mistake. But considering how I felt last night sleeping withoot ye in my arms, I think I would be making a bigger mistake if I didnae fight to keep ye here. With me."

A tear ran down her cheek and then another, but she continued to sit with her hands folded in her lap. "I never expected to meet you," she said, her voice unsteady. "I never meant, never intended, to find anyone with whom I wanted to share my life. I mean . . . who would want to? I didn't even want to."

"Marjorie, ye dunnae—"

"I do mean it," she cut in, as if she could read his thoughts. "I hated what I did, but it was the only way I could think to earn an income. I couldn't expect Gabriel to send me half his salary forever, and . . . he was a soldier. In a war. I couldn't rely on his salary continuing indefinitely. I felt awful for thinking that, but if something happened to him, it would be just me in the world. I literally have no other relations."

"I didnae realize that." Aye, he and the lads had been orphaned, but they'd had each other, Uncle Raibeart, a scattering of cousins, and atop everything else, clan Maxwell. Kin, whether or not they were family. "Ye grew up having to look after yerself."

She nodded. "It took the Crown six months to find an heir for the old Duke of Lattimer. That's how alone we were. We didn't even know." Her mouth curved in a slight, winsome smile that he wanted to kiss so badly it physically hurt to stay still. "For me," she went on, "one day out of the blue Gabriel appeared on my employer's doorstep, showed me his new signet ring, and said he was duke, of all things. I didn't even believe him at first.

"Within fifteen minutes he arrived, gave me the London house he'd just inherited, had his aide-de-camp write down his solicitor's address and send them instructions to give me whatever I wanted, and left for his new estate in the Highlands. That was nearly four months ago. I haven't seen him since."

"I dunnae like that ye were so alone, lass." It actually

made him angry. Not at her brother or anyone else in particular, but at the idea of it. At the idea that a woman as compassionate and sensitive and clever as she was had had to be so . . . self-contained.

"I'm not after your sympathy, Graeme. I do have friends. Women I met at school. They're nannies and governesses and companions and teachers now, scattered all across England." She sighed. "It sounds petty and pitiful, and I don't even know why I'm telling you this, but some of them feel that I lied to them or something because I have money now, and 'Lady' in front of my name."

Holding his breath, he took both her hands and drew her forward. She followed without protest, sinking across his thighs so he could put his arms around her. When it came to talking about herself and how hurt and frustrated and lonely she must have felt, she was more skittish than the foxes. He wanted her to understand that he was a protector—of his people, his brothers, and her if she'd allow it. Her, most of all.

"I want to belong somewhere," she went on, her voice muffled against his shoulder, her fingers twining into his coat. "I thought I had the secret password, once I owned a grand house in the middle of Mayfair and more money than I ever dreamed of. I knew what they knew: how to dance, how to chat, when to curtsy, how to dress—I didn't cheat or lie to be related to the old Duke of Lattimer. I just didn't know I was. But everyone in Mayfair thinks I'm an upjumped lady's companion and sister to an upjumped soldier. They're snobs. Mean, self-concerned, spoiled snobs."

"Then why fer God's sake do ye want to be one of them?"

A sob racked her slender frame. "It's the only . . . dream I had."

He kissed her lemon-scented hair. "*Mo boireann leòmhann,* ye need another dream. A better one. Mayhap I'm nae in it, but I'll fight to convince ye otherwise. I love ye, Marjorie. And if ye think that's easy fer *me* to say, then f—"

"I love you, Graeme," she interrupted, crying harder. "I just don't know what to do."

Graeme closed his eyes for a moment, warmed and troubled all at the same time. "I can tell ye what I want, lass, but I cannae tell ye what *ye* want. I do reckon that fer all our sakes, ye need to figure it oot soon."

She nodded against his shoulder. "I know. I will." Clearing her throat, she straightened. "Goodness. I don't think I've cried that much, ever."

"Aye, ye nearly drowned both of us."

With a damp smile she wiped at her face. "Mrs. Giswell would be very disappointed. A lady doesn't weep in front of a man unless she wishes to be thought a weak-willed watering pot."

"Who the devil are these ladies who dunnae do anything? They dunnae cry, they dunnae laugh, or get angry, or sleepy—what do they actually do, then?"

She looked him directly in the eye, her brow furrowing. "You know, I have no idea." Abruptly she gasped and pushed away from him to climb to her feet. "Samuel Cooper! I need to get him my letter."

"Write yer brother's name on it; I'll get it to Cooper." He stood beside her. "Ye sit fer a few minutes and get yer thoughts back together—unless ye care to explain to the duckling why ye've been crying."

"No, I do not." Leaning over the table, she wrote the Lattimer name and address on the outside of the folded note. She handed it to him, then rose up on her toes and placed a feather-soft kiss on his mouth.

That might well be his favorite kiss ever. He hadn't instigated it or even expected it. She'd kissed him simply because she'd wanted to—and he would never forget that moment. "I'll nae be sleeping alone tonight, lass," he murmured, smiling down at her.

With that he tucked her letter into his coat and returned to the meadow to find Marjorie's messenger. Aye, he didn't mind Lattimer knowing she was safe. Knowing where she was or coming to fetch her, though—that would mean a fight. He wasn't giving her up, even if it did mean a war.

"What the devil are they doing?" Sir Hamish Paulk reined in his horse, guiding the nervous beast in a tight circle amid the trees where they stood across the river Douchary from the Lion's Den.

Raibeart Maxton looked from his guest to his nephews spread across the meadow. "Young Connell likes to look fer treasures after a gathering."

"The castoffs of cotters and shepherds? In front of the men taking doon tents? Yer nephew doesnae know how to run a household, much less clan Maxwell."

After over a week of nearly continuous insults aimed at Graeme, Raibeart had become so accustomed to them he barely bothered to listen. Insulting the young lad, though, seemed both mean-spirited and pointless. "The bairn's but eight years old, Hamish. I've yet to meet any young lad who doesnae dream of finding treasure."

"The . . ." The Maxwell chieftain trailed off. "Did ye see that? Miss Giswell tossed a coin into the grass fer the boy to find."

"Nae, I didnae. That was kind of her."

"Aye. But where did Maxton find a well-educated English lass to tutor his brothers? And how did he afford to bring her up here? And how is he paying her enough that she can toss coins into the grass? Ye mark my words, Raibeart. Someaught's afoot here."

"If ye care to hear my opinion, Hamish, Graeme's done

as well as anyone could here. The Maxtons have always had more spleen than money, and he works with his own hands to support his cotters."

"They're nae his cotters. They're Dunncraigh's. That's what ye Maxtons keep fergetting."

"Ye need a new song to sing, my friend. This is a small corner of clan Maxwell, and one that the lot of ye, except fer Graeme, mostly ignore. Let it be. Let him be."

Hamish edged his mount forward a little. "What's this? The Sassenach looks like she's aboot to kiss that old lad." He chuckled. "If she's after a proper Highlander mayhap I should ride doon there and give her one."

"Dunnae be crude. If she can tame those lads some, she has my respect. And my gratitude. Now let's get back. I told ye the river here's too swift fer fishing."

"In a damned minute." He leaned forward in the saddle. "So she goes back to the hoose, then Maxton does. Do ye reckon he's plowing her? I would be."

"Ye've made that clear enough. What do ye think, he's going to walk oot of the hoose carrying enemy Campbell colors or someaught? Let's go."

Instead of leaving, Hamish swung out of the saddle. "I reckon I'll go after a trout or two here, anyway. Just because ye say there's naught here, ye dunnae expect me to take yer word fer it."

"T'would be nice if ye did, aye," Raibeart grunted, dismounting to unlash his pole from the back of the saddle. "Ye might just admit ye're spying on a man fer nae good reason."

Hamish jabbed a finger at him. "Dunnae ye try to tell *me* what's nae good reason," he growled. "I had my own niece at Lattimer, and trusted her to keep an eye on that Sassenach. We lost over a thousand of our clan because I trusted that damned female. And now she's marrying him.

I'll be keeping an eye on everything myself from now on, thank ye very much."

Raibeart blew out his breath. "I willnae comment, then, that what truly irks ye is that Fiona's aboot to be a duchess, *Sir* Hamish."

"Aye, ye'd best nae say such a damned idiotic thing. And . . ."

Paulk trailed off again. Beginning to wish, and not for the first time, that he hadn't bragged about the trout fishing on Loch Achall, Raibeart followed his friend's gaze. On the other side of the river Graeme approached the gray-haired stranger with whom Miss Giswell had spoken so intently earlier. They talked for a minute, and then Graeme handed him a folded missive and what looked like a five-pound note.

Five quid was a damned fortune for that boy. What the devil was he doing, giving it away with a handshake? As soon as the two men parted, the older one left the meadow to head up the road toward the old bridge and Sheiling beyond.

When Raibeart turned around, Hamish had already returned his fishing pole to his saddle. "Ye can stay or go back if ye choose, but I mean to find oot what in that letter is worth five pounds." He snorted. "Spying fer nae good reason, my damned arse."

They reached the bridge first, and had to wait a good half hour before the old man appeared. "Well met," Hamish said, sending his gelding in a circle around the man and his formidable mustache. "From yer tartan I make ye oot to be clan Stewart. What brings ye into Maxwell territory?"

"Work. I'm a builder. And I've the afternoon mail coach to catch, if it pleases ye."

"It'll please me more if ye let me have a look at the paper Graeme, Laird Maxton, handed ye."

The man's friendly, open expression closed down. "Whoever ye are, I was paid to deliver a letter. I aim to do it."

"I'll pay ye more fer a look at it."

Lately low-voiced tendrils of whispers had begun to spread that Hamish might have had something to do with the disappearance of his own nephew, Fiona Blackstock's brother, four years earlier. Raibeart had never paid the tales much attention—he knew his friend's reluctance to dirty his own hands. But he also knew Hamish still burned from the loss of face he and Dunncraigh had shared at Lattimer Castle.

"Thank ye fer the kind offer, stranger," the Stewart lad returned, "but I'll have to decline."

"That wouldnae be wise, friend."

"Hamish," Raibeart broke in, "let it be."

"*Sir* Hamish," Hamish corrected, his hard gaze still on the mustached fellow. "Sir Hamish Paulk. Chieftain of clan Maxwell. And ye'll hand me that letter, or I'll drag ye behind my horse to the Duke of Dunncraigh's doorstep as a Stewart spy."

The man blanched. "I'm nae such thing!"

Hamish held out his hand, palm up. "Prove it."

His own hands shaking a little, the man pulled a folded missive from his inner coat pocket and handed it up to Hamish. "Take it, then. Just leave me be."

With a flourish and a smirk that said as much about Paulk as his bombast ever could, he unfolded the letter. As his eyes scanned the missive, his mouth opened and closed like one of the fish they'd landed. At the same time, all the color left his face.

"Hamish?" Raibeart prompted, abruptly alarmed.

"By the devil," Paulk muttered, folding the letter again. "Take it, Stewart," he said, leaning sideways to hand it back. "Deliver it. And feel free to tell the Sassenach exactly what just happened here."

With a frown the stranger placed the missive back in his pocket, tucked his coat closer around him, and hurried up the road toward Sheiling.

"What did it say?"

Hamish wheeled his mount. "And ye said to leave it be. Did ye know, ye bastard?"

"What are ye going on aboot?"

"That Sassenach lass. Miss Giswell. She's nae who she claims." The chieftain sent his gelding into a gallop, headed back for Mòriasg, Raibeart's mansion. "She's Lady Marjorie Forrester."

Forrester. "Lattimer's kin?"

"His sister. And yer nephew's harboring her. What do ye ken Dunncraigh will have to say aboot that?"

Oh, God. Raibeart could imagine it all—and it wouldn't be pleasant. "Hamish, he's my nephew. And so are the other three. Connell's but eight."

Hamish looked over at him. "If ye want to spare them, ye'd best think of someaught fast."

Raibeart looked in the direction of the Lion's Den. What the devil had Graeme been thinking? The very second Dunncraigh heard about who'd been residing beneath Graeme's roof, and that the lad had been lying about who she was, the Maxwell would see him gone from the clan. He'd become an enemy in the middle of Maxwell territory, and likely find himself burned out of his own house.

"Take her to Dunncraigh yerself," he said aloud. "This is between the Maxwell and Lattimer, anyway. Leave the lads oot of it."

Hamish slowed to a canter. "That doesnae get me this territory."

"It does make ye the man who delivered Dunncraigh the means to be rid of Lattimer. Ye said the Maxwell wanted Lattimer to sell the castle and land to him, and leave the Highlands. Ye'll have the Sassenach's sister."

Slowly Hamish nodded. "Now that's an interesting idea. And ye'll be helping me with it."

Raibeart sighed. If he didn't, it would be his nephews on the headsman's block. "Aye. I'll help ye." And God help him, the Maxton brothers, and the poor lass.

Chapter Sixteen

M arjorie let out her breath in a shivering moan. With Graeme's fingers teasing up inside her and his tongue and teeth on her breasts, she felt like a quivering twist of shivering, trembling nerves. When his hands and his mouth traded positions, she lost the ability to speak.

"Graeme," she groaned, the only word she could conjure. "Oh, Graeme."

She gripped his hair in her hands, arching her back and trying not to suffocate him between her thighs. If a lady didn't indulge her carnal desires, she was well finished with being one. Because she was not going to give this up—give him up—for anything.

As she began to think she might faint from pure pleasure, he slid up her body, pausing to lick a sensitive nipple, and kissed her with an openmouthed growl. At the same moment he slid warm and hard inside her, and her fingers dug spasmodically into his shoulders. He'd said she no longer had to be alone. It was just words, hopeful words, until moments like this.

They were two people, but at the same time they were one, mingled breath, mingled sweat, no space between where she ended and he began. Even their hearts had the same fast rhythm. With every deep thrust she groaned, holding his gaze, watching to see the exquisite moment he climaxed inside her. She could feel it, feel both of them, rushing, quickening, rising, until with a deep groan he let loose, and she shook and shattered around him in response.

"Fer God's sake, lass," he murmured, lowering his forehead against hers. "Ye undo me."

She grinned breathlessly. "I'm undone, myself."

Graeme kissed her again, this time achingly gentle. "I love ye, lass, *mo boireann leòmhann*."

"I love you," she returned. They were words she'd never expected to say, and every time she uttered them, *she* felt stronger.

"I've been thinking," he said, shifting onto his back and pulling her over on top of him. "Ye ken what this hoose needs?"

"A new roof? Fresh paint?" she suggested, chuckling.

"A dog."

Marjorie snorted. "That should go well with the foxes, cats, rabbits, and the goose."

"It'll have to be a pup. By the time he grows up he'll reckon all this is normal."

She twisted her head to look at him. "You're serious, then."

"Aye."

"If I'm staying here, the dog has to be female. I'm outnumbered enough as it is."

His arms tightened around her, and he kissed her ear. "Oh, ye're staying. I still have that shackle, and I'm nae afraid to use it."

"Yes, I'm aware of that." If she *did* stay, as she wanted to, more badly with each passing hour and every time she thought about never having to return to London and those unkind, resentful gazes—she required one more thing from him. But while her comportment lessons had discussed flirtations and making oneself appealing to men, she had no idea how to suggest to a man—to this man in particular—that he needed to ask her to marry him. *Ask* her. Not demand or bellow at her. And since that mess had already happened and she'd turned him down, how was she to let him know that she might be much more amenable this time?

Now that she knew him, she would be happy to see her money going to improving the lives of his family and his tenants. But after endless lessons on ladylike behavior, she couldn't continue breaking the primary rule. Good heavens, what if she became pregnant? They'd certainly been having enough sex to make that plausible, if not probable.

"So, a dog—a bitch—it is, then."

Young footsteps and the quick click of fox feet rumbled by and down the stairs. Marjorie sat up and slid from the warm, comfortable bed. "Yes, of course," she said, knowing she sounded a bit brusque and not particularly caring. "First things first."

He sat up as well, the blankets falling deliciously past his waist. "Are we arguing aboot someaught again? I'm naked, so I reckon it's time fer a fight."

"That depends on your list of things you wish to do here." She pulled on her night rail. "I need to go get dressed before Connell comes back upstairs."

"I'm nae going to stomp after ye again, so come here."

So now he thought he could order her about. Narrowing her eyes, she started for the door. They did seem to end their rather excellent evenings and mornings with him naked and bellowing while she walked away. With a grimace she walked back and sat on the edge of the bed.

"Ye ken I started after ye because of yer money and yer brother," he said, trailing his fingers down her wrist. "But we have managed fer three generations withoot a spare coin to pitch. A time ago I'd nae have let ye go because I didnae much care how ye felt aboot all this. Now, though, I reckon I'd be after ye no matter whose sister ye were, or what yer income might be."

"I know that. And you know I said I'm not accustomed to wealth, either, but what I have is yours."

"Aye. Then why was I talking aboot a dog, when ye were talking aboot someaught else I cannae fathom?"

"Because you're a heathen Highlander, I suppose," she said with a sigh. "The one thing you insisted on before when I refused, is the same thing you don't seem to be offering now. If you can't decipher that . . . Well, I suggest you do so." Twisting around, she kissed him. Whenever they touched, the idea of living in sin seemed less significant than her need, she supposed it was, to be with him.

She didn't slam the door, which Graeme considered to be an improvement. The lass kept her true feelings buried beneath a lifetime of logic and propriety and disappointment, but he looked forward to a lifetime of discovering all her layers.

In the meantime, and as much a heathen as he knew he was, he had no intention of adding to her disappointments. Once he could hear her rustling about in the neighboring room he slipped out of bed and dressed in the shirt and kilt that were becoming as comfortable again as they'd once been—before he'd become so disillusioned with Dunncraigh and his use of clan Maxwell to make himself wealthy.

Once he'd shaved and cleaned his teeth and made an effort to comb his hair he padded over and quietly locked his door. Then he pulled open the bottom drawer of his wardrobe, dug beneath the stack of worn trousers, and removed a small velvet bag. When he tipped it into his hand, his grandmother's ring, a lovely thing twined with silver and a trio of blue sapphires that matched Marjorie's eyes, spilled onto his palm.

A few weeks ago he'd begun to consider selling it so he could afford to retrench all the irrigation ditches and replace the wooden water gates. When the lads had delivered their prize to him, he'd figured at least one of the few heirlooms they had left would be safe. Now, though, he could use it for what it was intended—a promise to marry a lass he'd never expected to find and never meant to let go.

Of course he meant to marry her, whatever she might think. But this time it mattered how she felt. She'd spent a quiet, solitary life without expectation of love. His own life hadn't been either quiet or solitary, but he'd been adamant about not risking his heart on something as fickle as love. Both of them had a bushel of surprises ahead of them, and he looked forward to every one of them.

Once he'd replaced the ring he left his bedchamber— only to have a plump female figure jab him in the chest. "Good morning, Mrs. Giswell," he said, stepping around her and continuing on to the stairs.

"Don't you 'good morning' me, Maxton," she returned in a low voice, following on his heels. "I don't know what you think you're doing, but Lady Marjorie has a home and a life in London. She could well wed a duke or a marquis."

"Ye're nae fooling me, woman," he returned. "There's nae a blue blood in London who even looks at her."

"Not yet, but they will. It will take patience and finesse."

Graeme stopped, facing her. "I'm a viscount, ye ken. I could have made her marry me."

"Yes, so you have a pinch of morality. Huzzah for you."

"In the two or three or four years it might take fer her to buy her way into parties and maybe find a beau who needs her blunt and happens to have a loftier title than I do, what do ye reckon'll happen to her?"

"You want her money, so don't pretend you're more noble than anyone else."

"I havenae. And aye, she brings with her someaught I

find very useful. But I'm nae asking her to change who she is or prove she's whatever those damned dandies require. I looked at her and I found someaught past her purse. And I happen to find her remarkable."

"I could say the same about a horse, sir. That doesn't make it so."

"Damned Sassenach. Ye tell me how often ye saw her laugh and smile before ye came to the Highlands."

Mrs. Giswell opened her mouth, then shut it again. "I notice when she smiles, Highlander. I didn't realize you noticed, as well."

"I do. I'm a keen-eyed heathen, Hortensia Giswell, and I love that lass something fierce. So dunnae ye try to come between us unless ye're ready fer a brawl."

She backed up the hallway a step. "Her brother could still cut her off if he disapproves of you, you know."

He'd figured that out weeks ago, when he'd reckoned Lattimer would be willing to trade some blunt for his sister's good name. Now, though, it needed to be a fair fight. "I ken. I reckon we'll go up to see him in a few days, once damned Paulk slinks away. If he hears word that I'm on my way to Lattimer, that'll begin a whole different battle."

The day he shrank from a fight with Hamish Paulk would be his last day, but he wanted any conflict to be between them, and not about Marjorie. And not about his brothers. That was the one thing that continued to trouble him, in fact; while his brothers had been born into this mess of clan rivalry, he'd kept them as far from it as he could. Marjorie, though, had no experience with clan politics or how deeply anger and resentment could run.

The Highlands was a different world, and one she hadn't learned about in finishing school. Was she ready for it? She was strong, but was she strong enough?

"Well, I see I've made you stop and think, at least," Mrs. Giswell said. "And that's something. We both want the best for Lady Marjorie, evidently, but I'm not certain we agree what that is."

Aye, she'd made him think. And now he wanted to heave the stout lass over his shoulder and dump her into the river. His fingers curled. "I reckon deciding what's best fer Marjorie will be up to Marjorie."

"True enough." She sketched a shallow curtsy. "Good day, Lord Maxton."

"Go soak yer head, Mrs. Giswell."

She didn't react to that, but he could swear he heard her faint chuckle as she retreated down the hallway to her own room. She could cackle if she wanted, but she wasn't going to win.

Cowen pulled open the front door, and Brendan appeared out of the morning room to join him in the foyer. "Ye're off to the Cracked Hearth, aye?"

"Aye."

"I dunnae ken why Ewen Sturgeon's scared to come to Garaidh nan Leòmhann," his brother continued, walking beside him as Graeme approached the stable. "If he's brave enough to marry Kitty Howard, coming to get yer permission should be easy."

"There's naught wrong with Kitty Howard. She's a tall, healthy lass."

"And Ewen's thin as a rail. Maybe he's worried he'll be crushed."

Graeme chuckled. "I dunnae want to hear ye saying that anywhere in their hearing. And I reckon Ewen would've come up to the hoose if I'd asked. But he says tall buildings make him dizzy, so we agreed to meet at the inn."

"I'll come with ye."

"Ye wouldnae expect to find a certain good friend of Kitty coming along with her, would ye?"

Brendan flushed. "I might." He squinted one eye. "Ye're going to marry Lady Marjorie."

Graeme stopped just short of the stable door. "I was going to marry her all along, if ye'll recall."

"Aye, but this time ye mean to ask her proper."

"I do. If she'll have me, after all this mess. Do ye have any difficulty with that?"

His brother kicked a clod of half-frozen earth. "Is it because ye dunnae dislike her now, and she's ruined because I kidnapped her? Are ye saving her reputation?" He lowered his shoulders. "Mrs. Giswell told me I was a ruffian, going aboot ruining women by taking them from their companions."

"Have ye kidnapped any other women?" Graeme asked, trying to stifle his amusement. Perhaps Mrs. Giswell would be handy to keep about the Lion's Den.

"Nae. Dunnae be ridiculous. But is that why ye mean to marry her?"

"I mean to marry her because I love her. And I'll ask ye once more, do ye have an objection?"

"Ye'd only throw me in the river if I did, but nae. She . . . She's nae what I expected from a Sassenach."

"She's nae what I expected, either." Graeme elbowed his brother in the ribs. "But dunnae expect me to thank ye fer grabbing her. Even if it does rescue the property."

Finally Brendan grinned. "Och, ye're grateful. Ye just cannae say it."

Well, that was true enough. What Brendan didn't realize was that Marjorie had done more than give *him* love and hope; she'd also helped Brendan and brought him back to his previous good-natured self. Two miracles, wrapped up in one precious, extraordinary, remarkable female.

"I'm nae looking fer orphaned rabbit kits," Connell declared, bending to turn over a rock. "I'm looking fer orphaned mice."

Oh, dear. "Mice? What does Graeme think about you rescuing mice?"

The boy shrugged. "I havenae asked him."

"Connell, he's been very good about your menagerie. But you can't go looking for things to bring home without asking him first. It's one thing to rescue a young goose from an attack. It's another to go take an infant from its parents."

"I suppose that makes sense." Changing direction, he clambered down the slope to the edge of the river. "I can find river rocks, though."

"Of course you can. We'll use them for your arithmetic."

"At least that's better than Dùghlas using his fingers. I dunnae mind counting rocks." Straightening, he looked up at her. "Are ye going to go back to London?"

"Do you want me to?"

He shook his head. "Nae. I like ye being here. I didnae know that lasses dunnae like profanity, until ye told me." Sending her a sly look, he returned to his search. "And I think Graeme likes ye. I went to see him one morning a bit ago, and he had some of yer hair clips in his bed."

Her cheeks warmed. That would have been the morning Graeme had pushed her off the bed to hide her from Connell. "I wondered where my hair clips had gone," she said aloud.

"And he makes Mrs. Woring buy lemons, and he sent to Edinburgh for a lemon tree to put in the sunroom. I think he traded his pocket watch fer it."

She hadn't known that. No one but her brother had ever sacrificed of himself for her. It made her want to cry and to spin in a circle with her arms out all at the same time. "Perhaps we should purchase him a new pocket watch," she suggested.

"There's a shop in Sheiling. They can order anything fer ye, as long as they have the catalog."

"Excellent. Let's go tomorrow, shall we?"

"Aye. I think I can manage that."

Marjorie grinned. Whether she'd ever wished to be a governess or not, Connell Maxton was a bright, curious, warmhearted joy. "Good. I'll . . ."

The sound of horses caught her attention, and she looked across the corner of the meadow slightly above where she stood. A dozen men in Maxwell plaid trotted in her direction. That didn't seem anything too extraordinary, until she recognized the gray-haired man in the lead. Sir Hamish Paulk.

Turning her back to them, she looked down at Connell still searching for river rocks. "Connell, get behind the boulders," she said, just loudly enough for him to hear over the sound of the river. "You stay there either until I tell you it's safe, or you don't hear anything. And then you get back to the house. Do you understand?"

His light gray eyes wide, he nodded and ducked behind the trio of cow-sized boulders at the edge of the water. Once he was out of sight she wandered a few feet to her right before she turned around again. The horses stopped in a half circle around her, cutting her off from every direction but the river. She swallowed, clasping her hands behind her back.

"Gentlemen," she said, inclining her head. "You're looking for Lord Maxton, I presume? Shall we go up to the house?"

"Nae, we arenae here fer Maxton." Sir Hamish looked her up and down, making her very conscious of the fact that she wore a slightly small brown muslin and an old overcoat—not a great deal of protection against twelve very solemn-faced men.

"Then how may I help you?"

"What are ye doing oot here all by yerself?" This time it was Graeme's Uncle Raibeart who spoke.

"The foxes decided to battle the cats up and down the

stairs, and I opted for a bit of fresh air while the house settles. What brings you here, if it's not to see the viscount?"

"Why, we're here fer *ye*," Paulk took up again. "I ken ye think we're nae but empty-headed barbarians, but we're nae so easy to fool, lass. Or Lady Marjorie Forrester, rather."

Damnation. She had a choice now—she could lie even though they clearly knew the truth, or she could try to use the truth, or part of the truth, to her advantage. Marjorie took a deep breath. "Well, that's a surprise," she said, pleased at how calm she sounded. "I do hope we can come to an understanding. If Lord Maxton discovers who I am, he's not likely to be very amused."

"Graeme doesnae know who ye are?" his uncle asked sharply, his expression hopeful.

"Of course not. My coach broke down near here, and I needed a safe place to stay for a few days. If he'd discovered I was the Duke of Lattimer's sister," she returned, using her brother's title deliberately, "I would not have been welcome. This is not friendly territory for me, as you know."

"Ye're a fair liar, my lady." Hamish continued to gaze at her levelly. "I half believed ye fer at least a moment, and I even saw Maxton deliver yer letter to that Stewart lad and pay him to carry it north to Lattimer." He gestured, and half the men dismounted. "Let's get this over with before someone from the hoose comes looking fer her."

Over with? Did they mean to murder her? She would have attempted an escape into the icy river, except for the fact that that would have exposed Connell. "I've said my brother is the Duke of Lattimer. Crossing him is not a good idea. Consider carefully, gentlemen."

"Fer God's sake. Get her."

As the first man reached her she swung out with her fist, smashing it into the side of his head. Then she turned and fled upstream. Hands grabbed at her, caught her gown, and she went down hard enough to knock the air from her lungs.

She gasped, and more hands pushed her down, binding her legs together and her hands behind her back. At least this didn't seem to be a murder, she told herself, working to calm down so she could use her head. When a cloth went over her mouth she wasn't surprised, but she was furious. A woman should never be kidnapped once—much less twice.

Wherever they thought to take her—and she could guess it would be to the Duke of Dunncraigh—she had no intention of making it easy. And as soon as Graeme heard what had happened, these cowards would truly have something to fear.

Chapter Seventeen

"Are ye certain it's Isobel who's caught yer eye, Brendan?" Graeme teased, sending the innkeeper a wave as they left the building for the stableyard. "Kitty had her gaze on ye the whole time, and she's a lass who willnae blow over in a strong wind."

"Ye have it wrong, *bràthair*. She couldnae look away from *ye*."

"Mm-hm. I'm spoken fer. Ye, on the other hand, shouldnae narrow yer choices so soon. The—"

"Graeme!"

The desperation in Dùghlas's voice turned his own spine to ice. "Christ," he hissed, turning to look up the road and then sprinting forward to meet the cart horse his brother rode.

Both brothers rode, he amended, as Connell jumped to the ground and ran forward to meet him. "Graeme," he rasped, sobbing, and threw his arms around Graeme's waist.

"What's happened?" he demanded, dividing his attention between Dùghlas and the top of Connell's head.

"He saw it," Dùghlas panted, swinging to the ground

as Brendan took hold of the pony's halter. They'd ridden a cart horse bareback.

"Saw what? Duckling, if ye please." With his three brothers there, his thoughts immediately leaped to Marjorie. *Damnation*. What the devil was wrong?

Connell lifted his head, his young face pale and streaked with dirty tears. "We were looking fer river stones, and then Ree told me to hide behind the grand boulders by the fast water and nae come oot. And then I heard horses and Uncle Raibeart and Sir Hamish and they said she was Lady Marjorie and some fighting and then they rode off with her. I waited until it was quiet because that's what she said to do and then I ran so fast to the hoose and found Dùghlas and we had to ride King George withoot a saddle and he didnae like it at all but I held on, anyway."

Even with the dizzying speed of the words flying about, Graeme caught the vital part. Paulk had Marjorie, and knew who she was. "Are ye certain ye heard Uncle Raibeart?" he asked grimly.

The bairn nodded his head. "I didnae want to, but I did."

Graeme hugged him again. He would bloody well settle with Raibeart later. "Brendan, get our horses."

"Aye." The sixteen-year-old set off at a run.

"I'm sorry I didnae help," Connell sniffed, backing away to wipe his nose.

"Ye did help, Connell," Graeme returned, working to keep his attention on this moment and not on what he meant to do next. "If ye hadnae stayed put like Ree asked, I'd nae have anyone to tell me what happened."

The lad's shoulders lifted a little. "We need to rescue her."

Brendan rode up, leading Clootie behind him. "Let's go, Graeme."

"Nae," Graeme said, as firmly and calmly as he could. "*I'm* going after her."

"Gr—"

"Brendan," he interrupted, "get yer brothers back home. Send word to Boisil Fox and his brothers and sons that they're to guard the hoose, get the staff inside, and bar the doors. Ye keep everyone safe. Do ye ken?"

His next oldest brother nodded, light gray eyes as serious as Graeme had ever seen them. "I ken. Duckling, ye ride back with me. Dùghlas, ye'll have to manage King George again." He edged closer to Graeme. "Do ye want my rifle?"

Graeme shook his head. "Nae. Ye may need it. I have mine with me." He swung up on Clootie, and with a last glance at his brothers, set off northwest.

They would be headed for Dunncraigh, and he doubted they'd risk stopping first at Mòriasg, no matter how closely Raibeart had been involved. Connell hadn't said how many men had been with them, if he even knew, but in his experience Hamish did little without someone else to supply the brute force.

And these wouldn't be boys uncertain what they were about and unwilling to do any actual damage. A month ago Dunncraigh had all but ordered him to murder Gabriel Forrester. And now they had Marjorie Forrester. If someone—anyone—hurt her, Dunncraigh *would* have a murder on his hands. Just not the one he'd expected.

He would be outnumbered. That didn't concern him overly much, though—advantage went to the man who was willing to pull the trigger first. For the moment he was a clan Maxwell chieftain, and any men with Paulk would be part of clan Maxwell. That alone could give him the edge he needed.

If worst came to worst, Brendan was old enough to look after his brothers. Without Uncle Raibeart available the lad wouldn't have an easy task ahead of him, but he could do it. Graeme didn't plan on dying, but it could happen. As long as Marjorie was safe, the rest was inconsequential.

Graeme topped a hill and pulled up Clootie. His land spread out before him, rough and rocky ridges cutting through glades and valleys of deep green forest, broken by silver-glinting streams and rivers. Marjorie and her kidnappers could be anywhere, but he didn't imagine they were more than an hour in front of him, if that.

A woman, a Sassenach he'd known for just over a fortnight, had hold of his heart. No, he'd never expected it, but now he wouldn't trade it for anything. With her by his side he didn't feel the struggle of trying to stay afloat, of being a parent to his brothers, a landlord to his tenants, a soldier to his clan—and all with barely a pound to his name.

Her wealth could ease that worry, but his focus on that prize had nearly cost him the greater one. Marjorie herself, her warmth and calm and underlying fierceness, eased *him* and excited him at the same time. It occurred to him that he'd never had a partner, an equal, someone willing to take on this gargantuan burden with him, someone to share the joy and the pain.

Graeme clenched his jaw. He'd found her through the most unlikely of circumstances, and no damned opportunistic power-hungry coward was going to take her away from him. No matter the price he had to pay to get her back.

A flash of color caught his eye and vanished into the trees again. That glimpse provided him with every bit of information he needed. "Up, Clootie," he ordered, and sent the gray gelding named after the devil into a dead run.

He was willing to die for her. As the thought racketed about in his brain he nearly steered the gelding into a tree. When Brian Maxton had lost his wife, he'd shot himself. Was it the same thing? Was dying to save someone equal to dying to avoid being without her?

Unexpectedly the answer came in Marjorie's matter-of-fact tones. He wasn't giving up. He was fighting, rescuing, protecting. It wasn't the same. *He* wasn't the same man his father had been. The fact that he'd stayed on at the Lion's Den, become a father and a brother to Connell and Dùghlas and Brendan proved that.

They traveled quickly, but he knew the land better, and he moved faster. He estimated it was early afternoon when he reached the edge of a clearing just as they headed back into the trees on the far side. He pulled his rifle from its scabbard to rest it across his knees.

As they started into the next meadow he kicked Clootie in the ribs. "Paulk!" he bellowed, crossing the edge of the trees to meet them broadside.

Hamish wheeled to face him. Before he could do more than open his mouth, Graeme slammed the butt of his rifle into the chieftain's face. With a grunt Paulk fell out of the saddle and hit the ground.

Graeme aimed the rifle squarely at the short, muscular man who had a bound Marjorie facedown across his thighs. "If ye want to see another sunrise, set her doon. Gently."

His uncle edged his bay forward a little. "Graeme, I'm trying to keep ye and the lads clear of this."

Keeping the weapon and his gaze on Marjorie's captor, Graeme scowled. "I dunnae know who ye are, but ye're nae kin to me. Now, *ye* put the lass doon. I'll shoot ye in the head and do it myself if ye make me ask ye again."

"Graeme, ye'll be starting a war," Raibeart pleaded.

"Ye already did that when ye stole my woman from me," he snapped. "The only question ye need to ponder is whether ye want to leave this meadow alive or nae."

"Ye cannae shoot us all, Maxton," one of the other men grunted.

In one quick move Graeme pulled the sharp *sgian dubh* from the top of his boot and hurled it into the man's shoulder. "Any other idiotic thing to say?" he asked, as the rider doubled over. "I'm nae jesting!"

His uncle took an audible breath. "Nae a man dies here today, lads. Give him the Sassenach."

Slowly the muscular man lowered Marjorie's feet to the ground. "Move back," Graeme ordered, urging Clootie closer and then hopping to the ground, his rifle still lifted. Swiftly he pulled a second knife from his waist, crouched, and cut the rope binding her feet and her hands.

Immediately she pulled the gag from her mouth. Clever lass, she took the knife from his hand and faced the tight group of Maxwell men. His clan, until today. Graeme swung back into the saddle, kicked his foot out of the stirrup, and held down his free hand. "Behind me," he said.

Marjorie took his hand and stepped up, settling behind the saddle with her arms around his waist. When she seemed secure Graeme toed Clootie again and the gray gelding backed slowly.

"This willnae end here, lad," Raibeart said, his tone glum and pleading. "Dunncraigh wants to be rid of Lattimer. She's the way to do it."

"Ye know where to find me, then. I'll be waiting."

As he turned for the trees Sir Hamish sat up, groaning and with blood dripping from his mouth and nose. Graeme shifted a little and kicked him in the face as they rode by.

"The lot of ye, get off my land. And take this pile of shite with ye."

They broke into a canter once they reached the trees, and kept up the pace until Graeme was certain they were well away. Marjorie had never ridden double, and her wrists hurt, but with her arms around Graeme's waist and her cheek resting against his shoulder, she felt completely safe and utterly content.

Finally he stopped by a stream and handed her down, then dismounted after her. Still without speaking he wrapped his arms around her, pulling her hard against him. He kissed her hair, and finally giving in to the fear and shakes she'd been fighting off for hours, Marjorie tangled her hands into the back of his coat and held herself as close to him as she could manage.

"Are ye hurt, my lass?" he finally murmured, swaying her slowly back and forth.

"No," she whispered, trying to keep from crying. For heaven's sake, she was safe now; the time for crying had come and gone. "I'm just a little tired of being kidnapped."

"It'll nae happen again. I'll nae allow it."

She nodded against his chest, then straightened, horrified that she hadn't asked earlier. "Is Connell safe? I told him to hide, but when your uncle arrived I worried that he would—"

"He's fine," Graeme interrupted. "He did just as ye asked, then ran back to the hoose and found Dùghlas. The two of them rode King George the cart horse to find me at Sheiling." He kissed her again, this time on the mouth. "I cannae ever—*ever*—thank ye enough fer keeping him safe, Marjorie."

"You trusted me with him. And he's . . . very dear to me."

"Aye. He's very dear to me, too. As are ye, my bonny, bonny lass."

She kissed him back, relishing in his warmth, and his strength, and his very presence. She'd *known* he would look for her, that he would find her. He'd told her the truth. She wasn't alone any longer. "I don't want to go back to London," she said, lowering her face against his pine-smelling coat again. "I don't ever want to see it again."

What had London ever given her, but a hatred for her own supposed failings—failings only brought to her attention by the very people with whom she'd wanted to mingle? The idea of returning to the sea of false smiles and ill-concealed resentments when she could instead simply turn her back on the entire maelstrom seemed utterly mad.

And she did pride herself on her logic. It was just unfortunate it had taken another kidnapping to rattle her brain to its senses.

"After this I was worried ye'd nae want to see the Highlands again. Two kidnappings in one month. That's a bit much even fer here." He kissed her again, slowly, his hands cupping her face as if she was something precious. But then she was precious, to him.

When they mounted Clootie again she opted to sit across Graeme's thighs, mostly so she could continue looking at him. "Your uncle said this wasn't over," she reminded him. "And I think you broke Sir Hamish's nose."

"I damned well hope I did," he returned. "I've been wanting to do it for nearly eight years, now."

"But what will he do to you in return, Graeme? He and the Duke of Dunncraigh? Because even if the Maxwell doesn't know about me yet, he will."

"He didnae like me before because I argue with his grand decrees when they aided him and hurt his people. He's claimed I'm nae loyal. Me flattening Paulk and keeping ye close'll give him more reason to want me gone."

"Gone from the Highlands?"

"Gone from clan Maxwell. He'd like it if I left the Highlands, and he may try to burn me oot to encourage me to leave, but this is *my* land. He cannae push me off it." She felt the deep breath he took. "I dunnae want ye taken by surprise again, Ree. He hates yer brother. Ye were a way to get to Lattimer. I doubt Dunncraigh'll leave it with harsh words and threats. Are ye prepared fer that sort of life?"

That was something she'd never considered. "I'd much rather fight to keep something I have and I believe in than for some stupid recognition from a group of people who mean nothing to me."

"We'll figure it oot then, lass. This is a new circumstance. Give my wee brain a bit of time to consider it. I reckon Paulk and his men'll all run away looking to Dunncraigh to tell 'em what to do next. That'll give us a day, anyway."

"My wee brain is also available," she reminded him.

"I'm nae likely to ferget that."

She wanted him to understand that they could be partners, that if he wanted to, he could tell her all his troubles, his thoughts and his dreams, and she would do everything she could to help him. Whether he ever asked for her hand or not.

"Lady Marjorie!" Mrs. Giswell hurried out the front door with more speed than Graeme thought the woman could muster. "Come inside! We'll draw a bath for you."

"I'm perfectly fine, Mrs. Giswell," the brave, bonny lass returned as he handed her to the ground. "Where are the boys?"

"I ordered them to remain in the morning room so you wouldn't be overset. We must get you changed. And oh, your hair!"

"I'm not overset," Marjorie protested, as the older woman bustled her into the house. "I want—"

"After you've cleaned off that dirt and fixed your hair, my dear. A lady never looks disheveled."

They headed upstairs, still arguing. Graeme wanted to follow, both to be certain she was unhurt and because Mrs. Giswell amused him. But as well as he knew anything he knew he didn't have the luxury of pausing for amusement.

So with a reluctant last look up the stairs he pushed open the morning room door. "She's safe, lads," he said, squatting next to Connell. "And ye, my duckling, are a hero."

"I was very brave," Connell agreed.

"Was Uncle Raibeart truly a part of this?" Dùghlas asked, his own expression more concerned than relieved.

"Did ye have to kill anyone?" Brendan added.

Graeme straightened again, nudging Connell toward a chair. "We need to have a chat, lads. And I need ye to listen."

"We'll listen, Graeme," the duckling said, sitting back in the chair so that his feet didn't quite touch the floor. Exchanging a glance, Brendan and Dùghlas sat on the sofa.

"Thank ye, lads. Sir Hamish meant to take Ree to Dunncraigh. I reckon the idea was to use her to convince Lattimer to sell his land to the Maxwell. That's what he wanted earlier, anyway." The idea of what might have happened to Marjorie made his jaw and his hands clench, and he pushed back against the anger. At this moment he needed to be calm. And logical. Later he could remind himself how satisfying it had been to smash Hamish Paulk's face.

"And aye, Raibeart was with Paulk. He may have been trying to keep the Maxton soot of any of this, but he'll nae be over fer dinner anytime soon. That's nae what I need to tell ye, though. Sir Hamish and Dunncraigh arenae going to let this lie. They may boot us from clan Maxwell. They may try to force us to leave Garaidh nan Leòmhann. The way I—"

"I dunnae want to leave Garaidh nan Leòmhann," Connell broke in, his eyes wide and worried.

"Hush, duckling," Brendan said. "Ye can talk when he's finished."

"Well, I will, too. Dunnae ye think I willnae."

Graeme hid his brief smile. "This is the thing, lads. They cannae make us leave our home. It's ours. They *can* encourage our cotters to leave, our sheep and shepherds to go missing, our fields to flood or to burn. That's what they did to Lattimer back when we still called it MacKittrick. The way I see it, we're going to war. But we can do it two different ways. We can stand up, buy more sheep, plant more wheat, build fisheries—and make ourselves both stronger and a bigger target fer them to aim at."

"But we dunnae have any blunt," Connell exclaimed, then covered his mouth with both hands.

"We dunnae," he ageed. "But Ree does."

Connell opened his fingers again. "Ye cannae take her money unless ye marry her." He covered his mouth again.

"Aye. I mean to marry her."

"Ye said that before," Dùghlas pointed out.

"Aye, but this time I've a better reason."

The duckling made a kissing sound behind his hand.

"Exactly," Graeme agreed. It wasn't very sophisticated, but it did represent the Maxton household fairly well.

"Then that's what we do," Brendan said. "Dunncraigh doesnae scare me."

"Me, either," Graeme seconded. "But there's one more point to consider," he said slowly, finding his way along the trail as he spoke. As long as Marjorie is here, Dunncraigh will see her as a chance to get to Lattimer. They took her today. I dunnae ken what these bastards might try next."

And that thought had begun to tear him up inside. She would be safer at Lattimer with her brother, where they knew the threats and had the men to protect her. Without her funds, though, Garaidh nan Leòmhann would be more vulnerable. *He* would be alone again, surrounded by family but without her to talk to, to hold, to argue and laugh with. But he'd given his word. He would protect her, no matter the cost to himself.

"Do we talk now?" the duckling asked, removing one hand from his face.

"Aye. We talk now."

"Good. Because I think—"

"Connell," Brendan interrupted. "Keep yer gobber shut."

"But—"

"I know one thing," the sixteen-year-old went on. "Ye mean fer us to be safe either way. That's who ye are. But nae one of us is going to tell ye what ye should do with Ree Forrester. We dunnae want the blame fer it either way."

"I'll tell ye what ye should do," Connell offered.

"Nae. Ye willnae." Dùghlas dragged the duckling over his shoulder. "We've a dozen men on the grounds, Graeme. Ye decide what to do next, and we'll follow ye. *I* think ye deserve to be happy, but that's all I mean to say."

As Graeme turned to watch them out of the morning room door, he caught sight of Marjorie standing there in the doorway, gazing at him. Her hair was combed, pulled back into a long, curling tail, but she still wore the dirty, ripped gown she'd had on when he'd rescued her.

"How much of that did ye hear?" he asked.

"Everything after you said Paulk and Dunncraigh can't make you leave." She tilted her head. "Are you going to attempt to send me to Lattimer or back to London and tell me it's for my own good?"

"Ye'd be oot of their reach in London, and ye'd be better protected at Lattimer."

"My well-being didn't concern you before, then?" she prodded.

Damnation. She was never going to forget that. "That was when I needed ye fer yer blunt and didnae much care what happened to the rest of ye. That's changed. It's dangerous here."

"I'd be even safer, then, locked in a room with a shackle on my ankle." She pulled the key from her pelisse pocket and walked forward to hand it to him. "Go ahead, then. Lock me away like some delicate, dainty porcelain doll that can't stand on its own two feet."

"Marjorie, y—"

"Don't 'Marjorie' me in your pretty accent, Graeme. I was dragged here against my will. I had no choice. You tried to make me marry you, and I stood against you. But then I *met* you—and Connell, and Dùghlas, and Brendan— and you introduced me to a different way of living. And to a great many other things that have literally changed my life. For the better, in my opinion."

"And all during that ye'd have been safer elsewhere," he made himself argue. She would be safer. *That* was what mattered. Now that he had time to move past being relieved, he needed to be logical. "That's twice as true now."

She stomped one foot. "Graeme Maxton, you told me that I didn't have to be alone any longer. And I don't want to forget this ever happened and go back to the way I lived before. I don't want to leave you."

"Jesus, Marjorie. Dunnae make this harder," he returned, pushing back. "We were an accident. We werenae supposed to meet."

"Shut up."

He lifted an eyebrow. "What was that, lass?"

"You've done this for the past eight years, haven't you?" she demanded, and punched him in the chest, keeping her palm over his heart. "You sacrifice everything. You would have married *me*—a Sassenach blue blood you detested, or so you thought—in order to provide for your people. Whatever life you had planned for yourself, every day that you spend helping your tenants when that still should have been your father's responsibility, it's a sacrifice of your time, your privacy, every spare penny. Well, I'm here to inform you, you stubborn man, that I love you. You don't have to sacrifice your happiness. *You* don't have to be alone."

No one had ever worded it that way before. Of course

he received applause and sympathy for taking over the care of his brothers, as if he could have chosen to do anything else, but he'd figured a long time ago that the responsibility had made him a better man. In Marjorie's interpretation, he'd always been a good man.

"You will be in danger," he said, as clearly and succinctly as he could, willing her to understand when he only wanted to keep his damned opinion to himself and kiss her. "Ye've nae lived in the Highlands, lass. Life isnae simple here. Ever."

"If the Crown hadn't found Gabriel, I would still be a lady's companion. In forty years I would be Mrs. Giswell. And I assure you, that frightens me far more than your Highlands." She paused, lowering her hand again. "Unless you've changed your mind. Oh, goodness. Am I being a fool? You're trying to find a kind way to be rid of me." She gave a humorless laugh. "If not for my money, you wouldn't—"

"Fuck," Graeme growled, grabbing her by the front of her torn gown and dragging her up against him for a hot, openmouthed kiss. "Ye're tearing me apart inside, lass," he murmured against her mouth, unwilling to part from her at all. "I dunnae want ye to go. Ever. But I dunnae want to see ye hurt, either."

"Then leave that decision to me, Graeme. This is the first place I've ever felt like I belonged. If you want me here, I want to stay and fight for it with you."

After being kidnapped twice she had a better sense of the danger of the Highlands than most other Sassenach lasses. And he'd never so much as sensed anything weak about her. Of course he was looking for any excuse to have her stay. "Ye're certain, my lass?" he asked quietly.

"I will leave if my being here puts those boys in more danger," she said fiercely. "Otherwise, I don't care about anything else, or what anyone thinks. They all detested me before; I don't give a . . . damn what they'll think of me now."

He grinned, relief and a stunned joy coursing beneath his skin. "Mind yer language, lass." Releasing the front of her gown, he caught her hand instead. "And if ye mean to stay, we need to see ye dressed proper." He pulled her into the hallway and to the stairs.

"I can change my gown later," she argued, but didn't try to pull free of his grip.

She wanted to stay, even with the trouble headed for them as surely as the heavy winter. That still didn't satisfy him, though; he wanted more, a promise between them as strong as any shackle. When they passed her bedchamber on the way to his, though, she balked.

"Graeme, everyone will know," she whispered, when he refused to loosen his grip.

"I want everyone to know, lass."

"But—"

Inside the room, he released her. "Dunnae move, Marjorie."

"What are you doing?" she asked, from her tone clearly thinking he'd lost his mind. If he had, it had been weeks ago, and he didn't want to find it again.

Keeping an eye on her, he pulled open the bottom drawer of his wardrobe, found the velvet bag, and returned to stand in front of her. "I'll nae have ye here against yer will for another damned second," he said, with his free hand brushing a straying strand of hair from her face. "But if ye're mad enough to want to stay, I mean to keep ye by my side always." He sank down on one knee, gazing up at her abruptly comprehending blue eyes. Eyes as clear and deep as a Highlands loch in summer. "We shouldnae ever have met, lass. And even after we did, we should have been enemies. But now I cannae imagine my mad life withoot ye in it. I love ye with every ounce of the heathen blood pumping through my heathen heart. Say ye'll marry me, Marjorie."

A tear ran down her face as he took her left hand in his. Her long, graceful fingers shook a little. He noted everything; the fading sunlight out the window, the tear in the gown that revealed a scraped knee, the distant sound of a rooster crowing.

"I'd stay with you even without this," she finally whispered. "I've been alone for most of my life. Almost from the moment I arrived here with a sack over my head and foxes nibbling at my toes, I've felt like I've been part of something. Part of this warm, chaotic family. And I haven't felt alone." Another tear trailed after the first. "I love you, Graeme. Yes, I'll marry you. Yes, yes, yes."

Abruptly his hands weren't quite steady, either. He slipped the sapphire ring over her finger, then pulled her down across his knee to fold her into his arms and kiss her until they were both out of breath. "I love ye, *mo boireann leòmhann*," he murmured against her mouth.

"They're kissing," Connell yelled from the doorway, angling his voice down the hall.

Then he strolled into the room. The lad had donned his Maxwell plaid; Graeme wondered briefly if this was the last time any of them would be doing so as part of the clan. "What do ye want, duckling?" he asked, helping Marjorie to her feet and then standing, himself.

"Ye cannae be kissing when damned—I mean blasted— Dunncraigh could attack any minute. I need to know what ye plan to do."

"I doubt Dunncraigh will be that swift, Connell. I'll put oot word fer a meeting here first thing in the morning and tell our tenants what's afoot. I'll give 'em the choice to pledge to Dunncraigh, or to stand with us." He reached out and took Marjorie's hand. "We may have to throw some blunt aboot to prove we have blunt to throw aboot."

She nodded. "I've never met this Dunncraigh, but I'm happy to do anything possible to annoy him."

"Oh, Graeme's sterling at annoying the Maxwell," Connell assured her.

"Good. Let's get started, then."

Chapter Eighteen

Y ou're purchasing sheep?" Mrs. Giswell said, both
  eyebrows lifting.

"I am," Marjorie returned, as she helped Cowen and
Ross clear the large table of plates and knives and the remains of what had been one very large roasted pig. Highlanders apparently liked to eat while deciding whether to
betray their clan chief or their local, much-loved clan
chieftain. And the consensus of deciding to wait and see
who ended up alive was not very reassuring.

"And where do you intend to graze them? In the Leeds
House garden among the roses?"

"Mrs. Giswell, are you being sarcastic?" Marjorie
prodded. After the tension of the morning and the disappointment over how few of Graeme's cotters had been
willing to stand with him regardless of consequences, it
was actually something of a relief to fall back on old familiar things like manners and etiquette.

The lady's companion took hold of Marjorie's left hand,
her gaze riveted on the lovely sapphires. "You mean to stay
here, don't you? After these barbarian boys kidnapped you
and brought you here against your will? After he tried to

force you to marry him? What about our plans to find you a place in Society?"

"There is no place for me in Society."

"You can't know th—"

"I can," she countered. "And you know it, as well. If I returned to London I would continue to be a resented pariah until I gave in to loneliness and married some fortune hunter, at which point I would be pitied and whispered about behind my back." Taking Hortensia's arm, she pulled the older woman to the tall ballroom windows. "Look out there. What do you see?"

"I'll tell you what I don't see. Almack's, Drury Lane Theater, stately houses, Hyde Park, or Bond Street."

Marjorie grinned. "Exactly. Isn't it wonderful?"

"And what about your years of studying at boarding school?"

A warm hand slid around her waist. "She can try to tame the local heathens," Graeme suggested, kissing her on the temple. "She's already reduced the profanity in the hoose by a good sixty-four percent, I reckon."

"But *he's* a fortune hunter," Mrs. Giswell insisted. "He told you he was. And now, before you're even wed, he has you purchasing sheep. How is that different than what you'd have in London, except for the superior shopping?"

Graeme opened his mouth to retort, but subsided when Marjorie put a hand over his lips. "Because before the boys dragged me onto his doorstep, he wasn't hunting a fortune. And because yesterday he tried to convince me to leave to keep me safe. And because I love him."

"Humph. What am I to do, then? Return to London alone, I suppose. I'll never work again, though, once any potential employer hears first about Princess Sophia and then about how my latest charge, an heiress, married a destitute viscount in the middle of Scotland."

Guilt touched Marjorie. Poor Hortensia certainly

couldn't be blamed for any of this. And the lady's companion had had such abysmal luck with employers. "I can certainly continue to employ you, Mrs. Giswell."

"There are lasses here who could benefit from yer expertise," Graeme added.

"Oh, pish. None of them could afford my expertise."

Marjorie smiled. "Isn't there space for a small schoolhouse in Sheiling?"

His fingers momentarily squeezed against her waist. "Aye. Doon beside the blacksmith's. If Ree agrees, we could build ye a ballroom fer yer dance lessons, a dining room fer cutlery practice, and a—"

"An academy," Mrs. Giswell interrupted, her color high and her eyes shining. "I've always dreamed, but with my reputation . . ."

"We're heathens here, Mrs. Giswell. We dunnae care aboot yer reputation."

"Oh, goodn—"

A rifle shot rang out, echoing across the valley.

Graeme's hand left her waist. "Visitors," he said, his expression going deadly serious. "They moved faster than I expected. Ye lasses and Connell head upstairs, lock the door behind ye, and stay away from the windows." He met her gaze, his eyes narrowing. "At least dunnae be seen looking oot," he amended, apparently reading her mind. He pulled a pistol from his pocket. "Be careful. It's loaded and primed."

He started for the hallway, but she grabbed his lapel and tugged. She might as well have tried to stop a volcano erupting, but he turned to face her again. "*You* be careful," she whispered, and lifted on her toes to kiss him.

"I will," he said with a swift grin. "I've a lioness to come home to."

"Good heavens, everyone's becoming a heathen," Hortensia noted faintly, but she patted Graeme's sleeve as he swiftly passed her. "Come along, Lady Marjorie. Let's get you upstairs."

Hefting the heavy pistol awkwardly, because no boarding school instructor anywhere had ever including shooting lessons as part of the curriculum, Marjorie left the modest ballroom and headed for the stairs, Hortensia on her heels. They met the boys in the hallway, Brendan and Dùghlas both carrying rifles and looking as grim as she'd ever seen them. The older boys nodded at her, and Brendan nudged Connell at her as they continued toward the front door.

She would much rather have kept all three of them locked away with her, but she also knew by now that the older two boys had been hunting for years and were far better with a weapon than she was. She also knew they would be hurt and insulted if she even suggested they remain inside.

"Come along, Connell," she said instead, taking his hand and ascending the staircase beside him.

"I'd go with the lads," the eight-year-old said tightly, "but Graeme ordered me to look after ye. And he said ye dunnae ken how to reload a pistol, and I do."

"Excellent. You shall be my strong right hand."

"I cannae always remember my right and my left, but I'll do what I can," he returned.

She could swear Mrs. Giswell muttered something about heathens behind them, but she ignored it as they reached Connell's room at the front of the house. From here they would have the best view of the road and the drive, from where she assumed any trouble would be coming. "Close your curtains but for two inches," she instructed, shutting the door and locking it. "We'll be able to peek out without having to move them."

"That's brilliant," Connell said, doing as she suggested. "I dunnae see anything yet, but I'll keep watch."

"Let me know the moment you spy anything." Marjorie sat on the edge of a chair, while Mrs. Giswell made clucking sounds and began straightening the boy's unkempt bed.

"Aye. I see Graeme and the lads rolling the wagon in front of the door and pushing it on its side so they can stand behind it, and the Fox lads on the stable roof and moving into the trees, but naught else."

She nodded, even though he wouldn't be able to see the gesture. Cowen, Ross, and Taog the underfootman, along with sturdy Mrs. Woring the cook, would be lurking behind the front-facing windows downstairs, all of them armed, while Johnny waited in the stable with a very large blunderbuss.

Despite his earlier concerns Connell now seemed to regard this all as a great adventure. For his sake she kept a calm face, as well. Inside, though, she couldn't stop the tumbling of her mind—the thoughts that said because she'd found someone she now had someone to lose, the worry that she'd somehow caused all this despite Graeme's assurances that the trouble had been simmering for years.

"I see horses," Connell said into the silence, making her jump.

"Whose horses? Can you tell?" Was it Paulk, or the Duke of Dunncraigh himself? Her heart caught in her throat, threatening to suffocate her.

"Nae . . . Wait. Maxwell plaid, coats . . . I cannae tell. But the horse in front is a big bay charger . . . Och, he's grand! And the rider . . . It's nae Sir Hamish, because he cannae ride like that."

"The Duke of Dunncraigh?" she suggested, setting the pistol on the side table and then picking it up again. She hated a man she'd never met. Judging by the actions of his men, he wasn't anyone she ever wanted to meet. And at the same time, she very much wanted to punch him in the face.

"Nae," Connell answered after a too long moment. "The Maxwell has gray hair. This one's got black hair. And he's nae wearing a tartan."

At the same time Marjorie heard a piercing whistle. A whistle she recognized. *Good heavens.*

"They've stopped," the duckling reported, even as Marjorie shot to her feet.

Rushing forward, hardly daring to breathe, she pulled aside the curtains. What looked like better than thirty men on horseback stood at the foot of the wide drive. At their head a bay warhorse stood still as a statue. And on his back, a tall man with orderly black hair, sharp gray eyes, and a long scar running down his left cheek. For a long moment she simply stared, not believing her own eyes.

"Hey," Connell protested, "ye arenae supposed to move the curtains!"

"My lady?" came Mrs. Giswell's anxious voice. "Do you know him?"

"I do," Marjorie said, scrambling to unlock the door. Graeme had no idea he was facing quite possibly the most dangerous man in Britain—Gabriel Forrester. The Duke of Lattimer. Her brother.

"Ye're close enough, I reckon," Graeme called, resting the barrel of his rifle across the top plank of the wagon. It wasn't a direct threat, but he'd made it clear he was armed and ready to defend the house and the lass inside it. "Whose dog are ye?"

The sharp-eyed man in front cocked his head, clearly taking in the Lion's Den's fairly meager defenses. Meager until the shooting started, anyway. "I'm here for Marjorie Forrester," he said, his accent unmistakably English. "Give her to me, and then we can discuss who the dogs here are."

Had Dunncraigh hired mercenaries, then? It was possible; even likely. Some former English soldier, from the looks of him, paid to burn out cotters and kill disobliging Highlanders. "I dunnae think I'll be giving ye anything but a lead ball between the eyes, if ye dunnae turn around now and ride back where ye came from."

The Sassenach didn't blink. "The only reason you're not dead already is because I am under the impression that you're not friends with Hamish Paulk. Give me my sister, Maxton, or I will revise my opinion."

Sister. Before Graeme had time to grasp anything beyond the fact that the Duke of Lattimer sat on horseback just beyond the point of his rifle, the door behind him slammed open. With Cowen trying to grab hold of her, Marjorie picked up her skirts and ran forward.

"Put your weapons down!" she yelled, charging the drive. "Gabriel! Don't shoot anyone!"

Lattimer swung out of the saddle, but his gaze remained on Graeme as he put his left arm around his sister, moving her to one side. The Beast of Bussaco, they'd called him when he'd served as a major in the army, and that had only been four months ago. The man was a fighter, and he had Marjorie. If one man in the would could remove Marjorie from him it was Gabriel Forrester, and Graeme wasn't going to allow that.

"What are you doing here?" she asked her brother. "And how did you even find me? I told you I was well and would write you within the week."

"No. First you explain why you're residing beneath the roof of a Maxwell chieftain. Then we can have a reunion."

Clenching his jaw, Graeme handed his rifle to Brendan and started around the wagon. "Why are ye giving me yer weapon?" his brother whispered.

"So I dunnae shoot my almost brother-in-law," he grunted back. He still had a knife in his boot and the one at his back, but if Lattimer thought he could talk to Marjorie like that, Graeme preferred to use his fists.

Marjorie saw him coming, and her eyes widened in response. "Graeme, he came all this way to make certain I'm well. I do owe him an explanation."

"From the sound of his barking, he came all this way to accuse one of us of someaught. And *I* want to know why."

The duke gave him an assessing look. "One Samuel Cooper delivered a letter to me yesterday. He told me that just before he took the mail stage north to Lattimer, a man who called himself Sir Hamish Paulk ran him down, read the letter, and then told him to make certain I received it. I then persuaded Mr. Cooper to tell me where he'd gotten the letter in the first place. And that led me here. To you. Your turn, Ree."

So Lattimer liked things straightforward. Good. It made for less confusion later. And Graeme wasn't in the mood to be polite, anyway. "First, ye might have thought to inform Ree that ye put yerself into the middle of a clan war with the Maxwell. If she'd known, I doubt she would have risked coming up here with only a lady's companion and two coachmen."

Finally the duke looked at his sister. "I didn't ask you to come up here."

"It was supposed to be a surprise. We've missed sharing every important moment in our lives. I wanted to meet Fiona."

"You came to surprise me. That still doesn't explain why you're here."

"Because my brothers kidnapped her. Because the Duke of Dunncraigh put oot word that any harm done to ye would be a favor to him. I'm nae on good terms with the Maxwell, and the lads decided bringing her to him would improve the situation. I objected. Yer turn."

A muscle in Lattimer's jaw twitched. "Why is she *still* here, then?"

"Two reasons. Hamish Paulk's been staying two miles from here with my uncle, and he stumbled across Marjorie. We—"

"I pretended to be Connell's tutor," she broke in. "He's Graeme's youngest brother. Graeme didn't want word about who I was getting back to Dunncraigh, and once I found out about your trouble with the Maxwell, I didn't want to risk traveling up to Lattimer Castle. Not while Paulk was about, anyway."

The duke nodded. "That makes a degree of sense." He looked back at Graeme. "What's the second reason?"

"Yer sister is a fearsome lass, and I didnae want her to leave." Reaching out, he took her left hand in his, and lifted it. "She wears my grandmother's ring. She's mine. I'm marrying her."

That made Lattimer blink. "Three months ago you announced how happy you were to be living in the middle of Mayfair. This is *not* the middle of Mayfair."

Marjorie looked around at the very attentive men surrounding them now on every side. "Perhaps we could go inside and chat," she suggested. Aside from the fact that a lady didn't want her troubles out on the wash line for everyone to see, Graeme looked very close to punching Gabriel. If that happened, she'd rather it be in front of fewer witnesses armed with fewer weapons.

"Your brothers aren't going to attempt to kidnap *me*, I trust?" Gabriel said dryly, glancing from the lads behind the wagon to where Graeme still stood holding her hand.

"Nae. There's nae chance of me making amends with Dunncraigh now."

"Is that the reason your trees are bristling with rifles?" her brother asked.

"Aye. More conversation fer inside."

"My men've been riding all night. They could use some breakfast."

Graeme nodded. "Kitchen's around the left side of the hoose, behind the garden."

Gabriel released his grip on Marjorie's shoulder and turned around. "Get yourself something to eat, lads. Those two," and he gestured at Brendan and Dùghlas, "will show you the way. We're all friends for the moment."

"Fer the moment," Graeme repeated. "I reckon the morning room'll do."

They trooped inside with Marjorie putting herself between the two tall men. Normally she would have been thrilled to see Gabriel; she saw him so infrequently that any time it happened was a treat. But nothing was normal today. And her brother's brusque manner pitted against Graeme's need to protect everyone around him—and her in particular—could be volatile.

Once they were all inside and the door closed, Graeme paced to the window and back. "Ye dunnae ken the first thing aboot yer own sister, do ye?"

"Graeme, *I'll* tell this story. And if either of you start punching each other, I'm going to get that fireplace poker and remind you forcefully that we don't have time for nonsense."

"Fine, lass. I like listening to ye talk, anyway."

Marjorie sat in the chair nearest the fire just to keep the poker close to hand, and she told her brother about how the past months had been for her. Graeme knew the tale, but he listened anyway, his expression an intent fondness that kept distracting her every time she looked over at him. No one looked at her like that—like she was something precious and rare and beautiful. For heaven's sake, he'd stood toe to toe with her brother, and was still doing so. The man about whom French soldiers had made a rather bloodcurdling song involving the Grim Reaper.

Because she didn't want a battle between them she left out the shackles and the attempt at a forced marriage and the other, more . . . personal parts of the tale, but she didn't spare any details about her second abduction or Graeme's swift rescue. When she finished that part, Gabriel put up a hand.

"You broke Sir Hamish Paulk's nose?" he repeated, shifting his attention to Graeme.

"I damned well tried to. Even withoot what he did to Ree, he's been after my cotters and my place in the clan fer better than seven years. The fact that he touched the lass topped it off."

Gabriel narrowed one eye. "You know I'm about to marry his niece."

"Aye. I also know how ye booted him and Dunncraigh off yer land and then exposed all the shite the Maxwell's been doing to his own fer the past decade or so."

With a half grin, Gabriel sat back in the old chair again. "And all the armed men outside are because you're expecting retaliation."

"Aye. I reckoned ye might be some Sassenach mercenary the Maxwell hired to burn me oot. I aim to object to that."

Marjorie sat beside him, twining her fingers with his restless ones. "Graeme told me what happened at Lattimer, Gabriel, when Dunncraigh tried to force you out. We promised the tenants here improvements and homes whatever their clan chief attempted, but they're scared."

"I dunnae have the men to stand against him in an out-and-out fight. And I've cotters afraid of what'll happen to them if they choose the wrong side—and I'd nae force them to do that."

Gabriel sat silently for a moment. "Marjorie and I need a word," he finally said. "In private."

She didn't need to look at Graeme to know he didn't like that. "I refuse to be kidnapped a third time," she said aloud, freeing her hand. "I'll be back in a moment."

He stood. "Nae. I need to go check on the lads. Ye stay here."

Marjorie watched him out the door, splendid in his heavy, dark coat and bright plaid kilt, then turned to find her brother gazing at her. "Are you pregnant?" he asked, with his usual abruptness.

A few weeks ago simply being asked that question would have mortified and offended her. Her world had tipped on its ear since then, and so had her sensibilities. "I don't know."

Gabriel cursed. "You were the one I thought was fit for this life we've had shoved at us. You're poised, proper, so-phisticated, I—"

"I thought I needed to fit into this new life, too," she interrupted. "But you don't, so why should I?"

"I didn't expect to meet Fiona, you know," her brother countered. "Or to find anything I cared to fight for here. I expected to be back on the Peninsula by now."

"And I didn't expect to meet Graeme, or to see anything of the Highlands except what I viewed through the coach window. I never expected any of this. But it happened, and I want what's here. More than I ever wanted to be a fine, admired lady in London."

He blew out his breath. "I'm not a clan chief. I can't tuck his people beneath my wings."

"Graeme said they call you Laird MacKittrick. And if I asked those men who rode all this way with you, would they say they're part of clan Maxwell, or clan MacKittrick?"

"They're Maxwells in everything but name, Ree."

"And the name they do use for themselves is . . ." she prompted.

"MacKittrick. But only because that's Lattimer Castle's old name, and the name of the Maxwell chieftain who re-sided there before one of the old Georges had his head lopped off."

She'd nearly forgotten how stubborn her older brother could be. "Graeme can provide for these people here. He's been doing it for the past eight years with almost nothing. I can help him make Garaidh nan Leòmhann profitable, if you don't get your back up and cut me off. But he needs to be rid of damned Dunncraigh."

Gabriel gave a surprised laugh, moving over to the couch to hug her and place a kiss on her hair. "Language, Ree."

The fact that he'd voluntarily embraced her, voluntarily allowed his arms and his attention to become entangled . . . "Fiona Blackstock has been very good for you, I think."

"Yes, she has. Did I tell you I resigned my commission? I realized I couldn't help these people without being here full-time, body and s—"

A rifle shot rang out, the second one this morning. Before she could finish registering the sound, her brother was already at the window. "It means someone's spotted riders approaching," she supplied.

With a nod he strode to the door and pulled it open. "Find somewhere safe," he barked, and vanished toward the front door.

Marjorie stood, ready to retreat to Connell's room again, but stopped herself in the doorway. The two men in her life did share one thing—the inability to keep from reminding her to go hide. However long the animosity between Graeme and the Maxwell had existed, it was her presence that had brought it to a head. Likewise Gabriel wouldn't even be here if not for her.

As Cowen hurried into the morning room, rifle in hand, to take his place by the window, she followed to crouch beside him. The butler lifted both bushy eyebrows at her. "Ye're meant to be in the duckling's bedchamber with the lad and Mrs. Giswell."

"I prefer being able to see and hear. And I want to be closer to the door."

"Laird Maxton'll have my head if someaught happens to ye, lass."

"It's my decision. And I don't plan on being foolish."

He likely would have continued arguing, but Gabriel's men flashed by outside, leading their mounts around to the back of the house. Did they mean to stay clear of this particular argument, then? From the standpoint of a soldier, it made sense to do so; her brother had no sound reason to wish to increase the antagonism between himself and clan Maxwell. Nor had he promised her anything, including his permission for her to wed Graeme.

A moment later everything looked as it had before, with Graeme and two older boys positioned behind the wagon and everyone else—such as they were—hidden in the house and among the trees. This time, though, she knew it was trouble approaching. The only question was whether it was Paulk, or Dunncraigh.

Roughly twice the number of men Gabriel had brought galloped up the drive, spreading into the semicircle she remembered all too well from yesterday. She even recognized some of the same men, from the one with his right arm in a sling to the previously distinguished-looking Sir Hamish Paulk, now with two black eyes and a thick swath of gauze across the middle of his face and tied at the back of his head.

Once her gaze found the mounted man on Paulk's right, though, she didn't look any further. White, close-cropped hair, deep-set green eyes, and an air about him that as much as said all these men belonged to him. A tremor ran up her spine. The Duke of Dunncraigh. This was the man to whom Brendan had wanted to deliver her, the man Paulk had attempted to drag her off to yesterday.

"I see ye ken ye're in some trouble, Maxton," the duke called in a flat, carrying voice. This conversation wasn't just for the two of them; he meant for everyone around them to hear it, as well.

"I'm fine," Graeme returned. "Ye're the one who's ridden into rifle range."

"If yer objection is to Hamish trying to steal the prize ye meant to deliver to me yerself, then I reckon he earned a broken nose." He tilted his head. "Is that what's happened, lad? A simple misunderstanding?"

"Aye," Graeme returned, to her abrupt confusion and dismay. Of course he would never give her to that man, but this sounded like he meant to antagonize his clan chief. Further antagonize him, rather.

Dunncraigh briefly looked surprised, as well, but the cool, stoic expression quickly settled over his face again. "Then mayhap ye're nae a lost cause, after all. Bring oot the Sassenach lass, and ye'll have my gratitude."

"And how would having the lass help ye?" Graeme pursued.

Oh, she hoped Gabriel was listening. Anything to convince her stubborn brother that his wasn't the only land that needed to be free of the Duke of Dunncraigh's influence.

"Dunnae pretend ye're innocent in all this, Maxton. What, were ye considering making an alliance with Lattimer against me? Turn her over to the bastard and say ye'd kept me from her?" The duke sneered. "Aye, that's what it was, I wager. I'll let it pass, though, if ye give her to me. Now."

At the corner of the wagon Graeme looked as relaxed as if he was chatting with a friend about the lowering weather. "I was agreeing that we've had a bit of a misunderstanding," he said coolly. "And so I've a counterproposal fer ye. Ye leave my land withoot the lass, and ye nae set foot on my property again, and I'll send ye the tithes due ye. My cotters will still call themselves Maxwell, and ye and Paulk and his broken beak will stay well clear of us."

For a heartbeat or two she hoped the duke would agree

to those terms. It wouldn't be perfect by any means, but it would likely leave Graeme's tenants the most comfortable.

"And have ye go to Lattimer behind my back? Nae."

She knew what would happen next. The insults would grow more savage, and then someone would shoot. Whether or not Gabriel's men charged in, it would mean a battle. And because it was what she feared and dreaded most, Graeme would be killed. She strode for the door.

"Lass," Cowen hissed. "Where are ye going?"

"To put a stop to this."

"I reckon we're at an impasse, then," Graeme retorted, motioning for Dùghlas to move farther into cover. This was about to get bloody, and he needed to keep the lads safe.

Dunncraigh's gaze moved beyond him, a very unsettling expression touching his face. "I'm nae so certain we *are* at an impasse," he drawled. "Welcome, Lady Marjorie Forrester. I'm glad ye dunnae see the point of hiding behind this *amadan*."

"What does *amadan* mean?" she asked in a calm voice, moving around the wagon and into the open.

Bloody hell. Graeme wanted to grab her, tackle her to the ground. Moving toward her now, though, would very likely encourage someone to start shooting. This wasn't her brother she'd decided to confront. This was a man who thought of nothing but his own power and pride. He took a shallow breath, ready to move if anyone dared approach her. "It means 'fool,' " he said flatly.

"Ah," she returned, nodding even though she kept her gaze on Dunncraigh. "Laird Maxton is a fool for not dragging a duke's sister across the countryside and then handing her over to you, whom everyone knows to be an enemy of said duke." She patted a finger against her chin. "Logically, even if you rewarded the viscount with sheep or wheat or something, the Duke of Lattimer would see him imprisoned for kidnapping." She dipped a shallow curtsy. "I am a member of the aristocracy, after all. My home in London stands between the residences of the Marquis of Pyegrove and the Earl and Countess of Adsam."

"I dunnae give a damn who yer neighbors are, Sassenach."

"That's Lady Marjorie to you, Your Grace," she returned, still as calm as if she was chatting over tea.

Watching her, listening to her, mesmerized Graeme, and he worked to keep his attention on Dunncraigh. Very rarely did anyone attempt to openly oppose the Maxwell, and whoever did make the effort never emerged successful, if he emerged at all.

"Since Lord Maxton is unwilling to risk being jailed," she went on, "I suppose it's a good thing—for you, Your Grace—that Sir Hamish *is* willing to take up residence at the Old Bailey." She glanced at the fuming Paulk, who looked ridiculous with a great bandage across the middle of his face. "Did you have any idea that five young lads were playing along the river when you grabbed me? That's five witnesses to the kidnapping of a duke's sister. Unless you mean to murder children of your own clan, of course."

That caused a stir among Dunncraigh's men. Whatever the lass was about, for the moment it seemed to be working.

"It's fortunate Lord Maxton stopped you, and persuaded *me* not to send to Fort William for soldiers, when you consider it." With that she returned her gaze to the tight-lipped duke. "While I was being dragged across the countryside yesterday, I also found myself considering the dilemma my delivery would have put before *you*, Your Grace."

"Oh, did ye now? Enlighten me. I'm curious to hear how hurt I would feel while ye rotted naked in an oubliette."

She nodded, apparently unmoved. Graeme wasn't; he

gripped the stock of his rifle so hard his knuckles showed white. One step. If anyone took one step toward her, he was opening fire.

"Certainly. I assume my captivity would be used to encourage my brother to sell you MacKittrick—or Lattimer, rather. If he agreed you could release me—in which case both you and Sir Hamish would have to face the English courts. Or you could murder me, which would give the Duke of Lattimer—also known as Major Gabriel Forrester, the Beast of Bussaco—every incentive either to hunt you down and murder you in return, or to inform his fellow soldiers of precisely what happened. And then *you* would be stripped naked and tossed into a cell at the Old Bailey. If you lived that long, of course. I personally doubt you would."

Marjorie lifted a finger in the air. "Oh, I forgot something. You came after me today. In person. Everyone here, those you can see and those you cannot, are *all* witnesses now. And I married Laird Maxton yesterday, so whatever happens to me, he has my entire fortune at his disposal. I imagine that's more than enough money to persuade even the most reluctant and loyal of men to speak up."

Dunncraigh's face went from mottled purple to gray and back again. Graeme wouldn't have been surprised in the least to see the Maxwell drop dead on the spot from an apoplexy. He bloody well wouldn't shed a tear.

"Once I consider all these fantastical thoughts of mine," Marjorie went on, clasping her hands behind her back, "I have to presume you *actually* rode all the way out here to make certain I'm uninjured, and to congratulate your chieftain on his marriage. In light of the past tensions between you, however, I'm afraid I can't invite you inside. So unless there's something else you wish to discuss, Your Grace, I thank you and bid you good day." With that she offered a deep, proper curtsy, turned around, and smiled tightly at Graeme.

That was the only sign of nerves he'd seen from her. Lowering the rifle, he strolled out to meet her, offered his arm, and headed for the front door. "Lads," he murmured, and Brendan and Dùghlas moved in front of them.

In the doorway Marjorie turned around again. "I do need to take issue with one thing you said, Your Grace. You called Laird Maxton a fool. He isn't a fool. He's a man who accepted, at age twenty, the responsibility of raising three brothers and being a landowner and a viscount and a clan Maxwell chieftain. He's delivered calves, shorn sheep, plowed fields with his own two hands because his tenants needed him to. Graeme Maxton is a true Highlander in the best sense of the word. I don't know what you are, sir, but I will have to be content with calling you gone from here."

"I called ye my fierce lioness, but fer God's sake, lass." As soon as the front door closed behind them, Graeme pulled her into a hard, relieved embrace. That wasn't enough, though, and he bent his head to kiss her.

"I suppose all those years of conversation and comportment and etiquette lessons *did* turn out to be valuable," she said breathlessly, holding on to his lapels. "My legs feel a bit wobbly now, though."

"*My* legs feel wobbly," Dùghlas put in.

Graeme swept her up into his arms. "Do ye ken how much ye risked oot there?" he muttered, kissing her again. She still wasn't close enough, but with the entire household pouring into the hallway, truly showing his appreciation would have to wait.

"As much as you risk every day," she returned. "If I'm to be your wife, I could do no less."

"Ye *are* to be my wife," he stated. "And now that ye've told all of clan Maxwell we're already wed, we'd best send for Father Michael before Monday."

"You haven't asked my permission," the Duke of Lattimer said, as he trotted down the stairs, his rifle held easily in one hand. "They've gone, by the way. Dunncraigh threw a shoe at Paulk. And you took away my best chance to shoot the bastard, Ree. I'm not certain how I feel about that."

"If you'd stepped in," she returned, pushing at Graeme's chest until he relented and set her down again, "someone would have gotten killed. And it might have been one of us."

"That's all well and good," Graeme said, figuring it might be a good thing to have both hands free now, anyway, "but let's get back to that first bit. I'm nae asking yer damned permission fer anything, Lattimer."

The duke lifted an eyebrow. "No?"

"Nae. Ye can ask yer sister if she's happy here, and I'll tell ye that I adore her. If ye want to fight aboot it, I'll oblige ye."

Marjorie pushed between them. "I *am* happy here, Gabriel, so you don't have to ask me. No punching."

"Let go of me, ye madwoman!" Connell's voice came from upstairs. "Cannae ye see it's safe?"

"We're to stay put until someone fetches us, young man!"

"I'm nae a man! I'm a duckling!" With that, he pounded down the stairs. "I need to know, Graeme. Are we still clan Maxwell?"

Graeme had to think about it for a moment. In all the chaos, he'd been so concerned with Ree's safety that their standing in the clan hadn't concerned him. "Aye," he said finally. "Thanks to a few well-placed threats and a bit of blackmail, we're still clan Maxwell."

"I knew it!" the bairn crowed. "Mrs. Giswell kept saying we were all done fer, but I didnae believe it."

Looking over his brother's head at Marjorie, Graeme didn't quite believe any of it, either. "The lot of ye stay here. I require a private word with Marjorie."

Without waiting for a response he took her hand and pulled her into the morning room, leaning back against the door to shut it. As she faced him, he drew her forward so he could slide his arms around her waist and breathe in the lemon scent of her hair. She rested her cheek against his chest, and he wondered if she could feel his heart beating.

"Ye're my lass," he whispered.

"I am," she returned in the same, intimate tone. "And you're my Highlander."

"I am," he echoed. "And please dunnae ever scare me like that again. I've just found ye. I'll nae tolerate losing ye. Anything else, aye. But nae that."

She knew as well as he did that while Dunncraigh might subside for a time, the trouble he represented likely wasn't going away. But she nodded anyway, lifting her face to gaze at him with those eyes the color of a loch in deep summer. "I've met a great many people in my life, Graeme, and you are the truest and bravest man I've ever known. I know how to use words, and today it happened to benefit both of us. I only stepped forward, though, because you would have given your own blood to protect me. So I'll do my best not to scare you, if you tell me every day that you love me."

"That's an easy task, *mo boireann leòmhann*," he murmured, kissing her again. "I love ye."

"And I love you."

A young fist knocked on the door. "Graeme, did ye tell Brendan we could get a dog? Because I would like a dog. A hound, I think."

Marjorie started laughing, burying her face against his

coat. She'd gone from a simple, hopeless life to a wealthy, restricted one, to this . . . warmth and noise and chaos. And to a man who made her feel strong, and hopeful, and loved. "Yes," she called, chuckling. "We should get a very large hound."

Coming soon. . .

Look for the next Scandalous Highlander novel from
New York Times bestselling author
SUZANNE ENOCH

The Good, the Bad,
and the Devil in Plaid

Available in February 2018 from St. Martin's Paperbacks

. . .and don't miss the other novels
in this bestselling series!

The Devil Wears Kilts
Rogue with a Brogue
Mad, Bad, and Dangerous in Plaid
Some Like It Scot
Hero in the Highlands

Available from St. Martin's Paperbacks